A KISS TO BUILD A GRUDGE ON

BRIANNE GILLEN

This is a work of fiction. Names, characters, places, and incidents either are the product of the author's imagination or are used fictitiously. Any resemblance to actual persons, living or dead, events, or locales is entirely coincidental.

A Kiss to Build a Grudge On: Phoenix Pictures, Book 3

Edited by: Michele Chiappetta of Two Birds Author Services, LLC

Cover Design by: www.DaybedBooks.com

Print ISBN: 978-1-7372403-6-5

E-book ISBN: 978-1-7372403-7-2

Published by Brianne Gillen

www.briannegillen.com

❀ Created with Vellum

*To the little red-haired girl who lived in her imagination
(and still does)…*
don't forget to savor this moment like Max's cheesecake.

Chapter One

Los Angeles, California
August 14, 1945
V-J Day

Max Mitchell wove through the narrow, smoky hallway leading to the crowded bar's side door. He shook his head as he walked, smiling at no fewer than three couples scattered along the hall, all locked in amorous embraces. He doubted any of the pairs had met prior to today's festivities… or that they'd be likely to remember each other come the next morning.

A trickle of sweat made its way down the back of his neck and under his uniform collar. He pushed the door open and stepped out into…another wall of heat. Serving in Europe, he'd nearly forgotten how warm summer nights tended to be at home. At least the air moved a little out in the alley. He fished into his pants pocket for his standard-issue envelope hat and waved it in front of his face to give the air an extra push along its way.

He hated to leave the celebration behind—the bar owner had defied city-wide orders and stayed open, after all—but better to be safe than sorry. Max felt all right at the moment, but vertigo was a sneaky bastard and he didn't want to push his luck. The bar was packed to the gills with revelers, every corner growing stuffier and more sweltering by the minute.

He paused his hat-fanning to take a swig of the fresh, ice-cold beer in his hand. He was thoroughly enjoying the cool relief sliding down his throat when he heard her.

"Celebration too much for you, soldier?"

Max turned at the rich, liltingly accented voice—*Scottish, perhaps?*—that slid over him like honey. A strikingly lovely woman sat on a crate against the wall behind him, nursing her own beer. She wore a gauzy, sleeveless blouse and a slim skirt, hiked up just enough so she could cross her shapely legs. A charm bracelet dangled from her wrist, winking in the dim light of the alley. Hard to tell in the shadows, but her hair looked to be a light brown, and her dark eyes sparkled up at him. A smirk lifted the corner of her blood-red lips.

Max grinned back. "Yeah, I've had enough of the tropical paradise in there."

The woman gestured around her. "So you traded it for the nice, balmy soup out here."

"What can I say? I like to mix it up."

That elicited a more genuine smile from her. "Clearly."

He ventured a couple of steps closer. "And what about you? Bored with the festivities already?"

She arched an eyebrow. "I'll have you know, things are rarely boring when I'm around."

"Of that, I have no doubt."

Her eyes narrowed, as if she wasn't sure what to make of him. But he held her gaze firmly, surprising himself a bit with his forwardness. He was no slouch in the flirting department, but he usually eased into it, at least waited until he knew a girl's name.

And god knew he hadn't exactly had any practice at it these last few years, what with the war.

But something about this woman drew out his mischievous side.

As they stared at each other, her eyes softened—then smoldered for the barest hint of a second, before she blinked and looked away.

With a tiny shake of her head, she returned to their conversation. "I guess I just needed a wee break."

"No one can be expected to be that scintillating all the time, after all."

She glanced up at him sharply, but at his wink, she smiled. "It's very true." She gestured to the space next to her. "Would you care to join me?"

Would I ever.

"You don't mind?"

"Nah." She scooted to her left, making room for him. "Pull up a crate."

"Thanks." He settled on the box and held up his hat. "May I offer you my fan?"

She chuckled. "I'm all right, but thanks."

Max dropped the hat over his knee, and they simultaneously lifted their bottles for another pull of beer. They glanced at each other as they swallowed, smiling over their mirrored action.

The woman inhaled a slow breath and looked across the alley, at nothing in particular. Max watched her for a moment.

"Are you sure I'm not interrupting?" he asked.

The corners of her lips curved up. "Trust me, I wouldn't have asked you to sit if you were."

"Fair enough."

They lapsed into a quiet lull as the sounds of celebration swirled around them, coming from all directions. The voices emanating from the bar were loud, even through the closed door. An impromptu band's music floated down the alley, along with raucous laughter and onlookers' periodic cheers for those showing off their dancing skills in the streets. A rousing chorus of "Boogie Woogie Bugle Boy" echoed from the alley's other end as its singers stumbled past along the avenue.

"So," he asked, "how'd you end up here in sunny California?"

She flashed him a saucy grin. "How do you know I wasn't born here?"

He lowered his voice conspiratorially. "Well...I didn't want to say, but...you're a little pale, considering all the sunshine around here."

She swatted his arm playfully. "Hey, some people simply can't hold onto a suntan." She scrunched her nose adorably. "No matter how hard they try."

"All right, I'll give you that." He grinned.

"You know, usually it's my accent that tips fellas off."

He pretended to consider that. "Yeah, I do detect a hint of something... Brooklyn, is it?" he teased.

She laughed, the sound again hitting him beneath his ribs. "Trust me, you do *not* want to hear me attempt a Brooklyn brogue." He joined her laughter before she continued, "No, smarty-pants, this is all Scotland."

"Ah, bonnie Scotland." At her dawning grimace, he held up his hand. "Don't worry. I would never attempt an undoubtedly terrible Scottish brogue."

"That's a relief. If I had a dime for every time someone's tried, especially with all the actors in this town..." She shuddered.

"Hey, can I ask a personal question?"

She cocked an eyebrow. "I suppose so."

He leaned in to whisper, "Ever seen Nessie?"

Her delightful laughter bubbled up. "Sadly, no. And not for lack of trying. I spent quite a fair bit of my childhood searching for her—*before* the rest of the world jumped on the bandwagon."

"Well, with that kind of a head start, I have every faith that if anyone can find her someday, it's you."

"Why, thank you, kind sir."

Their shared smiles heralded a charge of magic Max could practically taste in the air around them, like cinnamon mingling with vanilla.

Just then, another chorus of the Andrews Sisters' big hit echoed, louder this time, the same raucous group now moving toward the alley again.

Max huffed a laugh as he mourned the loss of the moment. "They sure like that one, don't they?"

His companion snorted in response. "I'll say."

He turned back in time to catch the tail end of her eye roll. "Not your favorite song?" he asked.

"Oh, no. I like that one a lot...usually." She glanced up at him, weighing her words. "It's only, it was on the radio when I left the office this afternoon. Right after I got fired."

He winced in sympathy. "Oof. I'm sorry."

"And the worst part is, I can't even escape much in all this reveling. Everywhere I turn I'm reminded..." She trailed off as she looked over at him, almost sheepishly—an expression that seemed very much out of place on this woman's face. "Never mind."

"I can go yell at those bozos to switch to another song, if you'd like." He bent his head to meet her eyes. "But I get the feeling it's not just the song...?"

"No, it's not." Her small smile masked her clear hesitation to say more.

"Oh, come on. You clearly need to get it off your chest. Tell me." He felt strangely protective of this woman he'd only just met.

She sighed. "The reason I was fired...was so they could give my job to one of the boys returning home from the war."

Max scrunched his brow. "Why? I mean, wouldn't there have been room for both of you?"

"That's precisely what I argued. But my boss wouldn't budge.

So now I have to get out there first thing tomorrow and hunt down something else to bring home the bacon."

"That's awful." As he looked down at his uniform, understanding dawned. "And here we all are, throwing it in your face."

Her head snapped up. "No! I mean...well...yes. But please don't take it personally. I'm incredibly appreciative of your service, really I am."

He rested his hand on her arm for a brief second in reassurance, trying to ignore the heavenly softness of her skin. "Don't trouble yourself. I get it." He gestured to the world around them. "And on behalf of all of us, let me say that I am sorry. I wish our return didn't come at your job's expense."

Her full red lips melted into a relieved—and dazzling—smile. "Thanks."

She absently brushed her fingers over her arm, in the spot he'd just touched, and he longed to do it again.

Her face relaxed further, and she asked, "So, what do you do? When you're not soldiering, that is."

"Hopefully not whatever it is you just got fired from."

She laughed. "That would be awkward, wouldn't it?"

"Indeed." He made a showy inhale before answering her. "I am a baker."

Her eyes sparked with genuine interest. "Well, that's one you don't hear too often." She reached out to brush his arm. "And you're safe, by the way." She pointed at herself. "Accountant."

"That's a relief." Not that his arm felt any relief, tingling now from the quick pressure of her fingertips.

"So, how does that work? Do you have your own shop? Or *did* you, before...?"

"Not yet." He squared his shoulders, in part to shore up his own resolve. "But soon. I hope." Max glanced at her, finding only interest in the way she studied him closely, so he continued on. "I was really close. Right before..." He gestured all around them.

"It sure put a crimp in everyone's plans, didn't it?"

"You bet. But I'm more determined than ever. With everything that's happened, the thought of waiting, going back to working for someone else…" He shrugged. "It's time I do this."

"Good for you." Her eyes sparked with admiration, which sizzled over his skin.

"You know, if you're still looking for something by the time I get started, it wouldn't be a bad idea for me to have some help with the numbers…" It was a bold offer, but he couldn't help himself around this beautiful stranger.

Her eyes widened slightly, before she schooled her face and arched an eyebrow. "That's a mighty nice offer. I'm tempted to take you up on it."

"What's stopping you?"

"How do I know you're any good? I'd hate to hitch my wagon to a dud." Her eyes sparked teasingly.

He took a chance and leaned a little closer. "Trust me, I know how to knead that dough."

"Well, that should give you a leg—or perhaps a baguette?—up on the competition."

The curve of her lips looked practically devilish now, and god, he wanted nothing more than to kiss her. The air shimmered around them. But her breath hitched, and she pulled back. He felt the loss keenly. When she drank from her beer, the metallic tinkling of her charm bracelet drew his attention, and he noticed the slight trembling of her hand.

She's feeling it too.

Again he reminded himself that he'd only just met her. On every street, in every bar, corners were full of couples who didn't care about that, not tonight. But Max didn't want to be one of them. He'd never been the "love 'em and leave 'em" type, and he wasn't about to start now.

Hell, she'd be damn near impossible to leave.

He blinked. Too soon, *much* too soon, to know that. He glanced down at his beer, still half-full. And only his second of the night.

She recovered her wits sooner than he did—if she'd ever lost them in the first place—and watched him, cool as a cucumber.

"So what's your specialty?" she asked.

"Sorry?"

She smiled. "I assume every baker has one, right? The best thing they make. What's yours?"

At least he knew the answer to this one. "I couldn't possibly say." At her raised eyebrow, he continued, "That's like asking a mother to pick her favorite child."

She laughed. "So your baked goods are like your children, are they?"

He arched his own eyebrow. "Nothing wrong with that, is there?"

"Not at all." Her smile softened. "It's actually a rather nice sentiment."

Warmth flooded his chest at the compliment.

She was quiet for a moment, before she leaned in. "There really isn't *one* thing that gets people coming back more than the rest?"

Max laughed. "You're a tenacious one, aren't you? Hmm...I have been told I make a mean cheesecake. My best pal raves about my chocolate version. Though honestly, he'd eat just about anything if it had enough sugar in it."

She chuckled. "Well, if it is really that good, I hope I get to try this fantastic cheesecake someday."

"So do I." He paused, needing to keep this conversation on neutral—and steady—ground. "And what about you? Are you any good at your accounting?"

She smirked. "All firing aside, you mean?"

"Obviously."

"Not to toot my own horn..."

"Oh, go ahead," he encouraged. "What are horns for, if not tooting?"

Her nostrils flared slightly, and she pressed her lips together, as if trying to hold in a laugh. Max winced inside. He hadn't meant to be so corny—or suggestive.

He cleared his throat. "Sorry, you were saying..."

Amusement warmed her eyes and softened her mouth. "Right. So, in the interest of horn-tooting, then… I am quite good actually. I aced all of my business school classes—much as my male peers hated to admit it."

"You ran circles around them, didn't you?"

"Damn right I did. Thought I was on my way to making a pretty good career of it, too." Straightening her shoulders, she held up a finger. "*Not* that I am giving up in any way. Today was only a temporary setback." She exhaled sharply, and added in an undertone, "God knows, I've had more than enough of those."

Their hands were now only a hairsbreadth from each other, on the edge of the crate between them. Max closed the distance with his pinky, brushing hers as softly as he could. Her finger pressed back against his, carefully, deliberately.

At the same time, her other hand floated up toward her neck, and she pulled out a chain, fingering what looked like a gold band.

He wondered suddenly if she'd lost someone. If he'd been too forward with his flirting. But she linked her pinky around his, prolonging their contact.

"Did your unit…see a lot of loss?" she asked quietly.

"Some. We were lucky in a way, didn't get as much action as a lot of others, but we saw our fair share." He squeezed her finger a little tighter. "Enough to make all this bittersweet. I'm beyond thrilled the war is over and I'm home now, but…"

"It's hard not to think of all the ones who aren't coming home."

"Yeah. I know I've got it pretty good. Even what I've seen…it's a far cry from losing someone close." He nodded at her necklace. "Your sweetheart?" He shook his head. "Sorry, that was intrusive."

"No, it's all right. I don't mind talking about him. And he was my husband, actually." She let out a surprised huff. "I lost him nearly two and a half years ago now."

"I imagine the when doesn't matter so much. You still wish he could be here."

"Aye. He would've liked all this dancing in the streets." She sighed. "So would my brother."

Max's heart squeezed. "I'm sorry. Did you lose him too?"

She shook her head. "No. At least…I don't think so. I hope not. He was serving in England, but…well…communication hasn't exactly been easy."

"That's for sure. It was pretty hard to get messages home."

"Is that where you were? Europe?"

"Yeah. What about your husband?"

"The Pacific." She flashed him a small smile, one that had him wanting to ease her burdens, even for a moment.

"Well, I hope you find your brother, at least."

"Thanks. Me too."

The impromptu band down the street began a new song. He recognized the opening notes of "I'm Beginning to See the Light." As did she.

Her smile brightened as she looked down the alley toward the music's source. "Now, this one I do love."

An impulse seized him, and he jumped to his feet before he could overthink it. He extended his hand to her.

"May I have this dance?"

She glanced between his hand and his face, her eyes wide with surprise. "What, here?"

"Sure, why not? I might not know your name yet, but I'm willing if you are."

Her lips curved slowly. "I do have to maintain a little mystery. But all right. A dance would be nice."

She stood and slid her hand in his. The heat of her touch sent shock waves throughout his entire body. He heard her small, sharp intake of breath, and as their eyes met, he knew she was having a similar experience. He wasn't sure who smiled first, but he felt almost shy as he slid his other arm around her waist and drew her close.

With a little more light hitting her face now, he realized her eyes weren't nearly as dark as he'd first thought. Up close, they shimmered an inky blue, much like the star sapphire in the ring his father always wore. She was so utterly lovely, it made his head spin.

They swayed to the music, and after a while she broke their locked gaze to rest her head on his shoulder. He took note of how perfectly she fit against him, the crown of her head barely brushing his jaw. He slid his hand further around her waist, splaying his fingers against her lower back. Max reveled in the fiery warmth of her skin, reaching through her thin blouse to singe his nerve endings.

He brought their joined hands in closer, to rest against his chest, and the breath of her sigh skated across the back of his hand. For a moment he worried, convinced she could surely feel his pounding heartbeat under her cheek—until he noticed the hurried thrum of the pulse in her wrist, nearly as frantic as his own.

Max had never felt such a sudden, intense attraction as he did for this woman in his arms. She'd done nothing but knock him on his ass from the moment he stepped outside the bar. And it wasn't simply that she was pretty, or that she fit wonderfully in his arms —though that was no small thing, either. But he admired her wit, her charm. Even when their conversation took a more solemn turn, a vivacious spark lurked beneath her surface. He wanted nothing more than to keep that spark burning. Feed its flame. Get to know all of her layers. He suspected one could spend a lifetime with her and still not unearth them all.

She raised her head to look at him again, eyes blazing. His heart skipped. A question loomed within the blaze, before she reached a decision.

"Kiss me," she whispered.

All breath deserted him. He raised his eyebrows in a silent question. She held his gaze and nodded.

And that was all he needed.

He tried to be gentle at first, brushing his lips over hers. At even that small contact, they both gasped, and he honestly had no idea who moved to deepen the kiss first. Their tongues tangled and their gasps turned into moans, and his blood rushed directly to his groin.

She slipped her hand out of his, sliding it slowly up his chest and around the back of his neck, pulling him closer. He followed suit, easing his arm around her shoulders, his other hand descending along her back to graze her ass. Sense flooded him momentarily, reminding him that he might be taking too much of a liberty—until she hitched her leg in a slow slide, hooking her foot around his calf. He growled a bit at that, palming her lush curves more brazenly as her teeth sank into his lower lip.

He'd never met a woman who made him so light-headed.

Shit, wait. Am I light-headed?

Max shook off the silly warning in his head. Of course he felt this way. He was kissing a beautiful, enchanting woman who…*oh, good lord*…who had raked her fingernails down his back and was now groping *his* ass. No wonder his head felt foggy.

Whew. Really foggy.

No, everything was fine. He needed to keep kissing her. She tasted so damn good.

She pressed even closer, and the motion pushed the metal of his belt buckle into his stomach…which felt pretty queasy, come to think of it.

Huh. Maybe I should come up for air. Just for a second.

Max managed to pry his lips away from hers, and she looked up at him, her pupils huge. They both breathed heavily, and she seemed as dazed as he felt. Well, maybe not quite as dazed.

A slight tilt of his head, and it felt like an entire, choppy sea sloshed against the inside of his skull.

Oh, no.

He swallowed hard in an attempt to ward off the dizziness. To no avail.

His stomach lurched, and he clamped his jaw shut.

Dammit. No. Not now.

His next attempt to swallow brought about disastrous results, as his throat felt like it was closing over, and a wave of acid stung the inside of his cheeks. He ground his teeth together. A sheen of cold sweat coated his face.

His lovely companion's dazed expression sharpened, and her eyebrows scrunched together. "Are you all right?"

He wanted to answer her, he really did. But he couldn't open his mouth. He didn't dare. So he settled for a nod.

He really shouldn't have.

The wooziness, nearly overpowering now, sent a telegraph right to his midsection.

No no no no no

He took a half-step back as her eyes widened. Somehow he managed to turn mostly away from her before… Max dimly registered her horrified gasp before the roaring in his ears drowned everything else out.

And he cast up the entire contents of his stomach.

Practically at her feet.

Fuck.

He closed his eyes and hung his head, bracing his hands on his knees, desperate to regain his bearings. The rushing sound died down enough for him to catch a fragment of her voice, the questioning word *drunk* the only coherent bit that broke through. He tried to hold up a hand, to tell her *no*, at the exact moment his body decided it wasn't through making a fool of him just yet.

As he finished—at least he hoped he was finished—his senses started to weave in and out of focus, like a wavering radio signal. The clearest sound, of course, was her grunt of revulsion, followed by the sharp click of heels on the asphalt. Disappointment pierced through the buzz, the loss of her good opinion making him feel even worse. Something else that might have been a door opening reached him amid the static, followed by a shout that sounded an awful lot like his best buddy Nick's voice.

A warm, steadying hand settled on his back, and another gripped his arm. "Jesus, Max. Are you okay?"

Yep, definitely Nick.

He let his friend lead him back to the crate to sit. "I'm fine, really," he croaked.

"Like hell you are." Nick handed him a handkerchief. "Do you need some water?"

"Nah." Max ran his tongue over his teeth. "Maybe."

Nick commanded someone who had apparently followed him out to fetch the water, then crouched in front of Max.

"The usual?" Nick asked.

"Uh-huh."

"It's been a while. I've gotta admit, I was wondering if it was going to catch up with you."

Max grunted in response. He'd been wondering the same thing himself, but hadn't wanted to dwell on the subject for fear of jinxing his luck.

Nick peered more closely at him. "You look a touch less green than you did a minute ago," he offered.

"Gee, thanks." His head *was* swimming a little less now, and— *Shit.*

He whipped his head up too fast and saw spots. But when they cleared, they revealed the truth he'd already known. She was long gone.

Max turned back to Nick. "Did you see…?"

Nick raised his eyebrows. "What?"

He was about to answer, but it didn't really matter. She wasn't coming back. "Never mind." He hung his head, rubbing the back of his neck.

"Huh. What's this?" Nick asked.

"Hmm?"

"Looks like someone lost a charm or something."

That got Max's attention. Nick held a tiny gold object that he'd picked up off the ground. Gently, Max took it from him and examined it. A little pencil. Exactly the kind of thing a fiery, beautiful accountant would add to her charm bracelet. He closed his fist around it and risked another glance down the empty alley, feeling pretty damn empty himself.

In under an hour, Max Mitchell had met—and promptly run off—a lovely Scottish lass who could easily have been the woman of his dreams.

And he never had gotten her name.

Chapter Two

Hollywood, California
Two years later…
December 1947

Frannie Haynes took a sip of her whisky sour, pleasantly surprised by just how delicious it tasted.

"You know, for a movie star, that Nick Bradley knows how to make a mean cocktail," Anna Yang commented at her side.

Frannie chuckled at how precisely her new colleague's assessment echoed her thoughts, as she absorbed the holiday cheer around her. Everything about the evening, the whole season, felt like a new beginning.

This was the first official gathering for the newly minted Phoenix Pictures, and Frannie's first as the newly installed head of the studio's finance department. She was thrilled—also a tad nervous, but mostly thrilled—to be back to her first love, numbers. Even better, her new boss was her dear friend, Lois Ashford.

The talented, if notorious, movie star had just stunned all of

Hollywood by acquiring an entire film studio in a marvelous coup. She and her husband, Nick—fellow actor and all-around good guy—had brought their friends and a select bunch of new colleagues together for a modest celebration at their home.

"That he does," Frannie concurred. Her smile softened as she spotted the cocktail connoisseur himself across the room with Lois, the pair beaming at each other. "And he makes Lois happy, to boot."

"Took me all of five minutes to figure out she deserves plenty of that." Anna snorted. "She's certainly a hell of a better boss than her asshole predecessor."

Frannie nodded. Anna was Lois's head office manager and a force of nature. She'd practically run the studio for the tosser Lois had tossed out on his rear, and now she was proving to be Frannie's greatest ally in winning over her new, male-dominated department. The two of them already made quite a team.

"How long have you two been friends, anyway?" Anna asked.

"A couple of years," Frannie replied, thinking back over the past two years and the hardships she'd faced. The career she'd had to cede to the boys returning home from war; the long hours working in a profession that wasn't nearly as rewarding, just to make ends meet. "Lois was one of my first clients when I started doing manicures, and we hit it off right away."

Anna's eyes held an understanding of everything that hovered beneath Frannie's words. "It must be nice to get back to accounting, though?"

"It is. Not that I didn't enjoy the other. The people always made it fun...mostly."

"But it wasn't your passion."

"No," Frannie admitted. "Though I'll always be grateful for that part of my life. It brought me here, after all."

She raised a glass in salute, and Anna returned the gesture, their glasses clinking before they each took a sip and resumed watching the rest of the party.

"How's your little girl, by the way?" Anna asked. "Lucy, right?"

Frannie warmed at the mention of her daughter, five years old and the light of her life. "She's fantastic—apart from her grave disappointment over not being able to come tonight."

Anna laughed. "She's got plenty of time to catch up on parties."

"That is precisely what I told her."

The two women shared a smile before something caught Anna's eye. "Uh-oh. My husband's about to corner Rex Tyler again. You'd think he'd run out of questions about the man's western films, but he's relentless. I'd better rescue them both."

"Good luck." Frannie waved her away with a grin.

It didn't take long for her smile to fade, her thoughts taking on a wistful edge as she watched Anna loop her arm through her husband's. Frannie's gaze drifted to Nick and Lois again, leaning into each other while engaged in animated conversation with a few of their other guests. She fought a sigh, her mind drifting to her late husband, Marty.

They'd married in a hurry, right after the attack on Pearl Harbor and before his enlistment. Barely over a year later, the war took him from her and their infant daughter. They'd never had the opportunity to mingle at a gathering like this.

A bit of her longed to find a partner again, someone to navigate parties—and everything else—with. But another bit of her remained more than reluctant to put herself through it all again.

She had tried from time to time, dating with mostly little success. The salon where she used to work was relatively fancy, but Enzo and Lorraine, the couple who ran it, were delightfully down-to-earth. They liked looking out for her, and Lorraine frequently tried to set her up with young bucks she knew.

She swore they were all dreamboats. Frannie had quickly learned, however, that the older woman was prone to exaggeration when it came to the gentlemen in question. What with her most recent disaster only the week prior, she really needed to learn how to start saying no to Lorraine's offers.

The few who lasted past a first date did a decent enough job of scratching her physical itches, but she'd yet to find any sort of meaningful connection with even one of them.

Well, you did find one.

Frannie chided herself. True, she'd spent a memorable evening with one gent who'd shown a hell of a lot of promise. But it hadn't even been a date, only a chance encounter...that ended disastrously. With vomit.

It was hardly fair to compare every date since with that handsome, charming stranger. And yet...

She sighed. It did her no good to dwell on it. While he hadn't seemed it, the man had been so drunk—or turned off by her kiss—that he'd gotten sick. The chances of her ever meeting him again were slim to none, anyway.

New beginnings, she reminded herself. She had a lovely new job, and her circle of friends was growing. While she had enough sense not to get involved with an actor, she'd be meeting plenty of other interesting people. Perhaps one of them would light an exciting spark.

Satisfied with her fresh line of thinking, Frannie scanned the room again, humming along with Billie Holiday's crooning of "I've Got My Love to Keep Me Warm" which was playing on the phonograph in the corner. She spotted her friend Natalie "Nate" Reynolds, the new head of Phoenix's costume department—whose damn husband was once again missing from the festivities, and at Christmas, no less—animatedly chatting with a dark-haired, vaguely familiar man.

Frannie studied him for a moment, trying to place him. She could see only his profile from where she stood, so her memory remained elusive. The man's full, close-cropped beard made him stand out; most men of her acquaintance with facial hair sported a mustache of some kind. She half-remembered a bearded man in the periphery of Lois and Nick's wedding photos—that might be why she recognized him.

The man turned his head briefly, a warm smile flashing across his face. Paired with the twinkle in his eyes that she detected even from a distance…

Frannie's heart stuttered, and she nearly dropped her drink. It couldn't be. Could it?

Looks like those odds weren't so slim after all.

She took advantage of the crowded living room to scrutinize him surreptitiously. The more she looked, the more certain she became.

It was her mystery man from V-J Day.

She gulped her cocktail in an effort to settle her nerves. Bloody hell, she'd practically conjured him out of thin air with her thoughts. And bloodier hell, he was even more handsome than she remembered. The beard was a new addition, but it suited him ever so finely.

Her entire body flushed with heat, all the potent attraction she'd felt that night two years ago roaring back to life. Their immediate connection, the fire in his kiss, and—

The way he'd only just missed her shoe when he heaved.

Embarrassment fueled her flush now. She chewed on her lip. What the fuck was she supposed to do? And who exactly *was* he, anyway? He'd told her he was a baker. Bakers didn't normally come to fancy Hollywood parties. Not that Lois and Nick were particularly fancy, but…

The beer bottle he held forced her attention back to the matter at hand. If he'd been blootered enough that night to get sick, it stood to reason that he likely didn't remember much, if anything, about it.

She couldn't say she was up to the disappointment if he didn't remember *her*.

But what if her own memory was faulty? The incident lived in infamy in her mind, but maybe she'd built it up, made too much out of it. Their connection probably hadn't been nearly as heady as all that. So really, no harm nor foul if he didn't recognize her. Tonight was about *new* beginnings anyway.

Nick's appearance at her side saved her from further attempts to convince herself.

"Enjoying the party?" he asked, all joviality.

"Indeed I am. And you?"

"Yeah." When his eyes landed on Lois, his smile took on a dreamy edge.

Her heart warmed on behalf of her friend. "Never dreamed you could be this happy, did you?"

He chuckled. "I really didn't." He returned his attention to Frannie, his grin sharpening. "Hey, come with me. I want you to meet someone."

"Okay."

See, this is how it should be. He'll introduce me to one of his friends, and I can forget all about drunken mystery men.

But as she followed Nick through the crowd, their target quickly became evident. No one new at all. *Shite.*

She had a matter of seconds to decide what to do, but her thoughts raced in a jumbled mess. If she began with a reminder that they'd met before…that could easily lead to epic, embarrassing disaster, if he didn't remember her. Or worse, they could renew their acquaintance only to find that it wasn't so special after all. She'd get her hopes up and have them crushed all over again.

Frannie supposed she could also play it cool, gauge his reaction first. Protect herself until she knew which way the wind blew. Although that would risk hurting him, if he thought *she* didn't remember…

But as Nick came to a stop, Marty's face flashed through her mind, unexpectedly. With that sting, the desire to protect her heart won out. She gathered her wits and dropped a mask of casual indifference over her features, waiting to see what her stranger would do.

He turned when Nick's hand landed on his shoulder, his handsome face…casual. Indifferent. Frannie's heart sank. So he didn't remember, then. She'd made the right decision. Even though it felt anything but right.

Willing her expression to remain neutral, she scanned his features. She thought she detected a small spark of...*something*... in his dark brown eyes. But it was likely only her sad imagination.

She brought her attention back to Nick, who'd started the introductions.

"Max, this is Frannie Haynes, our new accounting whiz at the studio, and Lois's friend. And Frannie, this is my oldest, dearest, most notorious friend, Max Mitchell." Nick lowered his voice in a conspiratorial stage-whisper. "He runs a bakery over in Burbank, and let me tell you, his cheesecake is to die for."

It was most definitely her stranger. *Max. His name is Max.* For all they'd shared that night, they had never gotten around to exchanging names.

Max shook his head at Nick. "So dramatic." He turned his attention back to her, extending his hand. "It's nice to meet you, Frannie."

She paused for a moment, hung up on the subtle emphasis he'd put on her name. But no, that was silly. Stupid wishful thinking again.

She returned his handshake, somehow maintaining a cool exterior despite the heat shooting up her arm at the contact. His skin felt every bit as warm and wonderful as it had been when they'd danced.

Which he doesn't remember.

Anger flared in her chest. "Likewise. Max, was it?"

He nodded.

"So if Nick's being dramatic, does that mean your cheesecake's not that great after all?" She worried briefly if the question was too mean-spirited, but her mounting disappointment, and attraction, felt overwhelming. Much safer to lean into her anger.

A glint of matching ire lit Max's eyes. "I don't usually like to brag, but I'm no slouch when it comes to cheesecake."

"And I am not being dramatic," Nick jumped in. "Not this

time, anyway." He flashed her an annoyingly hopeful smile. "I expect we're all going to be spending a lot more time together, so you'll have plenty of chances to try it and see for yourself."

Great. Just what she needed. The prospect of countless friend gatherings—forced to relive her embarrassment in the company of this handsome, aggravatingly oblivious man—yawned in front of her, churning her gut.

Frannie pasted a smile on her face. *New beginnings, my arse.*

MAX COULDN'T BELIEVE his luck. Or the fact that his luck managed to be so simultaneously wondrous and shitty.

After two long years, here she was. And he finally knew her name.

He'd been chatting with Nate when he spotted her. Thankfully, Nate was called away at the same moment, so he didn't need to invent an excuse for why his voice, and all sense, deserted him.

After that night, unable to shake the woman—*Frannie*—from his memory, he'd returned to the bar a few fruitless times in the distant hope of running into her again. Of getting another chance, to make up for the way things ended between them. Nick had finally talked him into moving on, warning him that even if he did find her, there was little chance she'd be as great as he remembered anyway.

And he'd tried, truly he had. Dated a couple of lovely women, who were very nice. But who failed to ignite even half the spark he'd felt with Frannie two years earlier.

Now, face-to-face with her once again, it turned out Nick had been right. She wasn't as great as he remembered. Between her still-staggering beauty and her fiery nature blazing hotter than ever, she was even better.

Aside from the fact that she appeared to have zero recollection of him.

Out of the corner of his eye, Max had watched her

approaching alongside Nick, his panic mounting over what to do. It hardly seemed like a good idea to lead with, "Hey, I'm the guy who puked on V-J Day, remember?" She'd probably turn around and run all over again. Suddenly and irrationally terrified that she might not recall their encounter at all—though how one could forget all they'd shared, good and bad, he had no clue—Max had decided not to do anything, instead letting her take the lead.

And she'd dashed all his hope. Even insulted his cheesecake. *His* cheesecake. All in that lilting, sexy accent, dammit.

But maybe he was being the dramatic one now. Perhaps she felt the same embarrassment he did. Anger would hardly solve anything. And she was *here.* He didn't intend to blow it all over again, not when he'd been given this beautiful—albeit fraught—second chance.

He should keep it light, reset the mood. Once they were all laughing, he could slip in a mention of that night. Make it casual, an amusing reminder.

Max inhaled a fortifying breath and picked up the thread of Nick's conversation. "Yeah, you really shouldn't knock my cake until you've tried it, lassie."

Frannie's eyes narrowed and her jaw clenched.

Shit. What is that look for? He'd had the sense to stop short of actually using a Scottish accent, which had to count for something.

"Did you just call me a *dog*?" she asked acidly.

Max stared at her in horror. "What? No. How... That's... *What?*"

She had the nerve to roll her eyes. "Lassie? Really?"

Understanding, or the complete lack thereof, hit him like a ton of bricks. "Are you kidding me? Why in the world would I call you, a woman I've just met"—*ahem,* for the second time anyway, but he'd deal with that later—"by the name of a famous, and heroic I might add, dog?"

"Exactly. It's ridiculous. Not to mention rude."

In his periphery, Nick's head swung back and forth as if he

were watching a tennis match. Max knew he should cut this off, but his annoyance, and humiliation, mounted.

He wished Lois and Nick had a well in their living room that he could fall down alongside poor Timmy.

But the strange glint lurking in Frannie's lovely blue eyes had him feeling suspicious, and his ire won out.

"It would be, if that's what I'd meant," he gritted out. "But my use of the word had nothing to do with the dog, and everything to do with the fact that you're Scottish, are you not?"

Frannie opened her mouth to retort, just as Nate returned to the group. "What'd I miss?"

A relieved-looking Nick steered the conversation back from the cliff's edge, but Max could hardly focus. His attention stayed on Frannie, now studiously ignoring him.

There had been a moment, before she'd taken offense, where she'd seemed to come to a decision—to eviscerate him. And then a flash, even more fleeting, when he mentioned having just met her.

His suspicion grew. Frannie Haynes might not be as forgetful as she let on.

The only trouble was, he'd just hit strike two. He should be thrilled that, as Nick said, they were about to start spending a lot more time together. Instead, he couldn't help the sinking sense of dread in his stomach, telling him that he was far from a home run.

Chapter Three

Burbank, California
Another Year-and-a-Half Later…
Spring 1949

Frannie surreptitiously peeked out her back door, full watering can in hand, ready to give the poor little tomato plant at the base of her porch some much-needed love. That affection would have to wait, however, if the coast wasn't clear. She gazed over the fence bordering the alley that separated her yard from the neighboring bakery. She and Lucy had moved into the house, along with her mother, two weeks prior. And she'd spent the entirety of that time successfully avoiding the neighboring bakery's owner.

Not that she wasn't neighborly. Generally she was. But this specific neighbor? She'd prefer to avoid him like the plague.

That was the trouble with finding a house through the recommendation of friends, like Nick. They knew of the vacancy through *their* friends.

Satisfied that all was quiet on the neighbor front, Frannie

approached her tomatoes. Well, her empty vines anyway. From all she'd read, they should have been sprouting *something* by now. But the sad little greens remained fruitless. She continued to tell herself the change of scenery simply arrested their growth—steadfastly ignoring the nagging suspicion that her lack of a green thumb might, in fact, be at fault. Either way, she was determined to nurture them into fruition, so, silly as it was, she crooned softly to the fronds as she watered them.

Her latest ministrations complete, and needing to get to work, Frannie had just turned to go back inside when a door slammed shut on the other side of the fence.

Oh, no.

She mounted the short set of porch steps, foolishly convinced that if she moved slowly enough he might not notice her.

A deep, dramatic gasp sounded across the alley.

Well, tits. There goes that theory.

She sighed. Might as well get it over with.

Frannie turned to find Max Mitchell's handsome—*no, not handsome, annoying*—face staring right at her, his dark brown eyes wide with disbelief. Which was odd. Surely Nick would have told him she bought the place. The man couldn't keep his mouth shut for anything. And even if he had neglected to mention it, Max must have seen her coming and going, as hard as she'd tried to slip past his notice.

Yet he continued to stare. And stare.

Och, what is wrong with him?

"Is there something I can help you with?" Frannie asked acidly.

He started at the sound of her voice, his eyes growing even wider as he walked toward her. "Oh wow, you're real."

"I beg your pardon?"

"I'm sorry, it's just…" He shook his head. "There was nothing but fog here earlier this morning. And now…here you are. It's… it's like a miracle or something."

"What the—" *Oh. Ugh.* He'd really just gone there. She let out a snort of disgust.

His face split into a positively shit-eating grin.

Her lip curled into a sneer. "A *Brigadoon* joke. Because I'm Scottish. How terribly clever of you."

"I thought so."

God, she wanted nothing more than to smack that stupid smile off his stupid face. Stupid man.

"Good morning, neighbor," he continued.

"If you insist. Neighbor." With that, she turned on her heel and opened her screen door.

"Welcome to the neighborhood!" Max called out.

She threw one more snarl over her shoulder and let the door slam in her wake. His laughter echoed across the alley, following her inside the house. Frannie dropped the watering can by the door and stalked to the kitchen counter to refill her coffee cup.

Why in the ever-loving fuck did I think it would be a good idea to move here?

Initially, she'd been under the mistaken assumption she'd only have to deal with the man during business hours. The day she realized he also *lived* above the bakery had been a grim one. But it was too late by then. She'd already fallen hard for her new home.

It was the perfect size for her little family, and exactly in her price range. They'd long outgrown their modest apartment, and it thrilled her that Lucy, now six-and-a-half years old and growing more active every day, had a nice little yard to play in. And it wasn't far from their old place, meaning she hadn't needed to change schools either. All in all, the house had charmed Frannie quite thoroughly from the moment she saw it.

If only *its* backside didn't face the world's biggest pain in *her* backside.

Too bad an actual wall of fog couldn't permanently take up residence between their properties, sucking him into its void for a hundred years, so she wouldn't have to deal with him. Or see that fucking handsome face of his.

Because he had to be fucking handsome.

She'd thought so from the moment she met him, nearly four years ago now. His dark brown hair nearly black in the dim light of that alley, eyes sparkling with barely banked mirth. And then she'd been blindsided by him anew at Lois and Nick's holiday party. His appeal couldn't have dimmed, couldn't have been less remarkable than she remembered—oh, no. He had the unmitigated gall to be even *more* handsome.

Hell, the man had a beard, for fuck's sake. Beards weren't stylish, but that didn't stop Max Mitchell. The bastard not only flouted convention, but he looked damn fine while doing so. That well-trimmed carpet on his face lent him an air of maturity. Mystery. Sex appeal.

Frannie growled into her coffee cup.

It didn't matter how obnoxiously attractive the man was. Or how much his bad jokes made her want to laugh in spite of herself. Or how she could still remember exactly the way his delicious mouth tasted when fused with hers.

No.

None of that mattered. Because he was still the man she'd spent a near-perfect, ultimately catastrophic, evening with, who failed to fucking remember her when the vicious fates had thrown them on the same path again two years later.

If he couldn't remember, she'd never forget.

She was a Scot, after all. Long-held grudges were in her blood. And much safer on her heart than the alternative, in this case.

"Mom, I'm ready!" Lucy's high voice pierced through her dark mood and brought a smile to her face.

"Be right there, love," she called back, before taking a final swig of her coffee.

She'd drop her daughter at school, and then make her way to the Phoenix Pictures lot for a productive day at work. Managing the numbers that she could always rely on, alongside the friends she'd come to trust so dearly.

Her neighbor from hell would absolutely *not* ruin this lovely day.

———

MAX LIFTED a corner of the towel covering the bowl on his huge kitchen worktable and tested the dough inside with one finger. *Perfect.* He'd taken it out of the refrigerator to warm up during the early morning rush, and now that things had quieted down out front, he was ready to get started on this batch of cinnamon rolls.

He hummed along with the radio as he dumped the ball of dough onto the floured board in front of him and picked up his rolling pin. This was one of his favorite times to work, taking advantage of the bakery's mid-morning lull to prepare some extra treats for the afternoon crowd while his assistant, Linda Talbot, manned—or rather, womanned—the counter.

The minute his pin hit the pliant dough, instinct took over, and Max enjoyed the warmth spreading through his arm muscles as they flexed. That was one of the unexpected advantages of owning a bakery—he had no need to join an athletic club.

Max let his mind wander as he settled into a familiar rolling rhythm, and before long he smiled. He'd been waiting two long weeks to try out that *Brigadoon* joke on his new neighbor. And it had provoked exactly the reaction he'd hoped for.

He rather enjoyed provoking Frannie Haynes.

Especially because she gave as good as she got—better than she got, as a matter of fact. The two of them had elevated bickering to quite a fine art over the last couple of years, and he'd be lying if he said it didn't give him a little thrill every time he got a rise out of her. After all, her Scottish fire usually came out in full force when it happened.

Of course, if Max was truly being honest, he'd much rather be kissing her than provoking her. She kissed even more sublimely than she bickered.

But the one time he'd done that, it hadn't ended too well, so he'd settle for the provocation.

Not that they ever talked about that night four years ago. It still stung like hell that the night destiny had deposited her back into his life at Nick and Lois's, Frannie hadn't displayed a single shred of recognition. Little wonder Max had clammed up at her indifference.

Dough flattened to his satisfaction—perhaps a little thinner than he'd intended, given the spark of ire his line of thinking brought out—he turned to the dish of melted butter at his side and began to slather it on.

Max still suspected Frannie wasn't as oblivious as she let on. Given the palpable contempt she'd been hurling in his direction since their introduction at the party—starting with her disproportionate, willfully obtuse response to that damn harmless joke—he could only assume that she did indeed recall V-J Day. And steadfastly kept that fact to herself while holding a grudge, rather than letting him try to explain.

Granted, the only way to find out for sure would be for him to bite the bullet, be the bigger person, and bring up the subject himself. Seeing as he'd only compounded the awkwardness surrounding the most embarrassing night of his entire life with his ongoing silence… It was fair to say he was hesitant to break that silence anytime soon. Besides, if she didn't care to hear an explanation anyway, why should he bother to offer one?

He was fully aware of the flaws in his logic.

But at the very least, he'd enjoy her reactions to his provocations more often now that they were neighbors.

Max sprinkled his secret cinnamon-sugar mix over the melted butter, just as Nick's voice called to him from the kitchen doorway.

"Please tell me I'm in time for some taste-testing." His best friend since forever smiled around the door frame.

Linda popped her head around the other side. "Sorry, he got past me again."

"Oh, please," Nick scoffed. "You've never been able to resist my charms."

Linda rolled her eyes and went back to the counter. The truth was, she had *always* been able to resist Nick's charms. She'd known the two of them almost as long as they'd known each other, as she and Max's twin sister, Vi, had always been good friends. One of the many things they had in common was the fact that they were two of the only women who'd never fallen prey to Nick's gravitational pull—Vi because she saw him as a second brother, and Linda because she was lured by charms of the female persuasion.

"Am I interrupting?" Nick asked, still hovering in the doorway.

Max continued sprinkling as he answered, "Nah. Come on in."

Normally, Max didn't let non-employees into his kitchen, especially during business hours, but he trusted Nick to be careful. Knowing the drill, Nick pushed aside his suit jacket and shoved his hands in his pants pockets—safely away from temptation—as he strolled to the opposite edge of the table from the spot where Max worked.

Nick's eyes lit up as Max set down the dish of cinnamon dust. "You gonna finish that?"

Max lifted his head to glare at Nick as he turned the board in front of him. "Yes. I have another batch to make after this." He began rolling the well-dusted dough lengthwise. "And you know you're not allowed to so much as lick the spoon of anything that's meant for my customers."

"Yeah, yeah," Nick grumbled. "You know, if I'd known how few perks I'd actually be getting, I might not have been so eager to invest in this place once upon a time."

Max snorted. "What are you doing here, anyway? Shouldn't you be…ya know…working?" Having finished off the roll's seam, he picked up his favorite knife and pointed it at Nick with a flourish. "Oh, that's right. You're sleeping with your boss."

"Try saying that without the knife next time and see how it

works out for you, jackass." Nick's broad grin—the one he wore whenever the slightest mention of his wife came up—leached any venom from his words.

Max grinned back as he sliced the dough roll into a dozen perfectly even pieces. "Empty threats. You know I can take you. *And* you'd never risk that money-making mug of yours."

Nick shrugged. "I suppose you're right. Lois, and my adoring public, do rather enjoy my face." He winked exaggeratedly, every bit the movie star.

"Ugh, spare me." Max reached for the pan he'd prepped and started laying the slices in it. "So, are you going to get to your point, or do I to have to give you something useful to do around here?"

"You'd really do that?" Nick's enthusiasm bordered on frightening.

"Of course not. You'd eat most of your work."

"No, I wouldn't—" He considered for a second. "Okay, yeah, I probably would. Anyway, I am here to make more work for you." Nick pulled a scrap of paper from his pocket. "Lois sent me over with an order for an event she's got coming up."

Max set a layer of cling wrap over the pan of cinnamon rolls and walked it over to the counter next to the ovens to complete the last rise, answering Nick over his shoulder. "She could've called that in, you know."

"I know. But I like doing things for her."

Max raised an eyebrow. "And you wanted a midmorning dessert."

"And I wanted a midmorning dessert," Nick echoed, resigned. "Can you really blame me?"

Max laughed. He wiped his hands on a nearby towel and reached for the list. A pretty standard order, by the looks of it, and he'd have all week to get it done. He very much appreciated all the extra business Lois threw his way on behalf of the studio.

"I did also want to say hello to my oldest friend, you know," Nick continued.

Something in his tone put Max on alert, given his friend's notoriously obnoxious matchmaking efforts.

"How are things going with your new neighbors?" Nick asked. Hard as he tried to sound innocent, Max saw right through him, as usual.

"Just fine, thanks."

He could sense Nick waiting for more as he grabbed a second bowl of dough and set to work with his rolling pin. Max let the silence drag out.

"Oh, come on," Nick finally exclaimed. "That's all you have to say?"

Max looked up from his rolling, widening his eyes in his own show of innocence. "What else should I say?"

Nick opened his mouth to retort, but stopped himself and crossed his arms over his chest instead, viewing him through narrowed eyes.

Max made no effort to hide his smirk as he focused on his task. "I thought you said we were a lost cause anyway."

"You are," Nick complained. "Still. You know I'm going to get to the bottom of…whatever's between you two…at some point, don't you? I mean, one Lassie joke—however unfortunate—could not possibly fuel this much sustained animosity."

Max dropped his rolling pin. "For fuck's sake! How many times do I have to tell you people, I was referring to the word for girl in Frannie's homeland, not comparing her to a damn dog! And she fucking knew it."

Nick's lips were sealed together in an effort not to laugh, and Max inhaled slowly, reining in his temper. He carefully picked up his pin.

"Anyway"—he cleared his throat—"you're wasting your time. There's nothing more to get to the bottom of," he lied.

What Nick didn't know wouldn't hurt Max.

Normally, he wouldn't keep anything from Nick, but his situation with Frannie felt different somehow. Max had been reluctant to reveal that she was his V-J Day mystery woman, fearful that

Nick's well-intentioned meddling could easily end up making things worse. What's more, if Max and Frannie had never gotten around to hashing out what happened that night, it didn't feel right for him to talk about it with someone else, even Nick.

Plus, a small, sentimental part of him liked having something only the two of them shared, however fraught—and despite how little actual sharing was involved.

"Bull. Shit," Nick retorted.

The man's optimistic insight was such a pain in the ass sometimes.

Max raised his eyes to Nick levelly. "Is that all you needed? Because, unlike you, I do have work to do."

Nick held his hands up in surrender. "Fine. I'm going." He walked to the door, turning around once more before he left. "But you know as well as I do, I'm not wasting my time." He gave Max a salute. "See you later, brother."

Max grunted a farewell at his so-called friend.

He threw a glance over his shoulder toward the back door, thinking of what—of *who*—lived beyond it now, and sighed. Nothing would ever come of Nick's meddling, even if he allowed his friend to meddle in the first place. But for a brief moment, Max let himself wish it could.

Chapter Four

Frannie strode across the Phoenix lot, enjoying the golden afternoon sun, all traces of the morning's neighborly encounter purged from her mind. Well, most traces anyway.

It wasn't her fault she'd been reminded of the man a few minutes prior. Upon leaving a meeting in the production building, she crossed paths with Heather from the makeup department and they stopped to chat for a few minutes. The woman's name always reminded her of her first home in Scotland, where the heather on the hills behind their town grew in wild abundance. The love song from *Brigadoon* then started echoing in her head, a perfectly natural progression. Which danced her mind right into an image of wide brown eyes hovering over a beard-framed smile.

Her lips began to curve upward of their own volition as she remembered—

No. Stop it right now.

Frannie shook her head. She would not find his joke funny. Because it wasn't. At all.

She focused her gaze determinedly in front of her, smiling unabashedly this time. Coming toward her was Colin Canfield, the best screenwriter at Phoenix, in her opinion. Granted, she might be a smidge biased, since he was also her brother, but she didn't care. He was the best, and that was that.

Colin matched her grin as he spotted her and waved. "Hi, Fish!"

I take it back. Best, my arse.

Frannie groaned. "How many times do I have to tell you, it is entirely unprofessional for you to call me that when I'm at work."

"Methinks the lady doth—"

"Oh, shut your hole, Chips," she snapped.

Colin laughed, and she stuck out her tongue, which only made him laugh harder. Frannie gave in and chuckled herself.

She'd always groused about—and secretly loved—the nickname. Their grandmother had christened them Fish and Chips when they were kids, and while Frannie protested plenty, it remained a lovely reminder of Gran. And Colin at least conceded to upgrade her to a mermaid on occasion.

After several years' separation during the war, Frannie was inordinately grateful to have her big brother back in her life.

"So, where are you off to this fine afternoon?" he asked.

"Back to my office. And you?" She glanced behind her, where the studio's wardrobe building hovered. "Off to see your sweetheart?" she sing-songed.

Frannie laughed at the telltale flush creeping into Colin's cheeks. He was utterly besotted with Nate Reynolds, and she couldn't be happier for the two of them.

He shrugged as he readjusted his glasses. "Perhaps."

"Well, do tell her hello for me."

"Will do." He smiled. "Are you all settled into your new place?"

Frannie narrowed her eyes. "Why, what have you heard?"

Colin snorted. "Nothing. Should I have heard something?"

"No, of course not." At his raised eyebrow, she continued, "But you're shite-stirrers, the lot of you, and over nothing, at that. Just because Max is now my neighbor, it doesn't mean there's going to be dirt for you to be digging up. So quit it."

Bloody hell, did that sound too defensive?

He held up his hands in mock surrender. "You have my word, no shite is being stirred here." He cleared his throat. "Though I would like it noted that *I* made absolutely no mention of Max."

Damn.

But really, could anyone blame her? Their mutual friends had wondered for some time what exactly had transpired to make the two of them so fractious in each other's presence, but they'd grown extra invasive of late. Now that everyone was all coupled up, she wouldn't be surprised if they'd made some kind of pact to team up and ferret out the truth. *Good luck to them.*

She made a valiant effort to control her own blush. "Right. Noted."

"Really," he replied mercifully, "I was only asking because we're pretty well set up in our new apartment, and we want to have you and Lucy over for dinner soon."

Frannie scrunched her nose. "We were just over last week."

"True, but that was informal. I think Nate wants to do something more official...or formal...or fancy?" Colin shrugged. "I really have no idea. Between you and me, I honestly think she's angling for a counter-invite. She's dying to see how your new place turned out."

Frannie smirked. Knowing Nate, it was more likely that she wanted to see some fireworks lobbed back and forth between her and the baker across the alley. It killed the woman if a piece of gossip existed that she wasn't privy to.

Frannie wasn't about to reopen that subject, though, so she kept her thoughts to herself. "I promise to have all of you over as soon as I get at least a few more boxes unpacked."

"I'll let her know." Colin gave her arm a squeeze. "But we really would love to have you. Perhaps this weekend?"

Frannie smiled. "That sounds fab. I'll check my diary. Lois has that brunch thing here on Saturday morning, but other than that I should be free." She paused, thinking. "It sticks in my mind that I have something going on Friday too, but I can't for the life of me recall it." She waved her hand absently. "No matter. I'll give you a ring."

"Deal. I'll see you later…Mermaid."

She grinned. "Enjoy your sojourn in Wardrobe Land, Chips."

They parted with a laugh.

Frannie made her way back to the building housing the finance offices. The sound of adding machines and typewriters beckoned her invitingly down the hall. She passed through the bullpen where most of the accountants worked, earning a few smiles and waves from those whose noses weren't completely glued to their facts and figures. Certainly an improvement from those early months after Lois had taken over the reins of the studio and appointed Frannie to her high-level position. It had taken a bit for everyone to welcome her, but with assistance from Anna—and Frannie's undeniable skill with numbers—she'd earned her colleagues' respect faster than expected. And no one dared ask her to fetch them coffee.

Arriving at her office, she tossed her leather-bound notebook on the desk and removed her jacket, draping it over the back of her chair. She smiled as she sank into her seat and glanced out the window. The finance department was one of the least glamorous buildings on the lot, but she at least had a window, and her second-floor location afforded her a decent view of all the more exciting goings-on.

Not that she didn't find her job exciting. She'd always encountered many a skeptic who simply couldn't fathom how crunching numbers for a living could be anything but boring. But Frannie loved it. She'd love it even if she was in some dingy bank office instead.

It just happened to be an added bonus to sit in the middle of a Hollywood movie studio, surrounded by actors and dancers in gorgeous costumes, making sure they had the funds they needed to create their art.

When she factored in that some of those artists were her very dearest friends… Well, life was good indeed.

Colin's invitation still fresh in her mind, Frannie picked up her datebook and flipped to the current week's pages. Her eyes fell on Friday's entry and…

Oh. Right.

She had a date. She didn't know how she'd forgotten it, since it was her first in longer than she cared to admit. Or perhaps that's precisely why she'd forgotten.

Frannie heaved a sigh.

She should be looking forward to going out, meeting someone new. Only she wasn't. The last few weeks had been exhausting, what with the move to the new house and getting Lucy settled in. She had no idea what had possessed her to agree to a date *now*, of all times.

Her memory landed with a thud on the phone call that set it in motion.

Her old boss, Lorraine, hadn't given up trying to find dates for her, despite the fact that Frannie finally started speaking up. She'd been successfully putting the woman off for ages.

Until that day last week.

Frannie grimaced in remembrance. She had been cradling the telephone's receiver between her cheek and shoulder, sweeping the never-ending parade of dust from all the moving boxes. She'd just opened the screen door to her back porch when she spotted Max emerging from his door, and ducked back inside before he could spot her. Her back flattened against the wall, peering around the corner of the doorframe, she'd barely heard Lorraine's question, but answered absently—affirmatively —regardless.

That blasted man had gotten her roped into a date she would very likely regret going on.

I wonder if he'd be jealous…

Frannie jerked her head up. Why in the hell should he be jealous? More importantly, why should she bloody care whether he was or not?

She shook out her shoulders. She'd given entirely too much

thought to Max Mitchell today, and it needed to stop. He was completely irrelevant, in every way.

With any luck, Lorraine had gotten it right for a change, and her upcoming date would sweep her off her feet. She was long overdue for some improvement in the love department—or the bedroom, at the very least. And maybe, just maybe, Friday evening would kick off a new, exciting adventure.

THE DELICIOUS SCENT of her mother's beef stew hit Frannie as soon as she walked in the front door. She dropped her pocketbook and briefcase on the hall table and made her way to the kitchen, a little surprised.

"Hey, Mum," she greeted her. "I thought I was in charge of supper tonight."

"Hi, love." Betty Stewart looked up with a warm smile. "You were, but the veggies at the market were beauties today, and I got home a little early, so…" She raised a wicked eyebrow. "I could stop and let you take over, if you're disappointed?"

Frannie snorted. "Oh, no, I'm fine, thanks." She leaned over her mum's shoulder and took a whiff of the warm, onion-y heaven that she'd loved ever since she could remember. "Smells like perfection."

"Of course it does." Betty gave her daughter a quick peck on the cheek before nudging her away from the stove. "How was work today?"

"Good. I ran into Colin. He and Nate want to have us over for dinner again soon."

"I'm so glad you two found each other again."

"You and me both." She leaned on the kitchen table and eased off her high heels with a sigh.

"How in the hell do you wear those all day?"

"Believe me, if I didn't sit as much as I do, I wouldn't last long." Frannie picked up the pretty—but painful—brown alligator pumps. "I'm going to go get comfy." She paused on her way to the door, the strange quiet of the house catching up to her. "Hey, where's Lucy?"

Betty glanced over her shoulder. "Off at the park with a few of the other wee 'uns from down the block."

Frannie smiled. "Oh, good. She's making friends fast."

She marveled at how quickly children, especially her child, adapted to change as she climbed the stairs to her bedroom. *Thank heaven for that.* Her wonderful little girl deserved the world. If the move to this house was good for her, then Frannie could certainly put up with a pesky neighbor.

She threw her jacket on the bed and had just opened her dresser drawer to fetch her blue jeans when movement outside the window caught her eye. She peered through the semi-sheer curtains and watched a pretty woman holding a pink box emerge from the little patio behind the bakery. Max followed.

When the woman turned to face him, he paused to lean against the space's lattice framework, hands in his pockets. *Honestly, what right does he have looking so—*

Frannie groaned, gripping the curtain harder. Here she went again.

She watched as the woman threw her head back, laughing at something he said. *He's not that funny.* She couldn't quite make out the expression on Max's face, but his relaxed posture indicated he liked the woman's attention. As if on cue, the woman reached up and brushed his arm. Frannie's nostrils flared. *Who is this dame, anyway?*

Not that it mattered. Not at all.

The lady rounded the corner of the patio, looking around surreptitiously as she headed back to the street. That was odd. For his part, Max pushed off the wall and strolled to his kitchen without a backward glance. All that apparent flirting, with a woman who clearly thought of her presence there as a risk, and she mattered so little to him that he couldn't see her off? *What an arse.*

Frannie shook her head. It was absolutely none of her business what—or *who*—Max did in his spare time.

She closed the drawer with extra force, then moved away from the window to slip out of her skirt. She shoved her legs into her jeans, focusing her attention on what she could control. Like cuffing her hems, since they were always too long for her slightly less-than-average height. She toed on her worn loafers and straightened the bottom of her short-sleeved sweater, taking a fortifying breath.

What did she care if Max Mitchell had a rendezvous with a customer? He was her sworn nemesis, and she had a date of her own to look forward to.

Nodding her head, she bounded back downstairs to the kitchen.

"Need any help?" she asked her mother.

"Nope, I'm fine," Betty replied. "Stew should be done soon, as a matter of fact."

"I'll go wrangle the little lass, then." *It'll give me something more productive to do.*

"Oh, I almost forgot. We don't have much in the way of dessert. If the bakery's still open, you might want to pick something up."

Believe me, I might not.

Since she'd prefer to avoid that subject, she gritted her teeth, hoping her mother didn't notice her utter lack of enthusiasm. "Sure. Be back in a jiff."

Frannie took a few deep inhales through her nose as she made her way around the corner and down to the park. Despite the fact that it resided directly across the street from the bakery, she proudly refrained from looking in the store's direction. Quite an achievement, really, as she scanned for passing cars.

An energetic hand emerged from the small group of children gathered near the jungle gym to wave at her, and all gloom vanished immediately.

"Hi, Mom!" Lucy trilled.

Frannie grinned as she approached. "Hey, Lassie-Lucy. I hate to break up the party, but it's time for dinner, kiddo."

"Okay."

"Uh-oh," another little girl—Nancy, was it?—moaned. "I've probably gotta go, too. My mom'll kill me if I'm late for dinner again."

A chorus of grumbles echoed as more of the children came to similar realizations.

"Bye, everyone!" Lucy called as the group dispersed.

Nancy followed as far as the sidewalk. Before turning to go, she nudged Lucy and nodded toward a boy who stood further away with another group of kids. "Hope he won't be here tomorrow."

"Yeah," Lucy agreed. They both made faces at the boy's back, before Nancy ran off in the direction of her waiting dinner.

"What was that about?" Frannie asked.

Lucy took Frannie's hand as they neared the street. "Johnny Aames." She scrunched her nose in disgust. "Always kicking up sand and pushing. He thinks he's better than everyone, but he's just a jerk."

"Want me to talk to his mother?"

Lucy smiled up at her. "Nah. It's okay."

"Are you sure?" Frannie narrowed her eyes. "Has he ever pushed you?"

"No, he mostly goes after the other boys."

The street was clear, so they crossed, Lucy swinging their hands between them.

"All right. But if he ever does, you tell me right away, and I'll take care of him."

Lucy giggled. "Okay."

Her girl might laugh, but Frannie meant it. The little twerp better not come for her daughter. She'd show him.

Lucy started toward home, but Frannie gently tugged her hand, hiding a sigh. "We have to make a stop first."

At her nod toward the Mom's Bakery sign, Lucy's eyes lit up. "Really?"

"Yup. Play your cards right, and I might just let you pick out what we get."

Lucy let out a little squeal, and now she was the one doing the tugging. Frannie braced herself for impact as they approached, trying to derive comfort from her daughter's bouncy brunette ponytail. She supposed she should be grateful for her previous streak of two whole weeks without Max-contact, but twice in one day felt highly unfair. The things she did for her lass...

Lucy opened the door, immediately enveloping them in a cloud of sugar and vanilla scents. With a little cinnamon and chocolate thrown in for good measure.

She'd say *this* for Max: he knew what he was doing when it came to baked goods.

The man himself looked up from his spot behind the counter as they came in. Frannie detected a hint of surprise, before he schooled his features.

"Well, don't you two have excellent timing?" Max greeted them with that damn devastating grin. "I was only a few minutes from closing up."

"Hi, Mr. Mitchell!" Lucy greeted him.

"Now, Lucy, what have I told you?" He was all sternness as he rounded the counter and crouched in front of her.

Frannie crossed her arms over her chest. What the bloody hell was he scolding her daughter for? Forget Johnny the Jerk. She'd be all too happy to kick the crap out of Max.

With a few of his teeth missing, at least his smile would be far less likely to put her twat in turmoil.

"Mr. Mitchell is my dad," the arse continued, oblivious. He pointed at Lucy. "You can call me Max, remember?" He finished with a wink.

Oh.

She supposed she and her twat had jumped the gun a bit there.

Lucy giggled in response, clearly charmed. Fantastic, she was raising a little traitor.

"Okay, *Max*," she trilled, before bouncing on her toes. "Hey, guess what? Mom said I get to pick what we take home today!"

"Did she, now?" Max looked up at her. "That's generous of her."

Frannie scowled down at him. He might have Lucy bamboozled, but she knew better. To her complete frustration, his mouth twitched as he tried to mask his humor.

He stood up and made a sweeping gesture at the glass-fronted counter. "So, what can I get you, Miss Lucy?" Before she could answer, he held up his hand abruptly. "No, wait. Let me guess."

Lucy grinned up at him as he raised his hand to his forehead and squinted, like some charlatan predicting the future.

"I think…" Max paused dramatically. "You're going to pick… hmm…snickerdoodles!"

Lucy gasped in delight. "How did you know?"

Max shrugged. "Eh, I have a sense about these things."

Frannie bit her lip in an effort to suppress a snort. The cookies were Lucy's absolute favorite—of course she requested them every time. Though Frannie supposed it was nice of him to play along.

He moved back around the counter, throwing Frannie a wink over his shoulder. For some unfathomable reason, heat crept into her cheeks. She looked away quickly.

Thankfully, Max turned his attention back to Lucy. "You're in luck, I happen to have some snickerdoodles left. How about a dozen?"

Lucy turned wide eyes up to Frannie. "Can we get that many, Mom?"

"Oh. Um…" Why in the world did her voice sound so raspy all of a sudden? She cleared her throat. "Sure." She nodded in Max's general direction. "A dozen will be fine. Thank you."

"You got it."

Frannie narrowed her eyes at his back as he pulled a pink box down from a shelf. She could have sworn she heard him chuckle before setting to work packing up the cookies.

"Oh, by the way, Lucy," Max began. Both hands occupied, he nodded toward the store's big front window. "I saw that Aames kid bothering you all before. I hope you know you can come get me if he ever gets too mean."

Frannie's head snapped up.

"Thanks, Mr.— I mean, Max." Lucy beamed up at him. "It's funny, Mom said the same thing."

He met her eye, all seriousness, and gave her a quick, definitive nod. The air vacated her chest.

Turning back to Lucy, he replied, "Well, good. Then there's two of us who have your back."

Lucy shrugged one of her little shoulders. "I'm not scared. There's more of us than him. And Mom's always teaching me how to stand up for myself, anyway."

"Of that, I have no doubt." Max failed to suppress a smirk. "Showed you how to throw a punch, did she?"

That stupid heat returned to her cheeks. And points south.

Lucy giggled. "No, silly. Mom said I shouldn't *actually* fight."

Frannie found her voice. "That's right."

Max nodded solemnly as he wrapped a length of twine around the now-full cookie box. "True. Especially with bullies like him. It never fails—they start it, but you're usually the one who gets caught. And then they laugh all the way home."

"Speaking from experience, are you?" Frannie couldn't resist teasing him.

He sighed. "Sadly, yes." He leaned over the counter and crooked a finger, beckoning Lucy closer. "I do have one piece of advice." He glanced at Frannie. "Not that you'll ever need it, but... If you find yourself needing to throw a punch, remember this." He held up a fist. "It is a truth universally acknowledged, that anyone who tucks their thumb into their fist will only hurt themselves more than their opponent. Keep that thumb on the outside."

He concluded with yet another wink, taking most of the seriousness out of his statement.

Max handed the box over to Lucy, and Frannie could tell it was all the lass could do not to lift the lid and steal one. Shaking her head, she stepped over to the counter, pulling some cash from her pocket.

"Do you always mix Jane Austen and boxing advice?"

"They are a natural combination, after all." He grinned.

She steeled herself against that bloody mouth as she paid him. "Thank you, by the way. For looking out."

"Of course."

The air hung heavy around them for a moment, transporting her back to that long-ago night. To the feel of his arms around her as they danced. To that melting kiss. Before—

She inhaled sharply.

"Right. Well." She turned to her daughter, waiting patiently. "Ready to go, lass?"

"Yup." Lucy took her hand as they made for the door. "Bye, Max!"

"See you later, Lucy. Enjoy those cookies."

If she didn't know better, she would've sworn she heard resignation in Max's voice. Frannie couldn't bring herself to look back as they exited.

Chapter Five

Max loaded a huge box, filled to the brim with pastries, into the back of his small truck. After a busy day, he was running later than he wanted to be with this delivery. He had been hoping to get it over to Phoenix Pictures earlier and perhaps run into some of his friends.

He glanced across the alley. In the growing twilight, he detected Frannie's mom, Betty, moving around in the kitchen. He wondered if Frannie had returned home yet.

"This is the last of it," Linda said, carrying out another box.

"Thanks for sticking around to help." Max took the last batch from her and set it with the others. "You sure Ronnie doesn't mind you getting home so late?"

An adorable touch of pink graced her cheeks, as it always did whenever her sweetheart came up. It bothered Max that Linda and Ronnie had to let most people assume they were simply "roommates"—but the two women usually took it in stride. They did, at least, have each other.

He fought the urge to glance across the alley again.

"She's fine," Linda replied. "After all, she's getting me all to herself on a Saturday for once." She grinned at him. "Thank *you* for that, by the way."

Max waved her off. "Don't mention it. It's been forever since Ronnie sang at a festival. You should both enjoy it."

Linda usually opened for him on Saturday mornings, but he'd insisted she take the day off this week to join Ronnie. While he normally would have preferred to deliver Lois's pastries right before her event in the morning, the smile currently on Linda's face made the evening trip worth it.

"You sure you don't need me to come with you?" Linda asked.

"No, you close up here and then get going."

"Okay." She nodded toward the small shed in the corner behind the building. "I still don't know why you haven't added a sidecar to that thing. Think of the fantastic advertising. You could be the only baker in town with a delivery motorcycle."

Max snorted. "As tempting as that sounds, I would not risk the safety of my baked goods by stuffing them in a sidecar."

She swatted his shoulder. "Oh, you're no fun. Don't you wish you could ride it more often?"

"Jealous, are you?" At her shrug, he laughed. "And I use it plenty, when I'm not on deliveries."

Linda raised a skeptical eyebrow at him. "If you say so."

"Okay, enough nagging me about my ride. Let me get these over the hill."

"Fine. Get out of here." She flashed him a downright evil grin before heading back inside. "You don't want to get there too late. Who knows, you might run into your neighbor."

Max narrowed his eyes at the door as it shut behind her, then sealed his baked goods in the truck with a grunt. It seemed everyone knew how he felt about his *neighbor*. Except for his neighbor, of course.

He jumped into the front seat and started the engine with a smirk. Linda didn't even know what she was talking about. It was Friday evening; Frannie was probably long gone from work. He'd likely miss her. His smirk promptly collapsed.

Max shook his head and turned on the radio as he pulled

away from the bakery. It made no difference whatsoever to him whether or not he met Frannie at the lot.

The radio crackled to life and… He bit back a groan. "I'm Beginning to See the Light," already in progress. *Of course.* He forced his focus on the evening breeze coming in the open window, on the pleasant winding drive through the hills.

On the fact that he'd enjoy it a lot more if he were riding his motorcycle—not that he'd give Linda the satisfaction of admitting it. The road was relatively quiet, with most people already at their destinations, be they home or some fun Friday locales. That suited him just fine, as he could take the canyon's twists and turns at a leisurely pace. He did have pastries to protect, after all.

Before long, he arrived at Phoenix. Bert, the night watchman, recognized him on sight and waved him through the gates, and Max parked the truck in the loading area behind the commissary. Given the frequency of his drop-offs, Lois had arranged a key for him ages ago, leaving him free to let himself in and unload.

Lois had also attempted, on many occasions, to hire him as a more permanent fixture in the commissary. As flattered as he was, Max steadfastly resisted. He loved his bakery. He'd built it into a nicely successful business in just a few years, though it could stand to be doing a little better. He'd love to hire more staff, so he could work a little less.

Max whistled to himself as he finished unloading. After locking the door, he paused to inhale the odd mix of scents around him. Eucalyptus trees bordered the studio, and he detected an early hint of night-blooming jasmine as well. Both of which contrasted with the unmistakable fragrance of freshly cut lumber, evidence of the many sets in progress.

He decided to take advantage of the quiet with a quick walk. He didn't know why he'd complained about being too late to run into anyone. As exciting as this place was when it bustled with all manner of movie-making activity, Max rather thought it had a certain magic when it was serene like this.

He'd always enjoyed the sweetness that came with a bit of

solitude. Sure, he'd been plenty active as a kid, but Nick was the one who'd really craved the action as they grew up. Max preferred the peace that tended to descend in moments like this one, or when he was elbow-deep in his baking.

Hands in his pockets, he ambled across the lot. It really was a nice night. A touch chilly, but the day's earlier warmth still hovered. A few stars had begun to wink overhead, despite the lingering light. If he looked closely, he wouldn't be at all surprised to see some sprites, maybe a ghost or two, prowling the studio, keeping watch.

Sprites and ghosts? He sounded downright Scottish.

He froze, eyes widening. *Maybe there's some magic around here after all.* There she stood, as if he'd conjured her out of thin air —Frannie.

She was here awfully late. He narrowed his eyes. And who was that guy with her? Not that Max knew everyone at the studio. But this one did not have the look of a movie-making type. Not even close.

Is she on a date?

A white-hot stab of jealousy shot through him. Which was silly, really. He had no claim on her. Chucking up your dinner didn't exactly count as marking one's territory. Not that he'd do that anyway. Women were not territory to be marked. Especially women who couldn't stand him. Because of the upchucking.

He groaned, but before he could settle his thoughts, his feet moved of their own accord, making a beeline straight for Frannie and her mystery man.

FRANNIE WALKED ACROSS THE LOT, half-listening to the man at her side enter his third hour of droning on about…she honestly didn't know what. She'd been tuning him out for a while.

She'd thought it a good idea to have Peter, her date for the evening, pick her up at work. Since her dates rarely made it to a second round, she preferred to keep them from meeting Lucy. The lot provided a nice alternative; it always made for a good conversation starter, or at the very least an exciting backdrop.

Plus, if things didn't go so well, she could hide behind the excuse that she needed to get some more work done, or pick up her things before the guard locked the gate for the night. Her companions didn't need to know that a guard was on duty all night, every night, and would let her in, no matter the hour.

The problem with her current suitor, however, was that he'd been more eager than a puppy to get a quick tour of the studio.

It surprised her, given that he'd never once let up talking about himself. But she supposed since she'd spent most of that time not entirely listening, she might as well give him a brief look around before she bid him goodnight. It would be his only chance.

She had to hand it to Lorraine; this one was at least mildly attractive. His darkish hair was a bit too light, his jaw a bit too smooth. Eyes a bit too dull a brown. But still, better looking than most of them.

Of course, he more than made up for that with his oh-so-riveting personality.

Peter let out a small gasp and stopped. "I say, is this where the writers work?"

Frannie looked up, startled. He hadn't paused enough in his conversation for her to point out much of anything, and she'd lost track of their location. "Oh, yes. My brother works in there."

Peter's dim eyes lit with a spark. "Does he really? My goodness."

Distant alarm bells sounded in her head, but before Frannie could form an answer, Peter continued. "You know, I just happen to do a bit of writing myself." He radiated a nauseating amount of self-pride.

"Really. I thought you were a..." *Shite.* What was it he did again?

"I must confess, most of us English teachers do harbor a secret longing to write our own masterpieces," he finished with a smug grin he hadn't come close to earning.

"Is that so?" *Please don't pitch me a script. Please don't pitch me a script.*

"Yes. I've just completed a screenplay, as a matter of fact."

It took tremendous effort not to groan aloud. Before she could craft a semi-appropriate response, however, another voice called out. A deep, all-too-familiar voice.

"Frannie, hello! Fancy meeting you here."

Max strode toward them—because her evening apparently hadn't gone tits-up enough. *For fuck's sake.*

"What the hell are you doing here?" The words escaped her before she could stop them. Not that she really wanted to, anyway.

The bastard didn't even flinch. "Dropping off Lois's pastries for her thing tomorrow."

Frannie arched an eyebrow. "At this hour?"

Max shrugged. "Sure. I have to open the bakery tomorrow morning. And Lois gave me a key to the commissary."

Frannie squinted in the dim light. It almost looked like Max was puffing out his chest.

"Anyone going to introduce me?" Peter interjected.

Whoops. She'd almost forgotten about him.

"Where are my manners?" Max extended his hand, with a bit more force than necessary. "Max Mitchell. In addition to owning a thriving bakery, I fill a lot of special orders for the studio."

Peter gripped the man's hand. "Peter Creavey. Mrs. Haynes was kind enough to give me a tour of the place as part of our date."

Frannie bristled at the emphasis he placed on that last word.

"She is kind." Max smiled, far too innocently.

She narrowed her eyes at him, at the same time Peter split a glance between them.

"And do you two know each other well?" he asked, unabashed skepticism in his voice.

Frannie fought the urge to roll her eyes. *I swear to god, if they whip out their pricks and start pissing…*

For some unfathomable reason, her eyes chose that precise moment to land in the vicinity of Max's potentially pissing member. And linger there. Her brain protested, so why weren't her eyes moving? *Huh. His pants are pretty drapey, and yet…* She swallowed, finally forcing her rebellious eyeballs upward.

She inwardly sighed in relief. He was too busy answering Peter's question to notice her scrutiny.

"Oh, Frannie and I are neighbors." Max's voice dripped with artificial syrup. "But we go way back, actually."

A vise-grip squeezed her lungs. *Wait a minute. I thought he didn't…*

"We had mutual friends when she started working here," Max continued. *Right.* Her chest loosened as he spoke. "My buddy's wife owns this studio, and so we've been to many a gathering with the two of them."

"Oh. Is that right?" Peter's face reflected conflicting impulses. His chest-pounding over her was quickly giving way to what looked like intrigue. *Swell.*

The intrigue won out as a realization clearly hit him. "Say, that Lois you mentioned earlier… Did you mean Lois Ashford?"

"I did." Max shot Frannie a look.

Believe me, I know.

Max returned his attention to Peter, eyes narrowing slightly. "Tell me, Peter, what is it you do?"

"Oh, I teach English by day." The man had the balls to square his shoulders. "But I'm also a screenwriter."

He'd graduated from aspiring to full-fledged. *Deliver me from asinine dates.*

"You're kidding," Max replied. "Imagine that. Have I seen anything you've written?"

Frannie stifled a snort. Max was baiting him, and the man had no idea. Given the way their date had been going, she couldn't find the desire to be offended on his behalf.

56 • BRIANNE GILLEN

Peter flushed a little. "Well, nothing yet, I'm afraid. But I've finished a banger of a script, and I'd love to see it go somewhere. I was just about to tell Frannie all about it."

"That is perfect. Frannie, did you tell him your *brother* is a screenwriter here?"

Okay, *now* she was going to kill him. "I did indeed," she said between clenched teeth.

Peter nodded. "She did." He leaned in conspiratorially. "And you know, since you know a lot of people here as well, I suppose it couldn't hurt if I told you about it too, Mr. Mitchell."

That settled it. Definitely a double murder on the bill for tonight. Surely her brother—and definitely Nate, come to think of it—would help her hide the bodies.

Max, to his credit, registered a bit of wide-eyed disgust at Peter's answer before gaining control of his features. He crossed his arms. "You're not going to leave us in suspense, are you?"

Peter straightened his suit jacket, mustering the most excitement he'd shown all night, a remarkable feat given how much he loved talking about himself. "It's a costume drama. A new spin on *Romeo and Juliet*."

Of course it was.

"How intriguing. Isn't that intriguing, Frannie?"

She wanted to kick Max in the shins. Instead, she pasted a smile on her face. "So intriguing."

With nary a clue, Peter continued. "Just wait. Let me set the scene. Our hero is a young English redcoat, out to prove himself."

Max gasped. "Don't tell me. The heroine is from a prominent colonial family during the Revolution?"

Peter grinned. Actually grinned. "Even better. Our story takes place a few decades earlier." Here, he threw an anticipatory glance at Frannie. "On the eve of the infamous battle of Culloden. Our intrepid heroine is from a Scottish family."

Kill me now.

"You don't say," she managed. She risked a peek at Max—and

regretted it instantly. His lips fused together tightly, holding in his smug mirth.

But Peter wasn't finished. "And of course, tragedy strikes, they both die, et cetera, et cetera." He inhaled dramatically. "Their entwined bodies are found among the aftermath of the battle, clinging tight even in death."

Frannie swore she heard a strangled sound coming from Max's throat, but didn't dare look this time.

"And in the end," Peter sighed, "reason prevails among those left behind."

Max recovered enough to find his voice. "The English decide to be merciful?"

Peter regarded him with surprise. "Oh, no. The Scots cast off their barbaric ways and adopt the more civilized English way of life, of course."

This. Howlin'. Bawbag.

Frannie's nostrils flared, and her eyes narrowed to slits, red flooding her vision. Little flames of anger sparked up her cheeks. She valiantly refrained from emitting the growl building in her chest.

Before she could retort, or clobber Peter over the head, Max spoke. "Hold on a minute. Did you just say the *Scots* were barbaric?"

"Well, yes. They were quite a ferocious warrior people for a while there." Finally realizing his audience—perhaps because of the noise she most certainly *did* make this time—Peter turned to Frannie. "I mean no offense, of course."

"Oh, that's too bad," she bit out, "because I take plenty of offense."

Peter's face took on a pale cast that had nothing to do with the growing moonlight.

"You know, buddy, you might want to rework that ending a bit"—Max clapped him on the shoulder with a generous amount of force—"considering it was the English who committed most of the barbaric atrocities after that battle."

The haze of her fury started to recede amid Peter's flustered sputtering, an alarming realization taking hold. *Max,* of all people, had just defended her. *Holy hell.*

She blinked up at him, utterly flummoxed, at the same moment he met her gaze. His expression was difficult to read, but it charged the air between them nonetheless.

Until the fact-averse arse-wit that was her date piped up.

"I say!" He leaned in toward her and Max. "I do rather like what I've come up with, but… You think if I make this change, I'll have a better chance with your brother and Ms. Ashford?"

Frannie shut her eyes and counted to five. Peter was damn lucky he'd mentioned Colin and Lois. Her deep appreciation for working with the people she cared about was the only thing keeping her from skelping the man to smithereens right then and there.

Max again picked up the slack while she contained herself. His voice heavy with sarcasm that sailed right over Peter's head, he replied, "You know, Mr. Creavey, I think that might be just the ticket."

She opened her eyes as Max shot her a look translating to *Can you believe this fucker?* She sneered and rolled her eyes in response. All the while, Peter's shoulders relaxed and his mood lightened considerably. He had to be the single most oblivious man on the planet.

And she'd had more than enough of his nonsense.

Before he could say another horrific word, she clapped her hands together. "As much as I hate to cut the festivities short, it's getting late." She gestured behind Peter. "Think you can find your way back to your car? The park's just on the other side of that building, and then it's a left out the gate."

"Oh." Peter deflated a little, but she didn't care. "Is your car there too? We can go together."

She laid a hand on his arm and physically turned him in the blessed direction that would take him away from her. "I have to nab my briefcase from my office before I head out, I'm afraid."

Like a dog with a bone, he perked up. "I could walk you. It is late, after all."

She waved absently behind her. "It's all the way on the other side of the lot. I wouldn't want to hold you up."

"It wouldn't be any trouble. I'd hate to see you go all the way there by yourself."

Jesus. Take a hint, pal.

Max intervened. "Oh, she won't be by herself. I'll walk you over, Frannie."

Peter shot him a venomous stare. "That won't be necessary."

Oh, god, here comes the pissing contest again.

"Actually, it will." Max smiled benignly. "I have to give Frannie my invoice." He turned to her. "I was going to slip it under your door, but this way I can save you a step and put it right on your desk."

Discombobulation punched her in the stomach. Again. She was...*grateful*...to Max. She shook it off, lest she lose her hard-won upper hand.

"That settles it, then." She turned to her date. "Peter, thank you so much for dinner. It really has been a thin slice of heaven."

He looked ready to protest, but—wisely, for once—held back. "Right. Of course." He glanced at Max and cleared his throat before turning back to her. "May I give you a call?"

"You know, things have been so hectic lately, I'd hate to miss that call. Why don't I ring you?" She flashed him her most angelic smile.

He hesitated before finally replying, "Sure. That would be lovely."

"All right, good night, then! Shall we, Max?" She spun around and started walking before anyone changed their minds and prolonged this disaster.

"Nice to meet you," Max called to Peter as he followed her. "Good luck with that script!"

"Shh. Don't *remind* him," she hissed.

He snorted beside her. "Right, sorry." Out of the corner of her eye, she saw him risk a squint over his shoulder. "Don't worry, he's not following."

"Don't jinx it." She kept up a brisk pace until they rounded one corner, then another.

Only then did she finally slow down, letting her body relax. Max matched her more casual stride.

"Okay, I've gotta ask," he ventured, "where the *hell* did you find that clown?"

She opened her mouth, her first instinct to protest out of sheer habit, but settled for the truth instead. "It was a setup." She groaned. "God, he really couldn't have been a bigger bozo."

"I suppose he might have tried to act out some of the battle."

Frannie shuddered. "Perish the thought."

Max chuckled. "Can you believe his nerve? I mean, pitching his script was bad enough, but then to call the Scots barbaric…to a Scot? Even *I'd* never do that."

As much as it pained her, she believed he wouldn't. Rather than admit it, she voiced a thought that had been nagging at her. "By the way, how in the world do you know about Culloden?"

"Lots of people do, don't they?"

"Not exactly."

He shrugged. "Oh. Well, I guess I must've paid attention. I always liked history in school."

"And they taught Culloden in your history over here?" She didn't bother masking her skepticism.

"Maybe not," he replied defensively. "But like I said, I like the subject and have continued to read about it over the years. Scottish-English history is especially fascinating."

She narrowed her eyes. It was hard to tell in the evening light, but she spied a bit of pink, high on Max's cheeks.

"Let me guess," he continued in a sarcastic drawl, "you're shocked that I read something other than pulp novels?" He narrowed his gaze. "Or that I read at all?"

"Of course not," she scoffed. "It's just rare to meet someone who's heard about my country's background."

"And gets it right?"

"And gets it right." She gave him a reluctant grin. "Thank you for your efforts on behalf of my people."

"Wow. Did you just show gratitude…to *me*?"

Frannie hung her head. "I'm afraid so."

He laughed. "Well, you're welcome. I was happy to correct that moron."

"The man truly needed to be put in his place." She hesitated, unsure if she should continue, but she supposed it couldn't hurt at this point. "I did appreciate your efforts in aiding my escape as well."

Max stopped in his tracks, staring at her. "Are you okay?"

She shut her eyes with a groan. "Probably not. You're going to hold this against me for a long time, aren't you?"

He regarded her with a small, private smile. One she had no idea how to decipher.

"Give me a little credit, won't you? I might let this one go."

"Oh. Well. You should." She leveled a finger at his face. "And for the record… Just because I expressed my appreciation for it does not mean that I needed defending or rescuing back there."

He held up his hands. "I, in no way, thought that you did. And just for my own record, it wasn't you I was rescuing."

Frannie's eyebrows inched toward her hairline. "Surely you don't mean that wanker?"

"Indeed I do. You were mere minutes away from dismembering the man, and I wasn't about to stand by and let that happen." He smirked. "I know how hard Lois and Nick have worked on this studio, and the last thing they need is a dead body causing headlines."

She smiled before she could stop herself. "Ah, that makes more sense." She resumed walking, and Max fell into step with her.

He darted his head from side to side and lowered his voice before continuing. "And actually, I was afraid he'd come back to haunt this place."

"If anyone would, it'd be him."

"Right? His transparent form, floating from person to person" —he executed a sweeping gesture—"pitching the most atrocious scripts?"

She laughed. "That would be truly terrifying."

He grinned, and this close, the dimples in his cheeks made quite the impression on her. *Jesus, how deep do those dimples have to be that I can see them through his beard?* She blinked. Thoughts like that were so damn inconvenient.

Luckily, his attention caught on the alley next to them—the lot's New York-inspired street, lined with the facades of various brownstones and storefronts.

Max squinted. "Are those…Christmas decorations?"

Frannie inhaled with relief at the distraction. "Yup. They don't usually make Christmas pictures this early in the year, but the actor they wanted for the Santa Claus character is booked up all summer, so it got bumped up on the schedule." Genuine excitement started to build in her. "You should see some of the shop display windows. The detail's unreal."

Max's eyes sparked with matching excitement. "Oh, yeah?"

"Yeah." She cocked her head toward the street. "Come on."

Frannie led Max over to the festive display and watched his expression grow steadily brighter with each window they took in. The art department had added even more cheer since the last time she'd passed through here, only yesterday. As the two of them strolled down the length of the faux street, she found herself relaxing, enjoying herself.

"You know," he marveled as they neared the corner, "it never ceases to amaze me how much magic they manage to create around here. Of all different kinds."

"I honestly don't know how they do it, time after time."

He smiled down at her. "Must make for a pretty fun place to work."

"It really does. There's always something new—Christmas in the spring, royal ballrooms, pirate ships…"

"Oh, hey, that reminds me. Nick was telling me they're starting work on a movie that takes place on an ocean liner?"

"They are. I hear the set's just about finished." She glanced to their right and pointed. "Stage Five. Want to see how far they got?"

She had no idea where the idea came from. Perhaps she'd pulled it from one of those dimples of his. Nothing about this night was going according to plan, but to her astonishment, she didn't want to go home yet. And with her mum watching Lucy, she didn't exactly need to rush.

Max's dimples pulled her under even more. "Sure. Lead the way."

She set off in the direction of the soundstage, with Max close behind.

The door was cracked open slightly, and she eased it wider to admit them. The stage's only illumination came from a ghost light in the corner. Frannie moved to find the bigger switch on the wall. She barely registered a small scraping sound before remembering what she'd heard about this soundstage earlier that afternoon.

"Oh, by the way," she called over her shoulder, "I had to approve an emergency repair guy today." She flipped the lights on and turned back to Max, still near the entrance. "That door— NO, DON'T!"

His eyes flew wide at her shout, which coincided with the firm slam of the door behind him—the *broken* door.

That had just locked them in.

Chapter Six

"No no no no no..."

"What the hell?" The question had barely made it past Max's lips when Frannie pushed past him—quite roughly given her small stature—to frantically pull at the door, netting precisely zero results. A sinking feeling arose in the pit of his stomach when she pounded the door one last time, before settling her forehead against it in clear defeat.

Shit.

She whirled to face him.

"What the bloody hell did you just do?"

He'd never seen her so livid. Which was saying something, given their history.

"I...moved the block?"

"Yes, exactly." She stalked toward him. "Why?"

"So no one would trip on it. You could easily break a toe on that thing." He pointed down at her shoes, where a few of her manicured toes peeked out. "Especially in shoes like that."

Said toes lurched a step closer to his own. "Never mind my damn shoes. It never once occurred to you that block might be there for a reason?"

"Honestly, no." She flapped her hands in frustration, and he narrowed his eyes at her, willing himself to stay calm as his sinking feeling grew to rival the *Titanic*. "Frannie, please tell me that block was not the only thing keeping us from getting back outside."

She shot him a venomous glare. "I would, but I'm not in the habit of lying."

He stormed over to the door himself, giving it a solid yank.

And nearly lost his balance when it didn't budge. In the same fruitless effort Frannie had made, he pulled the handle a few more times, to no avail.

Dammit. Dammit, dammit, dammit.

He faced her again, not bothering to conceal his mounting frustration. "That door cannot possibly be unable to open from the inside. This is a fully functioning movie studio, not an Abbott and Costello romp."

"I know that. Lois tried to option them from Universal last year, but they were too expensive," she muttered.

Max kept his tone dry. "So naturally, she installed self-locking soundstage doors. Perfectly logical next step."

She sneered at him. "You know she would never do that."

Max raised his eyebrows and gestured questioningly at the door.

Frannie's shoulders slumped slightly. "Under normal circumstances, of course not. But that one broke this afternoon. Too late in the day to get someone out here to fix it, so I had to approve an emergency order for early tomorrow morning." She squared her posture again, and poked him in the chest—which should've been painful, and yet… "As I was trying to tell you before you stupidly let it shut."

Oh, hell no. She was *not* going to blame this on him. He used his height to his advantage, leaning in to loom over her.

"Perhaps if you didn't want me to shut the door, you should have warned me *before* you waltzed us in here."

Indignation flared in her lovely—*no, not lovely, dammit*—blue eyes. "You should have read the sign on the door!"

"How could I? *You* opened it before I got close enough to notice there even was a sign!"

Her nostrils flared as she threw up her hands, the motion setting off a breeze that ruffled his hair. "Well, what kind of moron sees a block in a doorway and doesn't stop to think it might be there for a reason?"

They were now nearly nose-to-nose, breathing heavily. Her light floral scent teased at the edges of his anger, stirring up a memory. Slightly surprised, he inhaled sharply—a mistake, as it let in even more of her fragrance.

He stepped back. He needed to calm down and find them a way out of here before their argument escalated further. Or worse, before he lost all sense and pulled her in for a kiss.

"There's got to be another way out of here." He managed to keep his voice even—an impressive feat, if he did say so himself.

"There isn't."

He rolled his eyes at her stubbornness. Before he could retort, he spotted a telephone on the wall behind her. *Perfect.* He strode toward it. "Then we call the guards for help."

He picked up the receiver and held it up, only to hear…nothing.

"Shouldn't I get a dial tone or something?" He pushed down on the phone's switch hook a few times, but nothing changed.

"Ordinarily."

The defeat in her voice raised the hair on the back of his neck. He slowly turned his head to look at her, and found her thoroughly chewing on her bottom lip, studiously avoiding him.

"Frannie?" he practically growled.

Her eyes shot to meet his. "It's after-hours. The stages' phone lines are shut off every night." Defiance flared in her expression. "As a cost-cutting measure."

There was no need to ask who had issued that edict. Max clenched his jaw.

"Please do tell me again how this is *my* fault." He quirked an irate eyebrow at her.

He could practically see angry lightning flash around her. She gestured impatiently at the set looming next to them. "You're the one who wanted to see this stupid boat in the first place!"

He leveled a finger in her face. "After *you* suggested it. I was fine calling it quits after Santa's Village out there."

"Oh, please," she scoffed. "You were like a little boy, all wide-eyed and 'goll-ee.'" She punctuated this last with a sarcastic imitation that was anything but flattering. "If Santa had been there, you would've cut in front of actual children to sit on his lap."

"There is nothing wrong with recognizing the magic in life. I—" *Fuck it all.* "I don't have to explain myself to you."

He turned back to the door, needing to get the hell out, and banged on it a few times with his fist. "Hey! Help!" He paused in his shouting, another dreadful thought occurring to him. He turned back to Frannie. "The baffling on these walls—does it keep sound from getting *out* as well as in?"

She opened her mouth to respond, and then promptly closed it again, considering. Before he could express his astonishment that she could, indeed, shut up from time to time, she answered.

"I honestly don't know."

They stared at each other for a moment, before she joined him at the door to pound alongside him. The two of them made a concerted effort to make as much noise as possible to attract a guard who might hopefully be passing by.

"Is anyone out there?" Max called. At that, Frannie gasped, and he whipped his head around. "What. Now?"

A new surge of irritation flared behind her eyes, but she tamped it down in order to ask, "What time is it?"

Max glanced at his wristwatch. "A quarter to nine. Why?"

Frannie groaned as she rested her head on the door with a quiet thunk. "Bert starts his rounds at eight-thirty." She raised her head. "Typically on this side of the lot."

It took a minute for understanding to dawn. "So he's moved on already. Which means there is not, in fact, anyone out there right now."

Frannie shook her head as she pivoted to rest her back against the door.

"Is it even worth my asking how often he makes his rounds?"

"Unless some major commotion happens"—she gulped—"he's not scheduled to come back this way until nearly three a.m."

All the air vacated his chest. Max crossed his arms and leaned back himself. "So, we really are stuck in here. All night."

"Mm-hmm."

"Fuck me," he let out, under his breath.

Judging by her sharp, snort-like exhale, she'd heard him anyway.

As they leaned against the door in fuming silence, Max attempted to wade through the storm cloud roiling through his head. Part of him—a bigger part than he dared admit—wanted to dance a jig at the prospect of an entire evening spent in Frannie's company, despite the fact that she made no secret of her contempt for him. And currently blamed him for their predicament, which was, *in no way*, his fault.

The other, wiser part of him clearly perceived the utter disaster looming ahead of them. He'd assumed they'd be in here for an hour or two, tops, which was bad enough. But all night together? It would be absolutely nothing like his stupid, hopeful imaginings. No, it would most certainly involve bickering. Maybe even fisticuffs. Hell, Lois and Nick might end up finding a dead body or two at their studio after all.

The thought of Lois reminded him of the reason he was here tonight in the first place, rather than the morning. Max groaned, letting his head fall back against the door with a thud.

"What now?" Frannie asked, her voice full of ire.

He shot her a dirty look. It truly was unnecessary for her to hurl *that* much disdain at him, all the time.

"I gave Linda the day off tomorrow. Which means I'm opening the bakery." He inhaled through his nose. "By the time we get out of here, I'll be lucky if I get an hour's sleep."

"Oh. And I'll definitely be missing Lucy's bedtime now."

He let out an exasperated gust of breath, feeling like a selfish heel. "I didn't even think of that. I'm sorry. Is she with Betty? Will they be worried?"

Frannie's eyes widened, and he tried to ignore the sting of her surprise at his concern for her family. She considered for a moment before answering. "She is, and I suppose not. They knew there was a chance I'd be home too late to tuck her in. Just..."

"Not quite this late."

"No." She huffed. "I sure wasn't expecting my night to end up like this."

The lingering remnants of his anger evaporated. "Yeah, neither was I."

They let out simultaneous sighs. Max closed his eyes. Her lovely scent made its presence known again with his next breath, however. His eyes flew open, as his common sense mercifully sent him into fight-or-flight mode, saving him from his body's traitorous urge to throw himself at the woman who had been yelling at him only minutes before.

He pushed up off the door and started toward the massive set in front of them.

"Where are you going?"

Max shrugged as he answered her over his shoulder. "If we're going to be stuck in here for a while, might as well do what we came for in the first place. I've always wanted to explore a luxury ocean liner." He spun to face her, walking backwards now. "And with any luck, there'll at least be a few chairs we can sleep on."

Frannie's mouth formed a near-perfect *O* at that last, and he suppressed a snicker as he turned back around. The snicker died a quick death, however, as the impact of his words hit him, and another piece of the warped puzzle of this evening snapped into place. They'd likely have to sleep here. In relatively close proximity.

Dammit.

He mounted the wooden stairs behind the scenery flats that made up the massive ship facade, hoping the artifice was as big as

Nick had implied, so they could spread their chairs at opposite ends, as far from each other as possible. He reached the small faux hallway and pushed through a set of fancy doors onto the deck area, surveying the length of the set, and—

"Oh, you've got to be shitting me."

There was only *one* deck chair.

Nick hadn't been exaggerating—the deck stretched practically a mile long in front of him. And naturally, that huge expanse contained exactly one, single, solitary piece of furniture. Because of course it fucking did.

True, it was more of a double-sized chaise that could easily fit two people. But that only made it worse.

Frannie's footsteps echoed behind him, before coming to an abrupt halt.

"Oh. I guess they haven't quite finished decorating the set, have they?"

"It would appear not." He clipped his words in an effort to mask his rising panic.

She emitted a small grunt, then sent him a sideways glance.

Huh. She looks…nervous.

Before he could dwell too much on that fact, she breezed past him and strolled down the deck, running her hand along the railing. "It certainly is impressive, though, isn't it?"

"It is." He trailed after her, watching her take in all the details of the ship—and finding perverse comfort in the fact that she steadfastly refused to look directly at the chaise in her perusal.

Despite its awkward lack of furnishings, the boat was a marvel. Between the gilded porthole windows, wood-planked floors, and the lifeboats fastened to the railings—which appeared astonishingly sea-worthy—it felt very much like a real ship. It lacked only the gentle rocking of the waves—though it wouldn't surprise him in the least if they had somehow rigged it to move. Lois wasn't one to shy away from working with people who could create details like that.

"You know," Frannie said, leaning her forearms against the

railing to look out at the artificial ocean view, "they sprang for the extra expense and outfitted the backdrop to move so it mimics the rise and fall of the waves."

Max barked out a laugh as he came to rest his own arms at a small—but safe—distance from her. Her lips quirked into a quizzical smile.

"I was only *just* thinking that I wouldn't put it past Lois to sanction something like that. Though I would've guessed the ship moved, rather than the scenery."

Frannie chuckled. "You should've seen the look on her face when she came to me with the idea. She looked so resigned, like she really didn't think it'd be feasible. But there was this spark of hope behind it too." She shrugged. "So I crunched some numbers."

The pride in her voice was subtle, but very much present, and it warmed him. "You really like finding ways to make this stuff happen, don't you?"

She glanced over at him, startled, clearly assessing his face for signs of mocking. When she saw none—he resisted the urge to flash her a smug grin—her expression softened. "I do. It's a bit of a juggling act sometimes, but when I can balance it all and make the big things possible..." She paused, considering. "Numbers have just always made sense to me, you know? They're reliable, and if you know the tricks and the shortcuts, you can almost always find the solution." Gesturing widely, as if there really was an ocean in front of them, she added, "So much in this world doesn't make sense, doesn't add up, no matter how hard you try..."

"But you can rely on your numbers," he finished quietly.

"Exactly." She blinked, returning to the present. "And using all that to help these dreamers make magic? It's...well, it's pretty heady stuff."

Frannie finished with a small smile, and it took all his willpower not to close the distance between them, pull her into his arms, and...

And he really needed to clamp a lid on thoughts like that.

Thankfully, Frannie took that moment to turn her attention back "out to sea." He followed suit, trying to distract himself with the movie magic. Judging by the massive backdrop painted to look like the night sky over a watery horizon, they would obviously be filming from both directions on this deck. A giant half-moon hung in one corner, its reflection shimmering on the waves painted on the canvas below.

Once again it seemed they focused on the same details, as Frannie started humming "It's Only a Paper Moon" under her breath. He smiled, narrowly resisting the urge to finish the lyrics out loud.

He wondered what it would feel like if all this wasn't make believe. If she believed in him…

He held his breath against the wave of longing that socked him in the chest. Attempting distraction, he made the mistake of looking at his watch.

Only six more hours in here. Great. I am in such *deep shit.*

The sound of her sharp sniff pulled his attention. "What is it?"

"Nothing. It's only…" She angled her head to look at him. "You were in the service, right?"

"I was." He wondered where she was going with this, distinctly recalling that the two of them had never spoken explicitly about his service in the war—unless one counted that very first, ill-fated conversation on V-J Day. He held his breath, waiting to see if she would finally bring it up.

On the one hand, this might be the perfect opportunity, since they had plenty of time to hash it out. But on the other… Well, he wasn't too keen on the idea of the night watchman coming upon his dead body when he finally made it back here.

"Before, you said you'd never been on an ocean liner," Frannie responded, oblivious to his internal debate. "But you must have been. You had to get overseas somehow, didn't you?"

Oh. Well, there was his answer. Why bring up their disastrous first meeting—or admit she even remembered it—when she instead had a chance to trip him up in what she believed to be a lie.

Maddening woman.

He concentrated all his effort on shooting her a withering stare. "As much as I hate to burst your little 'caught Max in a lie' bubble..." She wrinkled her nose rather adorably, but he cut off her protest. "If you had been listening more carefully"—here she let out a little huff—"you would have noticed I said I'd never explored a *luxury* ocean liner."

Frannie abruptly closed her mouth at this, and he smirked as he continued, "Crossing the Atlantic in a giant, creaky tub with a few thousand other guys, all packed in like sardines, is hardly the ideal way to travel." He gestured around them. "Not like this would be."

She had the grace to look a little chagrined. "All right, I suppose I'll give you that."

He snorted. "What about you? Did you travel from Scotland on something like this?"

"Sort of. Though not nearly as fancy." A wistful look crossed her face.

"Have you been back there, since the war ended?"

She looked up, a bit startled at his curiosity. He fought that old, familiar sting.

"I haven't. I'd love to take Lucy someday, but things have been busy. And..." She considered for a moment. "I'm a little afraid to see it. Scotland fared better, I think, but Colin said parts of England, especially London, were..." She trailed off.

"I can understand that. It was pretty bad." He offered her a reassuring smile. "But from what I gather, the rebuilding is going strong."

"That's what I've heard too." She paused. "You and Nick served together, right? He mentioned once that your unit didn't see as much action as some others."

"Yeah, he was pretty pissed that his bosses pulled strings to keep him from the worst of it. But then, I saw even less." At her questioning look, he continued. "I technically should've been 4-F. Nick knew how much I wanted to be over there, though, doing *something*, and he…" Max huffed a laugh. "He figured if they were going to pull some strings on him, he could at least pull a few of his own. I don't know how he did it, but he got me on the roster. Restricted to mess duty, not allowed near any of the actual fighting. But at least I was there."

Frannie drifted toward the deck lounger. "Mess duty's nothing to scoff at, you know." She faced him again. "I remember one of Marty's letters, before he…" She cleared her throat. "He talked about his mess sergeant. Said their rations were atrocious, but the guy managed to make some pretty decent meals out of them anyway. He was really grateful." She met his eye, a small smile teasing the corners of her mouth. "You helped nourish your fellow troops. That's important."

Max suddenly found himself unable to swallow properly. Her candor, her *gratitude* meant more to him than he could put into words. He'd always been a bit insecure about the fact that others had risked their lives much more than he'd been able to. Including Frannie's late husband. But when she put his service that way, it made him feel as if, perhaps, he hadn't been so useless after all.

The moment hung in the space between them, breathing under that paper moon.

Frannie blinked a few times before blowing out a breath. "So. How did you come to be 4-F-adjacent, anyway?"

"Ah. Funny story." One he should absolutely *not* share with this woman. It was far too embarrassing on general principle. On top of which, it had already caused him more than enough embarrassment in front of *her*, on V-J Day.

But she watched him expectantly. *Swell.* He couldn't exactly leave it at that. He cleared his throat. "I, um, got a pretty nasty concussion when I was thirteen. It healed, and I'm fine now, but… it left behind a few lingering effects that pop up every once in a while, so… Anyway."

He turned back to the railing, fully prepared to drop the subject.

"And...?"

Max sighed. Maybe he could take a page from her willfully obtuse handbook.

He faced her again with a vague, "Hmm?"

Frannie promptly rolled her eyes. "Oh, come on. You can't just utter the words 'funny story' and then not tell me said story."

"As a matter of fact, I can."

"I could get it out of you. I have ways of making people talk, you know." She arched an eyebrow, her noir-dame delivery socking him right in his Jockey shorts.

"I'll bet you do." The words slid out before he could stop himself. He folded his arms over his chest in an effort to keep his stupidly salacious imagination in check, blundering on. "Trust me, you do not want to hear about the Mitchell Family Baseball Massacre of 1926."

He realized his error at precisely the same moment Frannie let out a gasp of delight. *Fuck fuck fuck.* He'd been so focused on curbing his lascivious thoughts that he'd completely neglected to curb his mouth.

He'd revealed the name of his family's infamous legend. There was no turning back for him now.

Worst of all, faced with the unfettered joy currently radiating off of her—toward *him*—he found himself far more eager than he ought to be to dive to his doom.

Chapter Seven

"Okay, now you absolutely have to tell me this story," Frannie demanded.

She gleefully watched the pink creeping up Max's neck. She'd surprised herself—and clearly him—by bringing up Marty and his thoughts about Army food. Not that she hadn't meant what she said. She did appreciate Max's service. She simply hadn't planned to tell him that. And then they'd had some kind of a…moment.

They weren't supposed to have *moments*.

So she eagerly seized on this change of subject—and Max's subsequent discombobulation over it. Who wouldn't be highly intrigued by a story with a name like the Mitchell Family Baseball Massacre of 1926, anyway?

Max cleared his throat roughly and switched the cross of his arms. "I most certainly do not."

She grinned. "Wow, you're really flustered by this."

"I am not. And you don't have to look so delighted," he muttered.

"Oh, but I do." She closed the distance to the deck chaise and sat down. Despite the furniture's disturbing lack of company, she wanted to get comfortable for the ensuing entertainment. Max shot her a withering stare as she propped her legs up and settled against the back cushion. She left him just enough room to join her if he dared—and wasn't sure whether to feel relief or disappointment when he didn't.

"Don't give me that look," she chided. "You waltzed yourself right into this, and I am going to enjoy it. Besides, you know I can get it out of Nick. So you might as well tell me."

He chewed on his lower lip in a self-conscious move that she refused to find adorable. "It's a long story…"

Frannie made a sweeping gesture at their surroundings. "We're not exactly short on time."

He opened his mouth to protest, then promptly shut it again. He cast his eyes upward, as if commending himself to some higher power, before meeting her gaze again with a heavy sigh. "Fine."

She rubbed her hands together in anticipation, which got a chuckle out of him.

He leaned his lower back against the ship's railing, crossed arms still shielding him, and began. "So, I was thirteen. We had a bunch of family over for supper, because my dad wanted to show off his brand-new Packard. He was so excited about that thing. We all were." His smile turned wistful for a second. "The grown-ups were all sitting around the backyard, talking. Naturally, us kids got bored and went out front to play, since it was still light out." He let out an amused huff. "My cousin Kit used to follow me and my sister around like a little puppy."

"Was Nick there too?" Frannie interjected, curious.

"Interestingly enough, he was not. I think his family was on vacation or something." He smiled, dimples out in full force. "It's about the only memory I have from when we were kids that *doesn't* include Nick. And ironically, the most notorious one."

"I'll bet that burns his arse tremendously, doesn't it?"

Max laughed heartily. "So much, you have no idea. It's part of the reason he still brings it up every chance he gets, telling it like he was there."

"See? Aren't you glad you're not letting me give him the chance, then?"

"I suppose." He smirked. "Are you going to actually let me get to it?"

She held her hands up in mock surrender. "*So* sorry. Please continue."

"Anyway, as I was saying…" He arched an eyebrow, and when she remained silent, he continued. "Kit wanted to do absolutely everything we did. He's about six years younger than we are, so…he was probably close to Lucy's age at the time."

"Ah, yes. The eagerness knows no bounds."

"It really doesn't," he agreed with a chuckle. "Kit wasn't annoying about it, though, so usually we let him tag along. At the time, Vi and I were both pretty obsessed with baseball. But Aunt Beth, who could be terrifying when she wanted to be, was adamant that Kit was too young for it, so we kept turning him away. We weren't about to cross her." He shrugged. "Well, not normally. For some reason, Kit finally wore us down that fateful day."

"Uh-oh."

"Indeed. Vi maintains it was my idea—which it was *not*."

"So eager to pin it on your sister, are you?" Frannie teased, unable to resist.

"Hey, I'm the one who fared the worst that day."

"I'll be the judge of that." She waved her hand. "But please, do go on."

He flashed her a look that was simultaneously skeptical and twinkly, which did not charm her in the slightest.

Not one bit.

"So let me set the scene." Max pushed up off the railing, really getting into his story now. "Kit was beyond excited, but he'd never played before. We figured we'd start with teaching him how to hold and swing a bat. No harm in that, right?"

"None indeed."

"Vi grabbed her bat, since it was a little lighter than mine—

though still pretty big for him. But he managed it okay, and we showed him the right positions." He took an exaggerated breath. "Then he asked us to let him hit a ball instead of just air."

Frannie winced. "You gave in?"

"Afraid so. He was just so earnest, you know?" He shook his head. "We positioned ourselves carefully. Got in real close, so we could intercept any contact he might make right away." He hunched into a pitcher's crouch. "I had the ball, and Kit was right in front of me." He emphasized this with a gesture. "And Vi was over there, where first base would be. We were ready for anything."

She leaned forward in her seat, completely enraptured in spite of herself.

"The first few pitches, Kit didn't even make contact. I could tell he was disappointed, but we were relieved. The last thing we wanted was to catch everyone's attention. Vi and I made him a deal." Max held up a finger. "One more try. And then we'd go inside."

Frannie inhaled sharply, and he gave her a grave nod before continuing.

"I got in position. Wound up to lob him a soft one, believing he'd miss again. I felt the worn leather as it left my hand…"

She held her breath.

"Then the crack sounded." He held up his hand in a steadying gesture. "Not a big crack, mind you. No home-run miracle swing." He rubbed a hand over his beard in a sad, slow motion. "No, in a somewhat inexplicable quirk of physics, the ball hit the top edge of the bat at just the right angle…" Max paused for dramatic effect, in a manner that was—just as inexplicably as the ball's physics—not obnoxious, but perfectly captivating.

"…to send it straight for me," he continued. "Before I could even think to duck, it got me." He pointed to a spot just above his left eyebrow. "Right in the head."

"Ouch."

"So much 'ouch.' Knocked me flat out."

A question popped into her head, and Frannie opened her mouth to ask before reconsidering. She wasn't entirely sure why she hesitated, since goading him was one of her favorite pastimes.

He cocked his head, watching her. "What is it?"

She waved a dismissive hand. "Nothing, really."

"Oh, come on. Since when do you hold back? Spit it out."

She let out an indignant—albeit half-hearted—huff before giving in to his request. "Okay, fine. It was a very entertaining story. And not to belittle your obvious injury, but..." She bit her lip. "It hardly seems to warrant a grand title like that."

Much to her surprise, she hoped she hadn't offended him.

His resulting smirk—followed by the *tsk*-ing sound he made—told her she had not.

"Now, now, Frannie. You know what happens when you assume..."

She narrowed her eyes at him. "And just what, precisely, did I assume?"

"That my story was over."

"I... Oh."

He grinned like a cat who had cornered a mouse, and it was all she could do not to give in and smile back at him. She waited for him to continue. And waited.

She finally shot him an impatient look, and he smirked once again. "I'm not sure I should tell you the rest. If you'd rather go on thinking that's the end..."

"You are such a pain in the arse!"

He threw his head back and laughed. Frannie hated how much the sound warmed her. And *where* it warmed her.

Thankfully, he had mercy on her and resumed speaking, giving her something else to attempt to focus on.

"Okay, I suppose it's only fair. So, the rest of this I will have to relay secondhand, since I'm sure you'll recall, I was pretty much out cold from this point on." He shook out his shoulders, getting back into storytelling mode. "The last thing I remember before I blacked out was the sound of my sister's yelp."

"Don't tell me…"

He nodded. "Yep. The ball ricocheted off my eyebrow and headed straight for Vi. My head slowed down its momentum quite a bit, so that should've been the end of it. However…" He held up a finger. "When she attempted to catch it, she was so flustered by having seen me go down that she accidentally put up her *ungloved* hand. She realized her mistake at the last minute, but in her haste to course-correct, she made it worse…"

Frannie's hand flew to her mouth as she imagined the scene. And his sister's pain. "Oh, god."

Max winced as he rubbed his wrist in sympathy. "Yeah. It wasn't pretty. Her flail put the ball right in contact with her wrist bone." He shook his head, his eyes brightening again.

"Wait. That's not the end, either, is it?"

He shot her a rueful grin. "Nope. You see, Vi's swatting reinvigorated the baseball's momentum. For a truly grand finale, she sent it hurtling toward a landing…"

Frannie's eyes widened, suspecting the story's conclusion. "No…"

"Right in the middle of the windshield of my dad's beautiful new Packard. Shattered it into more pieces than you would think possible." He hung his head.

"Jesus Christ. It really was a massacre."

"Told ya." Max chuckled. "You should hear the way my family describes the scene they ran out to find. Me, sprawled on the lawn, out cold. My sister, kneeling on the grass, curled around her hand, wailing. Glass from the Packard, sparkling everywhere. And my cousin Kit, frozen in place, still holding the bat limp at his side, eyes wider than saucers. All of the adults gathered on the front porch, surveying the carnage."

Frannie couldn't help the snort of laughter that escaped her. At his amused look, she said, "I'm sorry. It's just… I can practically hear that anthem-like dirge you have over here. What's it called?" She hummed a few notes, and he caught on quickly.

"The 'Battle Hymn of the Republic.'"

"Yes! That's it."

He joined in her laughter. "Vi and I have always joked that we should play exactly that tune underneath the story one day."

They laughed together for a long moment.

"God, your parents must've been furious."

"They were actually way more calm than I would've expected." He shrugged. "Probably owing to their worry about our injuries. I mean, it wasn't as bad as it could've been. I came to before the car had even pulled out of the driveway on the way to the hospital—my uncle's car, of course."

"Of course."

"But they were still pretty worried at first. My sister lucked out. As painful as it was initially, it was just a nasty sprain, and she got to go home as soon as she got her brace on."

"And you?"

"They kept me in the hospital for a couple of days, mostly to watch me. It was a concussion, after all. You should've seen the nasty egg I had." He touched his brow again. "Started forming before I even woke up."

"And you still have some lingering effects, even now?"

His hand traveled around to rub the back of his neck, a sheepish look crossing his face. "Yeah. It left me prone to bouts of vertigo, nauseousness. They're pretty rare at this point, but…" His eyes flitted up to hold hers in his gaze. "It does still happen once in a while."

A twinge of something suspiciously like guilt zinged through Frannie. Was it possible that vertigo rather than alcohol had been responsible for…? No, it couldn't have been. If so, he would have come clean about it ages ago. He clearly didn't even remember that night.

Right?

"Anyway," he continued, looking away, his suddenly cheerful voice pulling her out of the rabbit hole before she descended further. "The U.S. Army hardly wanted to hand a guy a gun if he could be getting dizzy at any given moment, so mess duty it was for me."

She managed a smile, grateful to latch back onto the subject at hand. "And did the three of you vow never to look at another baseball again?"

Max snickered. "That might be the funniest part of the entire story."

"Oh?"

The corners of his mouth quirked up. "My cousin Kit is now… a pitching coach for the Brooklyn Dodgers."

A bark of laughter burst out of her. "He is not."

"He is." Max held up a finger. "He gravitated more toward hurling the ball than taking up a bat again, but still…"

"And your sister?"

A warm glow of pride lit his eyes. "She always was the best out of all of us. Played for the women's professional league for a couple of seasons during the war."

"No kidding? That's bloody fantastic." He glowed even more, and she had to swallow hard before continuing. "You know, I've always wanted to take Lucy to a women's game, but never found the time."

"Vi still has some connections. If you'd like, I can talk to her, see if she can score you some tickets. Maybe even introduce Lucy to a few of the players."

"Thanks. I'm sure she would love that."

"But don't worry, I won't come along." He smirked.

She opened her mouth, in a knee-jerk reaction, ready with a quip about her relief—only it wasn't relief she felt. Something else, something she couldn't quite place, stopped the words on her tongue.

She settled for an innocuous question instead. "So, after all that, you're the only one who had his baseball dreams thwarted?"

"Nah, not really. It was never more than a fun game to me." He shrugged, leaning back, elbows against the ship's railing. "And it all worked out pretty well in the end."

"How so?"

"Right after everything went down, I had to take it easy for a while. You can imagine how thrilled my mother was to have a housebound thirteen-year-old boy on her hands."

Frannie snorted in agreement. Poor woman.

"Luckily, my granny took pity on us and decided to intervene. In an effort to keep me occupied, she came over nearly every day after school"—he shot her a sly grin—"and taught me everything she knew…about baking."

"Ah. The rest is history."

"Indeed. I fell in love with it, and never looked back."

Frannie couldn't help smiling. "Wow. That really was like your comic-book origin story, wasn't it?"

He crossed one ankle over the other and raised a rakish eyebrow at her. "I'll be damned. Are you comparing me to a superhero, madam?"

With that, her traitorous cheeks burst into flames. In spite of them, she narrowed her eyes and threw him what she hoped was her best glare. "Now who's assuming? The villains get origin stories too, you know."

He laughed, the sound echoing around the set, and shook his head. "Should've known."

Bloody fucking hell, why is it so hot in here?

She'd thrown a cardigan over her blouse for her walk around the lot, and it annoyed her now. She peeled one sleeve off and was just turning to extract her other arm when Max let out a small gasp.

"Frances Haynes. Is that a tattoo?"

She lifted her head, startled, to find him staring at the beribboned plaid heart near the top of her left arm. "Oh. Yes. It is. You don't have a problem with that, do you?" she finished archly.

Instinct had her defensive, but he looked…intrigued?

He held his hands up as he pushed off the railing and stepped closer. "Not at all. I'm only surprised I've never noticed it before."

"Oh, please, you'd have to be paying attention to me to notice," she scoffed.

His gaze heated. "Whoever said I'm not?"

She nearly swallowed her tongue. "Right. Well. I do tend to keep it covered up a lot. Some of the attention it raises…"

"More trouble than it's worth?" He'd closed the distance to the chaise and gestured to the empty side of it questioningly—finally taking the dare.

Frannie ignored her sudden onslaught of butterflies and nodded, at both his spoken and unspoken questions. "I certainly don't regret having it, but yeah, not everyone understands. And of course, when I'm here, I do try to maintain a professional appearance at all times."

"Of course," he replied, matching her haughty tone.

He perched on the very edge of the seat next to her, clearly bursting to get a better look at the tattoo. Feeling generous, she angled her arm toward him. He took the invitation with a grin and leaned forward.

"A tartan heart, huh?"

"Naturally. Had to honor my roots." She'd had to keep the pattern simple, and not terribly colorful—black and white, with a few accents of red—but she took great pride in it.

"A good choice." He paused, and she could guess his next question.

With a resigned sigh, she prompted, "Go ahead. You know you want to ask."

His eyes twinkled. "Isn't the little banner supposed to, you know, *say* something?"

"It doesn't have to," she retorted. At his patient—but amused—expression, she relented. "All right, yes, I know. It probably should. But honestly, when I got it, I simply wasn't sure what I wanted to fill it with. So I left it blank."

"Fair enough." Max regarded her for a moment. "What made you decide to get it in the first place?"

Heat crept up her neck. Best not to bring up *that* night. But he was waiting for some kind of answer.

"It was…right after the war. I had always thought about getting one, and I suppose I was seeking a burst of courage as I looked to the future. Something to remind me…"

"That you're brave?"

She was startled anew by how perceptive this man could be.

"Yeah," she breathed. "That was exactly it."

He nodded. When he glanced back down at her arm, his mouth kicked up into a wide smile.

Damn dimples.

"So, do you think you'll always leave it blank?" He raised mirthful eyes to her.

"I might fill it in one day. We'll see."

"What about Lucy?"

"She's a little young for a tattoo of her own."

Max snorted. "That she is. I meant"—he shot her a reproachful glance—"why not put her name on there?"

She grinned back at him. "I thought about it. But while she'd be delighted by it now, I worry that she might not like it so much when she gets older."

"Eh, I don't know. I suspect she'd be pretty open-minded."

She wasn't about to admit it, but his faith in her daughter's character gratified her.

Before she could formulate a response, he continued. "You could always go the obvious route and pay tribute to your mom." He paused, eyes going a little wider. "Ooh, does Betty even know you have this?"

"As a matter of fact, she does." She inclined her head in concession. "And I did offer the space to her, but she turned it down quite adamantly. For some reason, she didn't mind her daughter *having* a tattoo, but including her on it was a bridge too far."

Max chuckled. "Well, I have no such qualms, so you're welcome to pay tribute to me if you'd like."

She really should *not* enjoy his wickedly mischievous grin so damn much.

She arched an eyebrow at him. "I can assure you, Mr. Mitchell, that will never happen."

"I know. Figured it was worth a try, anyway." He shrugged, somehow resigned and flirty at the same time.

It was highly unsettling.

He shifted to lean back against the seat next to her, finally getting comfortable. Making her decidedly *less* comfortable. He at least maintained a few inches between them. This close, she picked up a whiff of sugar and vanilla. An occupational hazard, she supposed. Spend enough time in a bakery, and of course the delicious scents would cling.

In an effort to distract herself from how delectable he smelled, she reached down to brush some invisible lint from her skirt. The motion set off the ever-present tinkling of her charm bracelet, drawing Max's attention.

He nodded at her wrist. "I'm assuming those all have significance of some kind?"

She turned her head to face him. "What is it with you and all your questions tonight?"

He appeared to waver on the verge of honesty, but he settled for yet another shrug. "You said it yourself, we have nothing but time. I'm just trying to fill it up."

"Right."

"So... Your bracelet? Unless, of course, you're scared to tell me."

Frannie let out an affronted grunt. "Scared, my arse. Do you want to know, or not?"

"I do."

They stared each other down for a moment, before the quivering at the edges of his lips broke her. She rolled her eyes and offered him a grudging smile.

"Okay, then." She steadfastly ignored the jolt of warmth that sizzled through her at the low rumble of his laugh, and held up her jewelry instead. Luckily, the first charm her eyes landed on was the little letter *L* in a looping script. Always a safe topic.

She pointed to it. "That one's for Lucy, obviously."

"Obviously."

Frannie moved on to the thistle flower next to it. "A Scottish thistle, again for my roots." At Max's nod, she continued. "Nail polish bottle."

"A nod to your previous career."

"Exactly." She smiled wistfully. "I used to have a pencil too, in honor of my accounting, but I lost it years ago." On V-J Day, as a matter of fact—but, again, no way was she touching that. "One of these days I need to get a new one to replace it."

Max absently rubbed at his chest, before pointing at her bracelet. "And is that a mermaid?"

She smiled, glad to have something genuinely pleasant to dwell on. "It is. A gift from Colin, that one."

"Oh, yeah," he replied. "I seem to remember him calling you 'Mermaid' once. How'd that come about?"

She waved her hand in an effort to cover the sudden blush threatening her cheeks, her bracelet adding a hint of music to the quiet space around them. "Only a takeoff on a nickname he has for me. Nothing important."

"Yeah, I don't believe that. There's a story there."

"There is not!"

He cocked his head, skepticism wafting off him.

"I…" She averted her eyes. "It's embarrassing. Trust me, you do not need to know."

"Oh-ho, no. After I shared the Baseball Massacre with you? There is no way I'm letting you off the hook."

"I already told you about my tattoo."

He sniffed. "That's not embarrassing, and you know it." He turned to face her more fully and crossed his arms. "Come on. Out with it, Mermaid."

She glared at him. "All right, fine." She leveled a finger right in his face, almost skimming his nose. "But then we're even."

He inclined his head in silent agreement.

"I call him Chips. He calls me Mermaid." She stopped there, in one last-ditch effort to prolong the inevitable.

His dark eyes narrowed as he, unsurprisingly, saw through her bullshite. And then those not-at-all-lovely eyes widened.

"Wait a minute..." He brought his finger up to tap his lips, made fuller by the beard framing them. "Colin is Chips... And a mermaid is..."

"A fish, yes," she finished, equal parts impressed and frustrated he'd figured it out so quickly. Yet she couldn't help smiling at the utter amusement in his gaze. "We had a tradition with our Gran when we were kids. She took us to her local pub for fish and chips, and..."

"Then you *became* Fish and Chips."

She snorted. "We did."

"It pisses you off that the assignment of nicknames dovetails so well with your real names, doesn't it?"

"My god, you have no idea," she groaned, and they both laughed.

"But if you had to be a fish..."

She smiled. "Colin conceded that I could be a mermaid." She rolled her eyes. "On special occasions, when he's feeling generous."

"Ah, the privilege of older siblings."

"You're older than your sister, aren't you?"

"As a matter of fact, I am not." He sent her a rueful glance. "Vi has a whopping seven minutes on me."

Frannie inhaled sharply. "I had no idea you were a twin." Sympathy softened her features. "I'm guessing she likes to remind you of those seven minutes."

"Every damn chance she gets."

She'd lost count of how many times they'd laughed together tonight. Disconcerting, that.

"So, can I start calling you Fish now, too?"

She punched him in the arm, gratified by his startled *oof*. "Don't you fucking dare."

"Okay, okay. Don't worry." He settled back against his seat, and she followed suit. After a moment, he added, "Mermaid is pretty fitting, actually."

She tried not to warm at that. "Because I'm like a beautiful, enchanting goddess of the sea?"

"I was thinking more of a vengeful siren luring men to a brutal death, but sure."

She nudged him with her shoulder, with less force this time. "Oh, shut your trap."

Max snickered, and they fell into a companionable silence. She didn't know how long they'd been stuck in the soundstage at this point, but astonishingly, she didn't much care. Despite their earlier argument over the door, they were passing a largely enjoyable evening. They'd paused their animosity long enough to share quite a bit of themselves. The most they had since…

This Max was the one she'd met that first night, who'd prompted her to ask for that disastrous kiss. The one she'd tried so hard to forget in the intervening years.

The Max she'd liked very much. Before…everything that followed.

She sighed into a sudden yawn, unsure what to make of it all. She'd easily blamed him for everything that went wrong that night, because he'd been so drunk he didn't remember it. But doubts were beginning to tap on her shoulder.

Frannie didn't want to be wrong, but she also couldn't help the warmth that crept into her chest—and other bits—at all their interactions this evening. Hell, his storytelling skills were stellar enough for him to be honorarily Scottish.

She yawned again. It must be late, given the tiredness overtaking her. She supposed it was no use trying to figure out all of this conflicting mess while she was this wiped out.

As she settled into the cushion on the deck chair, she drifted closer to the warm body next to her. First, her arm brushed his. And before she knew it, her head found his shoulder.

Hmm. He's awfully comfy.

She inhaled deeply, encountering that intoxicating vanilla-sugar scent, stronger this time. And something else lurking underneath it. His cologne smelled almost…piney. Like a forest. Or a Christmas tree.

She stifled a giggle. Maybe it was because they'd been looking at all those decorations earlier, or the fact that he smelled like pine and cookies, but…

Her last thought before she drifted off to sleep was that Max Mitchell smelled like Santa Claus.

Chapter Eight

Max didn't dare move, let alone breathe.

He held said breath the entire time it took Frannie to slowly melt against his side. When her head settled against his shoulder, he couldn't believe his luck. He almost ruined it when she mumbled something about Santa Claus, their earlier stroll still clearly on her mind. But he managed to suppress his chuckle in time, and she drifted off.

He didn't know what he'd done to deserve this heaven, but he'd damn well do everything in his power to hold onto it as long as he could.

Even if that meant not moving a single muscle for the next several hours.

He risked a glance—eyeballs only—at the crown of her head. His gaze drifted a little further down, to where her startlingly long lashes rested against the tops of her cheeks. Her lips had curved into a sweet, private smile over Santa, and it lingered in her slumber.

Max's own mouth softened into a grin. What should have been an utter disaster had turned into a rather lovely evening. As reluctant as he'd been to share his baseball story, he was incredibly glad he had. Frannie's rapt attention—and morbid fascination—

had egged him on, and the more he talked, the more she herself opened up. It was as if a heavy curtain had finally lifted between them.

He suspected they might never give up their bickering, but most of their usual animosity had leached out, leaving only fun teasing in its wake. Things between them finally felt the way they had the night they met, before his vertigo-addled stomach ruined everything.

A twinge of guilt throbbed within him. He needed to come clean, clear the air about that night. Make up for all those occasions, shortly after their reunion a couple of years ago, when he'd gathered up his nerve, only to have their interaction turn inevitably disastrous before he even began. But now that she knew the story of his concussion, it should be easier. He had the perfect opening.

Her warm weight shifted as she snuggled closer. He swore he could feel his heart expanding in his chest. At the same time, heat zinged down his spine, heading straight for his balls.

He smothered a groan and squeezed his eyes shut.

He'd come clean soon. Another day. When she wasn't fast asleep. *I mean, it's not like I can wake her up to tell her right now. That would just be mean.*

Max pushed his breath out slowly. He attempted a calming inhale, bringing her flowery perfume in with the air, not resisting its pull this time.

This woman who drove him to all manner of distraction—and made him yearn like no other—was actually curled up next to him. He'd have plenty of time to agonize over their strange, fraught situation when they got out of this building. He might as well enjoy this peaceful moment while he could.

He snuck one more glance at her pretty face as he relaxed into the back of the chaise—as he relaxed into *her*. He closed his eyes and carefully brought his head closer to hers, the soft waves of her hair brushing the skin of his cheek above his beard.

She might be a siren, but he'd bash his head against the rocks for her every time.

MAX HAD no idea how much time had passed since he dozed off, but he drifted awake to find himself—and his companion—in a blissfully revised position. He'd brought his arm up and around Frannie's shoulders, holding her close. Not that she needed any help. His upper chest now served as her pillow, her arm curled firmly around his abdomen.

It was her tattooed arm, which he could now see with greater clarity. His lips curved into a slow smile. He found that tattoo so damn sexy, he could hardly stand it.

At the same moment he allowed himself a contented sigh, Frannie stirred with a hum. If the sound, along with the tightening of her arm around his middle, were any indication, she felt pretty contented herself.

He could get used to this.

Her leg shifted slightly. A leg which Max now realized, *very* belatedly, was hooked over his own.

His eyelids flew fully open.

If Frannie hitched just an inch or two higher, her thigh would come into direct contact with his—*shit*—raging hard-on. For the second time that night, he held his breath, petrified to move for fear of disturbing her.

His cock had no such hesitation.

It gave an excited twitch at the mere thought of potential contact with Frannie, and he bit back a groan. Maybe she wasn't waking up yet, only a restless sleeper. He'd give it a few more minutes, and then perhaps he could ease out from under...

She let out a longer hum this time, before inhaling deeply. Her eyes fluttered open, and she blinked a few times before tilting up to look at him. She didn't actually break contact to lift her head, but rather dragged her cheek up and over his chest, a fact his long-besotted soul noticed with relish.

Unfortunately, his cock relished it too.

At ease, soldier.

"I fell asleep," she rasped.

Max swallowed hard, his voice emerging like sandpaper. "We both did."

"Hmm. Fancy that." She held his gaze, her eyes still heavy with the remnants of slumber...and something else, something hotter. Something he didn't dare to hope for.

"How long were we out?" Frannie asked drowsily.

He carefully shrugged his free shoulder. "I'm not sure."

She glanced down at her arm, still wrapped around him, and huffed a small laugh. "Long enough to coorie in, at least."

He chuckled. Apparently her Scottish came out to play when she was sleepy. He tucked that information away into a cozy space in his mind. "*Coorie* in?"

She smirked up at him. "Yeah, coorie. You know...like..." She inched infinitesimally closer and squeezed him in demonstration.

Max rumbled in response, having found a new favorite pastime—until her leg joined the coorie party. He sucked in a sharp breath at the contact he'd forgotten to avoid.

She froze. "Oh."

Now he'd done it. She'd be up and out of his arms in a flash. Perfect interlude over.

"I..." His voice didn't want to cooperate. "I'm sorry, I..."

"Why?"

"Huh?" *Nice. Real intelligent response, Mitchell.*

"Why be sorry?" Frannie slowly raised her eyes to his. That heat he'd glimpsed earlier blazed to life. She paused for a scant moment, before her features settled in decision. A hint of challenge joined the heat, and—to his utter astonishment—she slid her leg purposefully higher, with more pressure this time. "I'm not."

Wildfire exploded through him, and for once he made no

attempt to hide it from her. He gave her an unabashedly wolfish grin, but before he could form a verbal response, she gripped the back of his neck and yanked his head down to meet hers.

One of them growled hungrily the second their lips fused together, and he dimly registered that it was *her* and not him. The sound was pure heaven. So was her mouth.

They licked into each other, hot and lush, both of them devouring as if they hadn't eaten in weeks, months. Years.

The sheer magnitude of his pent-up longing burst to life, no longer containable. Frannie matched him blast for blast.

Her fingernails raked over the back of his neck, into his hair, and when he pulled her closer, she pressed her breasts into his chest like she wanted to crawl inside him. Her peaked nipples seared him through both their shirts. She sank her teeth into his bottom lip, and it was his turn to let out a feral growl.

The hem of her blouse had come untucked while they slept, and Max took advantage of the opening, slipping his hand in to skate across the delectably warm, soft skin of her waist. They both moaned at the contact.

Matching him tit-for-tat, in predictably Frannie fashion, she wrenched open a couple of random buttons midway down his shirt and dove in. As if the way she rubbed her hand over the line of hair bisecting his stomach wasn't arousing enough, the resulting throaty purr of satisfaction she emitted had his cock practically bursting through his fly like Nessie breaching the surface of the loch.

In an effort to keep from coming right then and there, he grasped her leg and pulled it higher, off his groin and over his waist. All the while, their tongues slid over each other. He'd never tasted anything so perfect.

He ran his fingers over the silky nylon covering her calf, continuing up the side of her knee and across her thigh. Her skirt had ridden up to the top of her stocking, and Max stopped there, the tip of his index finger the only part of him grazing her skin directly. In spite of his unbelievable temptation to keep going, he paused, unsure if she'd want him taking that much of a liberty despite all they were currently doing.

Both sensing the precipice they hovered over, they finally broke the kiss, foreheads resting together, chests heaving. Max opened his eyes to find her watching him carefully, determinedly.

Frannie withdrew her hand from his shirt and slowly brought it to her leg. Her fingers brushed his with a quiet spark as she took hold of the edge of her skirt and pulled it higher. He took in the garter clip cutting across her newly exposed swath of skin. And above that, the lace border on her silky drawers, already plenty wet. For him.

He swallowed convulsively and returned his eyes to hers, now black with hunger. He was possessed of a fierce need to make her scream with that desire.

Max slowly traced his finger along the skin at the edge of her stocking, watching as her pupils blew even wider and her breath shallowed. He raised one eyebrow in question, giving her a chance to change her mind.

She narrowed her gaze, and with a smirk on her lips, took hold of his hand and dragged it higher, encasing the heat of her thigh.

All right, then, lass.

With a rumble deep in his chest, Max claimed Frannie's mouth and eased her back against the chaise, gripping her lush leg. Both of her arms tightened around his neck as she pressed into him. He slipped his thumb under the lace that shielded her, then dragged it slowly back and forth where her thigh met her hip. A feeling deep in his gut told him to draw this out, and her hungry, impatient moan at the contact confirmed it.

He brushed his other fingers over her thigh, getting closer— but not quite—to where she wanted them. She wriggled her hips, this time letting out a frustrated growl that did wild and wonderful things to his insides.

Maintaining his fragile hold on his self-control, Max chuckled against her neck. "My, someone's impatient." This he punctuated with a soft bite, careful not to leave a visible mark.

Frannie pulled back to glare at him. But unlike her usual glares, a potent haze of lust fueled this one.

Much more satisfying.

Max took another wandering detour into Frannie's mouth before trailing his lips down to the hollow between her collarbones. She gasped when he took the tip of one breast in his mouth, his tongue immediately going to work on her nipple. If she was this sensitive through her blouse and brassiere, he could only imagine what would happen when he met her skin-to-skin. He groaned at the prospect.

But before he could explore that option, she dug her fingernails into his forearm, above where his hand still teased at the edge of her panties. Her eyes were mutinously lusty. *I suppose I should give her what she wants, shouldn't I?* Holding her gaze, Max finally pushed the satiny, soaked fabric aside and brushed the backs of his fingers across her soft slit. He received a highly gratifying hiss in response.

He tested the waters with a few experimental touches—slides, zig-zag patterns, everything he could think of—gauging her responsiveness and reveling in the range of noises she made. Despite her building wildness, their eyes remained locked together, all while he teased ever closer—slowly as hell—to the spot where she wanted him most.

When he gave in and reached her clit, he gave the bud a gentle flick, and she whimpered, long and low. The sound hit him right between the balls, and he finally tore his eyes from hers to lean into her mouth for a slow, wet kiss. His fingers continued their study. It didn't take him long to read her, and he made it his mission to lean into what she liked.

He coasted his lips along her jaw, then pulled back to watch her. He'd always thought her gorgeous, but seeing her in the throes of pleasure was something else entirely. Lips parted, breath coming in shallow pants, eyes squeezed shut. She was so stunning, it made his chest—and his groin—ache.

He moved his finger off her pulsing, hot bud, and her face scrunched adorably in frustration. She opened first her eyes, then her mouth, but he stilled her protest with his free hand against her lips. He flashed her a slow, wicked smile as his thumb replaced his middle finger, which he brought down to join his index, pushing both deep inside her.

Her breath hit his other hand with a fierce exhale, followed by a glorious moan.

He eased off her mouth to cup her jaw as he bent to taste her neck, fingers working furiously. Her inner walls clenched steadily harder around his fingers, and he inserted a third. She was close. Having discovered that she needed firmer pressure, he ground his thumb in its hardest circle yet.

But not before lifting his head—because he *needed* to see this.

Frannie's graceful neck lengthened as she arched up into him with a shout that echoed through the soundstage. Unable to resist, he swallowed the end of her shout, tangling his tongue with hers as he continued to work her, wringing out every last ounce of her pleasure.

She slumped back against the chaise and he followed, resting his forehead against hers as he slowly withdrew his fingers from her still-throbbing core. His breath came almost as heavily as hers.

Max had a fairly sizable list of things he enjoyed doing to Frannie—provoking her, teasing her, *kissing* her—but every item had been knocked down a peg in favor of the new champion. Bringing her over the edge with only his fingers might now be his greatest accomplishment in life.

She finally opened her eyes and offered him a soft, almost shy smile. He grinned back, and they laughed quietly together.

"Well…that was…" She trailed off, still dazed.

He quirked an eyebrow at her, hoping a little teasing would mask his sudden insecurity. "Was it?"

She snorted. "Indeed it was."

Smug pleasure zinged through him, nearly overwhelming.

Frannie opened her mouth to say more, but the sound of an opening door brought life itself to a screeching halt.

"Hello? Someone there?"

Max's heart resumed its beating with a thud, as Frannie's eyes flew wider than he'd ever seen them. Bert's booming voice should've been a comfort, as it signaled their rescue, but crushing disappointment flooded Max's chest.

Unfortunately, he seemed to be alone in the emotion.

Frannie called out, "Bert! You're here!"

"Mrs. Haynes?"

"Yes! We got stuck in here." She sprang up and began righting herself with alarming speed.

"We?" Bert's voice grew closer, and the beam of his flashlight skittered across the ocean backdrop.

Max watched in a mix of fascination and horror as Frannie frantically smoothed her hair in the reflection of a porthole window, her voice disturbingly calm. "I was showing Mr. Mitchell the ship set, and we managed to get ourselves locked in."

Mr. Mitchell?

Without so much as a glance in his direction, she scooped up her sweater and swept through the door leading back downstairs. He supposed he shouldn't be so surprised, given who he was dealing with. But damn if it didn't leave a bruise anyway.

He rose to follow her, and— *Fuck.* His brain wasn't the only part of his anatomy that was slow to catch up. And Frannie had left him no choice but to go face Bert, with a highly unresolved situation in his pants.

Max grumbled to himself as he nabbed his jacket from where he'd dropped it earlier, trying to drape it in some semblance of cover as he limped off the set. He remembered to re-button his shirt just before he reached the bottom of the stairs. Frannie was still rambling to Bert, ongoing nonsense about their getting trapped.

"Mr. Mitchell," Bert greeted him affably. "Thought that was

your truck I saw. I wondered why you were still here, but figured you got another ride or something."

Max swallowed. "Yeah. Got locked in. Like she said."

Bert clapped him on the back, and Max nearly dropped his flimsy shield of armor as they all headed for the door. The fresh air provided a welcome slap in the face.

"Sorry I didn't find you sooner."

"At least you got here when you did." Frannie's strained cheerfulness grated on Max's last nerve.

But it also doused cold water on the situation in his pants, so he supposed he should be grateful. Or some such bullshit.

"Yes," he hummed. "Who knows what would've happened if you hadn't."

Her eyes finally snapped to his, far too briefly. He caught a mix of chagrin and apology, and a remnant of the heat she'd flashed him earlier, before she nervously tugged at her sweater and turned back to Bert.

"Well, I should be going. Thanks again, Bert."

"Need one of us to walk you to your car, Mrs. Haynes?"

"No, no." Frannie's words rushed out, as she practically sprinted away from them. "I'll be fine. Have to get home to my daughter, after all." She threw an absentminded wave over her shoulder. "Good night, fellas."

Max watched her retreating form, his mouth gaping open. A steady chorus of *what the hell?* kept time in his mind, to the tune of "Paper Moon" for some annoying reason. He blinked a few times, wondering if perhaps he'd been dreaming right before Bert walked in. But as he rubbed at his beard, he caught the scent of her, clinging to his hand. He narrowed his eyes at the dull click of her heels, echoing behind her. No, he *hadn't* been dreaming.

"Don't take it personal. Bet she's just embarrassed."

Bert's words took a moment to sink in. "Embarrassed?" *Shit. How much did he hear?*

"Sure. Let me guess." Max held his breath, terrified of the

guard's next words. "You two fell asleep, and you caught her drooling, didn't ya?"

Max's shoulders sagged in relief. "Something like that."

Bert shook his head. "Gals get so funny about that stuff. Too bad they don't realize how cute it makes 'em." He nudged Max. "Well, you have a good rest of your night, Mr. Mitchell."

"Yeah. Thanks. You too, Bert."

Bert ambled away, and Max let his head fall back. He shook his head at the stars hovering above him, more certain than ever that he would never understand Frannie Haynes.

Chapter Nine

Frannie paced around her bedroom, having existed as nothing but a ball of restless energy for the last thirty-six hours.

Between her attendance at Lois's event at the studio, and Max's likely busy day at the bakery, she hadn't seen her neighbor and fellow soundstage inmate at all the previous day. Not since she'd fled his presence like a ninny.

She regretted leaving him so quickly, but her embarrassment at nearly being caught by Bert had gotten the better of her. She didn't want the guard to get it into his head that something was going on between them. He was a lovely, fatherly gent, but the last thing she needed was him letting it slip to someone else at the studio. Or worse, joining her friends in their matchmaking efforts.

Frannie glanced out her window, across the alley to the bakery. No sign of Max. Maybe that was a good thing. She hardly knew what she'd say to him at any rate. *What is the proper etiquette when your sworn nemesis uses his fingers to bring you to ridiculous heights of pleasure, anyway?*

She groaned. Of course he and his fingers had to be damn talented. She'd tried all day and night to convince herself that it only felt so good because of how long it'd been since she'd seen any action. But she couldn't escape the nagging suspicion that her pleasure had a hell of a lot more to do with *him* than anything else.

As obnoxious as he was, Frannie was attracted to him like nobody's business. He was a hell of a good kisser. And an expert with those hands. *Bloody hell.*

Except he hadn't been obnoxious, either. She never would've gone as far as she had with him if she hadn't been enjoying his company so much. But he was still Max Mitchell, so where they went from here, she had no fucking clue.

With a frustrated grunt, she sank onto her window seat and leaned her head on the cool glass of the windowpane, letting her eyes drift closed. The memory of his kiss, his touch, flashed through her entire body, and she drew in a sharp breath. Good god, he'd felt sensational.

What if we…?

Her eyes popped open at the sound of a door closing across the alley. Max emerged from his lair…with some blonde holding a bakery box. Frannie narrowed her eyes. Not the same one she'd seen the other day, either. A new dame.

Who was touching his arm. And standing on her tiptoes to kiss him on the cheek. A low growl rumbled in Frannie's chest.

Well, fuck that.

She watched as the woman took her leave, and Max headed back into the bakery with a shake of his head. As if he felt surprised or humbled or… Shite, who cared?

Thirty-six hours. Only thirty-six hours ago, he'd been with *her.* And that bastard had already moved on to some other floozy? *Fuck him.*

Frannie vaulted to her feet, embracing her anger. Letting it fuel her. She'd trust her instincts from now on. At least she no longer had a dilemma.

She knew exactly where they went from here—and it was straight back into the rubbish bin for him.

MAX SMOOTHED his freshly combed hair as he dashed down the stairs from his apartment. He shot a nervous glance across the alley at Frannie's house, relieved to see no activity. He'd rather do this properly, go to her front door.

He inhaled a lungful of fresh air and made his way down the side street next to the bakery. He'd been almost glad not to run into her the day before. It gave him a chance to let everything settle. While he'd come no closer to figuring out precisely why she'd sped off after their encounter, he did at least have a theory.

He only hoped he was right.

As Max approached her street, he checked to make sure his shirt was neatly tucked before rounding the corner, suddenly questioning his decision not to wear a tie.

His heart sped up when he spotted her on her front porch, watering her plants. Her back was to him, so he took a moment to settle his nerves. And to appreciate her. Although…it might be his imagination, but he detected a tension in her shoulders, as if she was angry at the greenery in front of her.

He'd just ventured into her front yard when she turned, a frown on her face. Which turned into a proper scowl the second she saw him.

Uh-oh.

A pot of cheerful geraniums hovered in his periphery. *Flowers. Dammit, I should've brought flowers.*

"Frannie. Hi."

"Max."

He gestured at the porch. "Your plants are looking lovely."

"Thank you."

He wanted to ascend the few steps, get closer to her, but something in her posture warned him he wouldn't be welcome. He had to admit he hadn't offered the best opening line, but it hardly deserved this level of ice. It wasn't as if he'd pitched her a terrible script or anything.

He cleared his throat. "I, um…I'm sorry I didn't get a chance to stop by yesterday. It was pretty busy at the bakery, and then I figured you were at the studio anyway."

"I was."

Max fought the urge to grimace, reminding himself why he was there. Why she might have run from that soundstage so quickly. Maybe she wanted more, just like he did, but didn't know how to start.

"Right. Anyway. We got interrupted the other night…" *Did she just* flinch? "…before I could ask. But I did want to ask." He swallowed. "Would you…like to have dinner with me?"

He briefly wondered if he should've led with a confession about how much of V-J Day he remembered. But he dismissed the thought. She might not agree to the date after that. Better to set the mood first. *Then* he'd tell her the truth. Eventually.

She punctuated the ensuing silence with a snort of derision. "Dinner? Really?"

"Do you have something against dinner?" Max retorted.

Frannie set the watering can down on the ledge and crossed her arms. "Generally, no. With you…?" She scoffed.

He mirrored her posture. "I beg your pardon?"

"You heard me."

"I did. I'm having a bit of trouble understanding, though. After…everything that happened…I thought…" He trailed off when she rolled her eyes.

Okay, now she was making him outright angry.

"I'm sorry, did I do something to offend you since yesterday? Because you seemed to be enjoying my company the other night."

She shook her head with a mirthless laugh. "You say that to all your girls?"

"All my… What?"

"Oh, please." She descended one step. "I live right behind you. You think I haven't seen you and your endless parade of chickies?"

He tilted his head, trying to understand. "You mean, my customers?"

She huffed. "Customers, right. Is that why they use your back door? And they're all women?"

"Look, I don't know what you think you've seen—"

"Think? I don't think, I know," she snapped. "I saw one of them with my own eyes. Just this morning!"

Ah, hell. "You mean Mrs. Gregory?" Her sneer infuriated him. "For your information, some of my customers prefer a bit of discretion."

"I'll bet they do. Ugh. Customers."

Max threw up his hands. "What else would they be? As sorry as I am to disappoint you, I'm not dating them. And even if I were, do I need to remind *you* of the date I rescued you from the other night?"

Her expression held a perfect mix of disgust and shock, and it gave him a headache. He ran a frustrated hand through his hair.

"I am *not* dating those women," he repeated on an exhale. "I shouldn't have to reveal this, but I feel the need to defend myself —and them." He folded his arms across his chest again. "Do you know how to bake?"

That surprised her. "What does that have to do with anything?"

"Just answer the question."

"No. I don't. Is that a problem?"

He ignored her sarcastic question. "Neither do a lot of women. And yet, how many of them are expected to? How many of them are newlyweds, or have husbands who returned home from war with a whole new set of expectations? You know the pressure everyone puts on women these days to be the perfect happy homemakers."

Frannie watched him warily, but thankfully kept silent, so he continued.

"A while back, I had a woman come to me in a panic. She'd ruined a cake and had nothing to serve her husband—and visiting mother-in-law—for dessert. She looked so overwrought, I made her an offer in addition to the cake I sold her. Baking lessons. She burst into grateful tears right there on the spot." He chuckled softly, remembering. "Anyway, she took me up on it, and the next thing I knew, she'd recommended me to all her friends, and their friends. It turned into a nice little side business."

"So you…teach all those women how to *bake*?" He couldn't tell if the dismay in Frannie's voice was directed at him or herself.

"I do." He shrugged. "Well, not all of them. Some simply don't take to it; others have no desire to learn. So they get unmarked boxes of treats they can pass off as their own. Some develop quite a talent and move on after a few lessons. But every single one of them has their own reasons for wanting to keep our arrangement quiet. And while those reasons are none of my business, you can understand why I honor their wishes, every time." He leveled her with a stern look. "I hope you'll do the same."

She nodded, chagrined. "Of course. I'm sorry for assuming." She bit her lip. "That's…um…actually a really nice thing you're doing."

"You don't have to sound so shocked, you know," he muttered.

Frannie shook her head, voice nearly a whisper. "They really are your *bakery* customers."

Max snorted. "What other kind would they be?"

She laughed, and he should've paid attention to the nervousness behind it. Should've—but chose not to.

"What, did you think I was charging them for something else? Turning tricks out of the back of my bakery?" He chuckled.

And then froze at the furious blush overtaking her cheeks.

"Oh my god."

Heat quickly rose up his own neck, through all his limbs. It only grew when she peered up at him through her eyelashes—remorseful and defiant all at once.

"You thought I was… You *actually* thought I was… Fucking hell, Frannie."

"What was I supposed to think?" Her defensive tone did nothing to soothe his spirits. "I see an endless stream of pretty women, money changing hands. And then there's your obvious...skill..."

A strangled, cat-like sound escaped his throat.

"It's really not *that* big a leap to make."

"Are you shitting me? Of course it is!" He paced away from her. "I don't know if I should be more offended on behalf of ladies and gentlemen of the evening, or myself." He lapped back to her. "No, I think it's definitely myself. So eager to think me capable of illegal activity, aren't you?"

"Can you truly blame me?"

"Yes! Yes, I can!" He bolted away from her again. In the time he'd known her, this woman had surprised, annoyed, and angered him on more occasions than he could count. But *this*? This took the cake.

He whirled to glare at her again. "In all my days, I never thought I'd be turned down for a date because someone thought I was running a bordello alongside my bakery. So thank you for giving me this unique pleasure."

She glared right back. "Well, I'm sure you can forgive me for wanting to avoid getting the clap," she hissed.

He stormed right up into her face. "Funny, you didn't seem too worried about that when you pulled me in for a kiss. Or when you were *coming* around my fingers," he growled.

She reared back with a gasp.

As if *she* was the one who should take offense.

"Hi, there." A cool voice sounded behind him. "Am I interrupting?"

Max inhaled a not-so-calming breath and turned to find Lois Ashford—glamorous movie star, studio head, and love of his best friend's life—hovering cautiously at the foot of the house's walkway. Given that the woman was notoriously fearless and had witnessed all manner of altercations between the two of them, her current display of hesitance to approach said something. He could only imagine what his fury must look like. Hell, he hadn't even heard her car pull up.

He took one more breath and squared his shoulders. "Lois, hello. Fear not, you're not interrupting a single thing." He ignored Frannie's petulant huff behind him. "As a matter of fact, I was just leaving."

"Oh. Okay."

He strode down the path and paused to give Lois's arm a quick squeeze. "Lovely to see you, as always." He turned and pointedly inclined his head to the seething woman on the stoop. "Mrs. Haynes."

Her eyes narrowed to slits, but he didn't wait for further response. He breezed past Lois and stalked down the street, eager to lick his wounds in the comfort of his own home.

Max didn't know what he'd been thinking, asking Frannie for a date. He sure as hell wouldn't make that mistake again.

Chapter Ten

"Do I want to know what that was about?"

Lois's voice pulled Frannie's attention away from Max's retreating back. Much to her dismay, her anger deflated with each step he took, leaving her with a giant pile of regrets. She'd much rather be mad at him than submit to her growing sense of how colossally she'd just messed things up between them.

"I wish *I* didn't know what that was about," Frannie muttered. She shook her head as Lois approached the porch. "Sorry, is everything okay? What brings you here? Shite, we didn't have plans I forgot, did we?"

"No, no. Don't worry. I decided to surprise Nick with some of his favorite pastries from next door." She punctuated the last with an apologetic grimace. "And I figured I'd pop over to say hello to you first, but apparently my timing is lousy. I should've called."

"You didn't know you'd be walking into a hornet's nest." At Lois's eyebrow arch, Frannie snorted. "Okay, maybe you did."

"This one seemed to have more sting than usual. You want to talk about it?"

"No," Frannie grumbled. "Maybe. I don't know." She glanced

up at her friend with a sigh. "Can I be a less terrible hostess and offer you some iced tea?"

Lois smiled. "Always. And your hosting skills are hardly lacking. I'm the one who dropped by unannounced, remember?"

"That's right. You should be offering me a treat."

"I could pick you up some baked goods, but given the circumstances…"

"Fair point. Shall we?"

"Lead the way, my friend."

Frannie ushered Lois inside and to the kitchen. She hesitated briefly at the doorway, since the room faced the building housing a certain royally pissed-off baker. But a quick glance out the window showed no sign of him, so she soldiered on.

She busied herself preparing the iced tea while Lois settled at the kitchen table.

"So…" Lois began hesitantly. "If you don't mind my asking, this little dustup wouldn't have anything to do with the interesting report I got on my desk yesterday, would it?"

Frannie nearly overflowed one of the glasses. "Report?"

"Mm-hmm. I get all the security briefings for the studio. One of our night guards, Bert, made a special note about that soundstage with the busted door—which is fixed now, by the way."

"Oh, good." Frannie cut a couple of lemon slices, absently debating the wisdom of wielding a knife so close to her fingers during this discussion.

"Anyway, Bert mentioned that a couple of people actually got themselves locked in there the other night. He didn't name names, but the descriptions sounded awfully familiar…"

"Did they, now?" She turned to find Lois regarding her with a small smirk, and set their glasses on the table with a bit more force than necessary. "Okay, fine, yes. I ran into Max on the lot after a bloody terrible date, and before I knew it I was giving him a tour, and then the fool shut the door before I could warn him. And I should've known it was too good to be true, but I was actually having a nice time, and he should *not* be that good a kisser and—"

"Whoa! Hold on a minute." Lois's eyebrows had practically joined her hairline. "I assumed you two had an epic fight because you can't go five minutes in the open air together, let alone a situation with no escape." She sat forward. "But there was *kissing* involved?"

Frannie's cheeks burned. "Would you please keep your voice down?"

"Sorry. Is Lucy upstairs?"

"No, my mum took her shopping. But…" She jerked her head in the direction of her neighbor.

"I doubt he can hear us all the way across the alley." Her smile turned devilish. "And don't try to distract me."

Frannie opened her mouth to prevaricate, but deflated instead. No point in hiding it. She sank into a chair with a groan. "There was, indeed, kissing involved." And those fingers. Damn those fingers.

"Based on your current reaction, I take it Max delivers the goods?"

"Yeah," she admitted dejectedly. She pointed a finger at Lois. "But you can wipe that look off your face. Nothing is going to come of it. I did a fine job of ensuring that today." She heaved a forceful sigh, the memory of her accusation flooding back with a vengeance.

Frannie cut Lois off before she could say anything, unable to bear any potential sympathy. "I really don't want to talk about it."

Her friend nodded. "Okay." She took a sip of her drink. "This tea is delicious, by the way."

"Thanks. For the compliment and the subject change."

They shared a laugh, then slipped into a bit of small talk, mostly about the success of Lois's brunch at the studio. The distraction was far from successful, however. Before long, Frannie found herself blurting out the question she couldn't stop stewing over.

"Did you know that Max offers lessons and counterfeit dessert to housewives who can't bake?"

Lois's eyes widened slightly, but she took the inquiry in stride. "I did. He's mentioned it to Nick in front of me a few times."

"And you didn't think to tell me?"

"It's not something he talks to a lot of people about." Her expression turned arch. "And forgive me, but I didn't think you cared to know that much about the man."

"I don't. Usually. It just would've been useful information to have today, is all."

Lois simply watched her, waiting for her to elaborate.

Frannie gestured impatiently out the window. "You see what my house faces. A lass sees a constant stream of women parading in and out of there, women he calls his customers, and she's apt to draw some conclusions."

Lois snorted. "What, that he's turning tricks or something?"

Frannie bit her lip.

"Oh, no."

She slumped forward, her head hitting the table with a thunk.

"*Max*? Seriously?" Lois's chuckle descended into a gasp. "Jesus Christ. The fight I walked up on. Frannie, you didn't. To his face?"

She grumbled her assent into the tabletop.

"No wonder he looked so furious. And after you kissed?"

"And other things…" Frannie raised her head in time to see Lois's horrified expression. She rested her chin on her hands. "I know! But his timing was lousy. Just this morning, I saw him with one of those back-door customers—who was rather forward with him, I might add. And then he shows up, asking *me* for a date. What was I supposed to think?"

Lois's sharp intake of breath didn't make her feel any better. Neither did the sudden expression of pity in her friend's eyes— pity clearly *not* directed at Frannie.

Lois hesitated before speaking. "So…let me get this straight. Despite whatever's been roiling between you two for ages, you finally smooched. And other things. After which, that lovely man who makes the best cheesecake on the planet came over here—to your front door—to ask you on a date. Which you turned down…with the incredibly mistaken assumption that he runs a bakery-slash-*brothel*."

Frannie shut her eyes. "When you put it like that…it sounds even worse than I thought." She opened one eye to squint at Lois. "Bloody hell, I owe him a fucking huge apology."

Lois reached across the table to pat Frannie's hand. "Oh, honey. You really do."

She wanted to argue that she'd only been trying to protect her heart. But then she'd have to admit to Lois that her heart was demanding a say in the proceedings in the first place—and that scared her almost as much as the prospect of apologizing to Max.

"He's going to slam the door right in my face."

"Probably."

Frannie shot her a grimace. "Thanks."

Lois chuckled. "He might come around. You never know."

Frannie got up to refill her glass, mostly because she needed to move. The iced tea she'd already downed sloshed accusingly in her stomach.

"Frannie, can I ask… What exactly happened with you and Max? I know he didn't make the best first impression, what with the Lassie incident and all. But that's never seemed like…"

"Enough to justify my readiness to think the worst of him?" Frannie asked wryly.

Lois shook her head. "No."

It wasn't the first time Lois had asked. Colin and Nate had been trying to get it out of her for months. But she always held back—and not just because of their meddling. She also worried that the truth would only make things more awkward between everyone. Plus, if she hadn't admitted her memories of V-J Day to *Max*, it hardly seemed fair to fess up to all their friends.

But maybe she could tell Lois, at least. It would be nice to finally get it off her chest with someone.

"You're right. It's not about that. Max and I…" She slowly returned to her chair. "Your holiday party…wasn't our first introduction. We'd met a couple of years earlier, as a matter of fact. On V-J Day."

Lois inhaled audibly. "Noooo…"

"Yep."

"Don't tell me your V-J Day Vomiter…" Lois paused briefly at Frannie's snort. "That was *Max*?"

Frannie confirmed it with a mirthless huff of laughter.

"I always knew there was more to that story!" Lois leveled a finger at her. "And see, I still maintain that your kissing skills weren't the problem. He clearly enjoyed the reprise, or he wouldn't have come over here today."

"I suppose," Frannie begrudgingly agreed.

"But wait—I still don't understand how you got here. Did he botch his apology that badly when you met up again?"

Frannie rolled her eyes. "One would have to actually remember the incident in order to apologize."

"You've lost me."

"The man was so drunk that night, he still doesn't have the slightest recollection of it."

Lois blinked in confusion for a moment. "That…hardly seems right."

"No, it doesn't. And yet…"

Lois shook her head. "That's not what I meant. It's only…I've never seen Max drink more than one beer on occasion. As a matter of fact, I don't think he *can*. Something to do with an old injury, maybe?"

Guilt made an encore appearance, as the possibility she'd begun to consider on the soundstage gained momentum.

"Was that what he told you, that he was drunk?" Lois asked.

Heat flooded Frannie's cheeks, and she avoided her friend's piercing gaze. "Not exactly."

"Frannie."

"What?" She attempted innocence as she blinked over at Lois.

Who crossed her arms over her chest and raised one imperious eyebrow. "You've never acknowledged that night either, have you?"

Irritation flared. "Why should I, when his memory's a tidy blank?"

Lois cocked her head to one side. "You don't know that."

Frannie's hands flew up in frustration. "Then why didn't he say anything?"

There went that eyebrow again. "Maybe for the same reason *you* didn't. Embarrassment is a powerful asshole. And Max is the one who threw up."

"I..." She hated how much of a point her friend had.

"My god. All this time you've been back in each other's orbit, holding the mother of all grudges, and you haven't once talked about this." Lois shook her head. "You two are quite the pair, you know that?"

"Says the woman who couldn't admit she was falling in love with her own husband," Frannie retorted.

"I refuse to dignify that with a response."

Frannie attempted a comeback, but it died on her lips with a snicker, and the women shared a laugh. "Ah, hell," she groaned. "What am I supposed to do?"

"I assume actually discussing the nauseous elephant in the room is out of the question?"

Frannie bit her lip. "At this point, how would I even start?"

Lois smirked. "I have no idea. But at the very least, you owe the poor man an apology for the shenanigans I just witnessed."

"I'm never going to live this one down, am I?"

"Afraid not, my friend."

"Lois, listen. Max and V-J Day...you can't tell anyone. Especially not Nick. Or Nate. Or Colin. Please. If *Max* doesn't know that I know..."

Lois held up a steadying hand. "Relax. Your secret is safe with me." She flashed her a sardonic smile. "Mind you, it won't be easy. But you have my word."

"Thank you."

Lois finally took pity on her, lightening the mood. "Speaking of Nick, did I tell you he's trying to convince me to join him in his pirate sequel?"

Frannie couldn't help a slight grimace. "As what, a damsel in distress?"

"No. Fellow pirate."

That was more like it. "Good on Nick. You're going to do it, right?"

"My husband is very convincing."

They laughed together, and Frannie appreciated the distraction, however fleeting.

Chapter Eleven

Max glanced at the clock above his cash register—just about closing time—and pulled down the "day-old" basket for the next morning. On his way to the croissants, he passed a display of snickerdoodles and smiled.

While he'd successfully avoided his *neighbor* in the days following their disastrous confrontation, Lucy had skipped in earlier, all by herself, to pick up some treats on her grandmother's orders. Her expression was so adorably serious and responsible that he'd snuck her a couple of cookies. It wasn't her fault that her mother was such a pain in his ass.

Besides, his anger had largely dissipated since he'd left Frannie's front stoop. Hell, he could almost laugh at the absurdity of the situation. Almost.

He set the basket down. Since it didn't look like he'd be getting any last-minute customers, he might as well lock up.

He'd just reached the door when a familiar—and most welcome—brunette popped up with a grin and a wave. His sister. Max grinned back as he opened the door for her.

Vi Mitchell stepped through and yanked him into a big hug. "Mellow greetings, little brother!"

"Little, my ass," he grumbled good-naturedly. "I thought you were at Mom and Dad's for a few more days."

"That was the plan." Vi pulled back with a shrug. "But it felt like I was actually in their way. Their social life is strangely bustling since they retired."

Max chuckled. "Sounds like Santa Barbara's been good for them."

Their parents had sold the house where they'd grown up the year before and moved to a quaint bungalow a couple hours north, joining their aunt and uncle in their retirement. As much as Max missed having them nearby, he was glad they were thriving in their new digs.

"Yeah, I think it has." She clapped her hands together. "So, what's going on?"

"I was just about to close up. You have good timing."

"What can I say? My twin-tuition is impeccable, as always."

"Want to join me for a pastry out back? Or would that spoil your dinner?"

Vi swatted his arm. "You sound like Mom. And you know I never turn down your pastries. I'll help you finish up here."

"Thanks."

Together, they shuttered the front of the business, and Max loaded a plate with a selection of Vi's favorites—and his—before ushering her out onto his small patio.

"So, was Mom and Dad's busy schedule the only reason you came back early?" he asked as they settled at the little table.

"Of course," she scoffed. One look at his face had her rolling her eyes. "Okay, fine. I also wanted to get back to work."

Max frowned. "You hate your job."

"Yes, Mr. Know-it-all, I do." She snagged a hazelnut tart and took a generous bite before continuing. "But the sooner I get back to it, the sooner I can figure out how to leave. My new career path wasn't going to materialize out of thin air on Mom and Dad's couch. And at least the gossip is good." She currently worked as a fitness instructor at a salon and spa, catering primarily to rich people who'd rather chitchat than exercise.

A wave of sympathy washed over Max. It killed him that her ever-present spark had dimmed of late, due in large part to her career woes. She'd seemed a bit lost ever since leaving the baseball league, and he wished he could help her find her direction again.

"You know, you're still welcome to come work here while you figure it out," he offered.

"Thank you, but—*once again*—I'll be fine where I am a little longer." Her impatient tone softened. "Besides, that's the last thing you need."

"Says who?" he retorted. "You were the one who helped me find this spot, remember?"

Vi stared him down. "Max. My real estate skills might be top-notch, but you got all the baking aptitude in this pairing."

"You could work the counter."

"And what happens when I leave?" A shadow crossed her face. "Or worse, what if I…?"

"Get stuck here?" Max asked quietly.

"Yeah. No offense, but…it's way past time I start chasing my own dreams again. Whatever they are."

He gave her a reassuring smile. "I get it."

"Thanks." She finished her pastry and shook her head. "Okay, enough about my sad state of affairs. What's cooking with you?"

"Eh, not much." Part of him itched to unburden himself over his current situation with Frannie, but his sister already had a lifetime of blackmail fodder to hold over his head.

She glanced over his shoulder. "How are things with the nemesis next door?"

Stupid twin-tuition.

He tried for a casual shrug. "Okay, I guess."

"You sure about that?" The gleam in her eye bordered on evil.

"I…" He hung his head with a colossal sigh. "Yeah, it's been a lot worse than okay."

"Wow. I'm honestly not sure if I should razz you mercilessly or offer you some actual sympathy."

Max snorted. "I can top that. I'm not sure which I'd prefer from you either."

Vi pushed the pastry plate aside and leaned forward, arms folded on the table. "Okay, spill."

"You're worse than Nick, you know that?"

"I am not! Please, he'd be smooshing you two together like you were a pair of dolls. I've still never met the woman, and given what I know, I'm not sure she's worth the effort. I am firmly on *your* side right now. Talk to me."

He found Vi's show of solidarity oddly comforting, so he relented. He gave her an abridged version of recent events, careful to leave out the more salacious details—she was his sister, after all.

She whistled when he finished with the fight on Frannie's lawn. And then promptly bit her lip.

Max narrowed his eyes. "Are you laughing?"

"No, of course not." A snicker escaped, and she covered her mouth. "I mean, I am pretty furious with the woman, not only for hurting your feelings, but also for putting in my head the idea of you..." Vi grimaced, making a choking sound. "But at the same time...the idea of you..." She giggled, then tried again to rein in her control. "I'm sorry. It's just..."

"I know." He let out his own chuckle. "It really is."

Their eyes locked, and they both burst into laughter.

"Thank you," he wheezed. "I think I needed to laugh at the baloney of it all. I just wasn't sure if I should. It *is* funny." He sighed.

Vi rested her hand on his arm. "But it hurts too?"

He huffed. "It's so ridiculous. Why should it?"

She scoffed, seeing right through him. "Gee, I don't know. Maybe because you've liked her since the moment you met her, and after what I assume was finally a decent necking session—but please, do *not* confirm that—you put your heart on your sleeve, only to have it blow up in your face?"

"I do hate it when you're right."

"Right back at you, pal."

They shared a smile.

"I..." Vi hesitated. "Look, don't take this the wrong way, but... maybe you should actually talk to her? About V-J Day?"

"I shouldn't have talked to *you* about it," he grumbled. He'd let it slip during a phone call with her last year, when she'd been living up north, thinking it a safe bet the two women would never cross paths.

"Max."

"In my defense, I was going to, once I asked her on the date. Before, you know..."

"She labeled you the Gigolo Baker of Burbank."

Max barked a laugh. "I would call that clever, if it wasn't at my expense."

"I know you would." She grinned. "Really, though. A confession might clear a whole lot up for her, get her to start treating you better."

"Or give her even more ammunition." He rubbed the back of his neck. "I don't know, Vi. Too much time's gone by since we met again. And I'm not the only one who hasn't said anything."

She looked ready to argue more, so Max pulled out an old, familiar tactic. "I suppose I could make you a deal. I'll talk to her if you come work here with me."

Vi rolled her eyes. "Okay, okay. Touché." Her expression softened. "I just don't like seeing you hurt."

"Right back at you, pal."

She smiled wider at his echo of her earlier words, before slipping into a smirk. "Hey, if you want, I could at least go over there and defend your honor. Sling my baseball bat over my shoulder, real menacing-like."

Max laughed. "I don't think that's necessary. But thanks."

Vi glanced at her wristwatch. "Ugh, I should get going. I need to pop into the drugstore before they close. I'm out of curlpapers."

They stood, and Max pulled her in for a hug. "I'm glad you're home."

She squeezed him a little tighter. "Me too."

As he pulled back to smile at his sister, a movement out of the corner of his eye startled him.

Vi and Frannie were about to cross paths after all.

IT TOOK HER A FEW DAYS, but Frannie finally screwed up her courage and marched over to Max's bakery to offer that dreaded apology. This late in the day, she figured the back door was her best bet. She rounded the corner of the patio trellis, only to find…

Max embracing yet *another* woman.

Fate simply wouldn't make this easy on her. She inhaled a deep breath, clamping a lid on her judgment through sheer force of will. Quite the herculean effort, but she managed. Barely.

And then they broke apart, and Frannie got a good look at the woman.

Her hair was a couple of shades lighter, her eyes a fraction darker, but the slight upturn at the corner of her lips was the same —as was the spark of barely banked mischief in her expression. The resemblance was unmistakable.

"You must be Vi," Frannie exclaimed before she could stop herself.

The woman's eyebrows quirked up. "And by that accent, I'm guessing you're the neighbor."

The slight emphasis Vi put on that last word indicated she knew quite a bit more than that—and found Frannie sorely lacking.

She'd be offended, if she hadn't rather earned it lately.

Max snapped to life, emerging from his evident surprise at her arrival. "Right. Vi, this is Frannie. Frannie, my sister Vi."

"Nice to meet you."

Vi merely hummed in response.

Max folded his arms over his chest. "Sorry, did you need something? The bakery's actually closed. And Lucy came by earlier anyway."

"No, I know that. I…" She tried to ignore the frost emanating from Max's sister. Not that he was much warmer. "I wondered if I might talk to you for a moment. I wanted to…apologize."

Max's only movement was the widening of his eyes.

Vi split a glance between the two of them. "Okay, then. I'll let you get to it. Give you a call tomorrow?"

His attention refocused on her for a moment. "Yeah, sure." His expression softened and the dimples of distraction emerged. "Thanks, Vi."

She leaned in to stage-whisper, "Good luck." With a slightly thawed nod to Frannie, she breezed off.

Leaving her to face the one-man firing squad that was Max.

He faced her, arms still crossed. Which made it difficult not to stare at his rolled-up sleeves, the dusting of dark hair over his forearms.

All that dough-kneading certainly builds delicious arm muscles.

Frannie sniffed. She had a purpose for being here. If only she could remember it.

Max cleared his throat. One of his brows arched as he waited for her to speak.

"Right, then." She took a steadying breath. "Max, I am sorry about what happened the other day." She hated how stilted she sounded, but her blasted nerves overtook her.

"Wow. Did your mother make you come over here and say that?"

Out of sheer habit, she opened her mouth to retort, but caught herself in time. She hung her head with a groan. At least his dry tone released some of her trepidation.

"She did not. I came over all by myself." She finally raised her eyes to his. "And yes, that was a lousy apology." She took a tentative step closer, firmly holding his gaze. "I truly am sorry, though."

His expression softened the slightest bit, giving her the guts to keep going.

"I should never have said what I did. You were there to do something...nice." She gestured at the bakery. "On top of those other kind things you do. And I suppose I was still trying to wade through...being locked on that soundstage." Her cheeks flamed at the memory, but she pushed on. "I saw you with that woman and...I made a judgment. And then another."

She closed her eyes briefly, before squaring her shoulders and staring him down again. "But I shouldn't have. I insulted not only you, but all your customers. Not to mention prostitutes." The corner of his mouth twitched, and she let herself smile. "I'm sorry, Max."

His lips finally softened into a smile of his own, and relief coasted over her.

"Thank you. I appreciate that."

She nodded, unsure where to go from there.

Max looked like he wanted to say something more, but didn't. Instead, he uncrossed his arms and slid his hands into his pockets.

Bollocks on a crumpet, this is awkward.

She'd hardly expected him to repeat his offer of a date. And yet a strange sense of disappointment surged. She valiantly tried to stuff it back down with small talk.

"Your sister seems nice." She smiled at Max's snort. "I'm guessing from her reaction that you've told her about me?"

Max nodded, and Frannie's stomach dipped. Perhaps she was just hungry; it was nearly suppertime, after all.

"But apart from her...well-earned hostility toward me...she did seem like someone fun to be around."

His grin was genuine. "She is. I'm glad she's back in town."

Swallowing around an odd, sudden shyness, Frannie broached another, hopefully safe, topic. "I hope Lucy wasn't too much trouble earlier."

"Never." One dimple flashed again. "She took her task very seriously."

"She does like it when she gets to come over by herself."

Max chuckled. "Eager to feel grown-up already, is she?"

"Aye." Frannie sent him a sly smile. "But I think she really just wants the cookies you sneak her."

His eyes sparked above the slight rise of color in his cheeks. "I will neither confirm nor deny the exchange of any contraband cookies." He slipped into a comical accent. "I ain't no stool pigeon."

She let out a bark of laughter. *Finally.* "I'm not sure if I should be grateful my daughter has your loyalty, or worried about all that sugar."

"Eh, I wouldn't worry. I've been plying Nick with sugar since forever, and look how he turned out." He paused. "Okay, maybe that wasn't a great example."

He shared in her laughter, and relief swept through her. Though she'd better not tempt fate—and risk his renewed good-will—by lingering too long.

"I guess I should…" She gestured over her shoulder.

"Yeah, me too." Max nodded in the direction of the stairs up to his apartment.

They rounded the corner of the patio as an unmistakable call split the air, one that warmed her heart.

"Mom!"

Lucy emerged from the back door and spotted them instantly, her eyes bright even from a distance. She waved and bounded over.

"Hi, Max!"

"Hey, Snickerdoodle."

Frannie whipped a questioning gaze his way at the sweet new nickname, but he simply shrugged.

"Mom, Grandma says dinner's almost ready."

"Thanks, love."

Lucy turned her excitement on Max. "We're having spaghetti and meatballs!"

"That sounds delicious," he replied amiably.

He sure is cute with kids.

Before she could process her resulting tingle, Lucy tugged on her skirt. "Mom! Can Max have dinner with us?"

"Oh... I..."

Max cut in quickly. "Thanks for the offer, Lucy, but I wouldn't want to intrude on your family supper. And I have plans anyway."

"Okay."

Lucy took it in stride, but Frannie was another story. She wondered if he truly had plans, or was just being polite. Or perhaps he simply didn't want to share a meal with her.

Her daughter provided another welcome distraction when she looked up at the two of them, her little mouth twisting to one side.

Frannie smoothed the lass's hair back. "What is it, Luce?"

"Not much. Just, you guys are talking again. Guess you won't be growling out your window for a while." Blissfully unaware of the sudden dread in her mother's stomach, Lucy explained to Max. "Whenever something's weird between you, Mom ends up looking out her window and growling."

She blithely pointed a small finger up at their house. "That's her room up there! And whenever it happens, that's when I get to come to the bakery all by myself. It's fun." She shrugged. "Anyway. See you later, Max!"

Lucy scampered toward the house with a "come on, Mom!" and disappeared through the back door. Frannie could do nothing but stare after her in horror.

After a long, agonizing moment, she finally risked a glance at Max. He raised an eyebrow, his glee barely contained.

"So, you...growl out your window, huh?"

She raised her eyes skyward. "I'd argue, but I suppose I've earned this, haven't I?"

"You most certainly have."

"Okay, I'm going home now."

Frannie hadn't even taken a step when he raised his arm dramatically. "But soft, what light through yonder window breaks…"

"Oh, fuck," she muttered.

"It is…the oven. And Juliet is the growling…burning…cookie."

She let out an undignified snort, and he chuckled. She whacked him on his firmly muscled arm. "And you're impossible."

"*I'm* impossible? That may not have been my best work, but do I need to remind you why you came over here in the first place?"

"I know, I know. But terrible *Romeo and Juliet* puns? Do *I* need to remind *you* how that one ended up?"

Max lifted one shoulder. "Our friends do expect us to kill one another someday."

"I suppose they do. Good night, Max."

"Night. Enjoy your spaghetti."

He sauntered off to his apartment, leaving her wondering how he'd managed to make the word *spaghetti* sound suggestive. She sighed as she made her way back to her family. She'd survived her apology. And while she hadn't dared to raise the terrifying subject of V-J Day, and Max might not have renewed his efforts to date her, they'd returned to a semblance of their normal.

It was something, at least.

FRANNIE WOKE WITH A START. Followed promptly by a groan as she recalled the subject of the dream she'd been immersed in.

Max.

She'd had a restless night. So of course, when she finally settled into a deeper sleep, the inescapable man had to find her there, too.

She rolled to her side, which arrowed a stronger pulse of heat straight through her core. She squeezed her legs together—not that it helped much. As was the way of dreams, she hardly remembered a single detail, other than those dimples punctuating Max's smooth smile. But the sensations… Those lingered plenty.

The clock on her nightstand taunted her, and she flopped onto her back with a frustrated huff. Just after five a.m. Too early to get up for work, but late enough that even if she did drift back to sleep, her alarm would ring before she got any kind of quality rest.

She threw back the covers and shuffled over to the window. Perhaps some fresh air would help. She cracked it open and sank onto the window seat. One glance across the alley, and she chuckled ruefully. Leave it to innocent, oblivious Lucy to rat her out in front of Max. She hadn't realized her window-watching had become such a habit—or that she'd had an audience.

Frannie threw a quick look over her shoulder at her currently shut door and tucked her legs up onto the bench. The cool air coming in the window ruffled the hem of her nightgown, and she leaned her head back against the side of the alcove with a sigh.

Maybe she'd be able to get back to sleep if she relieved a bit of this pressure.

Between her view and the remnants of her dream—not to mention the fact that he'd been near-constantly on her mind of late—Max's image floated across her consciousness. She slid a hand under her nightgown, trailing her fingers up the inside of her thigh. Her breath caught at the memory of his hand working its magic.

Frannie's focus zeroed in on that recollection as she traced the same path, the same pattern, he had. She bit back a cry, forcing herself to go at his slower pace.

Christ, he'd been good that night.

She wasn't aware of closing her eyes, but she'd just brought her other hand up to cup her heavy breast when some instinct had her eyelids popping open. A light now illuminated the window directly opposite hers. She held her breath, easing her movement, but not entirely stopping. She froze when he appeared.

Dressed only in a towel. *Fuck me.*

Her eyes drank him in. Even from this distance, he captivated her. A liberal spread of dark hair fanned across his chest and trailed down under the edge of the towel. His arms were as muscled as she'd suspected, and his abdomen matched nicely. Though there was a softness to him as well—as if his definition came from frequent, everyday activity rather than any concentrated effort. She dragged her eyes up and enjoyed the way his hair curled against the back of his neck, wet from the shower he'd clearly emerged from.

Frannie bit her lip. The entire picture rocketed a new wave of desire through her, and she clenched around her fingers, still lingering at her entrance.

It wasn't until Max reached up to rub at his beard that she realized—he'd been watching her. For how long?

Their eyes locked, and she forgot to care. His dark, molten stare seared her from across the alley.

Feeling bold, and still a little remorseful over the way she'd treated him the other day, Frannie resumed her task. Her fingers went to work, mimicking his once again. By the violent bob of his Adam's apple, she knew he didn't mistake her actions. And that he liked what he saw.

She held his gaze as she went a step further, pinching her nipple through the thin, silky fabric of her nightgown. Her resulting shudder caused her strap to slide down her shoulder. His eyes tracked it, and she smiled at the increasingly labored rise and fall of his chest.

As excruciating as it felt, she continued at her slow pace, wanting to draw this out, to see how far she could push him. Push herself.

Max braced his hands on either side of his window frame, watching her with intense fascination. The sill unfortunately hit him just below his waist, so she couldn't make out what was happening below that towel. But his ever-tightening grip told her plenty.

His eyes pinned her in place. As if sensing her thoughts, he brought his right hand to his stomach. Slid it down the trail of hair to rest, for a second, on the fabric rolled around his middle. In a flash of movement, he whipped the towel off and over one shoulder.

Frannie gasped, her own hands still working herself as she strained to see below that damn windowsill. She could feel the force of his smirk.

He brought his arm down again, and she swore she could hear his hiss across the alley as he took hold of his cock. What she wouldn't give to see it.

The illicit tease of it all made her even hotter.

Their gazes never left one another as they writhed with their efforts. She was close, so close. With her last shred of sanity, Frannie clenched her teeth together to keep from waking the entire neighborhood as she shattered apart.

Only a few seconds later, Max snapped the towel off his shoulder to finish himself, slumping against the window.

They continued to watch each other, chests heaving, as they floated back to reality. Max recovered first, slowly pushing up off the wall. He straightened to his full height, lips curving into a seductive, sly smile. He inclined his head in a brief nod.

And then flicked his curtains closed right as he turned, giving her a maddeningly quick glimpse of his bare—and seemingly choice—arse before cutting her off completely.

She melted into the cushions of the window seat, frustration and utter satisfaction warring within her. Her interactions with Max in a nutshell.

Frannie blew out a breath, eyes still trained on the shuttered window across the way. Moving to this house hadn't been such a bad thing after all.

THE MINUTE he was out of Frannie's sight, Max dropped his confident veneer and collapsed onto his bed with a disbelieving chuckle. Definitely not the way he'd expected to start his morning.

Not that he was complaining. Hell, he'd start every morning like that if he could.

He gripped his towel tighter and ran his other hand through his hair. He needed another shower now, but honestly—it was worth every extra drop.

He'd lain awake most of the night, thinking back over Frannie's surprising apology…along with that little nugget of information Lucy had dropped in his lap. He grinned again, thinking of Frannie glowering out her window at him.

What he'd just witnessed was so much better than glowering.

He stared at the ceiling, still in a bit of shock. Most of the world remained tucked in bed at this ungodly hour. The last thing he'd expected was to find Frannie at her window, as if waiting just for him.

He'd felt like a voyeur, but his feet rooted to the spot. Her skin flushed, her breath labored—watching her work herself had brought back every minute memory of performing the task for her. And when she'd caught him staring…

Max shuddered.

Hope had flared back to life after their conversation on his patio. But he'd been burned before; he wasn't ready to ask her out again. Despite her apology, he'd feared that ship had sailed off into the horizon for good. But the fire he felt now…

Max sat up. Sadly, the bakery wouldn't open itself, and he needed to get moving.

He tucked his hope in the pocket of his heart, along with every new thing he'd learned about Frannie. Teasing responses out of her did seem to work wonders. He allowed himself a smile.

She was so delightfully easy to tease.

Chapter Twelve

rannie squirmed against the bench on her back porch, trying in vain to get comfortable as she watched Lucy play with her Tinker Toys in their small yard. She let out a long, slow breath, but it helped only for a moment. Another twinge, low in her midsection, made her grimace. Blasted cramps.

She wanted to curl up in a ball under her covers and sleep them away, but her mum was spending a well-deserved day with friends, and she didn't want to leave Lucy unattended for too long. She'd thought perhaps the fresh air would do her some good, but alas, it made no difference whatsoever.

She bit back a groan. How an ache could feel both dull and sharp at the same time, she'd never know.

As Lucy hummed to herself, Frannie snuck her umpteenth glance at the building across the way. Since their early morning encounter the other day, she'd run into Max a few times, mostly in passing, and once at the studio when he'd been making a delivery.

The man had not once come anywhere close to acknowledging what they'd watched each other do.

Not that she knew what to say either. But he'd been cool as a cucumber, while her insides flamed and she could barely keep a lid on her blushing cheeks.

Unfair, infuriating bastard.

Another hot pulse of pain punctuated her thoughts, as if her insides didn't want to be left out of the conversation.

Frannie was debating whether to finally give in and fetch a hot water bottle when his door opened. He emerged from his second-floor apartment carrying a rubbish bag, and wearing…

Oh, for the sake of all the fucks.

His pale blue shirt was completely unbuttoned, billowing out behind him as he jogged down the stairs, to reveal a crisp white undershirt tucked into his tan pants. And of course—*of course*—he had his sleeves rolled up all the way above his elbows.

What right does he have to look that good while carrying bloody garbage?

The tiny shadow of chest hair peeking over the top of his undershirt reminded her of the full picture she'd discovered *under* that undershirt, and a new, entirely different warmth spread through her. She surreptitiously clenched her legs together, trying to hold onto the feeling—and not just because it temporarily eclipsed her pain.

Max caught sight of her as he neared the bottom of the stairs, and his lips kicked up into a smile. Lucy spotted him at the same time.

"Hi, Max!"

"Hey there, Snickerdoodle," he called back.

Frannie's mouth watered inconveniently as he swung his arm up to toss the bag in the bin behind the bakery, and then strode over to their yard and leaned on the fence.

"Good afternoon," he greeted Frannie.

"Hi."

He glanced down at his open shirt, apparently remembering his appearance, and sadly tugged it closed in an attempt at propriety.

"Hey, Max, look—I got a new Tinker Toy set!"

Max politely obliged, stepping through the gate and crouching down to Lucy's level. "Wow, you're making some neat creations. Having fun?"

"Yep. Oh, I forgot! Shhh." She put a finger over her lips. "Mom's not feeling so good. We should be quiet."

Max's head snapped up at that, assessing her with oddly comforting concern.

She waved a hand dismissively. "It's nothing. Don't worry about it."

He looked about to protest or question her further, but Lucy—bless her—interrupted.

"Max, have you ever built with Tinker Toys?"

He paused only a fraction before responding. "A little. But I was much more of a baseball kid myself."

"I like baseball too!" She scrunched up her nose. "But Johnny Aames says girls aren't supposed to play."

Max scoffed. "Please. That kid doesn't know what he's talking about."

"I know! Hey, did you know there's whole teams of girls who play against each other?"

His answering grin made Frannie melt.

"I did. As a matter of fact, my very own sister played with them for two seasons during the war."

Lucy's eyes grew into saucers, and Frannie stifled a chuckle. "Wow," Lucy breathed.

"Next time she's here, I'll introduce you. I bet she'd love to meet you."

"Really? Thanks!"

Feeling suddenly restless, Frannie stood, but she proceeded with caution, closing her eyes for a moment while her body readjusted to the new position. She took a few steps and leaned on the porch railing, wincing as she did so. The entire time, Max tracked her movements.

A flare of deeper apprehension passed through his eyes, and he straightened up, flicking a glance at Lucy to make sure she'd gone back to playing as he walked over.

He kept his voice pitched low, despite its ferocity. "Are you okay?"

"I'm fine, really."

His expression took an exasperated turn. "Frannie. You're clearly in pain."

She matched his tone, without bothering to lower her voice. "Max. It's nothing I haven't felt before."

Another, hotter slash of worry pinched his features. "Should you see a doctor?"

Frannie couldn't contain her laugh. Or her eye roll.

"I fail to see what's funny about that," Max retorted.

"What's funny—or not, rather—is that I'd likely be laughed right out of any doctor's office I went to with this." She shrugged. "Not that there's anything they could do about it anyway."

Max was a portrait of warring disbelief and solicitude as he weighed his next words.

She sighed, cutting him off. "Do you really want to know?"

He gave a small nod. "Of course."

Frannie crossed her arms. "Menstrual cramps, Max. I have menstrual cramps."

"I... Oh."

"That's right. *Oh*. Every time I get a visit from my dear Auntie Flo, she brings with her a lovely band of sidekicks, some painful. They used to be milder, before...I had Lucy." She whispered the last, before returning to a normal volume. "But I refuse to shy away from it in front of her. She has a long way to go till it's her turn, but I don't want her blindsided when that turn comes. Those of us who experience it are just expected to grit our teeth and go about our business, pretending everything's fine. Because god forbid we actually talk about it in mixed company, lest we offend anyone's delicate sensibilities."

She paused for breath, a touch surprised that she'd unleashed on him. She certainly hadn't planned to. She squared her shoulders in an attempt at bravado. "I'll bet you're glad you asked now."

Max simply considered her for a moment, then offered her a small smile. "I'll be right back."

He headed for the gate, leaving her to stare after him. Lucy looked up as he passed, and he aimed an amiable finger gun over his shoulder. "Don't go anywhere. I'll be back in five minutes."

Lucy giggled and went back to her engineering feats. Frannie gripped the porch railing tighter, frowning at Max's retreating back.

That sure scared him off. Figures.

Frannie gingerly trudged back to her bench, angry at herself for feeling disappointed.

She barely had time to sulk, however. In what genuinely was only five minutes, Max reappeared from the bakery's back door, carrying a brown paper bag. True to his word.

He returned to the yard and paused in front of her daughter.

"Lucy, I wonder if I might ask you a huge favor," he asked, all earnestness.

"Me? Sure." Lucy hopped up.

Max squatted in front of her. "You see, I have a really big order to fill. For snickerdoodles, of all things."

She nodded sagely. "They are the best."

"Thank you. The only problem is, I'm worried about getting it all done. And I can't have just anyone help me—things don't turn out quite right unless you really love what you're baking." He paused for dramatic effect. "Then, all of a sudden, it hit me."

Frannie watched as Lucy's eyes grew wider, her entire little body frozen in anticipation.

Max continued, "Lucy, I know how much *you* love those cookies. How would you like to learn how to make them, and help me out something fierce at the same time?"

"Really?"

Max's expression turned somber. "I know it's asking a lot,

taking you away from your building project. And of course, it'd have to be okay with your mom."

Two heads turned in her direction, one serene and the other vibrating with excitement.

"Can I, Mom? Please?"

"It would take most of the afternoon," Max added, "but I promise I'll have her home in time for supper."

Frannie put aside her shock long enough to play along and pretend to deliberate. "I guess it would be all right."

Lucy hopped up and down with a delighted squeal.

"Thank you," Max breathed reverently. He turned back to Lucy. "Now, before we go over there, I have one very important rule. If you bake with me, your hands need to be the cleanest they've ever been in your whole life."

Frannie smothered a laugh as Lucy examined her hands with a touch of dismay.

Max did chuckle. "Don't worry, Luce. My friend Linda is an absolute expert on the subject. I told her you might be coming, and she's standing by with her favorite soap, ready to show you everything she knows."

"Whew."

"Why don't you run over and get started, while I talk to your mom for another minute, okay?"

"Okay!" She ran over and gave Frannie a sweet kiss on the cheek. "Bye, Mom!"

The two of them watched her skip across the way. Max waited until Lucy was safely inside the bakery before he climbed up the porch steps and held out his parcel.

"This is for you."

Frannie gingerly took the bag and peered inside, spotting a telltale flash of pink cardboard.

"I put it in the bag so it wouldn't distract Lucy."

She glanced back up at him questioningly.

"A couple pieces of my Chocolate Miracle cake." He held up his hand. "And before you make some crack about my unfettered ego, my sister named it, back when we were teenagers. She swears it has magical healing properties."

"Does it, now?"

"Yep. With the exception of those few years I was overseas, Vi's been coming to me for some of that ever since she named it. Nearly every month."

She didn't miss his subtle emphasis on that last word. A soft warmth coasted over her.

"Thank you, Max."

He inclined his head briefly, then gestured over his shoulder. "And don't worry, I won't let her eat too much of her handiwork and spoil her dinner."

She smiled. "I appreciate that."

He reached out and grazed a single, gentle fingertip over the back of her hand. "See you."

That minuscule touch stole her breath, and it didn't return until he'd disappeared into the bakery. Frannie remained in her seat, unable to move, for an indeterminate amount of time, before finally wandering back into her house.

She shook her head as she extracted the remarkably heavy pink box from its bag. She lifted the lid, curious, and let out an "oh." Damn, that was one hell of a good-looking cake. She hadn't planned to eat it right away, but she supposed she owed herself at least a taste-test.

Turning over the events of the last several minutes while she fished a fork out of the drawer, she struggled to make sense of it all. Her rant about period cramps hadn't put Max off in the slightest. Instead, he'd whisked her daughter off so Frannie could get a little rest in, and gifted her with some cake that—

Shut my hole.

She made a noise that she'd rarely emitted outside a bedroom…or a soundstage. One small forkful, and she was ready to lay down her life for this cake.

She took the entire box to the comfy couch in her living room, where she ate several more bites—okay, more than several—

before grabbing the knitted blanket off the back and curling up with a contented sigh.

Frannie hadn't expected to feel any contentment whatsoever today, let alone as a direct result of Max's ministrations. He'd been so very kind. And she'd once again been ready to think the worst of him. She chided herself as she sank into the cushions.

But introspection could wait. All that mattered at the moment was that she actually felt better.

Thanks to her baker next door.

MAX HAD JUST DRIFTED off when a knock at his front door jolted him awake. He tried to ignore it, pretend it wasn't real, but it sounded a second time. He rolled out of bed with a grumble and threw a robe loosely over his shorts on his way to the door.

He hoped it wasn't some kind of emergency. He hadn't been sleeping too well lately—due in large part to distraction in the form of a feisty Scottish lass—so he'd looked forward to a catnap this afternoon. The interruption had him feeling fractious. A third knock as he made his way down the hall whipped him up even more.

He called out an exasperated "What?" that poor Linda likely didn't deserve as he yanked open the door. "Oh."

It wasn't Linda.

Frannie stood there, looking slightly stunned. And awfully pretty in her cheerful peach dress. In his groggy state, he wasn't sure if that aroused or annoyed him. Or both. Probably both.

"Hello," she greeted him. "Am I interrupting…something?"

"Huh? Oh. No. I thought you were…" He shook his head, attempting in vain to clear it. "Doesn't matter."

"Right. I saw you come up here a bit ago, and I thought…" She blinked a few times. "Were you asleep? In the middle of the day?"

His annoyance won out. "Yeah. As a matter of fact, I was. I get up so early to open the bakery that it helps to come up and catch a few winks sometimes. In the middle of the day. So I can have some semblance of a life after work." He quirked an eyebrow at her. "Speaking of which, why are *you* here and not at your job?"

Contrition dominated her expression, but he caught a flash of her own pique as well. "Lucy had a dentist appointment, so I took a half-day." Color bloomed on her cheeks, and her gaze flicked down and quickly back up again, an action he realized she'd done several times in the last few minutes.

Max belatedly remembered his wardrobe choice of an open robe over nothing but a pair of Jockey shorts. He yanked the robe closed and fought the urge to shut the door in her face.

He didn't know why he should feel flustered—she'd seen him in nothing but a towel, after all. But this felt different somehow. More intimate, if that was possible.

I must really be out of it.

Frannie let out a small cough. "Anyway, I didn't realize you were…busy. I'll come back another time."

Shit. Relations were finally thawing between them, and here he was, making it awkward again.

"No, you don't have to." He rubbed a hand over his beard. "Sorry, I just wasn't expecting company. I guess I'm a little…"

"Cranky?"

He mock-glowered at her. "I was going to say tired."

"Oh, well…" She met his eyes with a teasing twinkle. "I'm sorry, too. I truly didn't mean to interrupt your time to yourself."

"Thanks. So, what does bring you by?"

"Right. I, um…" She seemed suddenly shy. It was damn endearing. "I wanted to thank you. For the other day. Taking Lucy for the afternoon. And the cake."

"Oh. Of course." He mentally kicked himself for not asking after her right away. "I assume you're feeling better?"

"I am, thanks. Your sister was right about that cake."

"I'm glad to hear it."

She swallowed visibly. "I've been meaning to come by. I was all ready to use the excuse of returning your plate, but…"

"All I gave you was a box."

"Exactly."

"Sorry," he stage-whispered.

She laughed, before growing serious again. She fished a colorful envelope out of her pocket and presented it to him. "I also wanted to bring you this."

He took her offering, but before he could open it, she forged ahead. "I'm throwing Lucy a party. Her birthday's in September, but with everything going on last fall, and being in a much smaller place, we didn't get to celebrate much. I thought it might be fun to do something a little different, now that we're in this house and Colin's back in our lives. So it's a half-birthday party, I guess."

"Yeah, she told me all about it during our lesson. She's so excited to be like Alice."

"Exactly." Her smile turned shy. "Anyhow, she wanted to invite you, so…"

"Oh, wow." He glanced at the envelope again, and a blush crept up his neck. "Thanks."

"There'll be other adults there, too, of course," she rushed on. "Colin and Nate, some of the kids' parents…"

"I'd love to come."

"Good. Great." She bit her lip, making him want to take over and do it for her. "Well. I should…" She gestured over her shoulder.

"Right, yeah." Now that he was fully awake, he wanted to prolong their conversation. "I assume you're going to Lois's big premiere tomorrow, and to her and Nick's for the pre-festivity cocktails?"

"Yes. You'll be there, right?"

It might be his imagination, but he spied a hint of hope on her features.

"Wouldn't miss it," he replied. "As a matter of fact, I'm making Lois a huge cheesecake. Nick said she's pretty nervous, with it being her first time directing and all."

"She is. A lot's riding on this picture." Her lips curved up warmly. "She'll love the cheesecake. That's very thoughtful."

Their latest truce hovered between them, balancing on the edge between awkward and promising. Max reached up to fiddle with the chain he always wore around his neck, a medal from his sister and— *Crap.* He hoped Frannie hadn't looked too closely at it.

Of course, she tracked his movement. He held his breath, but luckily his motion seemed to have inspired her into action as well.

"I should be going," she said, almost reluctantly. "Let you get back to your nap. Thanks again for the cake."

"Sure. And thank you for this." He held up the invitation.

"See you at Lois and Nick's."

"See you then."

Frannie nodded once, then headed down the stairs. He closed the door and leaned against it, lost in thought as he tapped Lucy's invitation against his palm, nap completely forgotten.

Chapter Thirteen

$\mathcal{M}$ax eased his truck into Lois and Nick's driveway, protective of his cargo. He'd outdone himself with this cheesecake, but he also needed to exercise caution. While it would no doubt taste perfect, there was a chance he'd made it a smidge too large, thus compromising its structural integrity. He'd already had a hell of a time getting it into its box, and then shoring up the bottom of said packaging. Given Lois's anticipation over her premiere, he'd never forgive himself if he dropped her gift before presenting it to her.

He carefully extracted the cake from the truck, taking nearly equal care with his tuxedo. Nate had helped him pick it out, and she'd kill him if he got sugary crumbs all over it. He slowly rounded the house to let himself in the back door. It made more sense to go straight to the kitchen, both for the dessert's virtue and the element of gift-giving surprise.

He had to admit, he also harbored a mass of nerves about facing one of his fellow guests tonight. Delaying the impact of seeing her would give him a chance to calm his breath…and avoid dropping the cheesecake.

Frannie's surprise appearance at his door had left him unexpectedly rattled. While their fragile cease-fire grew increasingly better, fragile it remained. One false move—like botching the execution of Vi's advice to come clean about V-J Day—and they'd be right back to square one. He was terrified to allow himself too much hope.

Max precariously turned the kitchen doorknob, then pushed the door open with his backside, weighing his options with Frannie as he did so. Maybe he'd start by asking her to dance at the party after the premiere. If that went well…

"Need help with that?"

Max froze. Just his luck. Why would Frannie be in the living room, when she could be in the kitchen instead?

He took a steadying breath and continued to walk backwards into the room. "Nah, I've got it balanced just right. If I let it go, who knows what'll happen."

He couldn't bask in her resulting husky chuckle, because he turned at that moment—and nearly upended the cheesecake anyway.

Her evening gown was a deep emerald green, its fabric gathered and folded in an almost Grecian style, nipped in at her waist with a crisscrossing cord belt made of the same fabric. The dress clung to her curves in all the best places. A little matching jacket draped around her shoulders, just covering her tattoo.

She skimmed appreciative eyes over his evening wear as well.

But none of that—no matter how glorious—was what imperiled his confectionary creation. No, that owed entirely to what she'd done to her hair.

He stared at her for a too-long moment, swallowing a few times before finally finding his voice. Which, of course, emerged as a half-croaked blurt.

"You're a redhead now."

Frannie appeared startled. "Oh, right. Yes." She raised a hand to skim the locks curling over her shoulder. "I mean, I always have been."

He couldn't keep the confusion off his face.

"At least, I was," she explained. "When I was a kid. By the

time I left my teen years behind, it faded to brown. But I always felt like a redhead." Max was incapable of doing more than blinking, which seemed to spur her further rambling. "It was about damn time I caught back up on the outside, so I made the change." She paused, eyes narrowing. "Does that meet with your approval?"

"What? Yes! Not that you need it!" Great, he'd been here all of five minutes and already he'd pissed her off. "But I...like it. A lot."

Talk about an understatement. Redheads were his own personal kryptonite. Always had been. Max had encountered a fair number of Nick's celebrity acquaintances over the years, and the one and only time he'd ever tripped himself up? Rita Hayworth.

Now Frannie, his *other* kryptonite, had added red hair to her arsenal. The imminent explosion of his head and his heart—and, yeah, his cock—would likely level the entire California coastline. He was done for.

And more than ready to be.

A hint of color stained her cheeks. "Thanks."

Max's brain told his head to nod, though whether he actually succeeded, he couldn't be sure.

"So...are you going to stand there holding a cake all night?"

The hint of impatience behind her words yanked him back to reality. He shrugged, finally able to return her volley. "I might."

"Come on. Let's hope there's actually room in their icebox for it." Frannie paused on her way across the kitchen. "It is going in the icebox, I assume?"

"Correct." Max stopped short when he reached the door she held open for him. "Huh." The fridge wasn't overly full—but not overly roomy, either.

Perhaps he'd been overly exuberant on Lois's behalf.

Frannie glanced between the box in his hands and the small space. "Jesus, how big did you make that cheesecake, anyway?"

Her sudden attack on his baking—along with the intoxicating

proximity of her perfume—provoked him. "I told you, I was trying to do something nice for Lois," he retorted.

"There is such a thing as quality over quantity, you know."

He cocked his eyebrow, unable to resist. "Why Frannie, are you saying you can't handle…quality *and* quantity?"

"Oh, shut up and let's make that damn thing fit."

"If you insist."

Max bit back a snicker at her resulting scowl.

She bent and started rearranging items, and after several rocky attempts, between the two of them, they got the dessert safely situated. Max closed the door and they leaned against it in unison.

"See, I told you it'd work out."

"Barely," she huffed.

With the refrigerator's cold air contained and thus no longer able to keep anything in check, the atmosphere grew heavy around them. Max took in Frannie's delectably full mouth, decorated in a darker red than usual. He swallowed, hard. Her eyes, bright even in the dimming light from the window, snapped up to his.

It took every last shred of his control not to pull her in and cement his lips to hers.

He reminded himself of Nate's potentially murderous turn should he muss his tuxedo this early in the evening. After which, in all likelihood, she'd proceed to insufferably gather all their insufferable friends around his corpse to gloat and speculate…insufferably.

Plus, he had to contend with his ever-present hesitation to push Frannie too far, too soon.

When her breath hitched, he almost plunged in anyway. But Lois's voice, echoing from the other room, saved him in the nick of time.

"Please tell me Max is here. I cannot be late tonight."

Moved by relief—and a sudden, fierce desire to leave Frannie as unmoored as she left him—Max straightened off the icebox and spun on his heel. Her tiny grunt of frustration echoed behind him as he strode out the door, cheerfully calling out to Lois and leaving Frannie to stalk in his wake.

MAX SKIRTED the edge of the supper club, observing the party in full swing. Ronnie O'Hara, Linda's sweetheart, crooned from her spot in front of the orchestra, keeping everyone entertained. He'd taken Lois for a celebratory spin around the dance floor before Nick cut back in, and he scanned the crowd to offer the same treatment to Nate, if she could tear herself from Colin.

He chuckled when he spotted her. She had, in fact, separated from Colin—because he was deftly leading Lucy in a dance, not their first of the evening. The pair had cut quite a rug earlier, but Colin had slowed his pace considerably for this number, as the evening was catching up to the little one. She valiantly stifled a yawn, barely able to keep her head from lolling on her uncle's shoulder. From her vantage point on the sidelines, Nate watched them, her smile comically dreamy. It wouldn't surprise Max in the slightest if her pupils actually turned into pulsing hearts like a cartoon character.

She wasn't the only one watching Lucy and Colin. Frannie stood on the other side of the room, nearer to him, a champagne flute in her hand. Her grin was more amused than dreamy, but it lodged right between his ribs. Before anyone caught him mooning like Nate, he shoved his hands in his pockets and closed the distance between them.

Frannie had been avoiding him since their encounter in the kitchen, but the time had come to remedy that. Maybe ask her for that dance.

"Think she'll make it to the end of the song before her eyes close?" Max asked, nodding toward Lucy.

Frannie's head swiveled in his direction, and luckily her smile didn't fade. "She's sure as hell going to try."

"Her effort is impressive."

"Well, I did promise her we could stay till ten." She nodded at the clock above the bandstand. "And given that she's got fifteen whole minutes to go, I have no doubt my child will milk it for all it's worth."

"As well she should."

They slipped into a lovely, comfortable quiet as they continued to watch Lucy and Colin. Frannie exhaled audibly and contentedly.

"It must be nice, having your brother back," Max offered gently.

"It is." She hummed thoughtfully. "For so long, I wanted to introduce them. And seeing them get along even better than I ever imagined… It's unbelievably nice."

Ronnie brought the song to a close, and Colin led Lucy over to a still-smiling Nate. Max held his breath, shoring up his nerve to ask Frannie for the next dance. In what was either a sign from the heavens or a cosmic joke, the opening notes of "I'm Beginning to See the Light" floated toward them.

Memories of holding her close, four years ago, washed over him. Before he could overthink it, Max held out his hand. "Would you like to dance?"

Frannie looked from his hand to his face, hesitant.

Which prompted him to keep talking. "They are playing our song, after all."

At that, her eyes widened and her mouth fell open on a small gasp.

Shit.

"You…" The rise and fall of her chest sped up, as those gorgeous blue eyes slowly narrowed. "This song… You *do* remember," she hissed.

He was on the verge of protesting, or apologizing, or…something, when her angry words caught up to him. He'd been right.

Frustration clouded Max's voice. "So do you."

"I—" She stared at him for a charged moment, then pivoted

with an indignant huff and stormed toward the French doors leading to the club's terrace.

"So I guess we're having this out now," he muttered, before following her.

It only took him a minute to catch up, but she'd already begun pacing furiously. Good thing most of the partygoers were spending their time inside with the talented orchestra, otherwise Frannie might leave behind a string of casualties, like scattered pins at a bowling alley.

Might as well dive right in. "I can explain. If you'll let me."

She whirled to face him. "There's no need, is there? It's perfectly obvious. You were drunk enough to flash your hash, but not so drunk that you blocked all memory of the incident. Which you have now failed, on multiple occasions, to tell me." She was practically vibrating. "What else could there be to explain?"

"Oh, I don't know," he spat back. "Maybe the fact that you've got it all wrong?"

She leveled a potent glare at him, but relented slightly, letting him speak.

He aimed her glare right back. "Clearly, we *both* neglected to divulge our memories of that night. But I was not drunk."

Another irate scoff escaped her. "Oh, please."

"It's true." Wary of being interrupted, he cut her off quickly. "I told you about my baseball injury. Because of that, I rarely let myself have more than a beer or two." He crossed his arms over his chest. "You know, due to the occasional vertigo? Often accompanied by nausea?"

Frannie opened her mouth to respond, but then closed it again. A hint of chagrin skated across her features, or maybe that was simply wishful thinking on his part. She stared at him for a moment, before pacing away in frustration.

"Then why the bloody hell didn't you say something?" She threw her hands up. "All this time?"

"Why didn't *you*?" Not his best comeback, he knew, but anger —and Frannie Haynes in general—tended to limit his vocabulary.

"You didn't remember me!"

"No. You assumed I didn't remember you. There's a big difference."

She narrowed her eyes. "Well, *someone* could've corrected me."

"Someone *else* could've asked for clarification. Or behaved like *she* remembered *me*."

She let out a high-pitched growl. "What was I supposed to do when Nick introduced us? Say, 'Right, you don't recall, but I'm the lass you met in an alley on V-J Day, the one you kissed before chucking your dinner at my feet. Nice to see you again.' *That* would've been fun." She pointed her finger in his face. "That shouldn't have been on me."

It was his turn to growl. "It sure as hell shouldn't have been on me! I'm the one who threw up, remember? And there you were, the woman who *ran away* in horror before I'd even straightened up, acting like it never happened. You honestly expected me to open with, 'Hey, funny story... Let me relive my most embarrassing moment,' just so you could shit on me all over again?"

He dimly registered a flash of remorse on her features, but his wounded pride—and a fresh wave of long-simmering hurt—kept him from dwelling on it. He ran his hand through his hair, heedless of the mess he left behind.

"God, Frannie. All this time. You've been holding it against me, all this time. I suspected you must remember, given how pissy and rude you've always been. And I was right."

Her voice sounded simultaneously small and mighty. "You could have said something."

"And if I had, would you have let me explain? Like you're doing now?" He didn't bother to curb the sarcasm oozing out of him.

They stared each other down, electricity sizzling around them.

Max felt more conflicted than ever. He wanted to explain himself, to yell until she understood. To lash out, bring her remorse roaring to life. At the same time, he felt desperate to erase her own hurt, and fix what he'd broken by not fessing up to his part in their misunderstanding.

Overriding all those urges was his need to take her in his arms and bring them back to their flirtatious cease-fire. The one that held such promise that maybe, just maybe, they could make a go of something wonderful after all.

Frannie broke eye contact first, hanging her head with a tremendous sigh. Letting the air out of Max's hope along with it.

"I can't do this," she breathed.

"Frannie—"

She held up her hand, refusing to meet his eyes. "I… It's…a lot, Max. I need…a minute." She glanced through the French doors. "And I should get Lucy home."

"Right."

When she finally looked at him, her unreadable gaze seared right through to his core. She hesitated, but remained quiet, and whisked back to the party.

Max watched her go, wondering—too late—if there was any way to salvage things between them. Or to survive the inevitable damage to his heart if he tried.

Chapter Fourteen

The cacophony of celebration slammed into Frannie's senses the minute she reentered the club, making it that much harder to curb the pressure in her midsection and behind her eyes. Her emotions reached a cacophony of their own, fighting for dominance within her—anger, disappointment, even relief. But the one that pushed hardest was the one she felt least ready to face.

Guilt.

She stubbornly focused on finding her daughter and escaping the festivities instead.

Frannie scanned the crowd for her brother, and spotted him sharing a besotted grin with Nate as he spun her around the dance floor. He threw an occasional glance at the table they'd all shared earlier.

She followed his gaze, and her anger melted. Lucy was curled up across two chairs, fast asleep. A quick look at the clock proved she had indeed made it to ten o'clock before turning back into a pumpkin.

She wove through tables and revelers, but stopped short when she reached Lucy. Now came the real challenge—extracting her daughter from her spot and getting her to the car without waking her. All while wearing a long gown and higher heels than usual.

Gathering her evening bag and Lucy's sweater bought her a little time, but there was nothing for it; she'd simply have to lift her and hope for the best. Before she could maneuver herself into position, she felt an unmistakable presence behind her.

"Here, let me."

She barely suppressed the heat-filled shiver his deep voice inspired.

Max stepped around her and, without another word, gently lifted Lucy into his arms. Frannie held her breath, but the lass stirred only enough to snuggle against Max's chest.

The resulting pang of longing in her own chest exacerbated her anger. At herself or him, she wasn't entirely sure.

Max hovered, waiting for Frannie to lead the way to the exit. The club's doorman flagged the driver of the car Lois had hired for them, and they stood in silence as they waited for him to bring it around.

A silence that was inexplicably awkward and comfortable at the same time.

His anger should match hers, yet here he stood, displaying kindness again—although she supposed that had more to do with Lucy than her. He let her slide into the car's back seat first, before delicately handing Lucy in, positioning her head to settle onto Frannie's lap. As if that wasn't enough, he eased her sweater from Frannie's hand and tucked it over her like a blanket.

With a brief nod, he retreated, and the driver closed the door behind him.

As they pulled away from the club, Frannie stroked her daughter's hair and closed her eyes against an even stronger wave of longing. She pushed down the lump in her throat, along with the idea of how lovely it would be to have domestic scenes like that with Max on a regular basis.

If only they hadn't shot it all to hell out on that terrace.

FRANNIE CRADLED Lucy on one shoulder as she pushed open her front door, feeling at once exhausted and so keyed up she might never stop buzzing. As desperately as she wished to ditch her heels, she didn't dare. If she tried to trudge up the stairs without the extra height, she'd surely trip on her dress's lengthy hem and send both of them straight to the hospital.

No light emerged from under her mother's bedroom door; she must have retired early. Just as well. As tired as Frannie was, she'd rather put Lucy to bed on her own. Her mum would sense her disquiet, and she didn't have the energy to try to deny something was wrong.

Or to pretend she wasn't imagining a different partner helping her guide Lucy through these bedtime rituals.

Lucy woke enough to sway on her feet while Frannie helped her out of her dress and into her pajamas. She nudged her into the bathroom and got her set up with her toothbrush, before escaping to her own bedroom to finally ditch her formalwear.

Frannie kept an ear cocked for evidence that Lucy had nodded off into the sink, but the steady—albeit agonizingly slow—sound of her brushing continued across the hall. A welcome distraction from the thoughts hovering on the periphery of her brain.

She stepped out of her dress with a sigh, swapping it for her favorite jeans and a cable-knit sweater she'd "borrowed" from Colin nearly fifteen years ago and never gotten around to giving back. It was worn in several places, which only made it cozier. The garment had seen her through many a difficult time, and kept her brother close during the years they were physically separated, so she wouldn't part with it for the world.

Returning to the bathroom, she found Lucy absently brushing the same tooth, staring into the mirror like a zombie. With a chuckle, she handed her a cup of water.

"Okay, kiddo, time to rinse."

Lucy blinked at her a few times before obeying. Frannie ran a washcloth over her daughter's face and led her back to her room. Once she'd scrambled into her bed, Frannie pulled the covers over her and Sir James, her beloved stuffed Scottie dog, one of the few gifts Marty had had the opportunity to give his newborn daughter. Lucy settled in with a deep, contented sigh that warmed Frannie's heart more than anything.

She smoothed her daughter's hair back off her forehead. "Did you have fun at the party, love?"

"I sure di—" Her words cut off with a jaw-cracking yawn.

Frannie stifled a laugh and leaned in to kiss the crown of her head. "I'm glad. Sweet dreams, my girl."

"Night, Mommy." She snuggled Sir James closer and went out like a light.

Frannie remained perched on the edge of the bed for a while, allowing the rise and fall of Lucy's breath to soothe her as she finally let herself analyze—and feel—everything that had transpired with Max.

Her anger lingered over how much time he'd spent pretending he didn't remember her, leading her to think he'd been drunk that night.

But, no. That wasn't fair. She'd done her share of pretending too. Of assuming, as he'd said. It was a wonder he could even stand to look at her.

She closed her eyes. If she had any hope of facing all this, she needed some chocolate courage. With one last caress of her daughter's hair, she slipped out of the room and downstairs to the kitchen.

Max hadn't been plastered the night they met. The night they kissed. Logically, a part of her had always sensed it. He'd been so *present* in that alley, so utterly charming.

Her foot hit the bottom step, and the crux of the matter hit her. That night, after several years of doing everything nearly on her own, of simply surviving one minute to the next, she'd enjoyed herself, and felt an awful lot of things she couldn't put into words. Hell, she'd *felt*. For the first time since losing Marty.

Perhaps even more than you felt for Marty.

That had scared the shite out of her. Still did.

She trudged into the kitchen, pushing herself to keep pulling on the thread, even as her heart resisted—it wanted to take the easier route, go back to her usual pattern of staying mad at Max.

As she took the tin of hot chocolate powder from the shelf, guilt flooded her chest like water in the burns where she grew up. She knew how to hold a grudge like nobody's business. Especially with him.

But the alternative made her shudder.

If she let him in, truly, she could lose him. She'd already lost so bloody much in her thirty years on this earth. While the specter of war no longer loomed, that wasn't the only threat. She could easily drive Max away. She certainly had a talent for it.

Frannie heaved a sigh as she opened the icebox to fetch the milk. She nearly dropped it when her gaze landed out the window, across the alley. Her breath hitched.

Max sat on the stairs leading up to his apartment, in his shirt-sleeves, having abandoned his tuxedo jacket. The dim light next to his door bathed his profile in a warm, ethereal glow. While it was impossible to read his expression from this distance, the lines of his body painted a pensive picture as he stared off into the distance.

The cool glass of the milk bottle beneath her fingers steadied Frannie as she came to a decision. She poured double her originally intended amount into a sauce pot, stirring in the cocoa powder when it was time, and filled two mugs.

She was no closer to sorting out her feelings for Max. Anger, fear…everything else. But one thing she did know. She owed him an apology, and the chance to fully explain his side of their shared history.

Carefully, she balanced the drinks and made her way across the alley. Max didn't look in her direction, but the stillness in his body told her he sensed her presence.

Frannie breathed through her nerves, inhaling the comforting scent of chocolate. When she arrived at the bottom of the stairs, he finally looked at her, watching warily.

She gave herself a moment to take in his handsomeness, the way he'd rolled his sleeves up and unbuttoned the first few buttons of his shirt, revealing that exquisite dark hair in both places. He twisted an unlit pipe between his hands, his only movement. Funny, she'd never seen him smoke one before.

"I made enough hot chocolate for two." She lifted one mug, fervently hoping he'd take the peace offering.

His chest rose and fell before he gave a small nod and scooted over on the step in silent invitation. Frannie climbed up and handed him the steaming cup before settling next to him, careful to leave a bit of distance between them.

Max blew on his chocolate before taking a sip, and Frannie followed suit.

"Thanks," he murmured. "This is nice."

"Sure." She suddenly realized she hadn't given much thought to what she'd say when she got here. The words bottled up inside her.

Taking the easy way out, she began with an attempt at humor. Pointing at the pipe, she said, "You know, I'm pretty sure you're supposed to smoke that thing."

"Where's the fun in that?" Max let out a rueful chuckle, and mercifully continued speaking. "Never had much of a taste for it, actually. My first attempt was a bit of a disaster. I snuck my grandpa's, wanting to be just like him. About a year after my concussion." He hesitated briefly, and her guilt poked at her, but he continued before she could interject. "I had no idea what I was doing, and practically coughed up a lung."

"Is that even possible with a pipe? Cigarettes, sure. Maybe cigars. But..."

"Trust me, it's possible. I spent two whole days trying not to" —he cleared his throat—"throw up. Permanently soured me on the pipe-smoking experience."

She took another sip from her mug, swallowing her follow-up

questions along with the cocoa, afraid to push him too hard, given everything still unspoken between them.

As if anticipating them anyway, he answered. "I may never light up again myself, but…the smell of pipe tobacco's always gonna remind me of my grandpa." His mouth curved into a slow smile, his dimples popping. "And all his stories, his advice."

"Is that his?" she asked quietly.

Max nodded. "We lost him when I was twenty. But just keeping this filled, having it nearby… It's like he's with me, you know?"

"I do."

She didn't miss the current under his words, the comfort he took from his grandfather's memory. The reason he needed comfort at the moment.

"I'm sorry, Max." He raised his eyes to hers, and the cautious hope in his expression gave her a boost of courage. "For not saying anything. For assuming." Frannie swallowed. "For running away that night."

His Adam's apple bobbed fiercely, and his voice came out in a rasp that was damn sexy, in spite of the situation. "I'm sorry too. I could've said something plenty of times. I was just…"

"Embarrassed."

"Yeah."

She huffed. "That makes two of us."

They sat there for a few minutes, sipping their hot chocolate, taking each other in while a light breeze kept them company.

Frannie broke the silence, her voice barely above a whisper. "What exactly did happen that night?"

"You really want to know?" The uncertainty in his voice pierced her heart.

"I do."

Max set his mug on the step next to him, but held onto his grandfather's pipe with both hands. "In a nutshell, the vertigo happened. It had been dormant for a while, but I should've known it would catch up to me." He shrugged. "In a way, I was expecting it. Just not…"

"Right then and there?"

He snorted. "Yeah. The entire time I was overseas, I was fine. The minute I came home…" He shifted to face her. "I suppose all that time, on the fringes of a war zone, took its toll. The constant stress. The relief of coming home. But then I had to cross the Atlantic in a huge destroyer packed to the gills with other guys… followed by a cross-country train trip, also crowded as hell. All the while trying not to worry that we might get shipped back out. It wasn't over everywhere.

"I'll never forget being on that train when the news came through, that it *was* finally ending. The conductor announced it over the speakers, and the cheer that went up…" Max shook his head with a small laugh. "We stepped off that train and into the biggest party I've ever seen."

"It truly was something else," she breathed.

"I don't usually drink more than one beer at a time, as a precaution. But it felt like a once-in-a-lifetime day, so I took a chance on starting a second one." His eyes, burning with a sudden intensity, held hers. "Two sips in, I walked into an alley to find a very pretty Scottish lass. Got up the courage to ask her for a dance. Kissed her." That last emerged as nothing but a hoarse whisper.

She swallowed hard against the memory of their magnificent, scorching kiss. "And then it all caught up to you?"

"It did." His voice sounded resigned. "It had been simmering, under the surface, for too long. I was just plain overstimulated. Overwhelmed. I got sick."

"And I ran away," she rasped.

"I won't lie, that hurt a bit. But you didn't know."

But she had assumed. And now she desperately regretted letting her fear propel her away.

Max shrugged, his tone lighter, almost forcibly so. "Besides, you only just missed Nick. He came along right away and found me. Took care of me."

It should have been me who took care of him.

"That's good," she said instead.

Max exhaled audibly. "I didn't know what to say that night we met again at Lois and Nick's. But I am sorry I let it go on as long as I did."

"It's not like I gave you much of a chance. Max, I—"

He raised his hand, cutting her off. "Look, Frannie. We've both made mistakes. What do you say we...start over?" He paused, swallowing. "As friends."

Hope and disappointment flared in equal measure. Part of her wanted nothing more than to take his extended olive branch...and the other part wanted to hit him over the head with it. If all she wanted was to be *friends* with him, they certainly wouldn't be in this mess.

But they did have to start somewhere. Or rather, start *over* somewhere, as he'd said.

So she nodded. "Friends. I'd like that."

"Okay, then." He turned away quickly, picking up his mug and taking a long sip. "I forgot to ask. Did you get Lucy to bed all right?"

Frannie smiled. Max knew precisely what subject change would put them both at ease. "She was a champ, as a matter of fact. Rallied enough for her pj's, though I did worry she'd keel over while brushing her teeth."

Max chuckled. "I'm glad."

"Thanks for your help getting her to the car."

"Don't mention it."

They took simultaneous pulls from their cups. Then proceeded to speak in unison.

"Speaking of—"

"I should—"

Their nervous laughter mingled in the quiet night air. Max gestured for Frannie to go first.

"I was just going to say, I should probably head back over. My mum's home, but still…"

"Yeah. Same." He pointed down the stairs at the bakery. "Early mornings and all."

They stood together, and as she looked up into his dark eyes, sparkling despite the low light, she resisted the urge to rise up on her toes and kiss him, even on the cheek. Though she wanted to. Very badly.

He handed his mug back to her, but didn't let go when her hand closed around it. "So…truce."

Their fingers hovered, less than an inch apart, on the ceramic, before one of them—or maybe both—closed the distance. It was the smallest of touches, but it delivered one hell of a powerful zing.

"Truce," she breathed.

Max withdrew his hand. "Good night, Frannie."

"Good night, Max."

She made her way down the stairs and across the alley, not daring to turn back around until she got to her door. She found him still standing there, leaning on his railing, watching her. He returned her small wave.

Once inside, Frannie leaned against her door, letting relief have its way with her. At last feeling a bit less scared of…everything…where Max was concerned.

Chapter Fifteen

Max tied a red ribbon around the cookie-laden pink box and stepped back to examine his handiwork. The design might not be overly artistic, but the ribbon elevated the look from his typical plain twine, so it would do just fine for the half-birthday girl.

He needed to freshen up a bit before Lucy's actual party, but he wanted to bring the cookies over early, so she could tuck them away if she didn't care to share with her guests. They were her favorites, after all.

And if it gave him a chance to see her mother before the chaos of the party descended? Well, that would be icing on the cake.

Max took his time crossing the yard, steadying his nerves along the way. It had been nearly a week since their near-disastrous evening of coming clean. But since they'd both been busy, they'd hardly done more than wave at each other across the alley.

The last thing he'd expected after coming home that night was to see her walk over to join him, let alone bring him hot chocolate. His entire body vibrated with gratitude that she had.

Even though he'd gone on to use the word *friend* when calling their truce.

But friend was a hell of a lot better than adversary, so he'd make it work. A big part of him believed it was the better way to kick off their new beginning, anyway. He had a heart to protect, and the two of them didn't have the most stellar track record with their cease-fires.

Frannie's back door stood open, and he caught a flurry of movement through the screen. He was about to knock when she spotted him, mid-whirl, as she paced around the kitchen.

"Max!" She made a beeline for the screen and nearly whacked him with it as she swung it open. "Thank god you're here."

He blinked. That was a new one. Not that anyone would hear him complaining…

She grabbed his arm and yanked him unceremoniously through the doorway, before letting go—much to his disappointment—to resume her frantic pacing.

"Everything okay?"

As he braced himself for the answer, he took in her appearance for the first time, amid her perpetual motion.

She had none of her usual polish. Her eyes were wide and a little wild, her newly fiery hair valiantly trying to escape the clip holding it up off her neck. The apron covering her casual, colorfully printed shirtdress was streaked with what looked like flour, some of which had also edged outside the lines to spill onto the dress. When she turned to face him again, he saw a telltale chocolate smudge near her temple.

Ah, a baking mishap. Tension he hadn't noticed gathering suddenly ebbed from his shoulders. *This, I can fix.*

"It's a disaster!" Frannie threw her hands up in frustration. "I have no idea how it happened. I have a houseful of children—and their parents—on their way over here, and a little girl who's been looking forward to this for weeks, and there's no time to fix it, and I—"

"Whoa, whoa." Max set the cookie box on the counter and gently rested his hands on her shoulders. "Take a breath." To his astonishment, she took his advice, though the panic didn't leave her eyes as she blinked up at him. "I'm guessing you tried to bake something?"

She nodded. "A cake. I don't know what happened. I followed all the instructions." Her chest resumed its rapid rise and fall.

"Hey, I'm sure it's not as bad as you think."

"Oh, no. It's far worse."

"Somehow I doubt that." At her protesting scoff, he pushed forward. "Why don't you let me take a look? I am an expert, after all."

That elicited a small smile from her, quickly chased by a flush of what looked to be embarrassment. "I guess that couldn't hurt."

She glanced over his shoulder, and he suddenly realized he still held hers. At some point, he'd even begun massaging with his thumbs. But she hadn't shrugged him off—a good sign. As much as he hated to, he let her go.

She stepped around him and moved to a big cake dome on the table. Her hand hesitated on the handle.

"Don't you dare laugh."

He put his hand over his heart. "I wouldn't dream of it."

Satisfied by his answer, Frannie slowly lifted the dome to reveal...a giant pile of chocolate crumbs, held loosely together by globs of what he assumed was frosting. Max did not, in fact, have the urge to laugh. He found it difficult to do anything other than stare.

"Fucking hell," she exhaled. "It really is that bad, isn't it?"

The despair in her voice snapped him to attention. "No. Not necessarily."

She cocked an eyebrow. "You don't have to sugarcoat it."

"I'm not. Honestly." He came closer to analyze her handiwork. "Though coating things in sugar does happen to be one of my specialties."

Frannie snorted. Good. He was determined to brighten her mood.

He continued to examine the wreckage—*ahem, cake.* As he did, Frannie took a step back to give him room, which better served his concentration in the long run. He peered more closely at the heap. It rather resembled a mud pie. One made with actual mud. But looks could be deceiving.

He started to form an idea about precisely what had gone wrong for her, and the harder he looked, the more his suspicion grew. He hoped, for her sake, he was right.

Max crouched lower. "How does it taste?"

"Taste?"

"Sure. Did you try it?"

"You can't honestly expect me to try *that*, do you?" She sneered with palpable shock.

He straightened, hands coming to rest on his hips. He took a second to enjoy the way her eyes flashed down, attention drawn below his waist, before answering her question.

"*You* can't honestly declare this a disaster until you've taken a bite. Trust me." He glanced at the table and pointed to a lonely fork next to the chaos. "Is this clean?"

"What? Oh. Yeah." Her cheeks looked awfully flushed. In much the same way as that morning, in the dawning light, framed by her bedroom window…

He ignored the siren call and focused on taking up a forkful that encompassed all the elements of her dessert, mentally crossing his fingers. The mess hit his tongue and…tasted decent. Better than decent, good even. *Thank fuck.* He made an appreciative noise.

Frannie eyed him as she chewed on her lower lip, her hand nervously rubbing at the base of her throat, setting off a perpetual tinkling of her charm bracelet. "Well? Was that a good *hmm* or an 'oh, shite' *hmm*?"

He shot her a reassuring grin as soon as he finished chewing. "Frannie. It actually tastes pretty damn good. Here, see for yourself."

He spotted a second fork on the counter and offered it to her, but she didn't take it.

"What's the matter? Don't believe me?"

She shook her head, but before she could utter a protest, he neatly scooped up a bite, bringing it to her mouth. He quirked an eyebrow in invitation.

Frannie opened her lips and let him feed her, and of course—*of course*—it sent a telegraph directly to his groin.

Thankfully, the corresponding heat in her gaze transformed to simple wonder the minute her tastebuds registered the cake.

"Oh," she breathed. "You're right. It is okay." She smiled up at him as she chewed. "What do you know?"

"I knew you didn't believe me."

"Can you blame me? I mean, look at it." She did, and her face promptly fell, all teasing vanishing in an instant. "Why the bloody hell *does* it look like that?"

Max considered the cake. "Could be a couple of things. How long did you wait to frost it after it came out of the oven?"

Frannie worried at her lip again. "Half an hour, maybe? Is that bad?"

"It can be. Cakes need to completely cool if you want the icing to adhere and not…"

"Let me guess…crumble into a million pieces?" she asked glumly.

"Afraid so."

"But it was already on its way before that. I noticed a big crack when I tipped it onto the plate."

"Hmm… Could have been the eggs, then, too. Sometimes you can over-whip them."

"Great." The exaggerated roll of her *r* was nothing short of adorable.

"Hey, it's really not that bad."

"Are you kidding?" She gestured at the table. "Look at it. I can't serve that."

"The most important thing is, it tastes good. That's way more than half the battle. Believe me, I know. Did I ever tell you about my first solo cake attempt?"

She shook her head.

He didn't know why he kept doing this to himself, but she managed to bring out every mortifying story he had. Her sad expression killed him, though, so he proceeded.

"I was so excited. My grandma finally felt I was ready to try on my own." He leaned his hip on the table, facing her more fully. "I thought I could listen to the ball game on the radio while I worked and not get distracted. Rookie mistake. I don't know if you've ever noticed, but sugar and salt look an awful lot alike."

"Oh, *no*."

"Yep. That cake had a teaspoon of sugar and a half a cup of salt." He chuckled at the memory. "I took one bite and promptly spit it right back out."

"I'll bet."

"And do you know what my grandma did? She proceeded to eat—and actually swallow—five whole bites before she gave up."

"You're kidding. Why?"

He softened his smile, getting to the other, more important point, of his story. "Because I'd made it by myself, and she loved me." He shrugged. "And she was brave as hell. But the point is, it was a lesson, and even though I'd messed up, she didn't want me to feel bad. She was proud of the fact that I'd made it just for her, no matter what it tasted like."

A hint of skepticism lurked behind Frannie's answering smile. "Why do I feel like there's a lesson in there for me, too?"

Max laughed and nudged her shoulder. "Because there is, lady." He pointed to her dessert. "You made that for Lucy, to make her day special. And I have a sneaking suspicion she's going to love it for exactly that reason."

"You think so?"

"I do." He gently took hold of her upper arms. "Look, if you really don't want to serve it, I've got a couple things at the bakery I can bring over instead. But that cake tastes a hell of a lot better than my salty disaster. And I'd be willing to bet Lucy would much rather have it at her party, because her mom, her *hero*, who she loves to pieces, made it. I think you owe it to her to ask her opinion."

Frannie's sapphire blue eyes coated with a sheen of moisture. "Thanks, Max."

He nodded brusquely, feeling a little misty himself. "And you know, if you play your cards right, I might even offer you some of my lessons before your next party."

Fire crept into her gaze. "At your usual rate?"

He rubbed his thumb against the spot where her sleeve met her skin. "For you, I'd be willing to negotiate."

Her cheeks flushed, and Max swallowed hard. But before he could act, the kitchen door swung open and Lucy bounded in. Frannie immediately tensed, and Max eased his hands from her arms.

"Hi, Max!"

He focused his attention on the happy little girl. "Well, if it isn't the gal of the hour! Ready for your party?"

"Yep." Her eyes slid to the beribboned pink box on the counter. "Is that...?"

"One dozen of my very finest snickerdoodles. All for you."

"Wow. Thanks."

Frannie stood between the table and her daughter, but Lucy's attention snagged on the cake anyway. She moved around her mother with a gasp.

Frannie's hand shot out and gripped his wrist tightly, snagging his heart in her vise as well. He enfolded her hand with a gentle squeeze.

"Mom. Is this my cake?" Lucy whispered.

Frannie swallowed audibly. "Um. Yes, love. It is."

Lucy stared at it for an interminable moment, before raising wide, reverent eyes to them. "It looks like a mud pie. This is the best. Cake. Ever!"

She flew around the table and tackled Frannie in a hug. Max was more than happy to part with her hand so she could bring her arms up to encircle her daughter.

"You really think so?" Frannie asked quietly. Disbelievingly.

"Are you kidding?" Lucy looked up at her mother. "Everyone always has the same boring cake. Round, with flowers. This is so much better. Thanks, Mom!"

"I'm glad you like it, my lass."

Lucy squeezed her around the middle one more time before pulling away. "I can't wait for my party," she squealed as she bolted for the door. "See you later, Max!"

"Bye, Snickerdoodle."

Frannie stared after her daughter for a long minute. When she turned back to Max, her eyes had glossed over once again.

"You can say it, you know. I've earned it."

"Say what?" he teased. "Lucy did give me an idea, though. I have some coconut flakes we could dye green, give the mud a grassy little garnish. If you want."

Frannie simply shook her head, smiling, and then the most miraculous thing happened. She wrapped her arms around his middle and held him for a moment. His arms came up to find their natural place around her, and he closed his eyes at the rightness of it all.

Far too soon, she pulled away. With a whispered, "Thank you, Max," she left the kitchen.

FRANNIE SURVEYED HER FRONT LAWN, party in full swing, and breathed her umpteenth sigh of relief. Deep down, she'd known Max was right, and that Lucy would enjoy whatever her party turned out to be, but it didn't change the fact that this was the first one she'd given for her. Frannie wanted to impress Lucy's friends —and their parents.

Luckily, it seemed to be working. Best of all, Lucy was having a ball. They hadn't reached the cake portion of the day's programming yet—Max's added coconut did lend it a lovely flair of authenticity, which eased Frannie's worries about its appearance

—but Lucy managed to preemptively brag about her cake to every arriving guest.

Colin and Nate had been the first to arrive, helping to set up the last of the decorations, and were now gamely engaged in being the bridge portion of a round of London Bridge.

Watching them, she felt a melancholy twinge, not for the first time that day, over Marty's absence from his daughter's life. From hers. But the ongoing sounds of laughter echoing all around reminded her that, as much as it hurt, she'd found room for other things too. New things. *Good* things.

Frannie's eyes landed on Max, hovering near the snack table with one of the other parents. She inhaled, the scent of him lingering in her memory from that hug. She couldn't quite believe she'd thrown her arms around him like that, but she'd been unable to help herself. His sweet generosity overwhelmed her —again.

He was so very warm. In every way.

As if sensing her attention, Max turned in her direction, catching her eye with a small smile. Before she knew it, he made his way over to her.

"Looks like the party's a rousing success."

"Thank god," she replied.

"Were you really that worried? Kids love any kind of party."

"I know. But this is the first I've thrown for Lucy, and I wanted it to be…"

"Better than everyone else's?" Max's face lit with a grin.

Frannie chuckled. "Better than everyone else's," she agreed.

He clinked his Coca-Cola bottle against hers. "Well, I think you can rest assured. She certainly loves her cake."

She bit back a groan. "Again, thank god." She paused. "And thank you. I know I was panicking back there."

Max lifted one shoulder. "With good reason. I would've been worried too, in your shoes." His smile turned sly. "It's lucky I showed up to reassure you."

Lucky indeed.

Frannie tried to mask her sudden blush with a mocking scoff. "So sure of yourself, aren't you?"

"When it comes to baking, always." He winked.

She truly didn't know what to do with this new, flirty side to their relationship. She rather enjoyed the way he melted her insides…which was more than a little terrifying.

Before she could spiral into another panic, Lucy's friend Nancy bounded up to the lawn, her harried-looking mother, Annette, in tow, precariously balancing a covered tray.

"Sorry we're late," Annette called out. "But Nancy insisted we walk."

"They'd fall over in the car, Mom." Nancy hopped as Lucy ran over. "Lucy, wait till you see what we made!"

"Can I help with that?" Max asked Annette.

"It's okay, I've got it," she replied, carefully easing her cargo onto a nearby table.

"Wait, weren't you bringing a fruit salad?" Frannie queried. "Is it that precious?"

Little Nancy's eyes lit up. "Oh, we didn't just make fruit salad. We made *candle* salad."

Frannie had never heard of it, but perhaps it was some American delicacy. She looked to Max, who simply shrugged. Perhaps not, then.

Annette split a sheepish look between the two of them. "I was going to make an ambrosia, but Nancy got this children's cookbook for her own birthday, and…she insisted we make this." After a quick glance to make sure her daughter wasn't looking, she mouthed an "I'm sorry" to Frannie.

What on earth?

"Show them, Mom, show them!" At Nancy's insistence, her mother lifted the covering from the tray to reveal…

And I was worried about my cake?

Frannie's eyes went wide, but she schooled her features in the nick of time, as she remembered that children—especially one who felt proud of her creation—were present. Her protective maternal instincts fought hard for dominance, and thankfully won out. Barely.

In front of her were a series of…desserts, apparently? Sitting on beds of lettuce, each sculpture contained a pineapple ring at its base, with a banana sticking straight up out of the center. Perched atop every banana was a bright red maraschino cherry, and—*oh dear god*—some sort of chunky white substance oozed from underneath the cherries, in some cases dripping all the way down the banana.

Max's hushed "wow" at her side nearly undid her, but Frannie bit her lip hard to keep herself together.

Think of the children, think of the children.

"Nancy, you made these?" she asked brightly.

The girl nodded enthusiastically. "Uh-huh! Aren't they neat?"

"So neat." Frannie noticed Annette's ever-reddening face out of the corner of her eye, but didn't have the heart—or the willpower—to meet her gaze. "And they're called…*candle* salads, you said?"

"Of course," Max piped up. "I definitely see candles."

A strangled sound escaped her throat, which she neatly turned into a cough. She was about to elbow him in the ribs when he bent forward to examine the *candles* more closely.

"These are really something, Nancy." Max flashed the child a genuine grin, all traces of irony vanished from his voice. "I'm impressed."

Frannie was impressed at how quickly he'd recovered his composure. Nancy beamed at his praise.

"Thanks, Mr. Mitchell!" She pointed at one of her creations. "I even included the wax, see?"

"I do." He nodded judiciously. "What an inspired use of…sour cream?"

"Cottage cheese."

"Right, I see the lumps now."

Frannie was amazed she didn't taste blood, given how hard she bit her lip. Poor Annette's face grew nearly purple.

Lucy chose that moment to join the conversation. "Hey, Max, you should sell these in the bakery!"

Max's fortitude wavered ever-so-briefly, but he soldiered on, and Frannie marveled anew at what a natural he was with children.

"Oh, I don't know, Lucy. I mean, it's not technically a baked good." The girls turned puppy eyes on him, and he talked faster. "Plus, I'd hate to steal Nancy's thunder. It's her talent, after all."

"Nice save," Frannie whispered under her breath.

Max gave a small, amused huff as he continued to focus on the delighted kids.

With the blessed tiny attention span of children, Lucy tugged on Nancy's arm. "Come on, we've got games. And wait till you see my mom's cake!" They skipped off, candles abandoned.

Annette shot Frannie and Max a smile that was equal parts relieved and mortified, before slinking off to join a few of the other parents. Frannie finally let out a breath, just as Max's chest collapsed as well.

"Jesus," he muttered as he pivoted partly away from the assembled group—and the candles. "It's not just me, right? They're fucking cocks?"

She tilted her head in examination. "Actually, I don't think any fucking's happened yet. See how proudly they're all standing at attention?" One of the bananas chose precisely that moment to start listing in slow motion, before hitting the tray with a sad plop. "Well, except for that one."

Max's resulting guffaw, which he quickly strangled into a snort, was immensely gratifying. "They should probably all see a doctor," he retorted, and she let out a chuckle of her own.

She shook her head. "I can't believe these came from a cookbook for *children*."

"I know." He inhaled a sharp breath. "You cannot let Lucy get hold of that book." He leveled a finger at her. "Promise you'll leave her dessert education to me."

Frannie rubbed at the strange, unexpected warmth blooming

in her chest, before holding up a hand in pledge. "You have my word."

He nodded. "Good."

She recovered enough to cross her arms with a smirk. "Tell me, is it the lewdness of these creations that offends you, or the lack of culinary skill?"

Max scoffed. "Please." He threw her a twinkly sidelong glance. "It's both. I mean, these are bad enough. Can you imagine the other travesties that might be lurking in that book?" He finished with a dramatic shudder.

"Is it weird that we're still standing here?" Frannie asked.

By unspoken agreement, they edged away from the table.

"Seriously, though," he said, "nice job keeping it together with the kids back there."

"Are you kidding? I barely managed. You're the one who held up a conversation and paid Nancy genuine compliments."

He'd been rather remarkable. And sweet.

He shrugged it off. "She was so excited. And had no clue what she actually made. The last thing I'd want is to make her feel bad. I've been that kid." He paused. "You know, minus the phallic imagery."

Frannie snickered, then resumed studying him. He caught her looking and raised a skeptical eyebrow.

"What?"

"Nothing. It's just..." She paused, weighing whether to explain. *Eh, what the hell.* "You get along so famously with children. You've got that unexpected generous streak. And on top of it all, you smell like cookies and pine trees, plus the beard... You're like some younger, alluring Santa Claus. It's a bit disconcerting."

"I'm sorry, did you just say *Santa Claus*?" Max asked incredulously.

She raised her chin in defiance. "Yes. I did."

"Huh."

Before she could parse out that single syllable—or why the

bloody hell she'd admitted all that—she caught sight of Nate across the lawn. She was leaning into Colin, head down and shoulders shaking.

Thankful for the distraction, Frannie embraced her genuine concern for her friend. "Is Nate crying?"

Max's head snapped in Nate's direction, but a spark of amusement quickly replaced the worry in his expression. "I don't think so. Judging by Colin's face, and the fact that he's looking everywhere *but* the table we just left? I'd say she spotted the Petrifying Prick Forest over there." He hitched a thumb over his shoulder at the candles.

Frannie snorted. "And here I thought my cake would be the most memorable thing about this party."

"See, I told you not to worry." He heaved a sigh. "I suppose I should show some mercy and relieve Nate from London Bridge duty so she can cackle in private, before the kids get impatient for the next round."

"I'm sure she'd appreciate that."

He'd barely taken a step before he huffed and muttered under his breath, "Younger, alluring Santa Claus."

Frannie's heartbeat sped up as he turned back and leaned dangerously close.

"You know," he continued, low so that only she could hear, "any time you'd like me to come down your chimney, you know where to find me. All you have to do is say the word." The corner of his mouth kicked up wickedly. "Or better yet…just put a candle in the window."

With that, he strode off, scattering her brain into more of a crumbled mess than her dirt cake.

Chapter Sixteen

Max leaned against the wall near the counter of his favorite Italian restaurant, flipping absently through a local newspaper while he waited for his sandwich. Gino's was down the street from the bakery, and the reason he refrained from serving cannoli at Mom's. While a little friendly competition never hurt anyone, he had tremendous respect for the family that owned Gino's—as well as a perfectly healthy addiction to their eggplant parm sandwiches. No need to rock the boat.

It was early enough in the evening that the sit-down section of the restaurant wasn't too busy yet, but a few families and couples enjoyed their dinners, illuminated by the wine-bottle candelabras on each table.

Candles. Max snickered at the memory of Lucy's party. Those desserts truly had been a travesty of inappropriateness. Warmth settled in his chest as he thought of what had followed, though.

It had felt so conspiratorial, so cozy, dissecting it all with Frannie. Laughing with her. *Flirting* with her.

He was still patting himself on the back for his chimney comeback line. It had clearly rattled her in the best possible way. He couldn't control the hope that she'd actually take him up on his offer someday.

He stifled a sigh and tried to focus on the newspaper. The bakery had continued its busy streak the last several days, owing to a few special orders amid the usual bustle. With things finally quieting down, he looked forward to taking his sandwich home and curling up with a book.

The weather was nice enough, he might even sit outside on his patio. And if he happened to catch a glimpse of his neighbor… Well, no one would catch him kicking up a fuss. The bell over the side door chimed, and in walked…

Speak of the Scottish devil.

Frannie stopped short when she saw him, eyes wide with surprise. "Oh. It's you."

Swell. We're back to this again?

"Good evening to you too."

Her cheeks flushed a delightful shade of pink. "Sorry. Hello. I didn't mean to be rude, I just…wasn't expecting to see you. Here." She hovered on the verge of saying more, but Gino emerged from the kitchen.

"Max, your order'll be up in a minute."

"Thanks, Gino."

The proprietor turned to greet Frannie. "And hey there, Mrs. Haynes. We're packing up yours right now. You having a party or something?"

"Not exactly," she replied, looking oddly embarrassed.

Gino's question sank in. Was she having some kind of gathering she hadn't invited him to? Not that she needed to, of course.

Aw, shit. What if she's got another date?

Oblivious to Max's sudden turmoil, Gino's face crinkled in a genial smile. "Well, sit tight, the both of you. Be right back."

As soon as he vanished, Frannie turned to Max, disappointment all over her face. "You ordered dinner."

"I'm not loitering here for no reason." He tried to assess her expression. Something about it felt off, but he couldn't put his finger on why. He wasn't sure he wanted to. "Is that a problem?"

"Oh, no. It's only…" She bit her lip, nearly sending him to his knees.

After so much time having the luxury of their animosity to hide behind, its absence of late left him defenseless against his attraction to her. And against his worry that he was about to get his ass—and his heart—handed to him on a platter.

Frannie let out a heavy sigh, pushing her next words out with the gust. "I bought you dinner too."

Max's eyebrows and jaw flew in opposite directions. "You…what?"

"You heard me. I bought you dinner." Despite her defensive words, she glanced up at him with a small smile. "You were so great the other day, talking me down from my cake disaster, and then sticking around to help with the party." The color on her cheeks deepened so slightly he might not have noticed if he wasn't so riveted to her. "Being so diplomatic over the candle cocks."

They both snickered, unable to help it.

Frannie's smile grew less tentative. "Not to mention the Chocolate Miracle that I never properly thanked you for. So I ordered you a meal." She rolled her eyes. "It was supposed to be a surprise, but…" She flapped her hand in his direction.

Max somehow managed to dampen the conflagration that had roared to life in his chest as soon as she'd started explaining. "But here I am?"

"Here you are. And with your dinner already sorted." Her face fell in defeat.

Which was thoroughly unacceptable.

He swatted the air dismissively. "All I got was a sandwich. I can throw it in the icebox and have it for lunch tomorrow."

"Yeah?" The hope in her eyes added a log to the fire inside him.

"Yeah."

"Okay, then." Her grin returned, fueling the blaze ever hotter.

But Gino, juggling three brown paper bags, once again interrupted them. He handed the smallest parcel to Max, then plunked two enormous sacks down on the counter. Max's eyes widened.

He leaned down to stage-whisper to Frannie. "You have a lot of confidence in my stomach."

At that, her face and neck flamed, in quite possibly the most charming sight he'd ever beheld. One of these days, she truly was going to be the death of him.

"I didn't know what you liked," she muttered. "So I ordered you a bunch to choose from."

"Thank you."

She looked up at the seriousness he'd injected into his tone, and answered his smile with one of her own.

"You need help getting these home, Mrs. Haynes?"

Gino really needed to work on his timing. Couldn't he see they were having a moment here?

"I got it," Max answered, still looking at Frannie. "Thanks, Gino."

Frannie held his gaze as she echoed him. "Yeah, thanks, Gino."

They each grabbed a bag, and Max heard the chuckle in the restaurant owner's voice as they headed for the door. "You folks have a good night."

The two of them spent most of the short walk back to their homes in companionable silence. Max wasn't sure he'd ever get used to this strange, newfound—and utterly wonderful— dynamic of theirs. As they neared the bakery, Frannie broke the silence with a small laugh.

"These bags are heavy, aren't they? I suppose I went a little overboard with the food. Sorry."

"Please, there's no such thing as too much food from Gino's." He nudged her shoulder with his own. "And it was a nice gesture."

"I'm glad you think so."

"I do. Not entirely necessary, but nice just the same."

She made a confused sound, deep in her throat. "I…I wanted to thank you…"

"I know. You're every bit the accountant." He leaned in a bit as they walked. "It's always got to be balanced, tit-for-tat, with you, doesn't it?"

"Not always," she huffed. She snuck a glance up at him through her lashes. "Sometimes I'm all right with tat-for-tit."

A laugh burst from his chest, her sly sense of humor utterly enthralling. "Fair enough. But just for the record, everything I did the other day, I did because I wanted to. Not because I expected anything in return."

"Duly noted."

They rounded the corner of his building to cut through the small parking lot, and Max debated the merits of asking her to stay and eat with him. She'd more than pleasantly surprised him with this dinner, but she might still have other plans, simply aiming to drop the food and run.

"So…are you taking some of this home to Lucy and Betty?" Easier to start with neutral ground.

"Oh, um…no, actually." She shifted her bag from hand to hand. "Mum's got her weekly bridge game tonight. And Lucy's having a sleepover at Colin and Nate's. She was awfully excited about it."

Max valiantly stuffed a cautious lid on the optimism that fizzed to life in his stomach. "Bet she's itching to play dress-up in Nate's closet, huh?"

Frannie laughed. "I almost feel sorry for Nate." She paused. "Anyway, I wasn't sure what I'd do with myself since I'm on my own tonight."

Fuck that lid.

"No, you're not."

Her eyes snapped to his. They'd reached his patio, and he took her bag and put it on the little table along with his, before turning to face her decisively, hands on hips.

"It's a gorgeous night, we're both on our own, and you graciously bought me this obscene amount of food. I insist you stay and enjoy it with me."

He held his breath, worried he'd said too much, but he was so damn tired of holding back when it came to her.

An extraordinary warmth began in her eyes and spread over her entire face.

"You drive a hard bargain, Mr. Mitchell."

He raised one eyebrow in question, still not daring to breathe.

"I'd love to join you."

BY THE TIME they gathered plates and silverware, divvied up the food—and set aside the copious amount of leftovers—the patio was bathed in the golden light of the oncoming sunset. Which set off lovely, mesmerizing sparks in the new shade of Frannie's hair.

"I know I said it before, but I do like the red," Max ventured. "It suits you."

She paused with a forkful of ravioli halfway to her mouth, her other hand absently coming up to brush a few strands over her shoulder. "Thanks."

He nodded, gratified by the upward curve of her lips as she chewed.

After swallowing, she cleared her throat roughly and glanced over at his plate. "So, eggplant parm is the winner, huh? Any particular reason?"

"It's always been my favorite. My mom used to make it all the time when I was a kid."

"And how does Gino's stack up against hers?"

"Mom's is absolutely the best, no question." He gestured at his plate. "But this comes pretty close. It's an excellent substitute when she's not in town."

"Good man." She speared another bite, but propped her chin on her fist instead of eating it. "Is she an expert baker too?"

"She's not, actually. A great cook, yes. But she never really took to baking, not like my granny. And me. Guess it skipped a generation."

Frannie chuckled, but then her brows drew together in confusion. "But wait… If your granny was the baker, then why name the business after your mom?"

He grinned slyly. "Oh, it's not named after my mom. I named it for myself." Her furrow deepened, and he leaned in conspiratorially, loving that she followed suit like a magnet. "My middle initial is O."

Her mouth resembled the letter for a brief moment before understanding dawned, and her face broke into a grin. "Ah. M-O-M."

"That spells mom."

Her resulting laughter was infectious. "Very nice."

Max nodded. "I'll admit, I did consider Max's Bakery for a while, but it never had the right ring to it. My sister suggested it should be something more homey, to draw in customers, and then it hit me."

"And the rest is history."

"Yep."

"I remember you mentioned…once…that your sister helped you find this place. But she didn't go into business with you?"

Max ignored the pink in her cheeks at the mention of that fateful night they'd met, instead focusing on her question. "Nah. Linda and I always wanted her to, but she's more like our mom, not much interest in baking."

His good mood deflated slightly at the thought of his sister's current job predicament.

Of course, Frannie noticed. "What is it?"

"No big deal, really." At her skeptical raising of an eyebrow, he relented with a chuckle. "I offered Vi a place here recently. She hates her job. More, I think, than she'll even admit. Twin-tuition tells me she's gotta leave there, so she can figure out what she *does* want to do, but…she's stubborn." He finished with a shrug.

Frannie opened and closed her mouth a few times, before shaking her head and finally setting down her forgotten fork. "First of all, your twin is stubborn? That comes as a complete shock." She gave him an exaggerated once-over that made him bark with laughter.

Her eyes twinkled as she continued. "Second... *Twin-tuition*? That is..."

"Adorable?" He batted his eyelashes at her, and it was her turn to laugh.

"As much as I hate to admit it...yes."

Max heaved a dramatic sigh. "As much *I* hate to admit it, I can't take credit for that one. It's all Vi."

"My compliments to her, then." Frannie sobered, and the gentleness in her expression punched him in the gut. "It really bothers you that she doesn't want to work here, doesn't it?"

"Yeah," he admitted. "But not because I particularly need her here. I mean, it would be fun to have her around, and I am looking to take on more help, hopefully sooner rather than later..." He rubbed at his beard. "I just hate seeing her so lost, you know? I want to offer her a safe space to find her spark again."

"That's quite admirable," she replied quietly. "But she refuses?"

He nodded. "As much as she appreciates the idea, she wants to figure it all out herself." No matter how many times he'd told her she didn't have to. "Plus, she maintains that I don't need to be hiring and training someone before I'm ready, especially someone who's temporary, only to start over again when she leaves."

Frannie pressed her lips together, impressively holding in her thoughts.

Max chuckled. "It's okay, you can say it. She's not wrong, and I know it."

She let out a comical exhale. "Oh, thank god. My wee inner accountant was screaming to get out." She paused. "I assume when you said you're not ready, you meant financially, right?"

"Right."

"So as much as you want to see your sister happy—and that is truly lovely..."

"At the end of the day," he finished for her, "it is a business I'm running."

"I realize I've only met her once, and under auspicious circumstances, but for what it's worth, I'm sure your concern and support mean an awful lot to her."

Her words—and the warmth behind them—reached his soul like a balm.

"Thank you, Frannie."

She nodded in acknowledgment, then bit her lip. Her eyes took on an analytical gleam, amid her lingering warmth. "Can I ask you something?"

Max smirked as he voiced his suspicion. "The wee accountant screaming again?"

She grimaced lightheartedly. "Afraid so."

"Go ahead, ask away."

Max tried to focus on her words as she eagerly propped her elbows on the table, resting her chin in her hands. "From an outsider's eye, the bakery seems to be doing well. When it comes to additional help, how…*not there* are you?"

"Not too far, actually. You're right, we're doing solid business." He paused to gather his words, so he could explain correctly. "But it's just me and Linda. We manage, but…it's still a lot for two people. I'd love to add one, maybe two more to our team. Even that would make a big difference, let us have a little more of a life outside work." *Start thinking seriously about dating, getting married, maybe raising a daughter…* But he didn't dare admit that, so he settled for, "I've wanted to get a dog for ages."

It wasn't a lie. He did want a furry friend too.

"I can see you with a pup." Before he could respond, she circled back to the subject at hand. "All that makes perfect sense. It's the natural growth of a business. You just need to be turning enough of a profit to make the addition comfortable."

"Exactly." He valiantly focused on the business, not the life he wanted outside it. *With you.* "And I am really close." *Business, business, business.* "Everything Lois and Nick have been throwing

my way with the studio is fantastic. But at the same time, my"—
he cleared his throat—"side jobs here have started to taper off.
Despite appearances." He raised his eyebrow.

Her cheeks flushed prettily. "Right. The lessons." She took a
breath, preparing to say more.

Max held up his hand. "You do not need to apologize again."

"Who said I was going to apologize?"

He simply smirked in response, and she huffed.

"What's the matter? Are the students becoming the master?"
she countered.

"What can I say?" He raised his hands in mock surrender. "I
guess I'm just that good." He narrowed his eyes with a wicked
gleam.

She bit her lip again, her expression a beautiful battle between
flustered and heated.

"Anyhow," she continued pointedly, "it sounds like what you
need is a sustained bit of extra income. Like what you have, at
least in part, with the studio." Her lips curved up. "Every time
your pastries show up on the lot, there's practically a stampede,
so that well's not running dry anytime soon. Although…" She sat
back in her chair and crossed her arms over her chest.

"What?"

"Given the quality of your product, and how much of a hit it
is, you could—and should—be charging the studio more for it."

Max mirrored her posture. "I charge exactly what I'd charge
here." A lie, but she didn't need to know that.

Frannie's head tilted to one side as she leveled him with her
piercing sapphire stare. "Have you forgotten who actually pays
the bills at Phoenix Pictures?"

Shit.

She laughed outright at the panic that he couldn't keep from
his features.

"Nick was an early investor here, so I…offer the…friends and
family rate," he bluffed.

"Don't."

The finality in her tone startled him.

"I mean it," she continued. "The studio can afford it. Lois and Nick would absolutely not begrudge you—hell, they'd probably insist on it—and you are running a business. Charge what you are worth."

Her eyes held his, the passion of her speech hovering in the air between them, filling him with a sense of invincibility.

"Okay. I will."

She eyed him skeptically at first, then turned analytical. "You've got a talent for boosting everyone else, but you don't always remember to do the same for yourself, do you?"

He wanted to protest, but her astute observation halted him. It chagrined him slightly to realize she was right. But at the same time, he was quietly thrilled that she'd noticed.

"You might not be wrong," he admitted. Another realization dawned on him. "But...how does the saying go? Takes one to know one?" He smirked.

Frannie rolled her eyes. "I am not ashamed to admit that it's probably true." She pointed a manicured, red fingernail in his face. "But we are talking about *you* right now."

He laughed. "Fair enough. Got any other wisdom to offer, Oh Mighty Accounting Whiz?"

"Maybe," she replied saucily. "You know, with your lessons tapering off, it couldn't hurt to come up with a replacement." She reached for a breadstick and munched thoughtfully on its end.

The sight of Frannie Haynes chewing while lost in contemplation, on his behalf, hit him with surprising aphrodisiacal potency. He shifted in his seat, hoping she wouldn't notice.

She sucked in a breath and pointed the half-eaten breadstick in his face. "Children!"

Okay, I'll make some with you. He blinked a few times. *The hell?*

Thankfully, his scrambled thoughts remained internal, and he instead uttered an eloquent, "Huh?"

"Your baking lessons."

Right. Business. Business, *dammit.*

"You should offer them for kids," Frannie continued. "Lucy hasn't stopped talking about that day she made snickerdoodles with you. She had so much fun. I'll bet there are plenty of other kids in this neighborhood who'd love to learn. God knows, Nancy needs to move away from those damn candle catastrophes. You'd be doing everyone a tremendous service."

He caught her grin and chuckled, as her idea began to sink in.

"Baking lessons…for kids. That's…" He met her expectant eyes. "That's pretty brilliant, actually."

Her entire face lit up, and he wanted nothing more than to ingest her sunshine with a kiss.

A sudden, unwelcome thought interrupted his daydream. "As tempting as it is, I'm trying to reduce my work schedule, not add even more to it."

Frannie simply shrugged. "So, offer group classes instead of individual lessons. Once or twice a month, maybe."

"Hmm. That's not bad. You really think enough kids would want to?"

"Max. I wasn't exaggerating—Lucy loved her lesson. And you get lots of kids coming through your doors. I'm sure they'd find it fun." The edges of her smile softened. "There are probably a fair number of them who'd need it as much as you did."

"Me?"

She nodded. "Necessity bred your passion, remember. Not everyone can play outside all the time. I was talking to Mrs. Henderson the other day about how much she wished Danny could go back to spending more time around other children."

"Oh, yeah. They live a couple blocks over, right? He had polio a couple years ago."

"Mm-hmm. He still can't do running, sports, any of it. A quieter, indoor activity like baking would be really good for kids like him."

"That's true." They smiled at each other for a long, wonderful moment. "It's a great idea, Frannie. Thanks."

"You're quite welcome."

The sun had all but vanished, and Max was struggling to make out Frannie's lovely features. He hated to get up, but did so anyway to reach inside and flick on the lights strung over the patio, casting an even more magical air over the evening.

He didn't want her to go.

"Would you like some dessert?"

"Got any dessert in there?"

They'd spoken simultaneously, and burst into laughter.

"Dessert it is, I guess," she said.

"Any requests?"

"Surprise me."

He'd like nothing more.

Chapter Seventeen

The entire night had held one pleasant surprise after another. Frannie waited for Max to return with their sweets, thankful for the breeze cooling her overheated skin. She was fast running out of reasons to keep resisting him.

And the biggest surprise of all was how little that bothered her.

She'd be lying if she said she hadn't hoped he'd invite her to join him. But from the moment he lifted the food bags from the counter at Gino's, everything about the night had felt like a date. A damn good one, at that.

Max's concern for his sister touched her heart. It reminded her of her relationship with Colin. A twinge of increasingly familiar guilt gathered in the pit of her stomach as she considered how long she'd steadfastly ignored Max's gentle, generous side.

He reemerged from the door with a plate, his dimples denting his beard. Frannie switched the cross of her legs in an attempt to curb the wave of longing that swept through her.

"I thought small bites might be good after that dinner." He set the plate on the table. "I had some tea cakes left."

Apprehension washed over her, given her complicated history

with this particular dessert. The last thing she wanted was to hurt his feelings.

These did look decent, though, so she picked one from the pile, determined to make the best of it. Luckily, she didn't have to feign her smile as the smooth, sweet texture dissolved in her mouth.

"Very tasty."

"But…?"

Her eyes snapped up to his. She couldn't possibly have been that obvious. The little cake truly tasted quite good, considering.

"But what?"

"You're clearly not convinced." His smile was easy, teasing. "It's okay if you don't like it, you know. Not everything I make is for everyone. And since when do you hold back when it comes to me?"

Since I started letting myself want to get into your trousers more and more?

She swallowed. "I'm not holding back."

He pulled a skeptical face, prompting her laughter.

"Okay, fine, maybe I am. I do like this, but… Let's just say, my relationship to tea cakes is a bit like yours with Gino's eggplant."

Understanding dawned across Max's handsome features. "Say no more. As much pride as I take in my skill, I will always concede to one's mom."

"That's a very healthy attitude." Frannie glanced down at the tea cake, nostalgia slamming headlong into her. "And it's my gran, actually. On my father's side. Him too, I guess."

"A family recipe, then." He kept his voice soft, sensing her mood.

"A secret one, at that. I don't know what she put in them, but there was something different, something…extra about them. I never could figure it out." She huffed. "And she'd never tell us. Made them constantly for me and Colin, and every single time, she'd declare them a special family recipe that her mother taught her and she'd taught our father. That he'd teach us when we reached the right age." Her mouth twisted into a grimace. "Part of me always suspected she only tacked on that rule to get Pop more involved with us."

"I know you and Colin have different moms, and he's English, so you didn't really grow up together. Was your dad…not around so much with either of you?"

"He was not." She shook her head. "You would've thought he'd remember the lessons learned from his first marriage, but no. He conveniently forgot that he wasn't cut out to be a family man, until after I was born and it all came flooding back."

Max reached out to cover her hand, his touch gentle. "I'm sorry."

"Thing is, he wasn't a bad guy. And I never doubted that he loved me, in his own way, even though he did it from afar. He was just…restless as hell. I don't think he knew what to do with children, either." Max's thumb caressed her hand, soothing the jagged edges of her heart. "He started reaching out more, the older Colin and I got. Those tea cakes were the one thing he did make and send to us over the years."

"Did he ever teach you the recipe?" he asked quietly.

She blinked against the sudden prickling behind her eyes. "No. He promised he would, swore that as soon as I got back from university here in the States, he'd have the both of us over." She swallowed around the lump in her throat. "But the Nazis who blitzed London had other plans."

"Oh, Frannie. The war took so damn much from you."

His recognition surrounded her like a warm blanket. Max squeezed her hand, and she flipped her palm over to squeeze back.

"It did." She inhaled sharply, determined not to cry over her father, not now. She'd done enough of that. "Anyway, we'd lost Gran a few years before that, so…" She shrugged. "The recipe got lost to history."

"It was never written down?"

"Not that I know of. Colin and I put on our detective hats more than a few times over the years, especially when we were kids, but if it was at Gran's house, I suspect even Nancy Drew couldn't have uncovered it." She shared in Max's chuckle at that. "Colin told me he looked through Pop's things too, after he... But he didn't come across it there, either."

Frannie tried for a smile, wanting to return them to their earlier pleasantries. Not that this was uncomfortable. Despite the melancholy nature of her story, sharing it with Max, along with his willingness to listen, brought her quite a bit of comfort.

As if sensing her change in mood, Max brightened his tone. "So now you're destined to go through life, tasting inferior tea cakes."

Her laugh was genuine, surprising her—and yet, not—with how easily it emerged from her chest.

"I have to admit, yours are not *that* inferior."

His eyes sparkled in the dim light of the patio. "Really?"

"Really. Closer than a lot of others I've tried. Not that I have any idea what made Gran's taste so different."

"Hmm." He tilted his head. His fingers drummed against the back of her hand as he considered her, as if he'd forgotten he still held it.

She pushed past the tingles his touch elicited to find her voice. "What is it?"

He paused briefly before speaking. "I...might be able to help."

"How so?"

"I'm pretty good at recreating recipes. I've done it on several occasions, figuring out the ingredients, piecing together the clues of what I've tasted."

She scrunched her nose, skepticism warring with a flare of long-buried hope. "You haven't tasted these, though."

"No, but you have." He beamed at her. "If you can describe them in enough detail and are willing to be my taste-testing guinea pig, we might just crack the case."

Her mouth curved up in answer. "You really think you can do that?"

He shrugged confidently. "Sure. You said mine are similar, which means they probably have the same base. That's the hardest part solved right there."

"Yeah?"

He nodded. "Baking's all about balancing ingredients, finding the right ratio that'll deliver the kind of cake, or cookie, or whatever, that you're aiming for. That'll do the right thing when you put it in the oven, or set it in the icebox."

He'd let go of her hand to gesture animatedly as he spoke, and while she felt the loss of the contact, watching his enthusiasm build made up for it.

"It's a bit like a mathematical equation, then?"

His eyes blazed brighter. "That's exactly it. Once you've got the foundation down, you can start experimenting with all the fun extras. Chocolate, fruit, nuts…the possibilities are endless."

His passion was infectious. "And with the foundation for the tea cakes already there…"

"All that's left is the fun part." His grin dimmed slightly. "If you want to, that is. I know it might be difficult, and I'd hate to presume…"

"No, you're not. I'd…appreciate it. Very much, as a matter of fact."

His dimples flashed, and he stood up, extending his hand to her. "Come on."

She glanced between his hand and his face. "What, now?"

"Sure, why not? The night's still young. We'll make it your first baking lesson."

The idea of watching Max at work, for her, felt dizzying. She staggered at the prospect. He must have mistaken her pause for hesitation, for he leaned closer, face full of mischief.

"You're not…afraid, are you?"

Truthfully, she was a bit terrified, but not for the reasons he suspected. For once, though, it felt tempting. Thrilling.

"Not on your life," she retorted, grabbing his hand. "Let's go."

"OLIVER? ORSON?"

"Nope and nope. I'm telling you, you're not going to get it."

Frannie scoffed, not deterred in the slightest. She and Max had settled into an easy rhythm of ingredient-mixing for their third round of tea cake trials. To her delight, baking came a lot more easily to her under his guidance. While Max tried to unravel the mystery of the recipe, she embarked on her own attempt to figure out what his middle initial stood for. She'd been on the case since somewhere in the middle of the second batch, still to no avail. Max provided no help whatsoever.

She continued to ponder as she sifted flour into the bowl, her foot tapping along to the music coming from the radio—Max having deemed it safe since, while she might be a rookie, he was long past any danger.

"Orwell? Or*ville*?" She couldn't help crinkling her nose at that one.

Max snorted, but made no other response.

"I will figure this out, you know." Despite her outward confidence, doubt crept in. She was running out of "O" names, not that there were many to begin with. "What about…Orving?"

Max's startled bark of laughter echoed through the kitchen. "*Orving*? Now you're just making shit up."

"No, I'm… Okay, fine, yes. I am. But it wouldn't kill you to offer me a breadcrumb here." She turned her face up to him, batting her eyelashes.

He watched her for a moment, amused, before his expression morphed into consideration. She'd only aimed for comedy when she deployed the eyelashes, so she marveled at the fact that it might have actually worked.

"I don't know," he said. "This is pretty powerful information."

"Ooh, it's that embarrassing, is it?"

He sent her a stern look that zinged all through her body.

"It is not embarrassing. I'd simply hate for you to use it against me, for any reason." He smirked.

"If you really don't want me to know…" She paused, but he cut her off, anticipating her next thought.

"And don't even think about threatening me with Nick again. I can get to him first, you know."

"That's what you think."

They both laughed at that, settling back into their task. Max handed her the sugar, while continuing his whisking of the wet ingredients, and she thought the subject closed for certain.

"Orsino," he said quietly.

Frannie paused in her measuring. "I'm sorry…what?"

"Orsino." He didn't look up from his bowl. "My middle name is Orsino."

"I…huh. As much as I hate to admit it, you were right. I truly would *not* have guessed that one."

"Told you." He watched her, clearly waiting for some kind of judgment.

She wouldn't give him that satisfaction. Not that she was judging. It was unusual, sure, but with something musical about it, something she liked. She'd heard the name before, though it took her a minute to place it.

"Hmm… Orsino's from Shakespeare, isn't he? The count from…*As You Like It*, was it?"

"*Twelfth Night*. And he was a duke." Max quirked a haughty eyebrow.

Frannie shrugged. "Close enough." She delighted in his resulting laugh. As she searched her memory of the Shakespeare she'd seen and read over the years, a thought occurred to her. "That's the one with…"

"The twins? Yep." He smiled down at his work. "It was my mom's favorite, even before Vi and I came along. She's always joked that she willed us into being."

"That's fantastic. Ahh…and Vi is short for Viola, isn't it?"

"Indeed it is."

They worked side-by-side for a few seconds, before another penny dropped.

"Wait a minute. By that logic, shouldn't...?"

"My middle name be Sebastian?" He hung his head with a sigh. "Yes, yes it should." He chuckled. "Believe me, it was not a quiet scene in the Mitchell household the day Vi and I figured that one out."

"Given the sheer number of your family's stories, you're practically Scottish."

He rested a hand against his apron-covered heart. "Why thank you, madam." He lowered his voice. "That was a compliment, right?"

She smiled warmly at him. "It was."

"Good. It's pretty nice, actually, to have someone new to share these stories with," he added quietly. "Someone who wasn't there to witness them firsthand."

"And who knows you now, rather than who you were then?"

"Yeah."

Frannie knew what he meant. It *was* nice, sharing with Max. And she felt rather touched that he'd chosen her as his audience.

"Anyway." He cleared his throat and continued, "My mom had a college sweetheart named Sebastian. And while she threw him over the minute she laid eyes on my father, Dad wasn't too keen on the idea of naming one of his children after the poor guy."

"So Orsino it was. Makes sense."

"Yeah, we couldn't really fault his logic after that. Not that we didn't have fun trying." He nodded at her bowl. "Is that ready for me?"

"All set." She poured her mixture into his as he folded it in. "Orsino's the 'music be the food of love' chap, right?"

"He is."

Frannie watched him stir as she recalled the line, and then sniffed.

"What?"

"I was just thinking." She gestured to everything in front of them and cleared her throat dramatically. "If cheesecake be the food of love, bake on."

Max laughed heartily. "Okay, that's a good one."

She dipped into a small curtsy that cracked him up even more. "Thank you, sir." She paused. "Though, I suppose in the original, he is trying to make himself sick of love so he'll get over the gal…"

"He did have a moody, dramatic streak. But I say we take it out of context."

"Me too. My version could be the motto for everyone we know."

"Nick would absolutely have it printed on a sign."

Frannie's chuckle tapered off as the meaning behind her new slogan for him sank in. She thought of all the cakes and cookies and pastries he showed up with at exactly the right moments. "It's really true, isn't it? All our earlier talk about business aside, food is love for you."

Max set down his spoon, considering. His lips curved into a soft smile. "It is. I've always liked looking out for the people I care about with what I bake."

The realization hit her, hard—this included her.

Her insides fizzed at the thought of his Chocolate Miracle cake. The snickerdoodles he always brought Lucy. His current efforts to restore a missing piece of her family.

She wanted to respond, but the words caught in her throat. Hell, she wasn't even sure what words *were*. Max's expression turned shy, and he returned his attention to the tea cake batter, reaching for a baking tin.

It was a relief, given her own state of overwhelm. Though she did regret the loss of their eye contact. Up close, in this lighting, she realized his weren't nearly as dark as she'd always thought. There was a brightness to all that deep brown. The color reminded her of…

"Maple syrup." *Bloody hell.* Those words had gotten past the blockage.

"Hmm?" Max quizzically looked up from his batter-spooning.

"Maple...syrup... Do you ever...*bake*...with maple syrup?" She wanted to sink into the floor.

Luckily, he was firmly re-entrenched in baker mindset, and picked up her subject change, however dubious. She focused on the spray of faint freckles across the bridge of his nose so she wouldn't fall into the trap of his eyes again.

"I don't use it a lot, but I have on occasion." He chewed on his lip while he continued filling the tin. "But it is certainly possible that's our elusive flavor. I'm not sure I have any on hand right now, but I'll add it to the list for the next round."

"Oh. Good. Thanks. So...you think we'll need a next round?" Hope infused her tone, despite her efforts to curb it.

The quick flash of his grin told her he'd noticed.

"We might." His maple-brown eyes twinkled at her. "Let's see when these are done."

He walked the pan over to the oven, and she took in his confident swagger. And that very lovely arse. She snapped her gaze away in the nick of time, as he turned back to her after setting the timer.

He nodded at the tray near her elbow. "The icing on those should be set enough for a taste test."

"Right." She willed her focus back to the matter at hand. With all his effort on her behalf, the least she could do was apply herself. And it would be marvelous to finally have her family's recipe back, despite how much she'd love another baking session with her expert tutor.

Frannie picked up one of the cakes, examining it instead of Max. "The color of this icing is certainly closer."

"That's good." He watched her expectantly as she took a bite.

The sugary coating and smooth cake dissolved against her tongue, and she tried to be analytical as she ruminated over the flavors. She'd already gathered some of the best ways to describe what she tasted, so that Max would understand, and she wanted to be helpful.

The more she sat with it, the more she liked this sample. She made a small humming noise after taking another bite.

"This one's...very good." *Not super eloquent.* She tried again. "Certainly the closest. It definitely captures a lot of the warm flavor I remember."

Max shook his head. "Nope. We're not there yet."

"How do you know? You haven't even tasted it."

"I can tell by your reaction." He crossed his arms. "This isn't it."

"But I said it's close. It might just be the one."

"Trust me, if you're still using words like 'close' and 'might,' this is not the one. When we hit the right combination, you'll have a tell." He pointed at her face. "And I haven't seen it yet."

"Oh, come on."

"I'm serious." He leaned his hip against the baking table. "One of the things I love about baking is how much of it is tied up with memories. Tastes from childhood, or weddings, or times people needed some plain old comfort." He waved his hand toward the door to his storefront. "I've seen it lots of times. One bite, and you know. They've been transported to another time, another place."

"It's really that obvious?"

"Absolutely. Slightly different for each person, but always visceral. They relax their shoulders, close their eyes..." His voice lowered, and he leaned in slightly. "Sometimes it's a little...noise in the back of their throat." She swallowed hard, at the same time he did. "Other times, a lip gets licked. Or even bitten."

Her teeth sank into her lip, of their own accord, and his eyes tracked the motion before silkily sliding up to meet hers. She found it hard to breathe.

He held her gaze, before his dimples flashed. "Anyway, I haven't made you do that yet, so I've got to keep trying."

She wanted to argue that he'd provoked exactly that reaction from her—especially since they were no longer discussing tea cakes—but she wanted even more for him to keep trying, so she held her tongue.

The sudden sound of applause startled laughs out of them. She'd forgotten they'd tuned into a live performance of Harry James's orchestra. Her breath caught yet again as they began the next song—"I'm Beginning to See the Light."

Am I ever.

Max had called it *their* song at the premiere party.

The two of them stared at each other, the kitchen suddenly charged. Trepidation flitted across his expression, but Frannie watched him chase it away and replace it with confidence. He held out his hand in invitation.

"What do you say? Third time's the charm?"

A wave of boldness joined with her newfound faith in him. She slid her hand into his, and the warm joy suffusing his eyes nearly turned her legs into jelly.

His palm slid around her waist, searing through her apron and her dress. She trailed her own over his strong arm, settled on his shoulder, and they began to sway to the music. She inhaled, gathering a whiff of his delectable sugary-pine scent, and the realization hit her—she could truly breathe for the first time in ages.

It felt so unbelievably good—so unbelievably *right*—to be dancing with Max again.

They remained quiet, letting the music surround them, inching closer together as their bodies sank slowly into each other. Just as he had on that night long ago, Max brought her hand to rest against his chest. She was torn between her desire to lean her head against his shoulder, and her need to see his face, and the banked heat igniting his maple eyes.

Those eyes won out, holding her in their thrall.

Despite everything that happened immediately following their first dance, and in all the time since, her body remembered the wonderful, enveloping feel of his—she'd been transported as surely as if she'd just tasted one of his baked goods. She smiled at the thought, but her mouth collapsed again right away.

She had been awfully hard on him, for such a long time.

Because their eyes were still locked—and because he was so damn perceptive—she saw the second he registered the change in her.

She broke their silence first. "I'm remembering the last time we danced. I am sorry, Max. For…everything."

His arm tightened around her waist. "Me too."

She did rest her head on his shoulder then, needing a moment to collect herself. And to take comfort in him. One question still lingered, one that had been nagging at her. One she wasn't sure she should ask now.

But if not now, she might never get up the nerve. She decided to take the risk.

"So it really wasn't my kissing skills that put you off that night?" she whispered into his chest.

The spasm of his laugh pushed against her cheek. "Of course not." Frannie let herself exhale. "You didn't actually think…?"

When she didn't respond, Max stilled.

"Frannie."

She raised her head, relief pulsing through her. In an effort to spare both their feelings, she tried to keep things light. "Don't be silly. I just wanted to check, that's all."

"Frannie," he repeated.

"I know, I know. It was the vertigo. Of course it was." She trained her eyes on their joined hands, suddenly embarrassed by her admission. "But you can't blame a girl for wondering. Some-times. Occasionally. Rarely."

"Look at me."

His voice was gentle but commanding, and she obliged.

He kept his words slow, deliberate, in contrast to the full blaze in his eyes. "While there was a lot that contributed to my vertigo that night, your kissing skills were, by far, the best of it all. Hell, some of the best I've ever encountered." She fought to keep looking at him as her cheeks heated. An intriguing grin spread across his lips. "Frannie, your kiss…made me swoon."

She laughed at that.

"I'm serious," he insisted. "I mean, swooning is just a more romantic way to describe vertigo. The dizzying sensation, the head rush, the stomach dip…" He grimaced. "You have no idea how much I wish I'd simply fainted instead of…"

She squeezed his hand in reassurance, unsure of her voice.

It worked, because he continued speaking, his eyes far away. She was right alongside him.

"It felt like so much…everything that night. When I took you in my arms to dance, and you asked me to kiss you." He lifted their hands, still joined, to trace her lip with one searing finger. "God, your mouth was so sweet, so hot…so magical. You went straight to my head." His gaze left her lips, snapping up to her eyes, arrowing back to the present. He lifted one shoulder in a tiny shrug. "And I swooned."

Excitement sizzled in her veins. She wanted to yank his head down to hers, to try for another kiss, another swoon. But a small, cautious voice broke through the delightful chaos inside her.

"What about that night in the soundstage?" She kept her voice low. "You didn't swoon then."

She shuddered, remembering all he'd accomplished instead of swooning.

His dimples flashed. "My life—apart from you—is a lot calmer lately. I had much better control that night."

You sure as hell did.

"And you knew what to expect with me."

His deep chuckle was laced with seduction. "I doubt I'll ever be fully prepared for you."

"The feeling's mutual," she whispered. She matched his sly smile with one of her own. "Tell me something, Max."

He hummed his assent.

"What about now?" A flash of understanding, followed by an

explosion of desire, lit his eyes. God, she was ready for it. "How are you feeling? Any danger?"

"Plenty of danger," he rumbled. "But I feel fantastic."

"Good."

She was so damn done hesitating. So she slid her hand around to the back of his neck, pushed up on her toes, and sealed her lips to his.

Chapter Eighteen

He tasted like heaven.

Neither of them wasted a second, delving into each other's mouths. Frannie didn't know if it was the lingering sugar from the tea cakes, or if the taste was all Max, but she'd never experienced anything sweeter.

All the pent-up longing she'd suppressed erupted inside her, and she couldn't get close enough to him. From the way his arm snaked further around her waist, grasping her tight, all while his tongue and lips plundered, she could tell the same blinding desire seized him. His other hand cupped her cheek, angling her to go even deeper.

The whiskers of his beard rasped against her skin, and it should have been abrasive, but the delicious, burning tingle fueled her desire. In contrast, the hair on his head felt thick and soft where she clutched it between her fingers.

He returned the gesture, hand curving around and through her hair, his fingertips tracing her scalp in a massage that was equal parts gentle and scorching. She moaned into his mouth.

He nipped her bottom lip, only breaking away to trail more kisses across her jaw and down her throat. His beard felt even better against the skin there, and she gasped at the contact. He pulled her ever tighter, his hips pressing firmly against her stomach—along with the hard length of him, growing firmer by the second.

She couldn't resist. "Do you always carry an extra rolling pin in your trousers, Max?"

The rumble of laughter in his chest teased her nipples, even through the layers of fabric between them. His teeth closed over the skin of her neck in a gentle tug.

"With you?" He pulled back to look at her, his eyes a molten river of maple. "Always."

Her heart thundered frantically in her chest, and their lips crashed back together.

How in the hell had she held back from this man for so long? And *why?*

"God, Frannie," he whispered against her lips. "You taste like heaven."

A giggle escaped her at his echo of her earlier thought...and descended into a needy whimper as his hand came around to skim the side of her breast. His thumb traced a line at the edge of her apron, entirely too far from where she really wanted him. Damn apron.

Reading her mind once more, he reached behind her to untie the blasted garment. He had it over her head in one fluid motion, but instead of tossing it aside and tugging her back to him, like she wanted, he paused to glance at the worktable next to them. He took another step away from her, spreading her apron on an empty space. He whipped his own off and added it to the pile.

Before she could express her frustration at his care for their flour-sprinkled smocks, when they had far more important things to do, Max pivoted back to her with a positively wicked grin. In a matter of seconds, his hands closed around her waist, her feet left the floor, and her arse came to rest on top of the fabric.

A startled "oh" escaped her. And then he stepped between her thighs and kissed the remaining breath right out of her. She circled her arms around his shoulders and snaked her legs around his waist, sealing them together.

Not that there was any danger of his bolting. While his tongue slid against hers, his hands roved over her back, and finally, *finally* slipped back around to his original target. He cupped her tits, thumbs tweaking both nipples simultaneously. She let out a long groan, as the sensation arrowed straight between her legs.

Max's hips twitched against her, but he kept his focus on her top half. He peppered more kisses down her neck. One of his hands continued to play with her through the layers of her clothing, while the other made quick work of unbuttoning the front of her shirtdress. The minute his warm fingers grazed the sensitive skin above the edge of her brassiere, she hissed.

He hummed his approval, and his fingers edged lower, easing the silky fabric aside. And then his tongue took up where his thumb left off, and her mind vacated her body for several long minutes.

As if unable to resist, he straightened to kiss her mouth again. Her legs tightened around his waist, and those talented hands of his came to rest on her thighs, skimming under her dress. Only skimming.

"Max." Her voice sounded plaintive, but she didn't give a single, solitary fuck.

His lips curved against her own. His hands slid further up, finding the edge of her underwear. One solitary finger traced the damp fabric at her center, far too slowly.

His breath fanned across her mouth. "So wet already." He licked along her lower lip. "I wonder if you taste as good there as you do everywhere else."

Her core spasmed.

A lazy smile spread over him as nuzzled against her cheek. "I bet you don't." He laughed at her outraged huff, then bent to whisper in her ear. "I bet you're even better there."

Frannie gasped. If he didn't get to work, and soon, she'd expire right there, on the table. Luckily, his hands moved to the outside of her hips, his fingers dipping below the waist of her pants in an enticing tease.

She let go of him to brace her hands on the table, lifting her arse a scant inch or two off the surface. It was enough for him—he masterfully slipped her panties down without dislodging the aprons beneath her, or even the skirt of her dress.

With seductive grace, he slid the silk all the way down her legs while his knees sank to the floor. He pocketed her pants before caressing her from calf to thigh. She slid her legs open wider as he pushed her dress higher, baring herself to him. He paused to take in the sight, tongue dragging over his lips. The pure, unfiltered hunger in his gaze when he lifted his eyes to hers was almost too intense to handle.

And then he lowered his head.

Just as he had with his fingers, he started slow, with kisses and nips across her inner thighs. Such a tease, this man. She was madly impatient—and yet she loved the way his agonizing, deliberate pace amped up her anticipation.

He rubbed his cheek against her skin and...*oh*. She'd thought his beard felt good on her neck? That was nothing. He made a satisfied hum at her full-body shudder.

Max's strong hands kneaded her legs as his mouth inched higher, and the massage felt extraordinary on her clenched muscles. To distract herself from his beautiful, torturing path, she cupped her breast, picking up where he'd left off. When her hips writhed, his hands stopped their motion to hold her in place. But her grumble of protest abruptly turned into a moan when the flat of his tongue finally found her center, giving her a long, lingering lick.

He finished with an extra flick against her clit, and colorful sprinkles danced at the edge of her vision.

"Max."

The combination of his rumbled laughter and the rasp of his beard nearly killed her. Her hand fell to the table at her side, a little puff of flour exploding into the air.

Max, meanwhile, got to work. His lips and tongue were even more talented than his hands—of course they were—and he nipped and sucked and ravished her as if he was finally tasting cheesecake again after years of subsisting on milk and crackers.

Frannie couldn't get enough of the pure pleasure he delivered.

She came apart—only he wasn't nearly finished. He added his fingers to the mix, diving into her, while his mouth focused entirely on her bud. Inhuman noises escaped her, another climax brewing already. She clutched his head with both hands, her heels digging into his back, riding his face and fingers as he wrenched a second wave of perfection from her.

He stayed with her, easing her down from the heights. As her heartbeat ebbed toward a more sustainable rhythm, her grip on his hair eased, and she massaged his head lightly, suddenly worried she'd hurt him. But when she pried her eyelids open, she found nothing but a wicked spark in his gaze. He pressed a lingering kiss to her inner thigh, rubbing his whiskers across her skin as he did so, and she shivered.

Max grinned up at her, beard damp and lips glistening. It was one of the sexiest things she'd ever seen, and she gave his hair a gentle tug. Getting the message, he surged up for a kiss.

They broke apart breathlessly, and rested their foreheads against each other. Frannie let out a satisfied sigh.

"I have no words," she admitted.

"Good."

They shared a chuckle, and Max pulled back to look at her. His arms caged her in, and his eyes raked over the crown of her head, down to her tits, still spilling out of her bra. When he brought his attention back to her eyes, his lips kicked up.

"Ravishment is a good look for you."

Frannie simultaneously preened and laughed, while she took in his full appearance for the first time. At some point she'd unbuttoned his shirt and it half-hung off his shoulders, his under-shirt clinging enticingly to his chest. His hair was an absolute mess, thanks to her, its waves sticking up in all directions. And no longer completely dark, either.

"You wear ravishment awfully well yourself." She reached up to brush a lock off his forehead. "Though I seem to have aged you." At his questioning look, she raked through his hair again, flourishing her flour-covered hand.

He smiled broadly, but then made a show of looking serious. "Do I look more distinguished?"

"Not in the slightest."

"Hey!"

One minute they were both laughing, and then, as if magnetized, their mouths fused together yet again. She wrapped her arms around his neck to pull him close. His hips settled into the cradle of her own, and she remembered that while she'd found her release—*twice*—he remained rock-hard.

It was time she did something about that.

The oven timer picked that precise moment to ding obnoxiously. Frannie and Max broke apart and turned to look at the offending appliance.

"Dammit," they cursed together.

Giggles overtook them. How unexpectedly *fun* lovemaking with him was turning out to be.

Max's laughter descended into a grumble, and he let go of her, much too soon. "I'd better grab those before they burn." He feathered one more kiss across her lips, before shuffling over to the oven.

Frannie watched him as he moved. The nice, firm arse she'd appreciated earlier, and the way his shoulders bunched as he righted his shirt... She swallowed. With the ease of long practice, he picked up a towel to protect his hands, and then rescued the pan from the heat. Something so mundane should not have been so damn attractive, but she found herself clenching her weakened legs against a new wave of desire.

He set the tray of cakes on a cooling rack, and with one glance at the front of his trousers, Frannie's focus shifted back off her own body. She readjusted her tits into her bra to reduce the potential for jiggling when they were already so sensitive, and hopped down from the table.

Something that looked suspiciously like disappointment flitted across Max's features, but he kept his voice light as he gestured to the tea cakes. "These'll need to cool before we ice them."

"Oh, right."

He smiled shyly. "I can finish them later, if you need to go."

"I'm in no rush."

"I don't mind, honestly. I can deliver them to you for the taste test."

Did he really think she was about to bolt? Well, she supposed she had done precisely that the last time. And the time before that. But they'd come a long way since then, and she wanted to make it up to him.

"Max. Come here."

His eyes snapped to hers at the command, his lips curving up.

She didn't give him time to weigh his response. "You said it yourself… We need to wait for them to cool. And I can think of an excellent way to pass the time."

"Can you, now?"

"Mm-hmm." She purposefully trailed her gaze down, below his belt. "You're still brandishing that rolling pin."

Wildfire roared in his eyes, but he still didn't make a move. "I am."

"So. Come. Here."

She reached out, grabbed his shirt front in both hands, and pulled him toward her.

"Frannie." His voice sounded strangled.

She pushed him against the apron-covered table and captured his mouth with hers. He moaned into the kiss, his hands circling her waist. Frannie pressed her fingers against his chest, feeling all that lovely chest hair through his undershirt. She continued her path down past his belt, palming him through his trousers.

"Wonder how good *you* taste there?" she purred against his lips.

His groan came from deep in his chest, and his cock gave an excited jump against her hand.

But the rest of him stilled. "Frannie. You don't have to…"

She arched an eyebrow at him. "What if I want to?" She cut off any potential argument with a firm squeeze that had him grunting again. "I'm a tit-for-tat gal, remember?"

He snickered. "I know, but…"

Her earlier realizations about his generosity with his food, with his love, came flooding back.

"Shh…" She unfastened the waistband of his trousers and slid her hand inside. "Max. You're always looking out for everyone. Offering your sister a job, baking comforts for Lucy, for your friends. Charging them less than you're worth." While she spoke, she stroked the overheated length of him, eliciting hiss after satisfied hiss. "Doing all kinds of nice gestures for me, even when we were at each other's throats…"

She stilled her hand, looking straight into his eyes. "But who takes care of you, Max?"

His only answer was the bob of his Adam's apple as he swallowed.

"Forget 'have to' or 'tit-for-tat.' Do you want me? Here?" She raked her nails over his hard, sensitive cock.

His eyes drifted closed, his voice a raspy growl. "So damn much."

"Then do me a favor?"

"Hmm?"

She brushed her lips over his. "Shut up."

His laughter echoed through the kitchen as she sank to her knees, easing his cock out of his pants. Moisture had already begun collecting at its head, and she ran her thumb over it. She deliberately waited until he met her eyes to lick her thumb clean, and his teeth sank into his full lower lip, nostrils flaring. He white-knuckled the edge of the table, tightly holding the leash of his control, and it gave her a new mission in life—to obliterate that hold.

Frannie planted one palm against his thigh, admiring the tautness of his muscles. With her other hand, she took a firm grasp of his prick, stroking once more before gliding a tantalizing lick around the crown. Max's growl arrowed straight between her legs, spurring her into further action.

She took her time, as he had, continuing to lap him up like an ice cream cone, enjoying every desperate sound issuing from his mouth. He called her name in a quiet moan, and still she teased. His hand found her hair, but instead of pulling or grasping, his fingers rested in a gentle hold. Even in his escalating frenzy, he was so careful, so tender.

And that made her abandon all moderation.

She circled him with her mouth, closing over his sensitive skin and sliding over the length of him. His fingers tightened, and she relished the possessive feel of it. Her lips dragged over him while her tongue swirled, and she punctuated every other movement with an extra suck at his crown once she saw how much wilder that drove him. Soon, his hips joined the party, bucking into her as both hands cradled her head.

With every one of his thrusts, the temptation to reach down and ease her own desire mounted, but she resisted. Not that she wanted to deny herself. She simply couldn't afford to lose focus, since she needed more than anything to see the moment he lost all restraint.

Max, in the throes of passion, was a beautiful sight.

His head thrown back, the cords of his neck standing out in relief, chest heaving. His delightfully furred forearms in her peripheral vision. When he opened his eyes to look down at her, his mix of raw lust and gorgeous affection would have made her knees buckle if she wasn't already on the floor.

Her eyes watered, and not just from the action of taking him deep. So she focused on her ministrations, cradling his bollocks as well. He moaned, and his hands flexed in her hair.

"Fucking hell, Frannie," he panted. "I'm close."

She could feel it too, his balls contracting under her fingers, the motion of his hips becoming more erratic. His hand slipped to her shoulder, as if to push her away.

No way in hell.

When this man finally shattered, Frannie wanted it all.

So she added her teeth to the mix, dragging gently down his length. His resulting bellow was the most satisfying sound she'd ever heard, and her chest surged with pride. Her lips curved in as much of a smile as she could manage around him. One more rasp of her teeth was all it took.

His muscles tensed and stilled, even as he roared, and a hot stream filled her mouth and coated her throat. A few tears did escape her eyes then, but she sealed her lips around him and continued to take him in. When he finally sagged back against the table, she released him with an audible pop and settled back on her heels.

They stared at each other for an infinite, sated moment. Watching Max unravel, driving him to it, gratified her even more than she'd expected.

She licked her lips, tasting him all over again, and he tracked the motion. It seemed to snap him back to life.

Max reached down to help her to her feet, then snatched a towel off the table. He gently wiped under her eyes, before moving on to her mouth. Her breath snagged all over again.

"If I say I didn't expect you to actually go that far, are you going to yell at me?"

"Probably."

"Okay. But I'm definitely thinking it." He leaned in to swallow her retort with a kiss.

But she had it ready when they broke apart. "Couldn't have you making a mess in your own kitchen, could I?"

He chuckled, before glancing around with a half-hearted groan. "Aw, hell. I'm going to get shut down by the board of health for tonight, aren't I?"

"Hey, what they don't know won't hurt you." She grinned. "But don't worry. I'll help you clean up just in case. My mum taught me all about the wonders of bleach. Although I rather successfully convinced her that I wasn't really listening, so don't you dare tell her." She wagged a stern finger in his face.

"Your secret's safe with me." He grabbed her finger and placed a kiss on its tip. Somehow, that small action had her blushing harder than everything they'd just done to each other.

Max noticed, his dimples joining the party, and leaned in to take her mouth again. A few glorious minutes later, they came up for air with matching sighs.

"I suppose we should clean up," he whispered, all reluctance.

"I suppose so."

They helped each other right themselves first, and then moved on to the kitchen. While they'd done a rather remarkable job of leaving little evidence of their post-dessert activities, their baking lessons were a different story. They had plenty of bowls and pans to wash, ingredients to put away, ovens and mixers to turn off or unplug. Max boxed up their untried cakes for Frannie to take home.

By unspoken agreement, they left the last batch un-iced. The winning formula might lurk among them, but if they delayed finding out, it meant future taste tests.

Once they'd set the kitchen to rights, Max locked up and walked Frannie across the alley to her back door. She climbed a couple of steps, until she was eye-level with him.

"Thank you for dinner," he said quietly.

"And thank you for the baking assistance."

She felt suddenly shy, but she took comfort in his equally bashful smile. Unable to resist, Frannie cupped his cheek, his beard softly rasping her palm, and leaned in. After a few delicious sips at his lips, she pulled back to meet his dark gaze. "I had a wonderful time tonight, Max."

"Me, too."

"Good night."

"Good night, Frannie."

She straightened and took the last few steps into the house. When she turned back, he lingered still at the foot of the porch. She hated to close the door.

The house was quiet, her mother still at her bridge game. Frannie slowly, dreamily made her way upstairs to her bedroom. That had been the best damn date she'd ever had.

Chapter Nineteen

Max steered his motorcycle through the Phoenix Pictures gates and headed for the parking area nearest the wardrobe building. Nick had left a message with the guard that he was busier than expected, so they'd have to tack their planned meeting onto the end of his costume fitting with Nate. Nick hadn't told him specifically what he needed, only that it wasn't a baked good.

Max had jumped at the opportunity. Not only did it give him a chance to get his bike out of the garage, but, more importantly, he'd have a chance to see Frannie.

His entire world had shifted last night. The glorious evening simply grew better and better as it wore on, and he'd completely forgotten to wait for the other shoe to drop.

As he eased his helmet off, his eyes drifted closed and he stifled a groan at the memory of her lips around his cock. And the way she'd come apart under his own lips… He might never recover. But the best part—she hadn't run, hadn't shied away.

Hope sustained his heart.

He kept an eye out for her as he smoothed his hair and started toward the costume department, more than eager to run into her.

Perhaps pull her into a secluded corner somewhere, cage her against a wall and let her ravish his mouth.

He pulled open the door to Nate's domain with a sigh. Even a secluded corner might be risky here, where any of their friends could happen upon them. Another reason he wanted to see Frannie. It hadn't occurred to him, cocooned in their blissful bubble last night, to wonder what came next for them, how public they could—or should—be.

As much as he wanted to shout it from the rooftops, instinct told him to keep this a secret for the time being. He had no idea if Frannie would agree, but given their history, it felt right that they take a beat to enjoy this newfound, precious thing between them, without the added pressure of their friends' excitement and meddling.

But that debate would hold for another time. Nate's assistant, Rose, directed him down the hall to one of the fitting rooms with a dreamy, borderline lascivious, wink. He knocked on the ajar door, and Nate waved him in with a smile.

"What brings you here? And more importantly, does it involve cheesecake?"

Max laughed. "Sadly, it does not."

The sound of hangers clanking together preceded Nick's voice, calling out from behind a curtained-off corner of the room. "I hope you don't mind, Nate. I asked Max to meet me here. I'm booked solid today." He paused, hangers stilling. "And what do you mean, no cheesecake?"

"You specifically mentioned that no confections were necessary today." He turned an apologetic grin on Nate. "Sorry. And like Nick said—I hope it's okay I'm crashing your party."

She fluttered a dismissive hand. "Ordinarily I'd say no, but the more the merrier this time. I'm outfitting Nick in something fun."

"Speaking of which…" Nick's tone brimmed with uncertainty. "Are you sure this is right, Nate?"

The designer's eyes narrowed at the curtain. "Since when do

you question my eye? You're usually game for anything. And I've costumed you in far wilder things than this."

"Okay…" He dragged the word out, piquing Max's curiosity. "But this feels like an oversight…?"

Nate huffed. "I do not overlook details, Nicholas. Stop stalling and get out here."

The curtain whisked open, and Nick stepped out, lacking his usual bravado. And with good reason. Max snickered.

The man wore some sort of historical pants with lots of buttons across the front placket, and knee-high riding boots. Draped over his shoulders was a dramatic, wintry cloak that skimmed the floor, its front open to reveal…Nick's bare chest.

"I think you forgot something there, buddy," Max teased.

Nate shot him a glare that rivaled his mom's, and he snapped his mouth shut. "Do not encourage him." She turned to bark at Nick, "Where the hell is your shirt?"

"You tell me."

Nate rolled her eyes. "I don't have time for pranks, Nick." She aimed a thumb over her shoulder at Max. "And judging by the fact that this clown is here now, I don't think you do either."

"Hey," Max protested.

"No offense." Nate didn't sound overly convincing.

Nick crossed his arms over his shirtless torso. "While I do love a good joke, I would not mess with your process, Nate. Seriously, I put on every item in there."

She glided past him and into the stall to see for herself, reemerging with a disgruntled hum. "I guess someone was asleep at the switch when they dropped these off. Because, believe me, you are supposed to have a shirt."

Nick took stock of himself in the three-way mirror.

"It is a bold look…" Max mused.

Nick cocked his head and put his hands on his hips, a mischievous gleam returning to his eyes. "It does scream"—he deepened his voice—"'I acknowledge the existence of cold, while remaining ruggedly impervious to it,' doesn't it?"

Nate swatted Max on the arm. "I told you not to encourage him."

He shrugged. "Sorry. Old habit."

She shook her head, but humor returned to her expression as she headed for the door. "You two behave yourselves while I go track down that shirt."

"You know, Lois would like it," Max added. Nick's resulting small, private smirk was nauseating, and he immediately regretted saying anything.

Nate whirled back around in the doorway, more worried than nauseous. "Do not, under any circumstances, let her in this room before I come back. She *would* like it, and the last thing I need is her overriding me. My reputation in this business is shaky enough after last year. I can't have a design choice as ludicrous as *this* calling it into question all over again."

Nick opened his mouth to retort, but she cut him off. "Zip it. Your wife can ogle your chest all you want at home."

And with that, she flounced out, leaving Max and Nick laughing in her wake.

"Okay, as much as I know you love staring at yourself…"

"Ha, ha," Nick sneered at him.

"Since we have a minute, what's up?"

Nick sobered, adopting a more businesslike demeanor. Well, as much as one could while wearing only a cape. He noticed Max's smirk and tugged the garment closed.

"I do have a favor to ask. I'm producing a picture that starts shooting soon, and one of the supporting characters is a baker. The fella we cast is a good actor, but…"

"He has no kitchen experience?" Max guessed.

"None whatsoever. And since he features in the background of several big scenes, he needs to look like he knows what he's doing." Nick's grin brightened. "So, I was thinking of bringing someone in to show him the ropes, make sure he looks the part. And who better to do that than my oldest and dearest buddy?"

"I've told you a million times, you don't have to invent reasons to taste-test my food."

"I know, but where's the fun in that? Seriously, though, do you think you'd be up for it?"

Max pretended to consider it. More time at the studio, where he could sneak off to find Frannie? Hell yeah, he was up for it.

But thoughts of Frannie brought to mind her business advice—and her impassioned defense of his worth. He stopped pretending and genuinely weighed Nick's offer. Might as well jump in and start heeding her suggestions with a friendly audience.

"I'd definitely be interested. But if you don't mind my asking—would there be some pay involved for my time?"

Nick didn't bat an eye. "Of course. I may have called it a favor, but I'd credit you as a special consultant, just like a fencing instructor or animal wrangler. I know your time's valuable, especially since it's just you and Linda at the bakery."

Max's chest deflated with relief. He should've expected the response—Nick had never been one to take advantage. Hell, he was one of the most generous people Max knew.

"Great, thanks."

Nick raised a questioning eyebrow. "You didn't really think I'd be that cheap, did you?"

"No! Not at all. It's only..." He cleared his throat. "A... friend...recently gave me some sound business advice, with regard to growing the bakery enough to hire more help. I'm trying to put it into practice."

"I'm glad." Nick watched him carefully, a smile playing at the corners of his mouth. "*Business* advice from a *friend*, huh? Anyone I know?"

Max kept his voice confident to throw him off the scent. "Nope."

"Speaking of business and money..."

So much for that scent-throwing.

"I haven't run this by our accounting department's head

genius yet," Nick continued, "so I will need to clear it before we bring you on officially." He waited expectantly for a reaction, but Max held firm, giving him nothing. Nick shrugged. "But I'm sure I can win her over with my charm."

Max chuckled. "Good luck."

The echo of approaching high heels in the hall interrupted them, but the footsteps didn't belong to Nate.

The accounting genius of his dreams appeared in the doorway. Frannie looked professional, in her stylish suit jacket and fitted skirt, but all Max could think about was the way she'd looked last night—disheveled, dusted with flour, and utterly satisfied. Judging by the way her cheeks flushed as she raked her eyes over him, her thoughts reflected his.

"Hey, we were just talking about you," Nick piped up behind him.

Oh, shit.

He darted a reassuring glance at her, but she seemed more curious than worried.

"Were you, now? I—" Her words cut off in a strangled laugh as she finally tore her eyes from Max and took in Nick's outfit. She made a sweeping gesture over his ensemble. "*What* is happening here?"

"It's supposed to be my new costume, but my shirt seems to have taken a holiday."

"I can see that."

"Rest assured," Max chimed in, "Nate's on the case."

"I'm glad to hear it. I'd hate to question her design choices, but…"

"Believe me, she'd hate for that too." Nick shuddered comically and turned to the mirror again. "Although I have to admit, the outfit is growing on me."

Frannie's attention stayed on Nick, and Max took advantage of the situation to focus on her. She was so damn pretty.

Her head tilted to one side. "You know, the more I look at it, it's not half-bad."

Max *tsk*-ed at her. "Uh-oh. Should Lois be jealous?"

She didn't miss his subtle, completely false emphasis on Lois's name. Her grin took on a wicked edge that sent heat sizzling down his spine.

"Please. Lois knows her husband is a handsome gent. And I once flirted with him right in front of her—as a test, of course—when they were first married. Both too caught up in each other to even notice. So, nothing to worry about there."

"Glad to hear it."

Their eyes held, full of tantalizing promise.

Nick cleared his throat pointedly.

Whoops.

"Anyhow…" Frannie nearly shouted the word, and Max would've laughed if he didn't feel so off-balance himself. She brought her voice back to a normal decibel as she continued, "What *were* you two chatting about when I walked in?"

Max seized on the opportunity to deflect. "Nick swears he can charm you into approving the funds for me to teach one of his actors how to bake."

"Hey," Nick objected. "Don't make me sound so crass."

"But you were going to try, weren't you?" Frannie asked, eyes narrowed.

"Well, yeah. But part of my charm offensive is not to admit up front that that's what I'm doing."

They all laughed at that.

"Honestly, though," Nick added, "I do need him to make Chris look convincing."

"It should be fine. I have to check, but I'm pretty sure set construction is coming in under budget, so I don't see why you can't hire Max."

"Good." Something highly suspicious glinted in Nick's expression. "Because Max mentioned some great counsel he got from a *friend* lately, and I want to make sure to pay him what he's worth."

Max shot him a withering glare. One of these days, he really was going to slug his best friend.

"Is that right?"

All thoughts of violence vanished at the honey in Frannie's tone.

He beamed at her. "It was good advice."

Out of the corner of his eye, Max saw Nick's eyebrow hitch up. *Uh-oh. Again.*

Nick crossed his arms over his chest, achieving a look of cheerful menace despite the ridiculousness of his wardrobe. "So, Frannie. You'd be okay with the idea of Max spending more time at the studio?"

She admirably held her chin high. "As long as it's for the good of the picture, I can manage the prospect."

Her fiery eyes darted toward Max on her last word. Unfortunately, Nick didn't miss a trick. His hands moved to his hips as he looked back and forth between them, a slow grin spreading across his face.

Max desperately steered them into another sidetrack, gesturing at what Nick had exposed when his elbows spread his cloak open wider. "Can you please put *something* on until Nate gets back?"

"Yes," Frannie added. "Think of my delicate sensibilities."

Max snorted, and flashed her a look that said, *Delicate, my ass.*

She merely shrugged and smirked back at him.

"I find it highly entertaining, the way you two keep forgetting I'm in the room."

Fuck.

Nick and his smug smile were right, dammit.

"Nick." The two of them spoke in simultaneous, identical warning.

Which, of course, prompted Nick to guffaw. "The scowls on you both! You look more like twins than Max and Vi." Before they could say another word, he held up his hands in concession. "Rest assured, I will say nothing more until you're ready."

Max and Frannie shared a relieved glance. He wasn't sure what calmed him more, the fact that she seemed to be on the same page, or Nick's surprising sensitivity over the matter.

Almost-sensitivity, that was.

Nick leaned closer and lowered his voice. "You should know, however, that I am doing a very happy jig inside my head right now."

Max groaned half-heartedly.

Frannie adopted a haughty air—though Max noticed she seemed pretty half-hearted herself—and pointed a finger at Nick. "I don't know why. I could easily tell Nate she doesn't have the budget left for your shirt, and then you'd be stuck in that getup."

Nick pulled a dismissive face. "Please. She'd be more upset with you than I would."

"Crap. You're probably right."

Nate's footsteps approached, bringing them all up short. "Found it!" she called, brandishing a flowy garment as she breezed through the door. "It got added to the aging pile prematurely. Oh, Frannie, hi." Her gaze swept the room. "This party keeps growing."

Frannie jumped in before Nate could catch on to the buzz in the air. "Yeah, I dropped your latest numbers by your office. Rose said you were in here, so I thought I'd say hello."

"Frannie's warming up to the idea of keeping my costume like this, too." Nick's provocation had the intended reaction, and Max felt inordinately grateful for the cover.

"No." Nate's tone brooked no argument.

Not that it stopped Frannie. "Lois would certainly like it."

"That's exactly what I said!" Max grinned.

"Okay, that's it. Party's over. Out! The both of you. Now."

Nate shooed Max and Frannie to the exit, ignoring their mirth —and their lack of animosity toward each other. Right before she shut the door in their face, Nick flashed them a wink over her shoulder.

Their chuckles descended into outright giggles. Feeling bold,

Max scanned the empty hallway, then pulled Frannie into the vacant fitting room across the way. He'd barely shut the door when she yanked him to her by his collar.

They muffled their groans with each other's lips. Too soon, they came up for air, both of them panting.

"That was a close one," Frannie whispered.

"It was. We probably shouldn't stay here too long, either."

She grumbled her agreement. "And how about Nick? I didn't think he had that much restraint in him."

"Same."

Her eyes sparkled, even in the dim lighting. "You really think he'll be able to keep it up?"

He nodded. "Surprisingly enough, yeah. I do." He paused, hating to ask. "And you…don't mind? Keeping this under our hats for a bit?"

"No." She worried at her bottom lip, already swollen from their kiss. "I have to admit, I wasn't sure you'd want to." Her next words came out in a rush. "Not that I'm ashamed or anything."

"Me neither," he assured her. "I guess it's just…given our history…this is so new. It'd be nice to have a little time to figure it all out before…"

"Our well-meaning but obnoxiously meddlesome friends swoop in and put all kinds of hopes and expectations on us?"

He met her shy grin with one of his own. "Exactly."

Frannie gasped dramatically. "Did we just agree on something?"

"Look at us."

He leaned down for another kiss, getting blissfully lost in the slide of his tongue against hers. A faint noise on the other side of the door brought them back to reality, and they grinned ruefully at each other.

"We really should escape while we can."

"Yeah." A wild and wonderful thought occurred to him. "Hey, how's the rest of your day looking? Busy?"

She shook her head. "Not too bad."

"Want to get out of here?"

"What, now?"

"Sure." He smirked, deploying what he hoped was a convincing weapon in his own charm offensive. "I took my motorbike here. We could go for a ride."

Judging by the gleam in her eyes, it worked. "I've heard it rumbling in on occasion, but I never make it to the window in time to see you on it."

"Now's your chance."

"You're very persuasive, Mr. Mitchell."

"And you're very persuadable, Mrs. Haynes."

Her laughter was a low purr. "Let's go."

They successfully made it out of the building without drawing anyone's notice, and Max drove his bike off the lot and around the corner, while Frannie gathered her things and changed into the spare pair of pants she apparently kept in her office for emergencies. As gorgeous as her legs looked in that clingy skirt, she would be a hell of a lot more comfortable on the back of his bike with the wardrobe change, and Max admired her practicality.

When she returned to him, her eyes traveled up and down his body, where he leaned against the machine, and the appreciative heat in her eyes melted him like a pan of caramel sauce.

He handed her his extra helmet, and when she settled behind him, arms circled tightly around his waist, he'd never been so excited for a ride. Frannie was proving to be even more of an adventure than he'd dreamed, and he hoped like hell he could hold onto her.

MAX PULLED the motorcycle in behind the bakery and cut the engine, but Frannie didn't stir from her spot. She rather enjoyed the feel of being pressed up against his back, her arms around his solid middle.

"So…what did you think?" Max asked, a smile in his voice.

"That's definitely the way to see the hills of Hollywood," she replied.

He squeezed her hand. "How do they compare to your Scottish homeland?"

Frannie rested her chin on his shoulder. "Not nearly as green. But they'll do."

"Someday, when you take Lucy for a visit, you could go on a motorcycle trip through the countryside."

"Are you trying to get yourself invited?"

His shoulder lifted under her chin. "Maybe."

She chuckled, and he placed a kiss on her temple. She sighed into the contact, not wanting to move, but did so anyway. As she swung her leg over the bike, she threw a glance at her house. Despite their agreement to keep things quiet with their friends, they hadn't discussed whether or not to tell Lucy. Part of her wanted to—her daughter was so observant, she'd probably put it together before long anyway. But Frannie also knew how excited Lucy would be at the idea, and she wasn't sure she was ready to get either of their hopes up just yet.

She was saved from further thought on the subject when Linda emerged from the bakery's back door.

"Oh, hey," she called to them. "I was just about to lock up." Linda's eyes drifted from Max, still straddling the motorcycle, to Frannie, cradling the helmet in her hands, and back again. "Did you two ride here together?"

An innocent enough question, but Frannie got the distinct impression they were about to have a repeat of their earlier scene with Nick.

"Yeah," Max answered. "I…gave Frannie a lift home from the studio."

"That was nice of you."

"It was a fun ride," Frannie chimed in.

"I keep telling him he should put a sidecar on it for deliveries. I don't know why he doesn't listen to me."

"Yeah, I can't imagine," Max retorted as he lifted himself off the bike.

"Oh, that would be bloody brilliant." Frannie had no trouble picturing it, and the idea delighted her. "Now, there's a way to bring in extra money."

"You're impossible, the both of you."

Linda perked up. "Hey, Frannie's an accountant. If she thinks it's a good idea..."

"For the last time, I am not putting a sidecar on my motorcycle." He ticked off each point on his fingers. "First of all, it would look ridiculous. Second—and more important—I will not risk my baked goods that way."

"Are you implying I'm more expendable than your baked goods?" Frannie batted her eyes teasingly.

"What? No! Of course not. I—" He cut off with a grunt when he caught her grin.

Linda beamed at her. "Don't worry, I'd say you're worth plenty. It's not every gal he lets on the back of that thing. Welcome to the club—it's pretty elite." She winked.

"Oh. Were you two...?" A sudden flush heated Frannie's cheeks. She knew Linda had grown up with Max and Nick, but it never occurred to her that she and Max might have their own special history. It shouldn't bother her. His past was none of her business. And yet... Jealousy, hot and irrational, surged through her.

"No, nothing like that," Max stammered, at the same time that Linda contradicted him thoroughly.

"Technically, we were engaged." She split an assessing look between them. "Did Max never tell you that?"

He shot her a glare. "No. Max did not."

"Oh. Sorry." Linda looked mischievous rather than chagrined. "Why not?"

"In part because it's not my story to tell." He folded his arms across his chest pointedly.

Clearly missing something, Frannie wasn't certain she wanted to be clued in. "It's really none of my business, anyway."

"Oh, please. If you two are getting serious about each other, of course you should know."

Max let out a strangled, surprised sound that matched Frannie's own. They shared a glance, and he hung his head.

"First Nick, and now you. Are we really that obvious?"

Linda laughed. "I hate to break it to you, but yes. You are." She shook her head with a wince. "And Nick knows? Good luck there."

Max groaned, and Frannie felt like a ping-pong ball was bouncing around in her head.

"Anyway, Max and I were engaged for a while. But don't worry, you have no reason to be jealous." Frannie started to protest, but Linda kept talking. "It was entirely phony."

"Linda."

She shrugged at him. "What? Since you seem to think it's my story to tell, I'm going to tell it." She turned her attention back to Frannie. "Despite people's incorrect assumptions that we'd one day end up together, Max and I have never had anything but platonic feelings for one another. But…there for a while, my family was putting a ton of pressure on me to settle down, at the same time I was nursing a broken heart, over a relationship I'd kept from them." She smiled affectionately at Max. "So this one stepped in and offered to pretend for a bit, to make things easier on me."

"That was kind of him," Frannie said quietly.

Max's cheeks flushed under his beard. "It was nothing, really."

"Nothing my ass," Linda shot back. "He was the best fake fiancé a gal could ask for. We had quite a good run."

Max snorted. "Till she dumped me for the real love of her life."

"I didn't realize you…" Frannie's gaze automatically went to Linda's empty left hand.

"Oh, I'm not married. Not allowed to."

Frannie's brows knit together in confusion.

"You should be," Max grumbled.

"We are in every way that matters," Linda replied softly. She turned back to Frannie. "This teddy bear hates that Ronnie and I let everyone assume we're just roommates."

The last piece of the puzzle clicked into place.

"Ronnie. Your roommate. Sure, I've seen her around here a few times."

"You've probably seen her perform, too. She's a fabulous singer."

"Of course! The lass with the gorgeous voice, from Lois's premiere party, right? I knew she looked familiar."

"That's her." Linda glowed with pride.

Frannie grinned back. "Oh, she's a knockout. Well done, you."

Linda laughed heartily. "I most definitely drew the lucky straw. Can you blame me for throwing this one over?" She gestured at Max.

"Absolutely not. It all makes perfect sense now."

"Hey!" Underneath Max's teasing affront, Frannie detected a bit of relief. And plenty of warmth.

"Seriously, though," Linda interjected. "I owe Max quite a lot, not only for the engagement. I almost let fear keep me from going for it with Ronnie, and Max gave me the push I needed. Drove the getaway motorcycle himself. Literally."

Max blushed in earnest now. "Anyone could see how perfect you two were for each other. I was glad to help." He turned and grabbed the handlebars of the bike, walking it toward the small shed where he housed it.

Linda watched him go, before turning intent eyes on Frannie. When she spoke, she kept her voice low enough that Max wasn't likely to hear.

"He's the best, you know. I like to needle him and Nick, but we all made quite a team growing up. Nick was always the showman, the ringleader. Vi was the rebel in a lot of ways. And I kept up a running commentary of sarcastic quips to egg them on." Her smile softened. "As for Max…"

"He was the glue," Frannie finished quietly, the full picture abundantly clear. "Holding you all together."

Linda's gaze sharpened with approval. "Yeah. Still is. He's got the biggest heart of anyone I've ever met."

"I'm learning that."

"Good." She sniffed, then raised her voice to carry across to Max, still putting his bike away. "Well, I'd better get home. Night, you two."

Max threw her a quick wave over his shoulder, and Frannie watched him work, thinking about Linda's warning.

Because it had been a warning. She'd shown plenty of encouragement, and Frannie felt deeply honored to be taken into her confidence. But she hadn't missed what lay beneath Linda's parting words—she would fiercely defend Max against anyone who broke his heart.

The more Frannie got to know of Max, the more she understood just how precious that heart of his was. She'd failed to see it for so long, failed to even let herself look.

But now her eyes were finally open, and she wanted very much to be deemed worthy of keeping it safe.

Chapter Twenty

With closing time approaching, Max decided he might as well start wiping down the cafe tables scattered around the bakery. He grabbed a towel just as Linda emerged from the kitchen.

"Want me to start packing up the day-olds for tomorrow?" she asked.

"Sure, that'd be great." He pointed a finger at her. "But I am still mad at you."

She merely rolled her eyes. "You know, I wouldn't believe you, even if I hadn't known you since we were five. Besides, it's been two days. Get over it."

He crossed his arms, feigning anger that—yes, she was right— he didn't feel. Not that it would stop him from goading her anyway. "You told my… You told *Frannie* about our engagement. Why the hell would you do that?"

"Because you were too chicken to do it yourself." Linda's smile softened. "And it is a nice story, Max." She dropped her voice to a whisper. "Makes you look really good."

He chuckled, in spite of his outward intentions. "Thought I needed help in that department, did you?"

Linda shrugged. "You two have been fractious with each other for so long, I figured it couldn't hurt to grease the wheels a little."

"Still. I know it's always a risk, sharing what you did."

"I had a hunch she'd react well."

"Oh yeah?" Max had had the same hunch.

"Yeah." She flourished a pair of tongs at him. "Admit it, you're thrilled she passed the test."

"First of all, I never said she needed to be tested." Linda simply waited, one eyebrow cocked, for him to continue. He relented. "And okay, fine. I was pretty happy about it."

Not that he'd doubted Frannie. But he'd spent a good many years being outraged—more silently than he cared to—on Linda and Ronnie's behalf, and he was accustomed to wariness anytime someone new learned about their relationship. Seeing Frannie's complete and immediate support only made him more smitten with her.

A sudden image popped into his head, of the four of them on a double date, laughing and joking around the table in Linda and Ronnie's kitchen. He couldn't wait to make it a reality.

"Aww, look at you with that big, goofy grin." Linda's tone skirted the line between affection and merciless teasing.

"Oh, shut up."

"Hey, do you remember what I told you when I was first trying to win Ronnie over?"

Max made a show of considering her question. "Hmm… That I was the best friend in the world, and you'd owe me one forever?"

"Don't make me hurl this croissant at you." She narrowed her eyes. "No. I told you that I could not wait until some fabulous woman came along and knocked you flat." Linda pointed her tongs at him again. "Many long years I have waited for this, my friend. So you better believe I'm going to enjoy the hell out of it."

He snorted. "Duly noted."

Max focused his attention on a table by the window, carefully wiping its surface in an effort to hide his blush at the truth of

Linda's words. He'd been knocked flatter than a pancake, ever since the moment he'd met Frannie in that alley. With the turn things had taken lately, he was practically a crepe at this point.

And he loved every minute of it.

He glanced up and spotted Lucy and a small group of her friends, playing on the jungle gym at the park across the street. His smile grew. Another lovely picture sprang to life in his mind —Lucy, swinging between him and Frannie, as they strolled through the Scottish countryside. His imagination was chugging full steam ahead this afternoon, and while slight warning bells chimed in the distance, he steadfastly ignored them. He'd denied himself hope for so long, he was overdue for some indulgence.

The sound of the kids' laughter bounced off the window as he moved to the next table. He looked up in time to see Lucy attempt a swing from one bar to another.

Her hand missed its connection, and time froze.

Max watched for a split second, helpless with dread, as Lucy plummeted toward the ground. Then he snapped into action. Despite feeling like he ran through molasses, he flew out the door in a flash. By the time he reached the park—with absolutely no recollection of how he made it across the street, safely no less— Lucy lay huddled on the grass, curled around her left arm, all the wind knocked out of her.

Max skidded to a stop, kneeling next to her. "Lucy! Lucy, can you hear me?"

She blinked a few times, before her eyes—the same dark blue as her mother's—widened and started filling with tears, the pain hitting her. An arrow pierced Max's heart.

Despite his mounting terror, he kept his voice level for her sake. "It's okay. You're gonna be okay. Tell me where it hurts."

"M-my arm…" Her voice trailed off into a whimper.

"Can I look at it?" At her nod, he carefully touched her arm. No blood, which was good, but as he started to gently lift, Lucy let out a sharp hiss. She'd probably broken a bone. Max gingerly laid her arm back down, visually sweeping the rest of her as he did so. A pretty nasty scrape on her knee, and a few scratches on her opposite hand from where she'd tried to brace herself. But otherwise, nothing else appeared to be amiss. Her arm seemed to be the worst of it.

Despite her clear efforts to hold it in, Lucy was crying in earnest now. He'd give anything to take away her pain.

By that time, Linda had followed across the street. The other kids started to gather, chattering worriedly—even that obnoxious Aames kid looked shaken. Lucy's friend Nancy hovered next to Max's shoulder, looking ghostly pale, but determined to be there for her buddy. Her attitude heartened him, and spurred him into further action.

"Nancy, can you ask everyone to give us a little space?"

She nodded briskly and whipped around to the group. "You heard Mr. Mitchell. Everyone get back! Now!"

Max fought back a smile. The girl had questionable taste in desserts, but she'd make an excellent drill sergeant.

Linda squatted next to them.

"Just her arm?" she asked quietly.

"I think so."

"What can I do?"

"Frannie gave me the number of Lucy's pediatrician in case of anything. It's tucked in the book by the telephone. Ring him, and then Frannie?"

Linda was in motion before he'd even finished. "Got it."

Max fished a handkerchief out of his pocket and brushed gently at the tears on Lucy's cheeks. "It hurts a lot, huh?"

"Yeah."

"You cry as much as you need to, sweetheart." He tucked the hankie into her uninjured hand. "Do you think it'll hurt too much if I try to lift you?" She shook her head, and he scooped her into his arms, tucking her against his chest as he stood.

She only made a tiny whimper at his motion, which he took as a good sign.

"I've got you," he whispered into her hair. "You're doing great, Snickerdoodle."

She sniffled, burrowing against him.

He tightened his arms as carefully as he could. "All right. Let's get you taken care of."

Max set out, back across the street, heart thudding in his chest but determined to stay calm. His Snickerdoodle needed him, and he'd do everything in his power to fix this for her.

FRANNIE RUSHED DOWN THE PRISTINE, pale green hallway of the doctor's office. Her heart hadn't stopped pounding since Linda's phone call, and she'd likely broken a few traffic laws on her drive over the hills from the studio. She clung to her one consolation—Linda's assurances that Max had gotten to Lucy immediately and had everything under control. Frannie knew, deep in her bones, that he'd take good care of her daughter in her absence.

One of the office's regular nurses, Carol, spotted her before she reached the nurses' station, and stood with a reassuring smile.

"Mrs. Haynes. Lucy's going to be fine."

The breath vacated Frannie's lungs in a whoosh, and she sagged against the counter. "Oh, thank god."

"She does seem to have a broken arm, which means she'll need a cast for six weeks. We're waiting on the x-ray results to confirm, but they should be back from the lab any minute now. Dr. Hart suspects it's a fairly clean, straightforward fracture, so it should heal easily. She has a few scrapes and bruises too, but otherwise she's fine. She's been a real trooper."

"That's good. Can I see her?"

"Of course. I'll take you back." Carol rounded the counter and led Frannie down another hallway. "Your friend Mr. Mitchell is with her. He's been a tremendous help. Not only did he get her here in record time, but he kept her entertained and calm while we worked."

Frannie's heart settled. "He is pretty great with her."

He's pretty great. Period.

Another nurse called out from down the corridor. "Carol, Dr. Magnum's asking for you in room five."

"Okay, thanks." She pointed Frannie down the hall. "Lucy's through the second door on the left. The doctor will be in to start that cast as soon as the results are in."

"Thanks, Carol."

As the nurse darted in the opposite direction, Frannie took a second to steady her breath. She didn't want to agitate Lucy.

She heard her daughter's soft giggle as she approached the door, which stood ajar. Frannie peered in, and a wave of affection helped loosen worry's grip on her heart.

Lucy reclined on an exam table, propped up against a few pillows, her left arm loosely wrapped and resting on another pillow. She looked the worse for wear, but her tired smile was genuine. Max sat on a stool beside her, animatedly acting out a story with what appeared to be a pair of tongue depressors sporting hastily drawn-on faces.

Frannie blinked against the sudden pricking of tears behind her eyes.

At that moment, Lucy spotted her. "Mommy!" Her smile remained big, but her chin quavered, and Frannie could see the sheen forming in her eyes from across the room.

She rushed to her daughter. "My love, I got here as quick as I could." She wanted to crush Lucy to her chest, but feared hurting her, so she settled for an arm around her shoulders. Her tears threatened to spill over as she inhaled the warm scent of her daughter's hair. "How are you feeling, sweetheart? Does it hurt very much?"

Lucy clung to her with her uninjured arm and sniffled against her shoulder. "Yeah, but it's better now. It hurt *so* much before." She lifted wide, tearful eyes to Frannie, whose heart cracked into a million pieces.

She brushed Lucy's hair back from her forehead. "Oh, my brave wee girl."

"So brave," Max murmured across from her. He'd stood when she entered the room, and she finally took a good look at him. Despite the soft smile on his face, he appeared completely wrung out.

"Max said it'd probably make me feel better if I cried a lot, so I did. I got his shirt all wet in the car."

Frannie pored over Lucy's sweet face. "Did you, now?"

Lucy nodded, her eyes brightening again. "And he was right! I did feel better when we got here. And the x-ray didn't hurt at all!"

"I'm glad to hear it, darling."

Lucy nuzzled against her shoulder again. After placing a kiss on the crown of her daughter's head, Frannie met Max's gaze and mouthed a fervent "thank you." A bit of pink crept across his cheeks, and he gave her a tiny nod of acknowledgement.

"The doctor thinks Lucy's arm is broken," he said softly.

"Her nurse told me. Sounds like he'll be in pretty soon."

Lucy's head popped up again. "Yeah, Doc Hart said I'll get a cast. I can't wait for everyone to sign it!"

Frannie and Max shared a chuckle. Her child's elasticity never ceased to amaze her. She wished she had half of Lucy's optimism sometimes.

"Did you ever have a cast, Mom?"

"I did. Twisted my ankle once. It wasn't fun."

Lucy grimaced before swiveling to Max. "What about you, Max?"

"I haven't, as a matter of fact. Although I did hit my head pretty hard once." He smiled wryly at Frannie. "Ended up in the hospital and everything."

"Wow," Lucy breathed. "Did someone have to carry you, like you carried me?"

Max cleared his throat, flushing a deeper red. "Yeah, my folks were there to help me out."

Before Frannie could dwell on the image of Max in full hero-mode with Lucy, Dr. Hart breezed into the room with a set of x-ray photos.

"Mrs. Haynes, hello. Has anyone filled you in?"

"Yes, Carol told me everything."

He nodded as he slid the photos onto a lightbox on the wall. "My hunch was correct. Lucy has indeed broken her arm. But it's a clean fracture, should heal nicely with a little time." He flashed a grandfatherly smile at Lucy. "And I thought the patient might like to see for herself."

He flipped a switch and illuminated the box, and Lucy's eyes and mouth went comically round.

"Wowzers," she whispered.

All the adults in the room laughed, but Frannie's mirth faded almost immediately. The image on the screen might be fascinating, but she zeroed in on the crisp line running across her daughter's bone at a slight diagonal. Rationally, she knew injuries like this were a natural part of childhood, that she'd sustained plenty herself. She believed the doctor when he said it would heal. But none of that changed the fact that her precious lass had been fractured, hurt.

She bit her lip, willing herself not to crack in front of Lucy. A warm hand settled on the small of her back. Max had stepped around next to her when the doctor came in. She leaned into his touch—technically a small comfort, but more than enough.

Before long, everything descended into a distracting bustle. Carol wheeled in a tray of supplies, and she and Dr. Hart got to work applying Lucy's cast. Frannie had phoned her mum before leaving work, and Betty arrived during one of the middle layers of plaster.

Frannie's attention remained on Lucy during the process. So much so, that it wasn't until they were ready to take her home, and she insisted on bringing Max's stick-puppets with her, that Frannie even realized he'd slipped out. Disappeared.

She pasted a smile on her face, took care of her daughter, and tried desperately not to mourn the intense consolation that had vanished along with him.

THE RISE and fall of Lucy's chest, firmly settled in slumber, brought back some degree of comfort.

They'd been at the doctor's office longer than she thought, so after getting her washed up and into her pajamas, Frannie settled Lucy right into bed. Betty brought in a dinner tray, and after downing a full glass of milk and some healthy spoonfuls of soup, Lucy's eyelids started to droop. After Frannie tucked her in, she drifted off to sleep the minute her head hit the pillow, broken arm propped up and the other curled protectively around Sir James.

Frannie didn't rush to get up, content to watch her daughter, more grateful than ever to have her safe and sound.

But she herself was hardly peaceful. Her body was weary as hell, but her mind, and her heart, hadn't caught up yet.

Now that Lucy didn't require all of her attention, one question nagged persistently at her. *Why did Max just leave? Without saying anything?*

She resolutely tried to curb her judgment, give him the benefit of the doubt. Knowing full well that she'd submitted to far too many negative assumptions throughout their roller coaster of a relationship.

But it didn't stop his absence from stinging terribly.

Betty appeared in the doorway with a soft smile, and Frannie finally rose from her seat. She feathered one last kiss on Lucy's forehead and slipped from the room, joining her mother in the hall.

"Our poor lass is exhausted."

"She's not the only one, is she?" her mother asked quietly.

Frannie shook her head. When Betty extended her arms, she fell gladly into her embrace, clinging for a long, blessed time. No matter how old she got, despite being a parent herself now, there was no place like mum.

"You should go talk to him," Betty suggested.

Frannie's head popped up. "What? Who?"

Betty gave her a skeptical look. "Max. It's been bugging you all night, hasn't it?"

No use denying it. "He didn't even say goodbye. It doesn't make sense."

"I don't know. Doesn't seem all that surprising to me." Her smile softened at Frannie's look. "This day's been shite for him, too. Don't forget, he actually saw it happen. He's probably feeling pretty overwhelmed. Maybe he needs a hug right now too."

"I hadn't thought of it that way," Frannie whispered. "But…"

Betty tucked Frannie's hair behind her ear. "Only one way to know for sure. Go talk to him, lass."

A good many of Frannie's instincts told her to follow her mother's advice, to run to Max. But every other instinct anchored her to her current spot. She shot a glance at Lucy's door.

"I can't leave Lucy, Mum."

Betty huffed. "She's fine. Snug as a bug in a rug, and like to be out cold till morning."

"I know, but…"

Betty rested her hands on her hips. "You're only going next door. And I'll be right here to sound the alarm if anything happens. Not that I think it will."

Frannie opened her mouth to argue further, but her mother firmly cut her off.

"Frances Grace. You need to talk to that boy." She cupped Frannie's face in her two gentle hands. "More importantly, I suspect you both need to lean on each other. A huge chunk of your heart is in there." She nodded toward Lucy's room. "But there's another bit that needs tending, too."

Tears sprang to Frannie's eyes. Betty kissed her forehead.

"Go."

Frannie managed a watery smile. "Thanks, Mum."

Her mother simply nodded and turned her by the shoulders, giving her a gentle shove.

Frannie made her way downstairs and through the kitchen, gathering her courage with every step. When she emerged from the house, she noticed light coming from the bakery's kitchen. *He doesn't usually work this late.*

Perhaps her mother had been right, and he wasn't handling things so well.

She approached the door and spotted him through the screen. His back was to her, and he kneaded a large hunk of dough. With a great deal of force. As she watched him work, her heart softened with every bunch of his back muscles, every thud of the dough against the counter. Though her question remained.

Why did you leave me?

When he finally heaved the dough into a bowl, heaving an even bigger exhale, Frannie found the nerve to open the screen door and step inside.

Max whirled around, and his expression punched her in the gut. His eyes were slightly red-rimmed, and an extraordinary mix of anguish and tenderness washed across his features.

"Frannie, hi." He rolled his shoulders, as if trying to decide whether to be relieved or concerned. "How's Lucy?"

She swallowed around the lump in her throat. "Fast asleep. Valiantly managed some soup and then, whoosh. Out like a light."

"That's good. I'm glad."

They stared at each other. Max's hands flexed a few times, as if he wanted to reach for her. Frannie sympathized. She had an overwhelming urge to throw herself at him. Instead, she spoke.

"Why the hell did you leave?"

Chapter Twenty-One

rannie's heart gave a shudder at Max's wince. She hadn't meant to blurt it out like that, in such an accusatory manner.

He considered his words. "I… I didn't want to get in the way. I was just a placeholder until you got there, and then when Betty arrived, you really didn't need me. Especially not after…"

He ran a hand through his hair, heedless of the light dusting of flour he left in its wake.

"After what?" She was genuinely confused.

"Are you really gonna make me say it?"

"I have no idea what you're talking about."

"I let it happen, Frannie! I watched, right from the front window, when she just…" He squeezed his eyes shut. "I saw the whole thing, and I…" He whirled around, slamming his hands on his worktable. "I didn't get there in time."

"Oh, Max…" She stepped up behind him, placing a gentle hand on his back. His muscles tensed beneath her fingers, but he didn't shrug off her touch.

"Why the hell would you want me to stick around after that?" His voice emerged as a rough rasp. "I couldn't stop her from getting hurt."

"No one could have."

He began to protest, but she cut him off. "I mean it. I don't blame you, so stop blaming yourself."

He hung his head further.

"Look at me." Frannie slid a finger under his chin, turning his head toward her. His dear face looked so very sad. "You're not bloody Superman, Max. You could not possibly have gotten to her faster than you did. Which, in my book, was pretty damn fast."

"I guess so…"

"Faster than I did. At least you were only across the street."

Max's eyes melted at that. "Frannie, don't—"

"What? Blame myself?" She raised an eyebrow.

He simply shook his head, chagrined.

"You know, my mother was standing right next to me when I hopped off a big rock and twisted my ankle. She assures me it's impossible to stop kids from getting into scrapes. Especially when they've got as much adventurous spirit as I had. And I passed that on to my daughter." Frannie gave him a wry smile. "Do I need to remind you of a certain baseball-related bout of carnage in your history?"

His breath gusted, part laugh and part sigh. "Slightly reassuring, but it still feels pretty awful."

"I know. But you didn't need to sneak out."

He faced her more fully. "You really wanted me there?"

Her heart liquified in her chest at the sincere doubt in his voice. She'd been so focused on her own disappointment at his leaving that she hadn't considered how broken up he'd be about what happened—and her past behavior toward him had likely contributed to his uncertainty.

Frannie cupped his cheek, his beard rasping softly against her palm. "Of course I did. And so did Lucy. You're absolutely wrong, you know."

Max's cheek lifted in a smile under her hand. "You're rather fond of telling me that, aren't you?"

"Yes, and don't you forget it." Her smirk softened. "But I especially want you to hear it now." She trailed her hand up his face to brush a little of the flour from his hair. "You are a hell of a lot more than just a placeholder. You swooped in and took care of my baby girl. The nurse said you were a huge help. And tell me, if you're so dispensable, then why did Lucy insist on taking your little stick puppets home with her?"

"She did?"

Frannie nodded decisively. "They're on her nightstand right now. The faces you drew are very cute, by the way."

Max chuckled softly. "Icing's more my medium of choice, but I can make do."

"Yes, you can. But I suspect Lucy would've wanted to keep them even if they were atrocious—for the same reason she loved my cake." She flattened her palms on his chest. "Because *you* made them for her."

He covered her hands with his own. "I'm not sure whether to be honored, or if it's time to start questioning her taste."

It was Frannie's turn to laugh. "A little of both, I'd reckon."

Max's exhale fluttered the hair around her face, and his thumbs began tracing a pattern on her skin. "I just wanted to make her feel a little better."

"Believe me, you did. And not only her."

His fingers stilled, and she took up the rhythm, softly caressing his hands.

"Today was bloody hard, Max. I've always worried about being at work if something happened to Lucy, about getting to her quick enough. And as terrifying and painful as the reality was..." She swallowed, holding his gaze. "The one thing that made it easier—hell, that made it even remotely bearable—was knowing you were there for her." Tears gathered behind her eyes, and she noticed a sheen forming in his as well. "I couldn't get to her right away, but you did."

His nostrils flared, but she pressed on. "You *did*, Max. Knowing that made all the difference to me. She was hurt, and scared, but she had her friend with her, someone she trusts. Someone *I* trust. And that is no small thing."

It appeared that words were a struggle for Max at the moment, but he nodded, and leaned in to feather a kiss across her lips. They collapsed against each other. Frannie slid her arms around his waist, leaning into his warm, solid chest. His own arms surrounded her, holding tight, his chin nestling against the crown of her head.

"Shite, what a manky day," she breathed.

Max's chest rumbled under her cheek. "So manky."

"Do you even know what that means?"

"Not exactly, but I get your drift."

They laughed softly together, but Max's descended into a sigh.

"God. All these years, I've so underestimated my folks' reaction to the Baseball Massacre."

"I'm sorry you had to see it happen, Max. I can't imagine what that…" She trailed off, finding she could imagine, after all.

Max's arms tightened, and he kissed the top of her head. "Better me than you," he whispered.

She squeezed him back, and they settled into a long silence, simply holding each other. Content to give each other strength. She'd had no idea how much she'd missed having someone to share her burdens with. Not just any someone, either. *This* someone.

Frannie nestled closer, rubbing her cheek against his soft shirt. As she did so, something shiny caught the light, next to her eye. Max always wore a gold chain around his neck, but usually kept it tucked below his clothes, so she'd never seen it in any detail. But it must have escaped its confines during his earlier work, because she noticed it now—a pair of charms weighing down the chain.

She shifted slightly to get a better look. One appeared to be a medal of some kind, while the other…

She laid a single finger against the little gold pendant. A pencil.

"You know, I used to have a charm just like this." Max went

utterly still. "I lost it years ago, on..." Frannie froze as well. Her breath shallowed. "On V-J Day," she whispered.

Her eyes flew to his. He stared back, holding his breath. Watching her warily, fearfully.

As awareness washed over her, she thawed, from her melting heart outward.

"You found it, didn't you? That night."

His Adam's apple convulsed. He gave the slightest of nods.

"All this time," she breathed. Her gaze drifted back to his necklace, and she absently watched her finger trace the small pencil—even as her awareness sharpened.

"I know... I should've given it back to you," he rasped. "I just..."

"You kept it. All this time," she repeated. "You kept it...right here." Her palm flattened against his heart, thudding erratically beneath her touch.

A dam of emotion burst in her chest. She cupped the back of his neck, and breathed his name against his lips before plunging into his mouth.

He groaned, relief and desire evident in the way he melted into her. For her part, Frannie poured everything she couldn't quite voice into the kiss. The stress of the day slipped away, as well as her guilt. She'd wasted so much time and energy misjudging this wonderful man, who had taken such extraordinary care of her daughter. Who took care of everyone around him, and made her laugh even while he pushed her buttons.

Who'd carried a torch for her, in the form of a pencil around his neck, since the night they met.

And good lord, could he kiss. His tongue slid against hers, and he tasted faintly of vanilla and sugar, which made her smile against his mouth. Until he nipped at her bottom lip, and she forgot her own name.

Frannie raked her hands through his hair, as much to incite him as to keep herself upright. A growl, deep in his chest, reverberated in her own, and they tightened their arms around each other. She slid her leg up and around his, at the same moment his hands found her arse.

He kneaded gently for a few moments, before his grip tightened. He lifted her to sit on his worktable, heedless of an apron this time. He trailed a string of kisses across her jaw and down her neck, and she arched into the contact.

The contrast of his soft lips and the rasp of his beard shot an arrow of pleasure straight between her legs, and she ground against him. His teeth joined the party, nipping at the base of her throat. One of his hands pressed into her back, while the other came around to skim her breast.

Together, they began to lean back toward the table's surface. Unfortunately, Frannie's lower back chose that moment to lodge a small protest, stabbing her with a tiny spasm. She groaned in frustration, her fingers tightening in his hair.

"Max, wait. I can't..."

His hands stilled, and he pulled back, chagrin written on his face. "Right. Sorry."

She softened her grip on him, brushing an errant lock of dark hair off his forehead. "Oh, god, would you let me finish before looking at me like that?"

He huffed a startled laugh.

"I was going to say," she continued pointedly, "that after the day I've had, my back isn't going to take too kindly to my being thoroughly rogered against a hard surface like this. Do you at least have a sack of flour you can lay me down on or something?"

Max's laughter deepened, and his mouth kicked up into a sly grin. "While I do have some extra supplies on hand, I think my financial advisor might yell at me if I used my resources like that."

"Is she truly so scary when she yells?"

"Hmm." He leaned in to trail his lips over her cheek, whispering against her ear. "On the contrary. I happen to like it. Very much."

She shivered.

He pulled back again, a playful, wicked gleam in his eyes. "But I also happen to have a bed upstairs, which I think you'll like more than a flour sack."

"I think you're right."

Max widened his eyes in mock surprise. "Will wonders never cease? Did you just admit I was right?"

"Oh, shut up. Are you going to take me upstairs or not?"

He made a show of considering it. "I don't know. I might need to write this in my diary first."

"Like hell you do," she muttered.

She pulled him in close for a kiss, intending to make him forget all about diaries and being right. By the time she finished, *she*'d forgotten her point completely.

Luckily, he hadn't. With a grin, he took her by the waist and lifted her off the table. After making sure she was steady on her feet, he quickly threw a towel over the bowl of dough he'd been working on, moved it next to the ovens, and grabbed her hand.

"Come on."

FRANNIE STEPPED over the threshold into Max's apartment, waiting while he closed the door behind them. Part of her wanted to be nosy, to take in every detail about the place he called home.

But the part that needed his mouth all over her again was far more insistent.

He was right there with her. They surged toward each other, moaning greedily. His arms banded tight around her as they kissed, and before she knew it, he had her pushed up against the wall. Desire flared strong, though a little less desperate now, between them. Fully aware that they had more time, more space to explore. Less need to rush.

Not that it slowed her roving hands.

She went to work on the buttons of his shirt, while he plundered her mouth with deliberate strokes of his tongue. She pushed the garment over his shoulders, reveling in the heat of his body under her fingers. He let go of her only long enough to peel his arms out of his sleeves, and then his hands roamed every-where—threading through her hair, skimming over her waist, settling on her tits.

His hips, his hard cock, ground into her stomach, as he flattened her against the wall with a groan of delight. But for some inexplicable reason, Max stopped. At her mewl of frustration, he laughed.

"I don't think this wall is going to do you any better than the table." His voice was a throaty whisper tickling her ear.

Frannie pushed against his chest and reversed their positions, pinning him against the wall. He took the opportunity to slide his hands under her sweater and whip it over her head. When she reached for his undershirt, he grasped her wrists to still her.

"Oh, no." He gave her a kiss as deep and drugging as it was quick. "I promised you a bed." Another kiss. "And I keep my promises."

Her knees went weak at the certainty in his words.

"So what the hell are you waiting for?" she purred.

Pushing off the wall with a delicious growl, he tugged her down the hall, the two of them shedding more layers along the way. He yanked his undershirt over his head, nudging her toward a doorway. She unfastened her jeans as they passed through, kicking them off along with her loafers. He followed suit with his own trousers, and they stood before each other in the dusky light of his bedroom, him in only his shorts and her in her brassiere and tap pants.

She reached around to unclasp her bra, and he swallowed audibly as she slipped free of it. They watched each other, their breathing shallow, as they both slid off their last remaining garments.

Neither of them dared to move. It was the first time they'd completely bared themselves to each other, and he seemed as afraid as she to break the spell.

Her eyes raked over the softly strong planes of his chest and abdomen, liberally dusted with dark hair. His arms, well-muscled from constant use in the bakery. His solid legs, with thighs that could support her easily. And between those legs, his cock, hard and straining for her, just the right size to fill her the way she wanted, *needed*, him to.

Between how beautifully made he was, and how long it had taken them to get here, her breath stalled in her chest.

And then there was the way he visually savored her.

His warm maple eyes blackened with desire as he took her in. The expression in them so raw, so full of tenderness and desire… and something suspiciously like awe.

His gaze traced over her with searing appreciation, and he took a step closer, reaching for her waist. She shivered immediately at his heated, featherlight touch. His fingers skimmed across and down her hip, and she belatedly recalled what he'd find there—the little translucent stripes peppering her midsection.

"Souvenirs from carrying Lucy," she whispered. She brushed her hand across her opposite hip, meeting his at her navel, ready to push him away.

Before she could, he took her hand and brought it to his lips. "A roadmap of where you've been." He pointedly raised the eyebrow next to his little scar from the baseball incident.

He bent to feather a string of kisses over her stretch marks, and she sucked in a sharp breath.

There's no way I'm getting my heart back, is there?

She found she was perfectly all right with that.

At least a fraction of that sentiment must have shown in her eyes, because when Max straightened up, his own breath hitched. The enormity of everything caught up to both of them, and the scant foot of space separating them was suddenly inexcusable.

They closed the distance in a flash, and his body felt glorious against hers—all smooth, hot skin married with the rasp of his beard, the hair on his chest and arms and legs. She couldn't get enough of him, and hopped up, wrapping her legs around his middle. He caught her effortlessly, gathering her close and safe.

Max walked her toward the bed, but stopped before he arrived. She let out a startled squeak when he dipped to root through the drawer in his nightstand with one arm, all the while holding her tight with the other.

"What—?"

He flashed her a lopsided grin and held up a tin of rubbers. Frannie laughed and pulled him in for another kiss. They tumbled to the bed, both laughing now. Much to her dismay, he let go of her and sank back on his heels to pull a condom out. He tossed the box back on the table and started to reach down for himself, but she halted his progress with a hand on his wrist.

"May I?" she asked.

His momentary surprise melted into a slow, scorching smile, and he handed over the rubber. She sat up, drinking in the sight of him all over again. "God, Max, you are gorgeously put together."

The extra tinge of pink washing over the already-flushed skin above his beard was adorable. "Thanks," he breathed.

The need to touch him overwhelmed her, and she thrilled at his hiss when she grasped his hot, eager cock and eased the protection in place.

"All set," she murmured.

"Indeed."

They allowed themselves a brief exchange of smiles, before anticipation got the better of them. Frannie snaked her arms around Max's neck at the same time he surged forward, and they crashed back down to the pillows.

"Damn, Frannie," he grunted into her skin. "You feel so good already."

His fingers found her entrance and she could only moan her agreement.

He hummed his appreciation as he toyed with her. "Seems you're all set, too."

She squirmed impatiently. "So maybe you should stop

talking."

Max chuckled against her neck, and replaced his hand with his cock, dragging himself through the wetness at her core. They both groaned. *If he feels that good before he's even inside…*

In one beautiful movement, he thrust home.

"Fucking hell, Max."

He was everything she needed after the awful stress of the day. Hell, everything she'd needed—but been unable to acknowledge —practically since she met him. She wanted to drag this out as long as possible. Neither of them moved.

They clung to each other for a moment, and Max leaned down to kiss her gently, slowly. But the motion shifted his hips against hers, and his cock twitched inside her. It unlocked both of them, and all attempts at patience went out the window.

Max withdrew almost all the way out and then slammed back in to the hilt, his movements smooth and sure. Fierce.

As delicious as it felt to be flattened into the mattress, Frannie was never one to be outdone. She met his thrusts with upward force of her own, her fingernails scraping across his back, digging into his wonderfully firm arse. His resulting hiss quickly turned into a growl, and he captured her mouth with his.

Their choreography became more frenzied, the sounds issuing from both of them less human. She couldn't remember when she'd last felt so free.

She longed to soar with release, and she chased it eagerly, rolling her hips to match his, to get the pressure right. Yet it remained elusive, so she finally tore her hand away from his skin and snaked around between them. She had almost reached her clit when Max's hand closed around her wrist, stopping her gently but firmly. His thrusts slowed but didn't cease.

He saw the confusion, the frustration, she couldn't keep from her expression, and smiled. Not a smirk, not a tease. A confident, playful, *tender* curve of his lips.

"May I?" His voice sounded rougher than she'd ever heard it as he echoed her earlier request.

"Oh." His never-ending desire to care for her took what remained of her breath away, filling her with an even greater need than the one she'd just been chasing. She managed a nod, and his dimples deepened underneath his beard.

He let go of her wrist and replaced her fingers with his own, lightly skimming the sensitive spot above his continued motion in and out of her. She gasped, though it still wasn't enough.

Sensing her mounting desperation, his expression turned delectably wolfish. In the blink of an eye, he flipped them, so she straddled him. The promise of relief spread through her, and she braced to push herself up and ride him more fully. But once again, Max had other plans.

His free hand splayed across her back, holding her in place against his chest. She wanted to protest, but the abrasion of his chest hair against her nipples did feel bloody wonderful. His fingers worked in a steadier rhythm against her clit, no longer simply teasing. At the same time, the new angle of his thrusts brought his cock into the perfect position to trigger an elusive, heavenly spot inside her.

Frannie let out a deep, guttural moan, as light glinted off the chain around his neck, morphing into a fireworks show behind her eyes. Her lids felt heavy, but she resisted the urge to close them. Her need to watch Max, to be present with him, reigned.

His eyes locked with hers and held. Even through the growing haze of pure sensation, she recognized every single thing he refused to hold back—his determination to wring pleasure out of her, his slipping hold on his control as he chased his own. And another, unnameable emotion, one that had lurked far longer than either of them dared to admit.

One that was steadily filling her own heart, harder and harder to ignore.

Her explosion detonated, unabated bliss shimmering through her from the inside out, and she succumbed, giving herself over to it. When it finally became too much to look at him, she buried her face in his neck, the breath leaving her in one prolonged whimper.

Max's fingers slowed, his other hand remaining firm on her back, and she vaguely admired the herculean strength it must have required to keep his hips steady, waiting for her to come down.

It took her what could have been an eternity, or only a few seconds, to get her breathing back to a slightly normal pace. He sensed as soon as she did, and his own control finally snapped.

"Oh, god, Frannie," he bit out.

His hips resumed a frantic rhythm, both hands tightening greedily on her arse. Frannie kissed her way up his throat while she moved against him, spurring on his release. She'd just reached his mouth when his entire body tensed, and she swallowed his shout as his cock pulsed against her still-sensitive insides.

When he finished, he melted into the mattress, his arms folding around her. She burrowed her face against his neck, surrounding herself with his vanilla-pine perfection.

His breath fanned the hair at her temple. "We're pretty damn fantastic at that, aren't we?"

"Yeah, I'd say so."

The rightness of it all enveloped her more fully than Max did.

He grinned up at her before pulling her in for a kiss. When they broke apart, resting their foreheads against each other, Frannie felt utterly boneless. She could have closed her eyes and fallen asleep right there on Max's chest, their bodies still joined, so she grumbled her frustration when he stirred, disconnecting them.

He tucked her hair behind her ear. "I'll be right back."

Flipping to her back, she watched him retreat to the bathroom, appreciating the unobstructed view of him. He reemerged quickly, having abandoned the rubber, and held up a washcloth as he approached. After gently, wordlessly ministering to her, he tossed the cloth aside and slid back into bed.

He gathered her close, and Frannie let herself relax into his warm safety.

Chapter Twenty-Two

For the first time all day, Max felt like he could truly breathe. He sank against his pillow, with Frannie nestled against him, and let go of everything. The terror of Lucy's fall, the blame that had sunken in once he got her to safety. The completely different fright that took hold when Frannie noticed her charm around his neck.

Her reaction had bowled him over. And then he'd lost his breath to her—repeatedly—in all the best possible ways.

He inhaled her lovely floral perfume now and savored the perfection of the moment. She snuggled—cooried—closer, and a slow smile spread across his face.

He never wanted to move again, but he knew she had responsibilities, so he risked a question. "Do you need to get back right away?"

"Lucy was fast asleep when I left, and Mum's keeping an eye on her. I can stay for a bit."

He tightened his hold on her. "Good."

The breath of her chuckle tickled his chest.

"So, Lucy really liked my drawings that much, huh?" It seemed like such a small thing to do to bring a smile to her face, so he was honored, and humbled, by how much it meant to her.

Frannie lifted her head and placed a kiss on his chin. "She did."

He brushed her hair back from her forehead. "She's a phenomenal kid, Frannie. You're doing a fantastic job of raising her."

Her eyes grew misty as she rested her chin on his chest, still holding his gaze. "Thanks," she whispered. "I do worry sometimes… Okay, a lot. I want better than the best for her." The corners of her mouth tipped up. "I don't know how much of it is due to me, but she is pretty phenomenal."

Max kissed her temple. "Believe me, she gets a lot of it from you."

She settled her cheek against his shoulder. Her fingers traced lazy patterns in the hair on his chest, and he nearly purred like a contented cat.

"Can I ask you something?" he ventured quietly, rubbing the soft skin of her back.

"Mm-hmm."

"Did, um…did Marty ever get to meet her?"

Her hand stilled, and he worried that he'd overstepped. But the rise and fall of her back remained steady, giving him the sense that she simply needed a moment to compose her thoughts.

"He did. Once."

He nodded, unsure how else to respond, and continued stroking her back. After a beat, her hand resumed tracing his chest.

"When he finished basic training," she continued, voice calm and steady, "his unit was stationed in Hawaii for a while. Before they moved deeper across the Pacific." Irony crept into her voice. "We were so in love, but only got to be married a little over a year. And hardly married, at that. I can count on one hand the number of weeks we actually lived under the same roof. No time to even memorize each other's habits, see how we'd handle days like…"

Like today.

The words hung, unspoken, in the air between them. Max squeezed her a tiny bit tighter.

"Anyway," she continued, "he was still in Honolulu when I went into labor. They got word to him, and his C.O. was simply wonderful. Granted him a short leave and put him on a cargo plane back here. We got to have a few days, the three of us."

"I'm glad," he whispered.

"Me too." Her lips curved upward. "We spent most of the time just passing Lucy back and forth between us. She was so tiny.

"We did manage to put her down for a wee bit, though. Talked a lot that night. Neither of us wanted to, me especially, but it was important to Marty, so…"

Her hand stilled, and she slid her arm more fully around him, clinging snugly. He reciprocated, holding his breath.

"I don't know if it was some kind of premonition, or only the worry of anyone going off into danger, but he needed to hash out the details about what would happen if…"

"He didn't come back?"

"Yeah."

Max held her close, his heart breaking for what she'd had to endure, everything she'd lost. He willed his strength into her as she spoke.

"Marty lost both his folks before we met, and didn't have much other family, but he had some savings socked away. He was awfully relieved I had an accounting job lined up. He had a lot of faith in me." She sniffed. "I wasn't so sure myself, but he knew I'd be okay. He wanted, more than anything, for me and Lucy to be happy. He was so thrilled he got to hold her, to hold us both. Before we knew it, his leave was up and he flew back to Hawaii."

Her next inhale was sharp, her voice now barely a whisper. "Only a few months later, he was gone."

He pressed a kiss into her hair. "I'm so sorry, Frannie."

She pushed tighter against his side, and they held each other, breathing and heartbeats eventually syncing.

Frannie finally broke the silence. "I'm eternally grateful for those few days. That he got to know her, even for that little bit."

"I'm sure he'd be awfully proud of the person Lucy's becoming," he mused. Frannie hummed her agreement. "And it might be a little presumptuous of me, but…I think he'd be proud of all you've done, too. For her, and for yourself."

He held still, waiting for her response. She blinked a few times, her eyelashes fluttering against his skin, and raised her head. Her eyes were full of tenderness and appreciation. Something else hovered behind it all, something he hardly dared to hope for.

She cupped his cheek, gently trailing her thumb along the edge of his beard. "Thank you, Max," she said fervently.

She leaned in to kiss him. It was lingering, much gentler than their earlier kisses. Yet it stole the air from him, and filled him more completely than anything else in his life.

When they broke apart, she settled back against his chest, and they both sighed contentedly. It only took a few minutes for Frannie to sink into sleep. As exhausted as he was, Max wasn't far behind.

He drifted off, arms full of Frannie, and heart full of her too. He fell more in love with this brave, beautiful woman with every breath he took.

MAX WOKE SOMETIME LATER. The two of them had shifted at some point in the night, and he lay spooned around Frannie, her arm clutching his tight to her chest. He'd slept soundly, and she still did as well—no surprise given everything, difficult *and* miraculous, that had transpired.

He allowed himself a few peaceful minutes to watch her sleep, but his internal clock registered the fast-approaching dawn. As much as he hated to, he should rouse her.

Unsure of the type of person she was in the morning, he thought it best to ease her into it, starting with a few light kisses on her shoulder. When she stirred, a slow smile spreading across her face, he ventured further, trailing his lips up her deliciously soft neck.

"Frannie?" he whispered against her ear.

Her contented hum dissolved into the sexiest uttering of his name he'd ever heard, and he had to forcibly remind himself why they should get up.

He continued his string of kisses while he spoke. "We've been here nearly all night."

She turned her head to stare up at him, her expression a perfect blend of dreamy and seductive. "It was a very nice night," she purred.

"It was," he agreed, as their lips found each other. He'd be perfectly happy to never leave their spot.

But reality lay close by, and for her sake, he didn't want to ignore it. He pulled his mouth from hers with a groan.

"As extraordinary as it's been, it'll be dawn soon. You probably want to head back home."

She shifted to face him more fully. "Trying to get rid of me, are you?" Her tone was playful, her little smirk teasing, but he also caught a flash of disappointment, a hint of the uncertainty that clouded her the night before, when she'd asked why he left the doctor's office.

It had pierced his heart then, and the sting sharpened now.

"I'd love nothing more," he rasped, "than to close the bakery today." He dragged his lips against hers. "Ask you to play hooky from work." This time he nipped her bottom lip with his teeth. "And keep you in my bed all day long." He finished with a shift of his hips, nestling his steadily hardening cock against her lush bottom. Her sharp inhale made him grit out, "Hell, I'd keep you here all damn week."

He scanned her face, making sure that trace of doubt had evaporated before he continued. "But…"

Her resulting growl, and pout, made him laugh. He kissed the tip of her nose.

"*But*…there's a little girl next door who'll be waking up before long," he said. Frannie's face softened immediately. "And while

I'm sure she's having a very good sleep and doing just fine," he reassured her, "I also know how much it would hurt *your* heart"—he brushed his fingers over the spot on her chest—"if you're not there when she wakes up."

She sighed around a smile. "You're right."

"Yeah, those two words are never going to get old, coming from you." He winked.

Frannie swatted his shoulder playfully, and he tightened his arms around her with a laugh. Despite his firm grip, she managed to wriggle around to face him, and pulled him in for a kiss. They melted into each other for a long, lovely moment, before resting their foreheads together.

"In all seriousness, though," he said quietly, "I know we have lots still to talk about. Certainly a hell of a lot more to *do* to each other." He pressed his erection against her stomach and they both groaned. "But we've got plenty of time."

She nodded, her blue eyes clear and sober, her desire to trust him evident. And god, he'd do everything in his power to earn that trust and keep it. He loved her so damn much.

He almost told her. The words hovered in his throat, but the fragility in the air around them gave him pause. He didn't want to ruin things by voicing it too soon, to risk scaring her away. Not yet.

Instead, Max trailed his finger down her cheek, holding her gaze steadily. "I'm not going anywhere, Frannie." He kissed her temple. "Go take care of your girl."

Frannie smiled, leaning in for one more kiss before she eased out of his arms.

They fell into an easy quiet as they rose and tracked down her clothes from the many places they'd been scattered the night before. Max threw on some shorts and his robe and walked her to the door. They paused on the landing, taking in the tiny wash of light blue hovering near the horizon, a sign of the impending fresh, new day.

"Want me to walk you over?" Max whispered.

She flattened her palms against his chest. "I'll be okay."

"Are you sure? It's quite a trek. You might get lost."

Her laughter provided an excellent buffer against the early-morning chill lingering in the air. "Don't worry, I can use the stars for navigation." She cast a glance over her shoulder. "And the porch light."

He drew her in for yet another kiss, their mingled laughter dissolving magically.

"I was thinking…" he asked. "Would it be okay if I stopped by later, brought Lucy some snickerdoodles?"

Frannie's smile dazzled him. "I'm sure she'd love that." She skimmed her hand over his cheek, and he leaned into the touch. "I would too." She rose on her toes to give him one last peck. "Good night, Max."

"Good morning, Frannie."

Her melodic laugh trailed her down the stairs, and he leaned his forearms on the railing as he watched her cross the alley. She must have sensed his attention, because she turned at her back door and blew him a kiss. He raised his hand in a wave, and she disappeared inside.

Max lingered there a while longer, surrounded by a blissful sense of peace, until the brightening sky nudged him back inside to get ready to open the bakery.

Chapter Twenty-Three

To Frannie's tremendous relief, Lucy bounced back quickly. Her pain subsided after a couple of days, and while Frannie kept her home an extra day, she was hopping to get back to school—mostly to start collecting signatures on her cast.

Frannie suspected the steady stream of well-wishers in those first few days had brightened her daughter's mood and set her recovery in motion even faster. In addition to her and Betty's fussing, Colin and Nate, along with Lois and Nick, came over for endless rounds of board games and charades. And of course, Max supplied endless batches of cookies—and smiles.

Since everything that transpired the night after Lucy's accident, they found it impossible to keep their hands off each other, if even for the smallest touches of comfort. A warm hand on her back had her leaning into his side; she'd skim the short hair at the base of his neck in passing. One afternoon, she came out of the kitchen to find a surprisingly contentious game of Chutes and Ladders in progress, and Max slung an arm around her shoulders and began filling her in on the gossip she'd missed. She slipped her own arms around his middle, and they stayed like that long after he finished his story, laughing at the increasing chaos before them.

The cat was well and truly out of the bag at that point, but neither of them minded anymore. Their friends, to their credit, didn't press for details, but simply threw them raised eyebrows and delighted grins every chance they got.

Frannie's heart became further ensconced in Max's capable care.

Somewhere along the way, she'd fallen in love with him. And it terrified her less and less every day. She'd yet to work up the courage to actually tell him that, but she'd get there eventually. She hoped.

After a few weeks and a thousand kisses—plus plenty of utterly glorious fucking—Frannie felt happier than she had in years. Maybe ever.

She derived particular enjoyment from her current evening's occupation, with one of Max's strong hands in hers, and his other white-knuckling the edge of her kitchen table.

"So you made it a practice to massage all your clients?" he gritted out.

"Sure did." She grinned as she focused on her ministrations. "Better tips that way."

He grunted in response, making her smile even wider. When he'd expressed his curiosity over her manicure style in her previous career, she'd pulled out her old kit and decided to show him rather than tell. It was extraordinarily satisfying watching his composure erode while she stroked his warm skin.

She pressed her thumb into his palm, and he sucked in a sharp inhale.

"You okay over there? Was that too much pressure?"

He swallowed hard. "The pressure is…fine." He shook his head and muttered, "I can't believe I thought this was a good idea. Hands… Touching of hands… So. Much. Touching."

She fought the urge to laugh, instead batting her eyelashes at him with mock innocence. "You don't like…touching?"

Max narrowed fiery eyes at her. "When your mother is in the house and could walk in any minute to find me levitating the table with this situation?" He gestured at his lap. "No. I don't like it."

She did laugh at that. "My apologies. Would you like me to move on to filing?"

"That might be for the best. You're very good at what you do."

Frannie heated at the compliment. "Thank you." She picked up her nail file, attempting to preserve her concentration before she flipped the table over herself and straddled his lap.

He took advantage of the transition to shift in his seat with a grimace. "You might need to distract me with some innocuous conversation too."

She chuckled again. "Fair enough. Let's see…" She considered, but the first thing that popped into her head made her hesitate.

"What is it?"

"Well, there is something I've been wondering, but…it's not exactly innocuous."

"Try me."

He regarded her with such guilelessness, as if he really was an open book. So she forged ahead.

"I know you and Linda pretended to be engaged, but wasn't there ever anyone…truly special for you?"

She was determined to keep her attention on his nails, but when he didn't answer right away, she risked a glance at his face. A soft smile played at his lips.

"Not really, no," he replied. "I mean, I've dated plenty over the years, and there were a couple of gals I got sorta serious about, but…nothing that ever worked out. Either they didn't understand my wanting a career with such odd hours, or…" He shrugged his free shoulder. "There was just no lightning strike, you know?"

She nodded.

Max's expression turned introspective as he continued, "My folks have a great relationship, too. I grew up watching them, always so smitten with each other, and it stuck. I wanted that for myself, and I guess I was content to wait till I found it."

His eyes finished the thought. *And I finally have.*

Her breath hitched. "I get it."

As they stared at each other, she belatedly realized that she'd failed in her distraction tactics. The table might be a goner after all.

Her mum bustled into the kitchen, breaking the spell. Frannie startled, barely avoiding filing her own fingernail in addition to Max's.

Betty gave them a knowing smile and headed for the stove. "Don't mind me. I'll get my tea going and be out of your hair."

"You're not in our hair at all, Mum."

Max shot her an *I told you so* look, and they shared a silent laugh before he turned his attention to Betty. "I agree with your daughter." He lowered his voice to a conspiratorial whisper. "Though maybe it couldn't hurt to knock next time. You surprised Frannie enough, I thought I might lose a finger there."

Betty laughed heartily. "I will try to remember that."

Frannie tugged lightly on Max's middle finger. "Hey! I'll have you know, I have *never* had a casualty."

His lips twitched with mischief. "With your regular customers, sure. But how do I know this isn't some grand scheme to have your way with me?"

"Don't you mean 'do' away with you?"

He shrugged. "Po-tay-to, po-tah-to."

Frannie snickered, darting a warning glance at her mother, who'd turned pointedly back to her tea preparations. She cleared her throat and resumed her buffing, ignoring the heat seeping through her entire body from his hand. "Regardless, your fingers are perfectly safe with me. After all, Lois and Nate would come over here and murder me in my sleep if I messed with the instruments of their cheesecake comfort."

Max grinned. "Nick would lead the charge."

"Hell, even my own brother would probably pitch in."

"It is good to know my skills are such a precious commodity."

The sound of Betty's muted chuckle doused the growing conflagration between them.

"So, Mum," she bit out. "All ready for your trip?"

"That eager to get rid of me, eh?" Betty smirked.

Max snorted, and Frannie let out a strangled sound of her own. "No, of course not!"

"I wouldn't blame you in the slightest. After all, you're two grown adults who…"

Frannie dropped her nail file and buried her head in her hands. "Oh dear god."

Taking pity on them, Betty dropped the subject with another chuckle. "Relax, I'll say no more. And yes, I'm all packed. Although…" She grew serious. "Are you sure you don't want me to delay? I know how lousy the timing is, what with my leaving in the morning and Lucy's school holiday tomorrow."

Frannie softened, and grabbed her mother's hand. "You deserve a lovely road trip with your friends. And we'll be just fine. It's only one day, and she has plenty of minders."

Over a lively group dinner the week prior, she'd been debating aloud the merits of letting Lucy spend the day with Nancy and her mom—and the possibility of all kinds of candle-making mayhem—when her friends collectively chimed in with a plan to have her spend the day at the studio instead. Touched by their kindness, and knowing how much Lucy would enjoy it, Frannie agreed.

"You're sure?" Betty asked.

"Yes, Mum," Frannie said, all tender exasperation. "Nate's going to put her to work helping 'organize' her accessories closet, and Lois generously offered to take her on a tour of the lot to see how many movie stars' autographs she can collect on her cast. I talked to Lois's manager Anna yesterday, and even she's going to draft Lucy to help with passing out new production schedules."

When she finally came up for air, Max chimed in. "I have another training session tomorrow with Chris for Nick's movie. I'd be happy to take Lucy home when I'm finished, if she's feeling worn out from all that excitement."

Warmth flooded Frannie's chest. Again. "Thanks, Max."

Betty gave his shoulder a brief squeeze. "He's a good egg, this one."

"He is."

Frannie grinned at the furious blush peeking past his beard.

"Well, all righty then," Betty said. "I'll hit the road. And now I'll leave you to your manicure." She picked up her teacup and headed for the door, flashing a wicked wink over her shoulder before she left. "Don't do anything I wouldn't do."

Frannie groaned, and Max snickered.

"We really need to do this somewhere else next time," he huffed.

"Next time, huh?"

"Sure." He dropped all pretense of the propriety he'd attempted to display in front of Betty. He examined his newly manicured hand and held it up to her with a slight waggle of his fingers. "Got to keep these in good working order, don't I?"

His crystal-clear meaning lodged right between her legs, and she rose from her chair, grabbing his flourished hand and using it to yank him up.

He nodded toward her supplies on the table. "Are we finished here?"

"Honey, we're just getting started."

Max laughed as she tugged him out the door and over to his apartment for a little of that working order. It was only right she perform a quality check on her services, after all.

AS FRANNIE'S pencil flew over a column of budget numbers, she absently wondered about her daughter's current location. She reached the end of her tallying, then blinked a few times, coming more fully back to the present. Standing, she moved to the window in her office for a stretch break.

From her vantage point on the second floor, she scanned the lot. True to their word, her friends and colleagues had pitched in with Lucy all day, and she was inordinately grateful. Not only because it gave her time to crunch her numbers, but because her daughter would be crowing about her adventures for a long time.

Speaking of the little lass... Frannie spotted Lucy coming from the direction of writers' building with Colin. Based on the lumpy bag slung over his shoulder, she suspected they were on their way to a tap dance lesson.

The pair had barely traveled a few steps when they encountered another duo—Nick and Max. Frannie's smile melted into a delicious grin, and she shivered. The feel of his hands, and the magic they'd worked last night, were firmly imprinted on her.

The quartet headed toward the building that housed the studio's rehearsal rooms, and Frannie nearly ran out to join them. But her work beckoned, so she sank back into her chair, picked up her pencil, and banished all distracting thoughts.

After an hour of successful banishment, Frannie sat back in satisfaction, having finished her set of projections. With nothing else terribly urgent on her desk, she shot up out of her chair and ventured out to see what mischief her little d'Artagnan was getting up to with the Three Musketeers.

She started with the rehearsal building, gratified to hear the sound of tap shoes—one set heavy and confident; the other lighter, less experienced—down the hall, along with lively music. Someone plunked out a fair piano rendition of that silly "Cement Mixer" song. She hadn't quite reached the room when two voices started singing the ridiculous, but fun, lyrics.

Frannie picked out Nick's voice right away. Nothing to write home about—he'd always said he had no future in musicals—but he could at least carry a tune. The other voice, though, sounded rich and deeply melodic, despite its exaggerated and comical delivery. It did all kinds of lovely things to her insides—and it didn't take long to realize precisely why. She recognized those warm tones.

She peeked through the half-open door, and sure enough, Max

was one hell of a singer. *Add that to his never-ending string of surprises.*

Frannie thoroughly melted in appreciation as she took in the scene before her, and since no one had noticed her yet, she indulged herself by leaning against the doorframe to watch.

Her brother and her daughter danced in the center of the room. Lucy giggled while struggling to keep up, thankfully being careful with her arm. Colin, meanwhile, beat out a steady rhythm, at the same time making funny faces to fuel his partner's giggles.

It nearly brought tears to her eyes to see Lucy with her uncle, the two of them getting on better than Frannie had ever imagined —and she'd imagined plenty in the years she'd been separated from Colin.

Then there was Nick, practically Lucy's other uncle at this point, gleefully accompanying them on the piano. Always ready with a laugh. Currently harmonizing—not well—at the top of his lungs with Max.

Bloody extraordinary Max.

She swallowed around the lump in her throat, owing to how many sizes her heart had grown in the last minute alone.

Max kept time with Nick, a huge smile on his face as he watched Lucy and Colin, his dimples more pronounced than she'd ever seen them. The adoration in his eyes for Lucy, so thoroughly mutual, was overwhelming and beautiful. He was fast becoming a tremendous father figure to her.

A band squeezed around Frannie's chest at the thought. Joy nudged its way over and through the walls around her heart. And yet...

A tiny, warning voice echoed in the recesses of her mind—so small she struggled to make out what it was trying to say. *What if...?*

Thank the stars above, Lucy spotted her at precisely that moment. Frannie shoved her tangled emotions aside and focused on the fun emanating from the group.

"Hi, Mom!"

"Hello, love. This is quite the soiree."

"I'm having the best lesson! And my cast is only getting in the way a little."

Frannie smoothed a hand over her daughter's hair. "I'm glad."

"You should've seen it," Lucy beamed up at her. "I almost fell over, but Uncle Colin *and* Max *and* Nick all caught me!"

"Wow." Frannie looked up to find the trio giving her shy but reassuring smiles. Max mouthed, "She's fine," and she relaxed, rather enjoying the matching swaths of pink blooming on the gents' cheeks.

"I'm sorry I've been missing all the fun," she added. "That might be the best rendition of 'Cement Mixer' I've heard."

Nick chuckled. "I'm not sure they'd let us on the radio, but thanks just the same."

"Well, maybe not you," she replied, laughing at his snort of mock affront. She leveled a thumb in Max's direction. "This one, however... I had no idea you had such a lovely voice, Max."

His neck and cheeks took on a delightfully deeper hue, and he shrugged. "It's nothing, really."

"Oh, please," Nick interjected. "I told him for years he should enter the crooning game, but he steadfastly refused."

"And I told you," Max retorted, "I have precisely zero desire to be in front of a crowd. I'm perfectly happy leaving the crooning to Ronnie and the acting to you."

"All right, all right," Nick sighed.

As they all laughed, Frannie pulled Max aside, whispering low so only he could hear. "Since I'm hardly a crowd, please feel free to croon to me anytime."

He let out a small groan, and the sudden, molten lava in his gaze promptly incinerated her insides. "I'll keep that in mind."

Before they could dwell on the subject, Lucy called out from her seat on the floor, where she'd begun removing her tap shoes. "Hey, Mom, did you know there's a hotel where a train actually runs right through the middle?"

"I did not." She had a sneaking suspicion she was about to get railroaded right into a vacation, but played along anyway.

"Nick told me about it. He's been there! And it's right near where Grandma went on her trip!"

Frannie raised her eyebrow at the man, who had the decency to look sheepish. "It's true. It's up in Santa Barbara."

"Can we go visit, Mom? Please?"

Frannie chuckled. "We'll see, lass. Let's at least get that arm of yours recovered first, okay?"

Lucy's expression dimmed slightly, but she didn't give up. "Okay. But it would be so much fun. We can get Grandma to bring us with her next time. And Max too! He said his parents live near there. We can all go together! *Please?*"

"I..." Frannie froze. She hadn't expected railroading of such epic proportions. The warning bells returned, louder this time. *Lucy's getting so attached. What if...?*

Max stiffened beside her, and Nick and Colin shared a loaded glance.

"That does sound like a lot of fun, but you know, I'm not sure what my parents have going on," Max said slowly. "Not to mention your grandma. She might not want to go back so soon. Why don't we wait and see, Snickerdoodle? Like your mom said, you've got to get all better first anyway."

"Plus, you have school," Colin added.

"And that hotel's not going anywhere, don't you worry," Nick chimed in.

Lucy's eyes darted around to each of them, her disappointment clear, but not dangerously so.

Frannie was grateful to the three of them for stepping in. It gave her a chance to get her panicked head out of her arse enough to turn a smile on her daughter.

"I guess," Lucy conceded. "But you won't forget, will you, Mom?"

Frannie swallowed hard. "I won't."

Colin intervened once again, ruffling Lucy's hair. "Lucy, why don't we go back to my office to get the rest of your things?"

"Okay." She hopped up cheerfully, regular shoes back on and her letdown cast aside.

Colin took her hand and split a glance between Frannie and Max before leading his niece to the door. "See you all later. Thanks for the music."

"Yeah, thanks!" Lucy gave them an enthusiastic wave. "Bye!"

Frannie fixed her eyes on the door in their wake, but felt Max's wary gaze on her.

Nick spoke up quickly. "I'm so sorry about that. When she told us about Betty's trip, it reminded me of the hotel. I thought Lucy would enjoy hearing about it, but I didn't expect her to run with it." He grimaced. "Or that she'd seize on my mention of Max's folks, either."

She attempted a smile. "It's fine, Nick, really."

Unsurprisingly, Max picked up on her fudging of the truth. "Do you want to get some air?"

One look at his concerned face, and a little of her strange worry slipped away. "Sure."

"You two go," Nick said. "I'll close up here."

"Thanks," Max answered.

"Thanks, Nick. See you later."

"See ya."

Max offered his own goodbye, resting a featherlight hand on her back as they left the room.

Frannie already felt better by the time they reached the bright sunshine. She kept telling herself it wasn't a big deal, and though she was most of the way to believing it, that small voice didn't go as quiet as she wanted it to.

The two of them started walking, with no destination in mind. After a minute, Max asked softly, "You okay?"

She took in a cleansing lungful of air before answering. "Yeah, of course."

It wasn't only him she wanted to convince.

He took her arm gently and stopped walking. "Frannie, I…" His eyes pleaded with hers, and it worked; the scary voice retreated a bit more. "I hope you know, that was not an ambush. I swear. It happened just like Nick said. And I sure didn't expect her to spring it on you like that." He sighed. "Although I probably should've. She's awfully excited when she gets an idea in her head."

"She is." Frannie smiled genuinely. "And I believe you."

Max nodded. "I mean, don't get me wrong, it would be fun to take a trip with you both. And I would love, at some point, to introduce you to my folks." His speech gained momentum, words running together. "I have no doubt you'd all get along great. But I'm not pushing. I wasn't about to suggest it, not yet. It…it's way too soon, I know that. We're still figuring all this out and…"

Her heart seized at his mounting worry, which only refueled her own turmoil. She truly hated wondering if she, and especially Lucy, were getting too attached to Max. If it was wise to reinvest her heart. Nor could she ignore the fact that she was indeed falling in love with him. She didn't want to push him away. Not anymore.

So she gave the nagging, vicious voice inside her a final shove, focusing instead on his beautiful eyes. She ran her knuckles over his cheek.

"I know, Max. And we'll keep figuring it out. Lucy caught all of us off guard for a minute there, but it's good. *We're* good."

His eyes softened. "Yeah?"

"Yeah."

He dimpled under her hand, and shifted his head to kiss her palm. "Okay."

"Want to join us for dinner later?"

"I'd love that. Still want me to take Lucy home now?"

"That'd be great. I should finish up a few things before I leave."

They parted ways with a quick kiss. And she hoped with all her heart that she had her fleeting panic well tamed.

Chapter Twenty-Four

*P*recisely four days later, Frannie came home from work to find an empty house, with giggles of delight echoing from the backyard. She headed toward the sound and spotted Max through the screen door, sitting on the porch steps with Betty, who'd returned the day before. They watched Lucy in the yard.

Frannie joined them with a cheerful greeting, then glanced over to where Lucy sat, or rather wiggled, in the center of the grass. It took Frannie a minute to discover the source of her mirth. And then she froze.

Lucy was playing with a puppy.

A brown and white, shaggy, spaniel-type puppy. Utterly adorable. And utterly the last thing they needed to add to the current chaos of their household, especially given the cast Lucy still had to wear for a few more weeks.

"Look, Mom! Isn't he the cutest thing you've ever seen?"

"He's very cute." She spoke around a tight smile. Her gaze snapped sharply down to Max.

His expression was bright, and he'd been about to speak when he caught sight of her face. His brows knitted together.

"Max, could I have a word with you? Inside?"

"Of course."

Her mum sent her a questioning look as Max got to his feet, but Frannie stayed her with a shake of her head and a slight nod in Lucy's direction. Max followed her inside, and she led him all the way to the living room at the front of the house, where there was less chance they'd be overheard.

"Frannie, is everything okay? Did something happen at the studio?"

The concern in his voice was too much to bear. She whirled around to face him. "I can't believe you got my daughter a puppy without asking me!" she hissed.

When his eyes widened, she dimly registered that her words had come out harsher than she intended, but it did little to curb her mounting exasperation.

He held up a placating hand. "I didn't—"

She waved hers dismissively. "Don't try to downplay this, Max. Did I hallucinate the puppy Lucy is currently wrestling with in my backyard?"

"Of course not, but—"

"What the bloody hell were you thinking?" As much as the rational side of her suspected she should let him explain first, she felt powerless to stop the onslaught of her consternation. So she surrendered and gave it free rein.

"This is a terrible idea! We have enough going on in this house, between my work and my mum's. And Lucy's arm is still mending!" She pointed angrily in the direction of the yard. "So you thought, let's add a *dog* to the mix? Not even a mature dog. A fucking puppy! One who'll need to be watched and trained and cleaned up after. And it doesn't matter how much she'll pledge to take care of him. You know who it's going to fall on. *All* of it.

"And that's not even the bloody worst part." She'd started pacing, and threw in a few wild gesticulations for good measure. "She's met him. They're out there bonding. And she'll look at me with puppy-dog eyes of her own, and I'll be helpless to deny her anything, especially after how tough she's had it lately. There is no way I can tell her she can't keep him. Not now."

She finally stilled, chest heaving. Max stood, eerily calm, arms crossed tightly over his chest. The only indication he felt anything at all was the frequent, steady flaring of his nostrils. Unlike her, he seemed to be keeping a tight lid on his anger.

"Are you finished?" he asked quietly.

Pure, stubborn pride made her deliver one more jab. "You should have asked me."

A muscle ticked in his jaw, and he took a long, slow breath before speaking. "It wasn't necessary to ask you."

Her temper flared, but he stilled her argument in its tracks with a look that revealed his own simmering, but no less potent, fury.

"It wasn't necessary," he repeated. "Because I didn't get *Lucy* a puppy. I got *myself* a puppy. And not even permanently, at that. Which you would know, had you let me explain."

"You… Oh."

"Yes. Oh." His voice remained deadly calm, which was more unsettling than if he'd started yelling. "Mrs. Hammond, from around the corner? Her dog had a litter recently, and she's not in a position to keep them all. That little guy is the last one she hasn't found a home for, but she needs to start weaning him from his mom, so I agreed to take him in until she finds someone for the long haul."

Her anger fizzled out of her, while chagrin flowed in to take its place.

"I believe I told you that I wanted a dog at some point?" He raised a questioning eyebrow, but didn't give her the chance to answer. "I figured this was a good trial run. To see if I was ready yet, or if it's still too much with running the bakery."

"That makes sense," she said quietly.

"And I thought, given everything Lucy's been through—and the puppy too—that they might enjoy each other's company for a little while."

"Right. Of course."

"If I'm not even sure *I* can deal with a puppy right now, I wouldn't foist one off on you without warning." His tone softened slightly. "You have to know that, Frannie."

"I do." At his doubtful look, she repeated, "I do. Really. I... jumped to conclusions."

His sigh was heartbreakingly weary. "I thought we'd moved past that."

"I thought so too," she whispered honestly. "I'm sorry, Max. It's probably just the stress of everything with Lucy, and the fact that this"—she gestured between them—"is all so new and different. And after everything the other day, with the prospect of Santa Barbara and your parents...the puppy hit me funny."

His chest deflated on a harsh exhale. "I knew you weren't okay." He rubbed the back of his neck before meeting her eye. "Why did you hide it from me?"

She wanted to go to him, wrap her arms around him—for her comfort as well as his—but she stayed frozen in place.

"I don't know."

"Frannie."

"I don't!" She started pacing again, more slowly this time. "I've been really happy lately, Max. I like this...thing between us." She hated reducing them to a *thing,* but she struggled, unsure of her words. Unsure where these feelings were coming from. "But everything's changing so fast."

"Not entirely." His voice was raw, rough as sandpaper. "No matter how much progress we make, we always seem to end up back in this same circle, don't we? Misunderstandings, assumptions. Instead of talking to each other."

The hurt in his eyes—and the truth of his assessment—killed her. She trusted him, she truly did. Only a few days ago, she'd pledged not to push him away. But here she was, doing it anyway.

"If we have any chance of making this work," he continued, "we've got to talk to each other. We've got to be *partners.*"

His words struck a powerful chord within her. She wanted that too. She'd been reveling in the partnership they'd begun to forge.

But what if you keep letting him in…and then he goes away?

And there it was. The scared, scary voice inside her, rising up. Growing more persistent by the day, despite her efforts to shut it out.

"I know, Max. I know." She raised her eyes to his, the pleading warmth in them squeezing her heart. She choked out the truth. "But I'm scared."

He melted at that. He cautiously raised his hand to brush her hair back from her face, his thumb caressing her cheek in passing.

"Aw, Frannie. I can only imagine. You have every reason to be scared. Of course you do."

His acknowledgment, his acceptance, of her fear brought tears to her eyes. It was a huge relief, while simultaneously compounding the problem. He was just too wonderful—she had no idea what she'd do if she lost him.

She opened her mouth to say something, anything, but no words would come.

He watched her carefully for a moment, and when she still couldn't speak, seemed to come to a decision.

"Frannie, I love you."

Her breath stalled. The temptation to say it back—because she sure as hell felt it—surged through her bones. But…

She wasn't sure if she was grateful or not that he didn't give her time to respond.

"I started falling the night we met, and I've never stopped. I want you to know, I'm all in, in all ways." He took a shaky breath, gently cradled her face in both of his hands. "And because of that, I'm not going anywhere." He said it slowly, deliberately, and she willed that foolish voice inside to listen to him.

He swallowed hard, and she braced herself for what might be coming next. "But I understand how much you've gone through, love. So if you need…time…I can give you time."

Tidal waves of emotion crashed through her. The relief alone nearly felled her, but it wasn't only that. Gratitude that he understood, worry that she'd make the wrong move.

And love. Of course, there was love.

A few of her tears spilled over, and Max immediately caught them with his thumbs, prompting a few more to follow.

Frannie sniffled. She wanted to wrap her arms around him, cling tight and bury her face against his big heart. To say *fuck time*, and hold onto him forever, starting right then and there. But another part of her, feeling somehow both foolish and wise at the same time, told her that Max was right.

She couldn't keep hurting him, holding him at arm's length, out of fear. So perhaps she did need time. If he was handing it to her, willingly, it might be the best thing for both of them if she took it.

Frannie looked up into his beautiful maple eyes, and wrapped her hands around his wrists, his steady pulse beneath her fingers steadying her. "Maybe…" she whispered, "maybe that's a good idea. A little time."

They watched each other, neither of them moving, until finally he nodded.

"Okay," he breathed. "Okay." He gave her a wavering smile, his eyes taking on a sheen of moisture to match hers.

He pressed a light, yet utterly searing, kiss to her lips, and her grip on his arms tightened, her nails likely leaving marks.

"I'm not going anywhere," he repeated against her mouth. And then he pulled back, taking her breath with him. He gave her one last, small smile, before stepping around her and moving for the door.

She inhaled shakily.

"Wait!" Suddenly, she wasn't quite ready for her time to start. She whirled to face him. "What about your puppy?"

"Oh, right." He glanced back toward the kitchen, a pained look crossing his face. "Lucy can play with him for a little longer. I'll, um…I'll send Linda over to get him later."

Linda, not him. To give her space, or because he simply couldn't face her, she wasn't sure.

"Okay."

He didn't move right away, drinking her in, memorizing her. She let herself do the same.

"I'll see you," he rasped.

She managed a nod.

Max turned hurriedly, as if he couldn't bear another second. The minute the door snicked shut behind him, Frannie sank onto the couch. Her breath was steady; no sobs wracked her chest. Instead, the tears rolled down her face in a slow stream.

It was only a little pause. A chance to catch her breath. To vanquish the fear.

And try not to make the biggest mistake of my life.

Chapter Twenty-Five

Max scribbled a few notes in his recipe book and resumed his contemplation of the tea cake in front of him. Between the afternoon lull and having Linda out making deliveries, he was alone in the quiet bakery, and he'd fallen into what had become a habit in the few days since he'd left Frannie's living room.

Pushing through how fucking miserable he felt by attempting to find the secret of her family's recipe. Without her.

He was fully aware that it might not be the best habit at the moment.

In his defense, he'd never really stopped working on the recipe since that perfect night in his kitchen, wanting to get it right for her and have something ready when they resumed their "lessons." Now he didn't know how he'd get the cakes to her to see if he did crack the code—or if he even should.

But when he moped, he coped by baking. And despite everything, he still wanted to deliver Frannie this comfort. Somehow.

She had good reason to be scared. Life hadn't been kind to her. He'd give anything to take away her pain, banish her fright. While he wished she'd opened up to him sooner, he also sensed, deep down, that this was something she needed to work through, mostly on her own. In his low moments, however, he wondered if she'd see it as him walking away from her, anyway.

And holy hell, did he miss her.

Not just her laughter and her kisses, the way she fit in his arms, how alive he felt in her presence. Somewhere along the way, her tit-for-tat had gotten under his skin as well. She'd pushed him to take some comfort of his own. Her massaging manicures, her business advice, her over-the-top dinners—they all meant more to him than he could even articulate.

He only hoped he was doing the right thing.

He didn't know how long he'd been staring, unseeing, at the tray of tea cakes in front of him, but the chime of the bell above the door brought him back to the present.

"Lois, hi."

"Hey, Max." She walked up to the counter, peering at the tray. "Find the meaning of life yet?"

"What?"

She nodded at the pastries. "The way you were contemplating them, I thought you might have found it."

He huffed a slightly bitter laugh. "Believe me, I'm trying."

Lois regarded him with an unreadable expression, and when added to his previous line of thinking, it amplified all his doubts, putting him on the defensive. Suddenly wary of her motivation for stopping by, he crossed his arms over his chest.

"So, are you here to tell me I'm a jackass for abandoning your friend to face her fears alone?"

"No." Her tone was simple, direct. Honest. "You are not a jackass, Max. Nor have you abandoned her. I believe—and I think she does too—that this is what you both need right now." Her lips curved into a smile. "And you're my friend too, you know. Which is why I'm here. To see how *you* are doing."

The fight went immediately out of him. He was touched by the sentiment behind her words. He started to answer, intending to bluff his way through and maybe even convince himself in the process. Then he caught sight of Lois's green eyes, assessing him sharply, kindly. But thankfully, without pity.

It broke his resistance, and his shoulders sagged. "I'm...not doing too great, actually."

"I suspected as much."

He was suddenly desperate for her calm, level-headed second opinion. "You really don't think I'm making a mistake?"

She shook her head. "As shitty as I'm sure it feels, no. After dancing around each other for ages, you two got serious pretty fast. Given everything in her past, it's understandable that Frannie might need a minute. And you have to protect your heart, too. It can't be easy, always waiting for the other shoe to drop, worrying that she'll bolt like she did on V-J Day."

Max blinked. "She told you about that?"

"She did. Right after that little tiff of yours I walked up on." She held up a finger. "And for the record, I told her she needed to get her head out of her ass and talk to you about it."

He fought through his haze of embarrassment to smile at her. "Thanks."

"Don't be too grateful—your head was up yours too, sir. I can't believe how long you went..." She trailed off with a shake of her head. "But that's neither here nor there. You got it together. And you're doing the right thing now."

As relieved as he was to hear her affirmation, it did little to make him feel better. "I know. I think. But why does it feel so godawful?"

Lois shrugged, and said simply, "Because you love her."

He hung his head with a groan. "I do. So damn much."

"Come here." Lois took his arm and tugged him toward one of his cafe tables.

"What...?"

She pointed at the chair. "Sit."

When he started to argue, she shoved him gently into the seat, then glided over to the counter. She pointed to the space behind it. "May I?"

Lois was in full regal empress mode, giving him the look that had leveled many a Hollywood honcho and made her an excellent studio head. There was no way he could refuse, even if he wanted to.

At his assent, she stepped into his domain, immediately washing her hands—which he greatly appreciated. She moved quickly, grabbing a plate from his shelves and pulling something from his refrigerated case. Before he knew it, she strode back over to him with a generous slice of chocolate cheesecake.

His lips curved into his first smile in days. "What's this?"

"A taste of your own medicine." She grinned as she set the plate in front of him. "Eat up."

He launched a feeble protest, mostly out of a sense that he shouldn't spend his workdays sampling his own wares, but she waved him off as she sat opposite him.

"Max. Take a bite. It'll make you feel better." Her smile softened again. "Trust me, I speak from tremendous experience."

He chuckled and gave in to her command. He closed his eyes as the smooth chocolatey bite dissolved against his tongue. Okay, maybe she did have a point.

"Was I right?"

"A little," he admitted.

"Good. Do you know how many wonders this cake of yours has worked? For me, Nate, Colin…Nick." She hummed. "You've been providing him with treats, looking out for him, forever. And I'll always be grateful for the way you picked up his pieces when I went to New York." She laid a hand on his arm, nodding at his plate. "So it's about damn time you let one of us take care of you for a change."

"Thanks." Her words brought back his earlier musings, and Frannie's voice suddenly echoed through his head. *Who takes care of you, Max?* He closed his eyes against the searing vision of her blue gaze, blazing with desire and affection. Longing pierced his heart with a fierce stab.

"I don't want to lose her, Lois. I don't think I could survive it."

She squeezed his arm. "For what it's worth, I don't believe you will lose her."

He opened his eyes and voiced his deep fears, the ones he'd been attempting to ignore. "But what if she takes this time and decides she can't do this? Or worse, what if she thinks I've given up on her?"

"I can't presume to know what's in her heart, but I have no doubt she knows how much you care about her, Max. It's plain to see." Her mouth twisted in a sympathetic grimace. "I suspect that's what scares her the most."

Max did too. The knowledge was only a small comfort.

He swallowed around the lump in his throat and risked another bite of cheesecake. It really did help, somehow. "How the hell did Nick do it?"

"Do what?"

He met her eyes, wondering if he was crossing a line by bringing it up again. But they were friends, so he risked it.

"When you were in New York." She winced slightly, but didn't break eye contact, so he kept going. "I watched him, all that time. And yeah, he was pretty miserable. Sorry."

"It's okay, I know. I wasn't having a ball myself."

They exchanged small smiles, and he continued. "But as lousy as he had it, underneath it all was this…hopeful certainty. Like he knew, deep down, you'd be back."

"That nauseating Nick Bradley optimism," she muttered, voice full of love.

"Exactly." He shook his head. "As much as he missed you, he was so sure. I've never been less sure in my life."

"I can't speak to you and Frannie, how open you've been with each other. And it's not my business unless you want it to be. But I can tell you about me and Nick." She lifted one shoulder. "Before the shit hit the fan, we'd admitted how we felt about each other. Fully. That's why leaving was the hardest thing I've ever done in my life."

"I'm sorry for dredging it up," he said quietly.

"Don't be. It all worked out the way it was supposed to." She smiled. "But I think the reason I was able to go, and to come back, was that Nick let me know, in no uncertain terms, how much he loved me. As terrified as I still was that I'd ruined everything, I knew in the very marrow of my bones that he'd be here, waiting, when I got back."

"And he was."

"He was." She paused. "I meant what I said before. I'm sure she knows, too."

"I hope so." He grunted. "I hope she *believes* it. I just…" He ran his hands through his hair. "I want to *do* something."

"Bombard her with baked goods?"

Max chuckled wryly. "So much, you have no idea. I've actually been working on something, a project we started together, before…" He cleared his throat. "I really want to finish it for her, give her some comfort right now. But I don't want to push her too far, either. I promised her time, and the last thing she needs is me butting in, going back on that."

"Don't forget, you're not alone in this. If you'd like, I can put out a few feelers, see if she'd be open to it." She smiled. "I might be a little biased, but everyone deserves comfort in the form of your sugary artistry. And I have no doubt, should you decide to offer it, that you'll find your own perfect, quiet, Max way to deliver it to her."

"Thanks, Lois." He gave her hand a squeeze. "Nick's a lucky guy."

She squeezed back. "I know." They shared a laugh. "Frannie's lucky too, you know."

He nodded his gratitude, and was about to dive back into the cheesecake when the bell above the door sounded a second time. He looked up to find Lucy, a subdued but hopeful smile on her face.

Max sprang up from his seat. "Hey, Snickerdoodle." He couldn't help a glance behind her, but she'd come alone.

"Hi, Max. Hi, Lois."

"Hello, sweetie," Lois greeted her.

Lucy held up a scrap of paper. "I came over with a list."

He immediately recognized Frannie's handwriting. A good sign, perhaps. His foolish imagination wanted to believe it was her tiny way of reaching out.

"I'll get right on this," he told Lucy. But he paused, wondering if he should ask after her mother. He settled for, "So you're on your own today, huh?"

Lucy nodded. She chewed on her lip for a minute. "Mom hasn't been growling out her window, though."

A splinter hovered near his heart. "No?"

"Nah. She's mostly kinda sad."

The splinter plunged all the way in.

Lucy looked up at him, eyes wide and curious. "I thought she didn't like the puppy."

Max blinked. "The puppy?"

"Uh-huh. She's been sad since you brought him over to meet me. I was gonna ask you if I could help walk him sometimes, but then I thought she might not like it, so I asked her, and she said that would actually be nice." She took a breath, absently scratching at the edge of her cast. "All she'd tell me when I asked why she looked sad was that it was some grown-up worries. I've been giving her lots of hugs, though, and that makes her feel better." She finished with a shrug.

Max's mind—and heart—reeled. He wanted to scoop both Frannie and Lucy up in his arms and erase any and all worries they'd ever have. As tenuous as things were between him and Frannie, he consoled himself that he could at least take care of Lucy.

"Once you get to be a grown-up, there are a lot more things to fret over, I'm sorry to say."

"Do you worry about the same stuff Mom does?"

"Right now? I'm afraid so."

Lucy nodded as if she completely understood, and Max

couldn't help smiling. Until a new worry popped up. He crouched down in front of her.

"Lucy, your mom and I have had our fair share of…disagreements."

"The stuff that makes her growl."

He heard Lois snort behind him and allowed himself a smile. "Yeah. But I hope you know, probably the one thing we've always agreed on, without fail, is what a fantastic kid you are."

Lucy beamed at him. "Really?"

"You bet." He gently chucked her under the chin. "And you know, no matter what happens between me and your mom"—here, he offered up a silent plea for more good than bad in their future—"I'll always be your friend. And there will always be a couple of snickerdoodles here with your name on 'em. I promise."

She giggled. "Thanks, Max!"

Then she cocked her head to the side, considering him.

"Max?"

"Yeah?"

"You look almost as sad as Mommy. Do you want a hug, too?"

His throat constricted around the giant ball of emotion suddenly lodged there. "Sure," he choked out.

She reached up and swung her arms around his neck, nearly clocking him in the ear with her cast. He bit back a laugh at her enthusiasm, and then let his eyes drift closed for a moment, taking solace in this delightful child, already a daughter in his heart.

"I hope Mom starts growling at you again soon."

"Me too, Snickerdoodle. Me too."

She pulled back to grin at him, and he matched it. Between Lucy and that cheesecake, he actually felt better, more sure of himself.

"What do you say to a cookie now, while I get this order ready?"

"Okay!"

He stood and made his way behind the counter, catching

Lois's misty, all-knowing smile as he passed. He ducked his head and fetched Lucy's cookie, along with a glass of milk. She joined Lois at the table, and the two of them immediately fell into easy conversation.

"So, snickerdoodles, hmm?" Lois mused. "I'm partial to the cheesecake myself."

"That's good, too. Did you know, Max taught me to make these once."

"I bet that was fun."

"It was!" Lucy's voice took on a proud edge. "Max said I'd be good at it because I loved them so much, and that's an important part of baking."

"Here you go, kiddo." He set her treat in front of her.

"Thanks, Max."

On his way back to the counter, Max trailed his fingers longingly over Frannie's words. He halted at the last item on the list. *Chocolate Miracle Cake, 2 slices.* The comfort he'd given her once.

A glance at Lucy, enjoying the cookies she loved so much, conjured a memory of Frannie's voice once again. *The food of love…*

Those words, and the affection she'd infused into them, wrapped around him like a warm blanket. All the while, Lois's advice and show of solidarity shored up his resolve.

He'd figure out those tea cakes for Frannie. Because they would be *her* warm blanket.

"Hey Lucy, do you think you can get a message to your uncle?"

Chapter Twenty-Six

At the same moment, Frannie sat on her front steps, chin propped on her hand, thinking about her daughter's current whereabouts. She wasn't ready to venture next door yet herself, but she consoled herself with the fact that she could at least reach out through Lucy.

She hoped Max fared better than she did.

Her doubts and fears loomed large, keeping her suspended and indecisive. Despite how much she really fucking missed him.

A car pulled up to the curb in front of the house, and the best possible distraction from her mood got out.

"Colin! You're early. Dinner's not for a while."

Her brother rounded the car with a bright smile. "I was finished at work, and Nate's on a deadline crunch, so I thought I'd head over first and spend some extra time with my favorite sister."

"I'm your only sister."

He waved a dismissive hand. "Bloody semantics." He paused on the bottom step, a world of concern reaching her from behind his glasses. "How are you holding up, Mermaid?"

The endearment brought a bit of mist to her eyes, and she heaved a sigh. "Oh, you know. Just fucking swell."

Colin settled on the step next to her and slid his arm around her shoulders. "I suppose there's nothing I can do to help?"

"Not much." She leaned into his side. "But this is nice."

"Then this I will do." He kissed the crown of her head.

She let herself take comfort in her big brother for a few minutes.

"I love him," she whispered into his sweater vest.

"I know."

"But I'm scared."

"I know that, too."

"I don't get it." She pushed up to look at him. "I thought I was ready. It felt so…wonderful, being with him these last few weeks. And yet my courage fled with the wind."

"Please. You're one of the bravest people I know." He squeezed her arm, in the spot where her tattoo was. "Hell, this little spot of ink alone took more guts than I've got."

"Says the man who had several surgeries to fix his leg?"

"Yes. That was a necessary evil." He rubbed her arm. "You volunteered for this bollocks." She chuckled with him. "Don't worry, Fish. Your bravery is still in there somewhere."

"Then why does it keep fleeing when it comes to Max?"

Colin's eyes held sympathy. "Because you've faced an awful lot of loss, Fran. More than anyone should. And grief's a funny thing. It doesn't exactly follow logical rules."

"I think that's part of the problem," she grumbled. "I'm falling hard for Max. The thought of losing him…I don't know if I could face that. Not again. Not this time." She blinked against her threatening tears. "Plus, Lucy adores him. How can I risk putting her through the loss of a father figure she actually knows…"

"Like we did?"

She nodded dejectedly.

"It's not quite the same, you know." At her skeptical look, he explained. "We lost Pop twice. When he died, yes. But we each had to grieve him long before that. When he left us." He brushed her hair behind her ear.

Frannie's throat worked. "You had it worse, though."

"How do you figure?"

She shrugged. "He left you and your mum because he couldn't handle it, but then turned around and tried again with us. I can't imagine how shitty that must've felt."

"Pretty shitty. But it wasn't all bad." He nudged her. "I managed to get you in the bargain."

She smiled. "A damn lucky break for you."

"Indeed." Colin laughed, before sobering again. "But that's my point. Good did come out of it. Not that that, in any way, diminishes what you've gone through. You have every right to grieve."

"I just don't want Lucy to ever have to." She held up a hand. "And I know, it's a part of life and I can't shield her from everything. But I want to protect her from having to wonder if…if she wasn't enough. Or too much."

Colin sucked in a breath. "Frannie. It wasn't you, or me. Or even our mums. It was him."

"I know that. I do." She met his eyes directly. "I did worry about it, when I was younger. But I know better now." She sighed. "And I know Max is a thousand times the man Pop was."

"He is. You two are only at the beginning of things, but he's already a more devoted father to Lucy than Pop ever was with us."

Which was precisely the crux of her other, main worry.

"That does nothing to allay your other fears, though, does it?" Colin asked quietly, astutely. When she shook her head, he added, "We're not at war anymore."

"No. But…anything could happen, Colin." She chewed on her lip. "Whether it's something awful, or simply him deciding he's had enough when I finally push him too far."

"I very much doubt that would ever happen. Think of all the endless ways you've annoyed me over the years, and I'm still here."

He let out a gratifying *oof* when she elbowed him in the ribs.

"You almost weren't, though," she admitted. "When I think of all the time we missed… I should've found you sooner."

He smiled crookedly. "But we did find each other, love. In spite of all of my unsuccessful efforts."

"You at least looked! While I sat on my hands…" *Out of fear…*

"Because you were scared." He fixed her with an obnoxiously big-brotherish look.

She wasn't sure if it was a blessing or a curse that he understood her so damn well.

"You know," he continued, "I blamed myself. I felt like I failed you. It took Nate's scolding to finally break me of that notion."

Frannie snorted. "She's a wise woman."

"That she is. And I'm about to pass that wisdom along. Look at me?" He waited until she did. "You've suffered tremendous loss, Frannie. And you've kept going. For Lucy, for yourself. I cannot even fathom it." His hazel eyes shone behind his glasses as he gave her another gentle squeeze. "And I would give anything to take that pain from you, my darling lass. But if I may say…?"

She nodded, unable to form words around her gathering tears.

"It's more than understandable for your grief to linger, to pop up and take charge sometimes, at less than opportune moments. And you can't ignore it, or pretend you don't feel it when it does. But, if you can, try not to lose sight of the flip side, either. The miracles."

"I…" The truth of his words lodged in her heart. She had indeed lost sight of the miracles lately. "Oh, hell." She narrowed her eyes at her brother, in an attempt to distract herself, if only for a minute. "Are you about to throw Irving Berlin lyrics at me? Blessings over sheep?"

Colin snickered. "He's not wrong."

She rolled her eyes, stubbornly refusing to admit to agreeing with him. But finally—*finally*—wanting to laugh.

The edges of his smile softened. "Pop may have been a shitty father, but he gave me the best sister in the world. And even when war separated us, you and I managed to find each other again—in a bout of astronomically unlikely, yet serendipitous, circumstances. The fact that we ended up across an ocean, and a continent, at the same studio…with all the same friends…?"

"Pretty bloody miraculous."

"Precisely."

We managed to find each other again.

Frannie's breath hitched. "We weren't the only ones…"

Colin's smile brightened. "No, we weren't."

A sense of wonder, of hope—*finally, thank fuck*—bloomed in her chest. So much so, she didn't even register Colin's knowing acknowledgment.

Her history with Max was fraught, yes. But it was also as bloody miraculous as her reunion with her brother. An aspect of their story she'd ignored for far too long.

"Oh, I've let my worries turn me into a right numpty, haven't I?"

"Perhaps." At her glare, he chuckled and held up a calming hand. "But the fact that you've identified the problem is a good step in the right direction."

"Thanks. I think." She groaned, as a new concern reared its head. "I am so fucking tired of being afraid. But Col, what if it's too late? What if all this is just showing Max he's better off without me to deal with?"

"Not bloody likely." He cut off her impending argument with a stern look. "I mean it. Not only is Max a tremendously decent chap, but he's been smitten with you for ages. Long before either one of you would deign to admit it."

Frannie let out a grunt of indignation, despite Colin's utterly correct assessment.

"Besides," he continued, tapping a finger against the charm bracelet on her wrist, "the man's been wearing your charm around his neck for years. I think it's safe to say he won't be making a run for it anytime soon."

"I suppose you've got a point there." But then his words landed with a thud, and she twisted to face him more fully. "Wait a minute. How the hell did you know about the pencil? Did he tell you?"

Colin's cheeks flushed. "Ah. No. Nate, with her fantastic eye for detail, and adornments, and…" He trailed off when Frannie crossed her arms over her chest. "Anyway, she noticed Max's necklace—only a couple of weeks ago, actually. And when she mentioned it looked like a pencil…well, we started piecing it all together."

Frannie's mouth dropped open.

He rushed to explain more. "Between the various bits and pieces you'd told each of us—when you lost the charm, what else happened on V-J Day, that inexplicable animosity between you two…" He gave an awkward shrug. "It didn't take us long to finally figure it all out."

She stared at him, speechless, for a moment. "Why didn't you say anything?"

"You two were together by that point." His mouth kicked up into a smile. "You were happy, and we didn't want to rock the boat."

With a groan, Frannie buried her face in her hands. "Yeah, I'm plenty good at doing that all on my own."

Colin rubbed her back gently. "So the poor man threw up on you, and you really held it against him for ages?"

She sat back up and swatted his arm away. "If Max and I managed to move past all that, I am not rehashing it with you."

"Fair enough. But I believe you just dropped a key piece of information there…" He cocked an eyebrow.

We did *manage to move past it.*

Frannie nudged him. "You're a pain in the arse when you're right, you know that?"

"I do." He paused. "You love him, Frannie."

She exhaled, the truth settling around her like armor. "Awfully."

"Then I think you owe it to yourself to take the risk. You deserve to be happy, Mermaid."

No matter how she teased Colin, he *was* right. Max made her happy. And she was so fucking tired of pushing him away, of being afraid. She rubbed absently at her tattoo, letting it remind her, not for the first time, of her bravery.

Max was worth all the risks.

"Don't lose sight of the miracles," she whispered, echoing Colin's earlier words.

"I'm reminded of a tremendous piece of advice you yourself once gave me." He cleared his throat, his clipped English baritone slipping away. "What's fur ye'll no go past ye."

She choked out a laugh at his atrocious brogue.

"Colin Canfield, what have I told you about attempting a Scottish accent?"

He grinned, unrepentant. "That I'm terrible at it and should thus never even try, especially in your presence."

"And yet, you still haven't learned." She *tsk*-ed at him.

"You wouldn't have me any other way, and you know it." He tweaked her nose. "But my point still stands. You and Max are fantastic together. Meant for each other, even. All you have to do is take the leap."

"Easier said than done."

"True. But one thing Nate and I are learning is that burdens are a lot easier to bear when you can share the load. And Max seems to have very capable shoulders."

"He does." She wrapped her arms around Colin's middle. "Thanks, Chips."

"You are quite welcome, Mermaid." He gathered her against him, and she burrowed into his embrace.

As she leaned into her brother, her certainty mounted. A plan began to take shape. She needed to talk to Max, yes. To let him in, let him help ease her burdens.

But she also needed to ease his.

She'd come to love him with all her heart, and it was about damn time she let him know that.

<hr>

AFTER A FEW DAYS of getting her ducks in a row, Frannie vibrated with anticipation. She'd cemented her plan, put some of it into action already, and rehearsed everything she wanted to tell Max. All that remained was to get him in her presence.

So of course, she was wildly busy at the studio. With two huge productions about to begin, her entire workweek had been filled with crunching numbers and lining up last-minute funds for the various departments. And while it provided a soothing distraction from her churning anticipation, her patience was swiftly running out.

She bustled around the lot, delivering a final round of budget reports. She could have assigned the task to a page, but she preferred to be on hand in case anyone had any issues. Plus, the walk allowed her an outlet for her pent-up energy.

And helped quiet her remaining nerves.

She hoped like hell that Colin was right, and Max still wanted her. Still loved her.

On the way back to her office, she mentally crossed her fingers that she wouldn't find a slew of messages waiting for her, from people who'd belatedly decided they had questions about their budgets.

She swung open her door—and stopped in her tracks. Not in response to her blessedly empty inbox, but rather to what sat in the center of her desk.

A pink bakery box.

She whirled around to glance at the main office floor, but no one paid her any attention. Nor was there a handsome baker lurking nearby.

After closing the door, she approached the desk, barely daring to breathe. A note bearing her name sat atop the small box. She unfolded it slowly.

A wise woman once told me that I made the food of love, so I baked on.
I hope I got it right.

Love,

M.

P.S. Colin has the recipe…
P.P.S. Please don't feel you need to respond. I just wanted you to have a bit of comfort. If you need it.

Frannie gasped, blinking against the growing moisture in her eyes. She set the note down and carefully lifted the box's lid. A pair of tea cakes, looking *exactly* like her grandmother's, and her father's, stared back at her.

A sob escaped her throat, and her remaining nerves finally shut up.

"Oh, you wonderful, baking man."

She gulped a great, freeing breath, and glanced at her watch. It was barely two o'clock, but she'd met her deadlines, and any work that remained could bloody well wait for another day. Frannie gathered her things as quickly as she could, shut her office door, and hustled off the lot.

It was time to put Operation Woo Back Max Mitchell into effect.

She couldn't fucking wait.

Chapter Twenty-Seven

Max escaped to his apartment for his semi-regular afternoon break. He was far too keyed up to nap, but he suspected his combination of distraction and restless energy had been annoying the shit out of Linda all morning, so he'd removed himself from the situation.

He collapsed on his couch. He meant what he'd told Frannie about not expecting a response, but he was still dying to know how his cakes had gone over.

Colin had assured him, between sips of Alka-Seltzer, that he'd nailed the recipe. The poor guy had valiantly consumed an obscene number of taste-test samples, and then further cemented his application for sainthood by volunteering to deliver Max's gift to Frannie.

Now, all that remained was the waiting. The hoping.

He propped up his feet with a sigh. He'd always been a fairly patient person, but this was going to be agony, he just knew it. Sensing his need for a friendly face, his puppy rounded the couch, let out a tiny bark, and leapt up to join him.

"You know, Rudy, I should be training you *not* to be on the furniture with me."

Rudy responded by licking Max's chin and then sprawling—as much as one his size could—across Max's chest.

Max chuckled, scratching Rudy's head. For all his youth, the little fella was proving to be a pretty mellow dog. And exactly the friend he needed at the moment. Practically on cue, Rudy cuddled closer. "Thanks, pal."

The two of them lay there for a while, and Max enjoyed the dog's calming presence. But it wasn't long before Rudy started squirming slightly. He was a fast learner, but he was still a puppy, so Max brought him outside before he wound up with the aftermath of an accident all over his shirt.

He tried not to look at the house next door while Rudy did his business. He doubted anyone was home at this hour, but he assumed even the sight of her windows would trigger a fresh wave of longing, and he was trying to be mature. Calm.

Rudy yipped, and Max smiled down at him. "All done, buddy?" He started to lead him back to the stairs.

Just one glance couldn't hurt...

He risked it, and immediately stopped in his tracks. He blinked a few times, unsure if his eyes played a trick on him. But they didn't. There was definitely a candle in the kitchen window.

He peered closer. Not a candle. A candle *salad*.

He threw his head back, the bark of his laughter echoing through the alley and prompting Rudy to reply. His gaze tracked past Frannie's bedroom window, and he snorted. She'd positioned a second candle-cock monstrosity there.

All you have to do is say the word. Or better yet...just put a candle in the window.

His own promise came back to him, and his heart began to pound out a fierce, hopeful beat.

He scooped Rudy into his arms and bolted up the stairs to his apartment. "Sorry, pal, but you're on your own for a bit." The puppy licked his jaw, which he took as a gesture of solidarity and good luck. After setting him down, however, he paused, considering the damp spot left behind and whose lips could potentially, god-willing, be on his face next. And what a long day he'd put in at the bakery already.

With lightning speed, he washed up, ran a comb through his hair, and added an extra spritz of cologne for good measure. Feeling generous, he threw a few extra treats in Rudy's bowl to keep him occupied.

He'd never dashed across the alley faster.

FRANNIE WATCHED the back of the bakery like a hawk. She'd calculated that Max might be on his afternoon break, and hoped she hadn't set the "candles" out too soon. She had confidence in her construction skills, though, so she remained cautiously optimistic that her banana sculptures would hold up better than Nancy's.

She didn't have to wait long. Her breath caught as Max brought the puppy downstairs. The little lad was awfully cute, now that she had a chance to give him a proper look. And Max... Well, he was a heavenly sight for her sore eyes.

She grinned, reveling in the sight of his amusement. When he charged inside, it took every ounce of her self-restraint not to open the window and call out to him. But he *had* laughed, so she willed herself to believe that he'd come back.

Her heart soared when he did.

She opened the back door to find him with his fist primed to knock. He lowered it slowly, a shy smile on his face. Suddenly, she felt shy as well.

"Hi, Max," she whispered.

"Hi." He cleared his throat, gesturing toward the window. "Nice candle."

"Thanks. I hoped it would do the trick. And here you are."

"Here I am."

All the words she'd ever known bottled up in her throat. She wanted nothing more than to throw her arms around him and kiss him until neither one of them could breathe. But her words were awfully important, so she stepped back to usher him inside. She inhaled her favorite scent as he passed, and it buoyed her.

Max stood before her, hands in his pockets, with a stunning amount of affection in his eyes.

"I, um…" she croaked. She chuckled nervously. "I thought we could…talk."

"Of course."

He watched her patiently, letting her take the lead. So, naturally, everything she'd rehearsed in her head repeatedly over the last few days took a flying leap, right over her candle salad and out the window.

The pink box on her kitchen table caught her attention, giving her a lifeline to seize.

"Thank you for the tea cakes."

His lovely smile widened. "You're welcome. I…" He rubbed the back of his neck. "I wanted to give you a little comfort, a taste of home, in case you needed it. And, um…"

"And to let me know you were still here?"

He chuckled sheepishly. "Yeah. That too." He raised suddenly anxious eyes to her. "But I meant what I wrote. I promise, it was not my intention to put extra pressure on you."

Her heart overflowed at the care he always displayed so freely. "I know, Max."

He took a step closer, started to extend his hand, then stopped as if unsure whether he should. "Truly, Frannie. If you need more time, you've got it." He made up his mind and reached out to gently squeeze her upper arm.

She winced, unable to stop herself.

Max immediately retreated, his face falling. *Oh, fuck.*

"Sorry," he murmured.

"Max. It's not what you think."

"It's okay, Frannie. Really."

Her eyelids fell closed with a grunt of embarrassment and frustration. "No, I mean it." She closed the distance between them again. She wanted to reach for him too, but didn't dare. Once she touched him, she'd lose what little focus she had. "Max, look at me."

When he obeyed, she explained, "I added to my tattoo. The evening before last."

Relief wafted off him in a palpable wave. "Oh." His laugh held a tinge of his own embarrassment. Then his eyes widened, and his hand hovered over her arm, careful not to actually make contact this time. "Aw, geez, did I hurt you?"

She shook her head. "No, it's just a wee bit tender, is all. You took me by surprise more than anything." Frannie rolled her eyes with a groan. "I *was* saving it for a big, slam-bang finish, you know. All the places you could've touched me, and you...had to pick that one."

The prospect of all those places, all that touching, hovered in the air between them. His eyes heated and darkened, and she bit her lower lip. He tracked the movement, his throat working on a swallow. Frannie sucked in a sharp breath.

No. Get all this out first. Then *you can touch the hell out of each other.*

"Anyway. Finale. Supposed to be." She shook her head. "But I might as well open with it instead."

Max gave her an amused smile. "Okay."

She stepped back and slipped off her cardigan, tossing it on the chair next to her. She presented her tattooed arm to him, holding her breath.

He peered at it, his face oddly quizzical. "So Betty relented, huh?"

"What? No." She huffed a laugh. *Poor, clueless Max.* "If that were the case, it would say *Mum.*" She flattened her tone to a more American, nasal pronunciation. "Not *Mom.*" Nodding to her arm, she added, "Look closer."

He bent to do so, his breath coasting over her skin. She fought a shiver, not wanting to disturb his concentration.

"What am I supposed to be seeing?" He paused. "Those little

dots after each…letter…?" *There it is.* She felt, as well as heard, his breath hiccup. "They're…initials."

"M-O-M."

Max Orsino Mitchell raised his eyes to her slowly—eyes suffused with hope and joy and affection. Her answering wave of love began deep in her chest and made its way outward to her smile.

"Frannie. Really?"

She shrugged. "You started imprinting yourself on my heart the night we met. It might have taken me an unforgivably long time to admit it to myself, but I figured it was about damn time I broadcast it to the world. And to you."

His watery laugh was the best thing she'd ever heard.

She cupped his face in her hands, the familiar bristle of his beard a balm to her soul. "I love you, Max. I'm sorry I didn't tell you sooner."

He shook his head. "You're telling me now. That's all that matters." He laughed again, trailing his finger below her tattoo, careful not to graze anywhere that might hurt. "And here you swore you'd never put me on there."

Frannie chuckled. "You're the Shakespeare man. You should've recognized a lady protesting too much."

"Well, I didn't want to say…" He winked, before growing serious again. "And I guess my poor, besotted heart didn't dare hope."

She drew in a breath. The words that eluded her earlier returned—a good thing, since she was more than ready to say them now. She stepped back a fraction, not to distance herself, but to look at him more fully.

"That night on the soundstage, I didn't tell you the whole story about when…and why…I got this tattoo. It was the day after we met, as a matter of fact."

His gaze filled with understanding. "And you needed an extra shot of bravery."

She smiled softly. "I did." She clasped her hands in front of her, knitting her fingers together. "When Marty died, I...I was devastated. But I also had a baby girl who needed me, who I loved beyond words. I had a decent job I liked, and my mum was here with me. All that got me through. But at the same time, I shut off a big part of myself, and I didn't realize just how tight I'd locked that door."

She leaned on the back of a chair, gripping tightly. "Then the war was ending, and I lost my job. And, of all things, that started to unlock me. I was so angry over getting fired, over the reason for it."

"I remember."

"It was the first time I let myself truly get mad, since... I'd bottled it up, I think. We weren't supposed to talk about it, to be angry. Noble sacrifices, and all that. But finally, I had an outlet. A specific place to put it all." She closed her eyes. "And it felt *good*. It was awful losing my job, but...it felt so good to let go and be angry."

Max nodded, but remained quiet, letting her speak.

"Then you stepped into that alley, and a whole lot more of my puzzle pieces snapped back into place. I felt...things I hadn't felt in so very long. I felt like myself again. Only, in a different way." She shrugged. "If that makes sense."

"You can't go through all you did without it changing you, at least a little." His voice was calm, steady. Reassuring.

She let out a hum of agreement. "Spending time with you that night was exactly what I needed. *You* were exactly what I needed. All at once, it was completely freeing and...utterly terrifying." She took a deep, fortifying breath. "The fear won out. It'd already started tapping on my shoulder when..."

He smiled wryly. "I puked."

Frannie snorted. "You puked." She held his gaze, determined to convey what she needed to say, what he needed to hear. "I let it be the flimsy excuse my fear needed. I convinced myself that this wasn't anything special, that I'd be a fool to open my heart up again, that you were just some drunken soldier who wouldn't remember me in the morning. I ran away." She huffed. "You know, the reason I was at that bar in the first place was because of the tattoo parlor around the corner. I'd heard of it because one of their artists was a woman."

Max smiled at that. "Yeah?"

"Mm-hmm." She cocked an eyebrow. "I forgot all about it when I encountered you. So, the next morning, when half of me was congratulating myself on a bullet dodged, and the other was kicking myself, I went back."

"For some bravery," Max said. "Did it work?"

"Mostly." She gestured to her ink. "Except for the little banner, the one thing I couldn't figure out. I was ready to move forward… only I wasn't entirely sure what direction I was headed in. Not yet.

"And I suspect there was a piece of me, buried deep, that recognized, even after such a brief encounter, who should be on that stamp." She put every ounce of her affection into her smile. "Only I hadn't gotten his name."

He laughed heartily at that. "But you know it now."

"I do." She grasped both his hands in hers. "Max, my fears have a tendency to be loud. And I've listened to them quite a bit. That first night, and when we met again at Lois and Nick's. All the times I tried so hard to push you away." His fingers flexed in hers, as if he wanted to interject, but she squeezed back and continued speaking.

"But Colin helped me realized something, finally. Something I wish I hadn't let myself miss, all this time."

"What's that?" Max asked quietly, his thumbs tracing a gentle, steady path over her skin.

"There are miracles, and magic, in my life too. Extraordinary ones. It's past bloody time I gave them the lead."

"We've always felt pretty magical to me," he whispered. "From the very first."

"Me too." His eyes melted even further at her admission, feeding her oncoming tears. "I recognized it, even then, how great we could be together. And how much you could devastate me, if things went south."

"Frannie."

"But by some magical miracle, we've managed to find our way back to each other. Over and over."

He brought their joined hands up to graze a kiss over her knuckles. "Like magnets."

She laughed, and a tear slipped free. "Exactly like magnets. I've spent an awful lot of time facing the wrong direction, hitting that invisible wall. But you never gave up on me, and you turned me around." She tightened her grip, heedless of how much she scrunched his fingers.

"I love you so damn much, Max Mitchell. The way you push me and never let me get away with my shite." He laughed. "The way you bring me chocolate and give me back long-lost bits of my family. The way you marvel with me over the wrongness of desserts that look like pricks, and always make me laugh, in spite of myself, at your bad jokes."

"Hey."

She ignored his interjection. "I love your handsome face and your unstylish beard and your talented fingers and your enormous heart." Her tears fell in earnest now, but she didn't dare let go of him to wipe them away. "And the way you are with my little girl, caring about her not because of her connection to me, but for the person she is.

"I'm all in, in all ways, too. My heart's all yours, Max."

"Good," he sniffed. "Because mine's always been yours."

They beamed at each other for a moment, and Max leaned closer, ready for a kiss. As ready as Frannie was too, she hadn't quite finished her speech.

"Listen, I am so sorry I let my fears snap at you that day with the puppy. It was myself I was truly mad at. I can't promise that I won't get afraid again sometimes. Hell, I can almost guarantee it. But I am done letting it control me. I'm going to try my damndest to make sure you don't get caught in the crossfire."

"I would never begrudge you those feelings, Frannie. I know where you've been, and how much courage all this, with us, must be taking. How much courage you *have*." He hesitated. "Can I ask one thing, though?"

"Of course."

"Will you tell me when you're feeling that way?" He shook his head. "I don't need you to go into the gory details, if you don't want to. Of course, I'll listen if you do. But if you need some time to yourself, if you're overwhelmed and want to be quiet for a while, I will absolutely understand. Just…give me a heads-up if you can?" His mouth hitched up in a crooked smile. "So I can at least be standing by with cake when you're ready."

It was her turn to feather a kiss across his fingers. "I can absolutely promise that. As long as you do something for me."

"Anything."

"Hold me to it. Please. You may have noticed by now that I need a little push from time to time. But I don't need kid gloves. Your heart is so very dear, Max. And I want you to feel that it's safe in my hands. So push me if I need it."

"Deal." His smile was soft and steady. "Tit-for-tat."

She shot him a look of mock dismay. "I don't know. We might be hopelessly unbalanced after all. Can we ever truly achieve tit-for-tat, since I'm the one who's got both in this relationship?"

His eyes took on a wicked gleam. "Lucky for you, I love your tits and your tat."

"And I love you."

He let go of one of her hands to caress her cheek. "Frannie?"

"Yes?"

He released a frustrated exhale, his eyes drifting closed for a moment. "Can I please fucking kiss you now?"

She threw her head back and laughed, a tremendous peace washing over her. Along with blazing desire.

"I thought you'd never ask."

Frannie didn't know who moved first, nor did she care. All that mattered was their mouths, fusing together around their joint, satisfied moans. The magic that had bloomed between them from night one exploded to life, stronger than ever. Because she'd finally let go, listened to her heart. Surrendered to the miracles.

Nothing had ever tasted sweeter.

She twined her arms around Max's neck as he lifted her against him, his embrace a perfect symmetry of safety and wild exhilaration.

Her fingers found purchase in the soft waves of his hair. His resulting groan trailed off far too soon, and he drew in a breath. Magnet that she was, her lips tried to follow his as he wrenched himself away.

"I should probably tell you something," he panted.

"Let me guess. You're keeping the dog permanently?"

His mouth, gratifyingly swollen from their kiss, dropped open. "How did you know?"

She chuckled, raking her fingers through his hair again. He shook off her distraction and cleared his throat, quirking a cocky eyebrow.

Frannie grinned. "He is rather a cute little pup. And you're a big softie."

Max started to protest, then gave in with a laugh. "I am, that. But in my defense, he's a real sweetheart."

"Like attracts like."

He nipped at her lower lip.

"So tell me," she asked, trying to remember what words were, as he forged a trail down her neck. "Does the little lad have a name yet? Because I might have a suggestion."

His beard tickled her skin as he spoke against her throat. "Sorry to disappoint you, but he does, as a matter of fact. I've taken to calling him Rudy."

Frannie hummed in absent approval, tilting her head to give him better access. She froze as the name sank in.

"Rudy." She pulled back to assess him. "That wouldn't happen to be short for Rudolph, would it?"

Max grinned mischievously. "Seeing as I have been compared, quite favorably, to Santa Claus…it did seem fitting."

She buried her face in his chest, laughter bubbling up out of her. "As if I needed confirmation."

"Of what?"

Frannie met his eyes, her smile uncontrollable. "Of our magic."

Understanding dawned. "That's the name you were going to suggest."

She bit her lip, nodding. His laughter was warm and contagious as he gathered her in tightly. They leaned against each other, and time stopped, cocooning them in a blissful bubble. Frannie felt more at home, more herself, than she'd felt in ages, maybe ever. It was perfect.

"Oh, I nearly forgot," his voice rumbled delightfully through his chest, against her cheek. "Did I get the tea cakes right?"

Frannie hesitated, glancing up at him through her lashes. "I don't know," she admitted. "I didn't try them yet."

Max stared at her, his confusion evident. "Why the hell not?"

Her cheeks heated. "You made such a big deal about knowing my tell when you saw it, so…it seemed only fair to wait till you could witness it."

His eyes softened to the warmest maple, his dimples magnificent. "I love you."

She'd never tire of those words. "I love you, too."

"So, don't keep me in suspense." He slid his arms away and reached for his box on the table. Pulling a tea cake out, he held it up in offering.

Frannie closed her lips around the dessert, her lips brushing his fingers as she took a healthy bite.

She promptly closed her eyes with a gasp, a flood of childhood memories surrounding her as the warm sweetness dissolved on her tongue.

"Oh, god, Max," she breathed. "That's it."

She reopened her eyes to find him beaming at her. And underneath the blinding brightness, a conflagration of desire lay in wait, ready to consume her. She was desperate to do some consuming of her own.

He tossed the remaining cake on the table, and their arms were around each other in a flash, their mouths devouring the last of their patience.

"Is Lucy home?" Max whispered between kisses.

"Nancy's mum is taking them to the pictures after school. She won't be home till after dinner."

His hands tightened on the back of her blouse. "And Betty?"

"Also has dinner plans."

"Perfect."

She squeaked as he scooped her into his arms, heading for the stairs.

"And just where are you taking me?" she asked, teasingly.

His eyes shone with exquisite wickedness. "Your bed, that glorious window seat...anywhere you'll let me."

They laughed all the way up the stairs, and then, in true Max fashion, he made good on his promise.

A year later…

ax studied himself in the full-length mirror in Nick's dressing room on the Phoenix lot, adjusting his jacket. His friend appeared behind him.

"You really sure about the outfit?" Nick asked.

Max shot him a glare through the reflection. "I trust Nate. And she assures me Frannie's going to love it."

"Yeah, you're probably right." He clapped Max on the shoulder. "And I know I don't need to ask if you're sure about everything else," he added with a grin.

"Indeed, you do not."

Max had never been more sure of anything in his life.

The two of them headed out, making their way to Soundstage Five. In a lot of ways, getting locked inside it had finally pushed Frannie and Max together, onto the same path forward, so it seemed more than appropriate that they return to the scene of the crime to begin this new leg of their journey. Nick and Lois had generously offered to decorate it in style, and then throw them one hell of a party on the lot.

He and Nick rounded the last corner, just as Frannie came from the opposite direction, flanked by Colin, Nate, and Lois.

Max stopped short, Frannie's beauty robbing him of breath.

Her hair, still that alluring shade of red, fell in soft waves to her shoulders, one side pulled up with a gold clip. The neckline of her dress skimmed her shoulders, and the silky, soft green fabric hugged her waist before flaring out into a full skirt that stopped mid-calf. One side of the skirt was gathered up to reveal a hidden layer of multi-hued tartan—the very same that made up the kilt currently circling Max's hips.

Frannie gave him a hungry perusal of her own. Her eyes roamed over him, but she kept coming back to the kilt, a seductive smile curving her full red lips.

Thank you, Nate.

They were perfectly content to ogle each other, but their friends had other ideas. Nick grabbed Max's arm.

"Hey, isn't it bad luck to see the bride?"

Frannie's smile deepened. "We make our own luck."

Max grinned back. "And magic's on our side."

While they mooned unabashedly at one another, Lois stepped in and pried Nick's fingers from his sleeve, and Nate promptly smoothed the wrinkles left behind.

"Don't worry, darling," Lois assured Nick. "After all, we saw each other before our ceremony, and look how well that turned out."

He snaked his arm around his wife. "That is true."

Max stepped closer to Frannie, offering her his arm. "What do you say? Shall we get this party started?"

Her hand slid into the crook of his elbow. "Ready when you are." She paused. "Oh. Unless…"

She turned to Colin, nodding down at her arm, intertwined with Max's. "Had you wanted to…?"

Colin gave them a wide smile. "Please. No one gives you away but yourself, Mermaid."

She laughed and grasped her brother's hand with her free one. "I'm so glad you're here, Chips." After a beat, she turned to look up at Max. "And it would be nice to walk in together, you and me."

He covered her hand with his own. "Sounds perfect."

Their friends prepared to file in ahead of them, leaving them a moment to themselves.

"You look beautiful," he said quietly.

"Thanks. You wore a kilt for me."

"I did. I've gotta tell you, it's surprisingly comfortable."

"Glad to hear it." The way she raked her eyes over him again sent a shiver down his spine. "It looks mighty good on you."

Another shiver hovered perilously close to the base of his spine.

"Okay, you need to stop looking at me like that."

"Why?"

"Because we're about to stand before a preacher and all our friends and family, and I'd prefer not to be pitching a tartan tent when I say, 'I do.'"

She laughed huskily. "Fair enough. I'll behave." She lowered her voice to a whisper. "But we'll be pitching that tent later, yeah?"

"Oh, *hell* yeah."

They chuckled together, all the way down the aisle constructed just for them in the soundstage.

***

IT WAS the best party either of them had ever been to. Strings of twinkling lights lined the canopy above, and the sounds of love and laughter surrounded them. The warm, dulcet tones of Ronnie's voice floated above the din, currently delivering an upbeat melody along with the small band behind her. Betty chatted animatedly with Max's parents, the three of them getting along famously. Linda had insisted on making them a big chocolate cake, with the help of Regina, the bakery's new hire, who was already a splendid addition to their team.

A good thing for Linda the cake was utterly delicious, because she more than needed to make up for the other wedding present she'd conspired with Vi to give him—a fucking sidecar for his motorcycle, emblazoned with the Mom's Bakery logo.

They were lucky he was too blissfully happy to yell at them.

He stood with his arms around Frannie, her back nestled against his chest, and reveled in the new weight on his ring finger. It felt like it had always belonged there.

The two of them contentedly watched the festivities—flanked by Nate and Colin on one side, and Lois and Nick on the other—when Lucy approached. Her typically buoyant nature held an edge of seriousness. She'd been thrilled with the idea of their marriage ever since Max had asked for her blessing to propose to Frannie, and he hoped nothing had happened today to upset her.

She stopped in front of them, uncharacteristically nervous. "Max? Can I ask you something?"

Her blue eyes were wide and solemn, and his heart stuttered in his chest. He glanced at Frannie, but her expression gave nothing away. "Of course." He let go of his new wife and crouched in front of Lucy. "You can ask me anything, Snickerdoodle."

She darted a quick look at her mom, and heaved a breath, squaring her shoulders. Whatever it was, was clearly important to her.

"I wondered… I never met my dad. Well, actually, I did, but I was too little and I don't remember it." His heart cracked as she continued. "But I asked Mommy, and she said she didn't think he'd mind at all. So…" She blinked up at Max, and he forgot how to breathe.

"Do you think it would be okay if I called you Dad? Instead of Max? Because I already felt like you were my dad, but now you

and Mommy are married and it feels even more like it. And I…
was just wondering."

Max felt as if an entire cheesecake was lodged in his windpipe, his heart having expanded to a size that could engulf all of Holly-wood. He blinked dazedly up at Frannie, who'd moved to stand behind Lucy. She smiled around the hand pressed to her mouth and nodded. At least, he thought she did—she was a bit blurry due to his gathering tears.

He returned his attention to Lucy, his beloved little Snicker-doodle, and forced his voice out.

"Lucy," he croaked, "I would be so incredibly honored if you called me Dad. Because I'm honored to call you my daughter."

She beamed at him and threw her arms around his neck. He clutched her tight, completely and perfectly starstruck. Frannie's hand found his, and they exchanged watery smiles over Lucy's head.

Lucy pulled back to split a look between him and Frannie. "I think this is the best day ever."

Frannie smoothed her hair. "I quite agree, lass."

The lass grinned up at them, then blithely scampered off to rejoin the party, as if she hadn't just dropped a grenade of joy on Max's head.

A loud honking echoed as he stood up, and he turned to find Nick blowing his nose into a handkerchief. Lois was misty as well, and a glance to his other side revealed Colin wiping his eyes behind his glasses, and Nate fishing her own hankie out of the pocket of her dress.

Max returned his attention to Frannie, smiling so tenderly it nearly sent him back to his knees.

"She ran it by me the other day," she whispered, running her thumb over his wet cheek. "But I didn't know when she was going to ask you."

He nodded. "And you're okay with it?"

"Are you kidding? I couldn't be happier that we both have you, Max."

"The feeling is mutual, love." Max leaned in for a kiss.

Later, the opening strains of "I'm Beginning to See the Light" filled the reception, and he scooped Lucy up with one arm, and wrapped the other around Frannie, leading them both to the dance floor.

Frannie had been right; they did have their own, beautiful magic between them. He swayed to the music, overwhelmed with happiness—but at no risk of swooning. Not this time. Because he had the loves of his life, a charming little lass and her beloved mother, holding him up.

Lucy giggled, pulling their attention.

"What is it, Snickerdoodle?"

"The song." Her grin widened. "I'm really glad you two saw the light."

Frannie and Max locked eyes, joining in Lucy's infectious laughter.

"Us too," they said together.

In perfect agreement. Would wonders never cease?

Max & Frannie's "Hit Parade"

A PLAYLIST

Music plays an important part in Max and Frannie's love story, so I wanted to share a playlist of their favorites, especially since the music of the 1940s might not be so familiar to everyone. I've also added a few "bonus" songs that more peripherally influenced this book—including a pair of much more recent tunes that make pretty good theme songs for Frannie and Max, respectively. Happy listening!

- "I'm Beginning to See the Light" — The Ink Spots & Ella Fitzgerald
- "Boogie Woogie Bugle Boy" — The Andrews Sisters
- "I've Got My Love to Keep Me Warm" — Billie Holiday
- "The Heather on the Hill" (from *Brigadoon*) — Gene Kelly**
- "It's Only a Paper Moon" — Nat King Cole Trio
- "Cement Mixer" — Alvino Rey
- "I'm Beginning to See the Light" — Harry James & Kitty Kallen

Bonus songs:

- "A Kiss to Build a Dream On" — Louis Armstrong
- "Count Your Blessings" (from *White Christmas*) — Bing Crosby
- "Easy on Me" — Adele
- "I'm Gonna Be (500 Miles)" — The Proclaimers

** In 1949, Frannie & Max would only have known the Broadway version of this song, but I've included the film version from 1954 instead, because Gene Kelly was simply magic.

A link to the full playlist on Spotify can be found on my website (www.briannegillen.com)!

Author's Note & Acknowledgments

This book will always hold a special place in my heart, in part because it is the conclusion of my first series, and also because I love Max and Frannie so much. These two might a bit less flashy than their friends, but getting them to their HEA brought me a lot of joy, and I hope their journey did the same for you! Writing about the entire cast at Phoenix Pictures has been an adventure, and I must admit it's a little bittersweet to bring things to a close. These characters have seen me through a lot of ups and downs (and vice versa!) and I am so grateful I've had the opportunity to share these stories with you. And rest assured, you haven't seen the last of Lois & Nick, Nate & Colin, or Frannie & Max—I know I won't be able to resist inviting them to pop up from time to time for cameos in future books!

A couple of quick historical notes about elements in this book... First of all, I am sorry (not sorry?) to report that the candle salad is a mid-century culinary phenomenon that did, indeed, exist. The recipe goes back at least as far as the 1920s, and really took off a couple of decades later. It did actually appear...somehow...in a children's cookbook. Though the most well-reported version of this cookbook dates to 1951, there may have been earlier versions as well—like the fictional one Lucy's buddy got for her birthday!

I also make brief mention of the Irving Berlin classic "Count Your Blessings" which features most famously in the film *White Christmas.* I wanted to include it as a nod to one of my family's longest-running holiday traditions, so I hope you'll forgive my slight fudging of the song's timeline, since it hadn't quite been written yet in 1949. I'd like to think that perhaps Colin was an acquaintance of Mr. Berlin, and got to hear an early version of it, which he then shared with his sister.

And now…on to my gratitude! As always, I need to thank my wonderful Sploosh Sisters—Amanda Pereira, Jillian Graves, Daria Vernon, and Genevieve Kersten—for not only their friendship, but their tremendously helpful insights when it comes to writing in general, and drafting this book in particular. Thanks especially for helping me fine-tune the physics of the Mitchell Family Baseball Massacre of 1926, and sharing in my horror/fascination over candle salads. And Amanda, the credit for Frannie and Max's fateful second "first" meeting appearing on the page goes to you!

My editor, Michele Chiappetta, was, yet again, so instrumental in helping me polish this book. Thanks a million for your expert feedback and answers to my questions, not to mention the continued support and cheerleading. Your rooting for Max and Frannie meant a lot!

The absolute beauty of all my Phoenix Pictures covers is due to Daybed Books. I am impressed anew every time at how perfectly you capture the vibe of each book and its characters, and make magic out of my vague ideas.

I'd like to give a special shout-out to two of my favorite independent bookstores. Everyone at The Ripped Bodice in Los Angeles has been tremendously supportive along my writing journey. Thanks especially to Katie for taking the chance on putting my books on the shelves, and Teresa for helping me organize this book's launch event!

Equally supportive is the crew at Love's Sweet Arrow in Chicago. Huge thanks to Roseann and Marissa for making into reality my idea for a virtual event series connecting classic screwball comedies and romance reads! And to all my fellow authors who joined me this past year, thank you so very much. I had an absolute blast chatting with you.

To the vast community of romance reviewers, bloggers, podcasters, librarians, and more—thank you. You do so much for not nearly enough credit, and give us all so many hours of reading enjoyment through your recommendations.

Of course, as ever, thanks to my wonderfully supportive family, friends, and colleagues. All of your excitement and encouragement over my books means more than I can express. To my Dad especially—my love, always. And my Mom—I miss you every day, and I wish I could share Max with you. You would *love* him.

And finally, my enormous gratitude goes out to all of you readers. Those of you who have reached out with your excitement and lovely, kind words about my series have touched me so much, and made all of this so very worthwhile. Thank you for inviting my characters onto your bookshelves. I can't wait to keep sharing more of them with you.

See how Linda & Ronnie fell in love!

(WITH A LITTLE HELP FROM MAX)

Sign up for Brianne's Newsletter to receive *First Harvest of Love*, starring Linda Talbot & Ronnie O'Hara, for FREE! This Phoenix Pictures prequel short story is now available exclusively for subscribers!

Plus, you'll be in the loop for all the gossip—including news, updates, & other bonus content!

Subscribe at www.briannegillen.com

The Phoenix Pictures Series:

DIFFICULT (Lois & Nick)

SINGLE INDEMNITY (Nate & Colin)

A KISS TO BUILD A GRUDGE ON (Frannie & Max)

First Harvest of Love: A Lughnasadh Short Story

(Newsletter exclusive; originally part of the *Flames, Flirts & Festivals* anthology)

From the Phoenix Pictures Vault:

SEA CREATURES PREFER REDHEADS (a novella)

***

Did you enjoy this book? Please consider leaving a review!

…on Goodreads, Bookbub, or your retailer of choice

About the Author

Brianne Gillen is a romance author, costume designer, theatre educator, and life-long storyteller, based in the Los Angeles area. She loves classic films, especially the screwball comedies of the '30s and '40s, and will never turn down the opportunity to browse the treasure troves otherwise known as vintage clothing stores. She is also a voracious reader and firm believer in happily-ever-afters. She has done a bit of playwriting, and in recent years, has contributed her opinions to a few online publications centering on the art and craft of costume design. Her Phoenix Pictures Series centers around fierce dames and cinnamon-roll gents finding love in late-1940s Hollywood.

www.briannegillen.com

 twitter.com/BooksbyBrianne
 instagram.com/booksbybrianne